SPIRITs of Retribution

ROD JOHNSON

A Josh Morgan Publishing novel.

ISBN: 0-578-48912-0
ISBN-13: 978-0-578-48912-4

DEDICATION

To the brave men and women of our military and intelligence agencies who keep us safe.

"And ye shall know the truth and the truth shall make you free." John 8:32

Bible verse on a wall in the Lobby of the Central Intelligence Agency's Original Headquarters Building

CHAPTER ONE

Day 1 – Saturday

With six white columns standing in contrast to its pale yellow walls, the over two-hundred-year-old church shone majestically.

The slightly overcast sky permitted just enough sunlight for a barely perceptible shadow in front of the westward facing portico. Though sparse, the clouds still managed to release a few snowflakes that created a slight shimmer on the rectangular pavestones in front of the church.

On the northeast corner of H St NW and 16th St NW across from Lafayette Square, St. John's Episcopal Church was enormously significant in Washington, D.C., not only in a religious sense but also historically and politically. Beginning with its first service on October 27, 1816, the church had been inextricably intertwined with the District. The parish grounds had seen treaty signings and other historic events, and for a time before the Civil War, it had served as the site of the British Legation to the U.S. The church boasted a half-ton bell cast by Joseph Revere, son of the War for Independence patriot and even had a pew, number 54, reserved for the President of the United States. From the fourth commander in chief, James Madison, until the present, every chief executive had visited the church at one time or another, leading to its being known as "the Church of the Presidents."

For most people, Washington was synonymous with nasty rhetoric and self-serving ambition. The political climate had been an abomination in the eyes of most of the electorate forever, it seemed, and few expected that to change in the near term, if ever. So more than mere history, St. John's Episcopal Church existed as a symbol of something different, a moral presence in the governmental center of the nation, just a stone's throw from the heart of that political organism, the White House. And throwing stones

1

was prevalent in public discourse with nobody feeling the least bit hypocritical for casting the first one, despite their not being without sin. The political constituency might have even launched a few literal stones in the direction of the elected officials, if given the chance to do it and to do so without consequence.

So, given the incredible beauty of the church, it was terribly incongruous that what stood out to every observer weren't the beautiful stained-glass windows that portrayed scenes from the Gospel of John. Nor was it the soaring steeple. Since two days before Election Day the unavoidable focus of every passerby was the damage to the two center pillars. More substantial to the southernmost of the two columns and minimal to the other, the cavities in the colossal white supports had been caused by an out-of-control truck belonging to the District Miracle Plumbers.

The decision had been made to delay repairs until after the Thanksgiving Eucharist. So, while the orange tape around the columns was an eyesore and disappointing to the visitors whose photos would be less than ideal, decision-makers deemed it to be less intrusive to the Thanksgiving event than construction equipment. The problem it presented was the relatively short window of time to get all the repairs done before January 20. That was the constitutionally prescribed date on which the president-elect would be sworn in. And as was customary, her day would begin with a short visit to St. John's.

So, with only three days left until Inauguration Day, the final review of the work was nearly complete. Present were the general contractor who oversaw the restoration, the St. Johns rector, and the church's Executive Director for Operations. Also, in attendance were a construction consultant retained by the church, a high-ranking representative from the insurance company paying for the repairs, and the legal counsel for the church. And certainly not the least among the individuals present were representatives from the Department of the Interior and the National Park Service, owing to St. Johns' designation as a National Historic Landmark.

"13,775 feet versus 555 feet." It was more a condemnation than a statement of fact.

"What?" Maggie Loughlin peeked around the doorway from the spare bedroom/office to see Josh Morgan gazing out the window over the cityscape.

"Grand Teton – Washington Monument. Tallest thing in Jackson Hole. Tallest thing in D.C." He let out a wistful sigh.

Maggie walked to her fiancé and reached both arms around his chest and lay her head against his back as she often did.

"You know, that's thirteen thousand above sea level. It's not really that 'tall.' I guess it's probably…"

"Seven thousand, thirty feet. It's seven thousand and thirty feet, valley floor to summit," he said.

Maggie moved around to Morgan's side, duplicating his gaze toward the skyline.

"I thought you were good with this move."

"Oh, I am," he reassured her. "I'm very excited, Maggie." Josh turned and pulled Maggie to face him, taking both her hands in his. "But I miss home. That's okay, right? It's not as bitterly cold here as it is in Wyoming but this time of year…"

He turned to look out the window again.

"The snow on the peaks; on the trees; on the rooftops. It's beautiful there."

He noticed the misgivings in Maggie's body language and took her hands again.

"But here… with you… it's right. You know me. It's been a long time since I've taken much of a chance on anything as big as a move across the country. I think it's mostly that I'm out of my comfort zone."

Maggie wondered what exactly his "comfort zone" was as she recalled the events that occurred just over a year and a half earlier. She didn't know all the details, but she did know that over those couple of weeks that July, Josh had been attacked at his home outside Jackson where he had killed one of the attackers. Maggie mentally skipped over the part where she had killed another one by crashing her pickup into him, pinning him against the outside wall of Morgan's garage. Then Josh had chased a terrorist across northern Mexico, catching up with him on the Texas Gulf Coast. God only knew what happened there, but her fiancé returned home battered and bruised but with a strong friendship with an ex-U.S. president who was at the center of the whole affair and who had quietly had Morgan's back years earlier when he had gotten into a mess at CIA. So, this was out of his "comfort zone," he said.

✦

Assistant Interior Secretary Sean Mathis took a seat at the large table in the conference room inside St. Johns where the group had moved to discuss their inspection. He blew gently over the top of his cup of coffee and leaned over to Jana Murphy.

"So, tell me again how this could happen. I mean, jeez, look how far off the street those columns are."

The attorney who had served as the church's legal counsel during the whole fiasco that was a truck crashing into the church shook her head.

"Beats me, Sean. Here's the story. This asshole…" The attorney suddenly remembered where she was and surveyed the room. She began again, "The plumbing company's truck driver was stopped at the light on H Street. He was first in line when it changed. His story was that his accelerator went full open and stuck there. Van was off like a shot and made a beeline for the church portico."

"And the guy doesn't try to turn the key off? Put it in neutral? He could've steered away from the church, I'd think. Why didn't he just turn away from it?"

"That's the thing. Not only didn't he steer away, he turned straight toward it."

The Assistant Secretary's head lowered as he leaned in and said softly, "No shit?"

The lawyer nodded her head. "He maintains he was worried about people in the crosswalk, but traffic cams showed no one there. Believe me, we checked. We think he just panicked and made up the story about pedestrians and stuck with it."

Mathis reflected a moment. "At least they did a great job on the repairs" was all he could think to say.

"Well, it looks good. But it's still a repair. This old church has witnessed a lot and this asshole..." – she didn't care who heard her this time – "...damaged her."

Once everyone had taken a seat, the St. John's Episcopal Executive Director for Operations quickly polled the group to get everyone's assent that the repairs were adequate and complete and that the terms of the settlement had been fulfilled. All agreed, signatures were affixed, meeting adjourned.

✦

When President Wendell Mercer had resigned "for health reasons" something over a year earlier, Vice President Sandra Melton-Hendrickson had ascended to the office of president. This past November, despite suspicions among some in the United States of some unknown scandal bringing down Mercer, she was elected to the office in her own right. Apparently, the public didn't suspect Madam President of any complicity in whatever it was that was assumed to have happened. And because she had served less than half a term upon becoming president, she would be eligible to run for reelection again in four years.

When she succeeded Mercer, President Hendrickson dropped the hyphen and her maiden name for simplicity's sake. She had for the most part kept Mercer's staff with a few notable exceptions. Henry James was out as chief of staff, as was NSA Director Stanford Grayson. Secretary of State Susan

McGregor offered her resignation. President Hendrickson tried to refuse it, preferring instead to allow a measure of latitude and perhaps even forgiveness, mostly for naiveté on the part of SecState rather than any culpability in the Weston affair. But McGregor, perhaps weary of politics and diplomacy, insisted.

President Hendrickson knew every detail of what her predecessor had done with regard to Trenton Weston – his turning a blind eye to the Saudi plot to kidnap Weston and try him as a war criminal. She knew he had abetted NSA Deputy Director Everson Blake in his attempt to thwart the kidnapping but only so he could himself kill the ex-president to satisfy a personal vendetta.

In the aftermath, the current president deftly played the hand she had been dealt in the crisis as it involved the al-Qaeda leadership of the Holy Islamic Republic of Saudi Arabia. More than they feared condemnation by the international community if their role in the plot were revealed, Saudi leaders were horrified that its failure would weaken their standing among sympathizers. So, they resumed petroleum exports in an arrangement immensely favorable to their American trade partners. They quietly made many other concessions to the Great Satan and meekly accepted all sanctions. Oil prices began to plummet in the U.S. and the economy began to rebound. This was rightly attributed to actions taken by President Mercer before his "health" forced him to step down; just not for the reasons people thought. So, as was customary in the current political reality, whatever scandal was really behind his departure was forgiven for the sake of the dollar. And now-President Hendrickson benefited, and she was easily elected.

President Hendrickson kept the secrets of the ordeal with the dignified grace that was characteristic of her. Then she moved on to prepare for her campaign for the office. Once elected to a full term she would pursue the personal goals she had set for her own administration.

Sandy – at home, Madam President was simply "Sandy" or "Mom" – sat at the dinner table in the executive residence of the White House with her husband Adam, thirteen-year-old daughter Noelle, and fifteen-year-old son Adam Jr., or "AJ." Whatever the demands of her job – and people only thought they knew how tough it was – whenever she was home for the evening meal, her time belonged solely to her family. No briefing papers, no phone calls, nothing – just "Sandy" or "Mom."

And she likewise expected their time to be hers. No texting, Instagram, Snapchat for the kids. No Wall Street Journal or spy novels for her husband. No television.

"Two days and a wake-up, hon."

Sandy smiled across the table at the first gentleman.

"What's that mean, Mom?" enquired the first daughter.

Dad answered. "Tuesday morning your mom will be sworn in as President of the United States."

"But she's already the president," insisted AJ with the smirk and attitude that only a teenaged boy can muster. Not even the son of the chief executive was immune from that.

"Well, she became president because she had been President Mercer's vice president. She was elected because people wanted *him* to be the president. This time's different. This time the people elected *her* to be the president. It's a vote of confidence specifically for your mom."

"Whatever," said the first son.

"Well, I think it's cool!" the first daughter offered in her most supportive tone.

"Thank you, sweetheart," Mom said.

Later in the executive residence's master bedroom, Sandy momentarily resumed the role of POTUS and scanned the draft of her inaugural address, the hoped first of two. She lined through a word here, inserted another there. She underlined ideas that she wanted to emphasize. Madam President even drew a smiley face in a couple of places where she hoped to inject a little levity. Finally, she laid the notes aside on the nightstand with her pen and reading glasses. She rubbed weary eyes and then massaged her temples.

"You know, honey, this will be a bit of a fresh start for me. Despite how things ultimately worked out, I always felt like everything I did was in Wendell Mercer's shadow."

Adam placed his toothbrush in its holder, rinsed his mouth, wiped his face, and moved to the bed where he crawled under the cover with the World's Most Powerful Wife.

"I'm sure it'll be a relief. It's a chance to begin to work on your own agenda. Quite a bit of staff turnover, too."

"Uh-huh. Initially, I kept a lot of Mercer's people on simply because it was easier, but this is a logical place for a lot of them to leave. Not just because they were his people but also to just bring in some fresh faces. And a lot of Mercer's staff still credit him for President Weston's rescue."

Her husband's face took on an immediate scowl at the thought of that. As a former Deputy Attorney General, Adam Hendrickson had the highest of security clearances and, of course, he was the current president's most trusted confidant, so he knew the truth about Weston's abduction and rescue.

"That must be hard to stomach; you know, having to listen to their praise of the scumbag and not say anything."

"You have no idea! Speaking of President Weston, there is one interesting new hire."

"Oh? Who's that?"

"Marie Ginnetti is bringing in Margaret Loughlin as her new Principal

Deputy Press Secretary."

"Who?" The name wasn't familiar to Adam.

"Maggie Loughlin," said the president. "She's Josh Morgan's fiancée."

"Really? What's her background?" asked the first gentleman, turning out the lamp on his side of the bed.

"Degrees in Public Relations and Political Science from USC. Then time at some PR firms, including her own in Jackson Hole."

"And that gets her to the White House? How'd Ginnetti even hear about this...what's her name?"

Sandy snuggled up against her husband. "Loughlin. And I might have put her name in front of Marie."

"You did? Why?" Adam was surprised.

"Because President Weston put her name in front of me. And I kinda figured the White House owed him some consideration." The president was starting to nod off.

Her husband understood. "Because of her connection with Josh Morgan. I get it. But what about Morgan himself?"

"Weston's looking out for him, too. I suppose he'll never be back at CIA but at least he's off everyone's shit list. It's really up to him now to pursue whatever opportunities he wants without having to look over his shoulder. He's at Georgetown right now."

"The University? What's he doing there?"

Adam's answer was only the soft steady breathing of his wife getting some much-needed sleep.

CHAPTER 2

Day 2 - Sunday

Outside, the morning broke clear and cold. Inside, Josh stretched in the warmth of his bed and rolled over.

"Good morning," he said to... nobody.

Josh propped himself up on an elbow and looked around the bedroom.

"Maggie?" he called. He slipped on the sweat pants that Maggie had bought him with "Georgetown" emblazoned down the left leg in Georgetown Blue and Georgetown Gray. It looked incongruous with the burnt orange t-shirt with the white imprint of a Longhorn's head and the single word "Texas" splashed proudly across the chest that he donned next. Walking toward the kitchen, he pulled the shirt down and sniffed the welcome aroma of fresh-brewed coffee wafting its way down the hall.

"You're up early," Josh said to his fiancée who had her gaze fixed intently on her laptop screen, tapping a pen on a legal pad with several pages folded up.

"Mmmm. Yeah. 'Spose so," she mumbled.

Morgan was almost always the first one up. Even on those long cynicism-infested nights in Wyoming that he passed by drinking more than he should, he always managed to rise early, even when he didn't feel like it. So, it was a surprise to see Maggie up first.

The ex-CIA spy added a spoonful of sweetener to his coffee. He took a sip and turned up his nose. One of the benefits of being the first one out of bed each morning was that he could make the coffee like he wanted. Maggie always made it too weak.

The native Texan straddled a chair and rested his arms on the back of it. He gazed across the table at Maggie and sat quietly as she read the display and jotted notes on the yellow pad. She finally reached a stopping point. She dropped the pen on it with some frustration and reached up and pulled at her auburn locks.

"I don't know if I'm up to this," Maggie finally said. As excited as she was to be working at the White House, it had all happened so fast. She had felt so thrilled at the job opportunity that it never occurred to her to consider if she was in over her head.

Morgan moved to the chair beside hers and took one of her hands.

"They must think you are… No, they must be *sure* you are, or they wouldn't have hired you. And *I* know you'll be fantastic."

"I would've been happier to start in a more junior position."

"No, you wouldn't," Josh countered. He took another sip of his coffee and got up to get a refill and to top off Maggie's lukewarm cup.

Maggie Loughlin knew he was right, but it didn't do anything to calm her jitters. Immediately after Election Day, almost all of Press Secretary Ginnetti's staff resigned. There had never been any love lost between the secretary and her crew, largely because, despite her public posture, Ginnetti had always had a personal disdain for Mercer. She inherited her staff from the man, and they were loyal to him. They had quietly hoped Hendrickson wouldn't run or would perhaps lose in the primaries. Some even held no party loyalty strong enough to keep from wishing that her opponent would win the Oval Office. The last scenario wasn't optimal because if the incumbent lost, they would be gone, too.

So less than a week after the nation reelected Hendrickson, almost the entire White House Press Department tendered their resignations. To keep from being completely unprofessional, or at least mitigate the appearance of being so, some agreed to stay through March to help bring their replacements up to speed.

The most surprising of those leaving was Principal Deputy Press Secretary Anson Carter. He had a long history with Ginnetti. She had hand-picked him, so he was extremely loyal. However, just before the day voters elected Sandra Hendrickson to continue as president, Carter had learned he had Stage 3 lung cancer. Against his doctor's advice, he stayed on to get his ultimate boss, POTUS, past the election. Nobody in the administration knew except his friend and mentor Ginnetti.

The bottom line to all this was that an entire West Wing department had to be rebuilt and it had to be fast-tracked. So, with virtually no junior staff – rather, practically no staff at any level – the position of principal deputy was open and on the recommendation of a former president, the press secretary hired Margaret Loughlin.

The press secretary completed interviews and made her eventual decision to hire her by Christmas. Since Maggie had been on the short list – in fact, she had *been* the short list – background investigations had begun with her very first consideration.

Maggie and Josh made the decision to relocate to D.C. very quickly. Finding a place to live wasn't as difficult as one might expect. The beginning of a new four-year term always brought with it a host of people coming and going. Even when the incumbent won a new term, it was commonly used as an opportunity to reconfigure and retool an administration so there was usually significant turnover.

Morgan, despite having left CIA in disgrace, received a full pension, again thanks to Trenton Weston. He had made a great income as a photojournalist and had invested wisely. Though not wealthy by any measure, he was easily able to pay his share of the substantial rent on his and Maggie's townhouse at The Wharf, a development not far from the National Mall and a short ride to the White House.

As Maggie resumed her self-orientation for her new position, Josh considered where this move had brought him. Their new home was about four miles from his new office.

"'Office.' That's weird," he thought. He had really never had one, he realized. Whenever he was at Langley during his days with the Company, he would take one of the on-demand cubicles there. Back home in Jackson Hole, his "office," to the extent that he actually worked, was a converted bedroom in his log home. He wondered how often he would really have to go in. The courses he would teach were in the late morning and afternoon.

Courses! The realization that he was about to be a visiting professor terrified him. He had no course outlines. He also had no clue. As much as the prospect of working in the White House intimidated Maggie, she at least had done similar work before. With the exception of teaching a couple of community education courses in photography through the Jackson Independent School District, he had never taught a course in anything.

That seemed like a lifetime ago.

✦

"Dump" didn't even begin to accurately describe the motel he was in but with Inauguration Day upon him, Ed Broussard was relieved to have gotten a room anywhere. The Xcalibur Motel was some distance from D.C. and the White House area, in particular, but he could make it work. Yes, he would just have to get an earlier start on January 20. In the meantime, Eddie would try to keep from being distracted by the men and women – lowlifes, he thought – that came and went at all hours of the day and night. They certainly put the "X" in Xcalibur, he observed. Sitting on the open tailgate of his pickup, Eddie laughed out loud at his joke, took out another beer, hooked the cap on the edge of the metal tailgate. A slap downward on the cap with the heel of his hand, and he lifted the frothing bottle to his lips.

✦

Josh and Maggie had seen the Westons enough over the last eighteen months that the couple no longer intimidated them but the occasional realization that they were friends with a former president and first lady... well, that was always an overwhelming thought.

As they were being seated at Fiola Mare, Morgan noticed that the gait in Trent Weston's step had slowed but that his bearing was unbowed, still demonstrating the strength and character of one who had been through much but who had not been conquered by any of it. He and Alicia Weston held hands the way a young couple who had just begun dating would. The other patrons in this restaurant, accustomed though they were to celebrated people in the dining room, were nevertheless unable to keep from taking notice of the former first couple. A few hushed words were shared throughout the dining area. Some fellow diners stared, though their gazes didn't rise to the level of rudeness.

President and Mrs. Trenton Weston never presumed themselves to be of sufficient importance to wave or gesture in these types of settings but rather nodded slightly and smiled. Still, the former chief executive felt at once humbled and excited at the warm acknowledgement that everyone seemed to offer. It was as if the other diners wanted to applaud but did not.

Weston leaned over to Morgan and whispered, "I guess they've never seen a globetrotting photojournalist before. Do you get this attention everywhere?"

Despite the humor his elderly friend's tone conveyed, Morgan couldn't manage even the slightest chuckle and felt a flush creep throughout his face. Weston gave him a soft elbow in the ribs and whispered again. "Lighten up, son. We both know our ladies are the real stars of our little group." This time, Morgan allowed himself a laugh and a nod in agreement.

They took their seats at a table with a view of the Potomac, the gentlemen holding the chairs for the ladies and Secret Service Agents Jack Johnston and Jeff Coulter taking not-so-discreet positions nearby.

After the quartet ordered wine, they settled into the type of conversation that was more like that of relatives than mere friends. The two men had a bond forged by shared experience that few people could appreciate.

While the older couple listened as Maggie spoke about their move to the District, Morgan gazed at Weston. He was frailer, he decided. He also realized that he felt about the former president much as he had his grandfather, Silas Houston, who had passed away only four months earlier.

While they never spoke of the ordeal they shared, President Weston had remarked many times immediately after it that he owed Josh his life. Josh could never quite make Weston comprehend that the older man had in fact saved his life, twice to be precise. The first time, Saudi Agent Fadi Al-Majeed held a tactical advantage from which he might finish off Morgan as they fought in the cabin of the *Jezebel* at Gulf Mariners Marina in Texas. Weston stabbed the agent in the back with a kitchen knife, disabling him enough for Morgan to regain control of the contest. Then, a mere minutes later, the ex-president pulled him up from submerging and undoubtedly drowning after he had jumped clear of the exploding twenty-eight-foot power boat.

But it was in the emotional and moral sense that Trent Weston had really saved Josh Morgan. And that was of far greater significance and it was something that his older friend could never quite get.

"Right, Morgan?" The question jolted him back into the here and now. He had no clue what Maggie was asking him to agree to, but the nature of the enquiry made him certain that he was expected to. So, Josh squeezed his fiancée's hand and said, "Right, sweetheart."

His three dinner companions all burst out laughing, so Morgan laughed, too, never realizing that Maggie had previously said, "But my guy isn't listening to a word I'm saying," to which he had unwittingly confessed.

It was 6:30 PM. The wine arrived, toasts were voiced, and the foursome perused the menu. Every dish, mostly Italian and largely centered on seafood, and as beautiful as it was superb, was crafted into a sumptuous blend of art and culinary perfection.

The Westons were in town for the inauguration and Josh and Maggie were both about to start new jobs. Unsurprising to Maggie, Josh figured he could just wing the first couple of days at Georgetown until he got a clearer idea what he was supposed to do as a visiting professor. In stark contrast, Maggie was immersing herself in preparing for the new position. And though she felt she really couldn't spare the time from her crash course in her job duties, it would be difficult to refuse a dinner invitation from political royalty. More than that, she and Josh would never miss the opportunity to spend time with people who had been such an important part of their recent lives.

"I don't know if I'm up to this job, to tell you the truth," Maggie admitted. She looked around among the three pairs of eyes, in her heart really hoping to hear an affirmation that she was. No matter how confident she was as a professional, a little encouragement never hurt.

Three voices competed to see who would first offer that moral support. Alicia Weston's broke through.

"They all know you're the right person for the job. They wouldn't have even interviewed you had they thought otherwise." Josh and President Weston reinforced Mrs. Weston's comment with their nods and "yeses." Josh took her hand in his.

Maggie continued, "I just feel that I would've been happy to start a little lower down the org chart. The only reason I got the number two is that practically the whole department was vacant. If Deputy Press Secretary Carter hadn't resigned, Press Secretary Ginnetti sure wouldn't have been looking to replace him. Maybe that would've been best."

Trent Weston took his turn at reassuring Maggie. "They had the whole country to pick from to fill these jobs. Maybe if the position of Deputy hadn't been open, you would've hired in at a lower grade. But it *was* open, and you got it. And even if it hadn't been open, that wouldn't have meant you weren't qualified. I think the whole thing was lucky for you. And for them."

President Weston knew of Carter's health issues but figured it wasn't his place to spread the news. He also knew that Maggie Loughlin would be a great fit in the press department.

He reached across to take Maggie's hand and continued with a very earnest look. "I do have one problem."

Maggie furrowed her brows.

"Problem?"

"You're working for the administration that got me voted out of office." The current president was the running mate of Wendell Mercer when they defeated Weston and his vice president, sending him into forced retirement in his adopted state of Texas.

Neither Maggie nor Josh knew how to react. That is, until the former president grinned.

✦

The snow was beginning to fall in earnest now, a departure from the otherwise clear sky throughout the day. The city lights cast an uneven glow on the low clouds and the reflected light fashioned soft shadows on the rapidly mounting accumulation. The dramatic drop in temperature made for a drier precipitation than the wetter snow that had manifested on and off through the last several days.

"*Da, papochka. Ya tozhe tebya lyublyu,*" came the young boy's voice.

The affirmation that his son loved him brought a bittersweet smile to Gennadiy Valeryevich Borzilov. He "hung up" his mobile phone and sat on the lower step of the Lincoln Memorial a few moments longer in silence. There was so much more he wanted to say – to his son, his infant daughter, his wife. But what would he say? Besides, after attending the U.S. inaugural ceremonies, he would see them. Their lives would change markedly in their new home in a new city. Gennadiy wondered how "retirement" would suit him personally.

Regardless, the plan was, as the Americans say, cast in stone. Earlier the Muscovite had visited the Vietnam Veteran's Memorial. There were the Three Servicemen Statue and the Vietnam Women's Memorial, but the central and best-known part of the complex was the nearly 250-foot long wall of highly polished black granite. It seemed a bit odd to the Russian that the

Americans would celebrate a war they lost, but The Wall did after all appropriately memorialize the nearly sixty thousand men and women who died in the conflict. The *Amerikanskiy* preferred to portray their departure not as a surrender but as an honorable withdrawal. But, however they chose to characterize it, withdraw they did, never to return.

Borzilov had sat for several minutes under the gaze of the Americans' sixteenth president. When he stood, the just-beginning snow shower left an imprint of his presence where it had fallen around him onto the step. Though the weather in the American capital was not nearly as cold as it would be in his native Moscow, his three years in Washington had acclimated him to its weather so he felt cold, very cold. He raised his collar, placed his phone in his pocket and left his hands there, too.

Gennadiy's walk took him to the Korean War Memorial that depicted nineteen soldiers advancing – or perhaps retreating, the man thought – through a triangular lot. The backlighting provided a respectful though eerie atmosphere to the tribute.

Though he was a child of Russia, borne a few years after the U.S.S.R. had fallen apart, he had been taught in his childhood of the proxy wars between the Soviet Union and the United States. The Korean Conflict was the first military confrontation in the "cold war" and it began almost as soon as the uneasy alliance of the two superpowers came to an end at the conclusion of the Great Patriotic War, Russia's term for World War Two.

Tensions never entirely ended with the Americans. Relations between the two nations alternated up and down, ranging from merely frosty to a tantamount resumption of the Cold War more recently.

Current tensions existed largely because of the annexation of the Ukraine in 2014. The hostility simmered during the Trump presidency, later reaching a boiling point in open military action. Though technically the conflicts were between Ukrainian rebels and Russian forces, everyone in the world knew that U.S. forces were involved in training and it was widely suspected that U.S. Navy Seals had made surgical strikes against Russian outposts. Such was the world that Gennadiy was born into, grew up in, and lived in as an adult. His current world involved steady tensions between his home country and the one where he lived while serving *Rodina*. The only thing that pushed Russia into a less prominent role with the Americans was the year-long period of heightened tensions with China.

The snowfall increased from simply steady to heavy in the blink of an eye. Gennadiy Valeryevich Borzilov knew he would have difficulty sleeping but he decided he should return to his apartment and at least try.

The Russian moved his eyes through the monuments around him – toward the Lincoln Memorial and Washington Monument at opposite ends of the Reflecting Pool.

Peace was never easy, despite the hearts of the men who wished it.

CHAPTER 3

Day 3 - Monday

The morning broke with the sun rising into a clear sky. The overnight snow had left about three inches on the ground. Washington, D.C. covered in snow was a beautiful sight on all days, but with the promise of a blue dome above it, the day was off to a great start.

Despite the relatively early end to the evening with President Trent and Alicia Weston or more likely because of it, there had been no lovemaking for Josh the night before. He had hoped that getting home as early as they did from a night out would provide an unexpected break in Maggie's intense preparation for her new job in the White House. And though he understood that you don't just show up on your first day there and wing it – or West Wing it, Morgan thought, proud of his pun – he had hoped for some overdue intimacy. But it wasn't to be.

So, Morgan went to bed long before Maggie had and though he was up at his customarily early hour, he rose well after she had. He noticed that she hadn't made coffee.

"You make it to bed?" he enquired, opening the cabinet to collect the coffee and two cups.

"For a couple of hours." Maggie began to sort through all her papers and put them in a neat stack. "I thought I'd go in today."

"In where? The White House? You don't have to be there until Wednesday."

The White House had arranged to have most of her things delivered to the West Wing the previous week and even though in a normal change of staff personnel, newcomers would have begun to settle in at least a few days prior to Inauguration Day, Marie Ginnetti had suggested that Maggie be allowed a later arrival, owing to the tardiness of her hiring.

"I know. But I think I'm about as prepared as I can be short of sitting in my chair at my desk with someone looking over my shoulder telling me what I'm even doing there." She laughed weakly. "So, I'm going in today, first to make sure my credentials really work, and this hasn't all been some sort of bizarre practical joke. Then I'm gonna put my few personal things in place. That will let me take tomorrow off from all this cramming and just enjoy the swearing-in and all the pomp and circumstance of Inauguration Day and make a serious start the next day.

"But for now…" she walked over to her fiancé and slipped her hands inside his shorts. She rose up on tiptoes and gave him an extraordinarily passionate kiss. Josh pulled her to him as well as he could. Once he placed the unused coffee and empty cups on the kitchen counter, he resumed his embrace, this time caressing Maggie's ass with both hands. He lifted her; she wrapped her legs around him. Josh walked them into the bedroom.

A couple of miles away another couple was rising from a rare moment of passion. POTUS and her husband snuggled for a few minutes longer – minutes President Hendrickson really didn't feel she could spare, but minutes Sandy Hendrickson needed, nevertheless.

She had little on her official agenda. There were inaugural festivities, some of which required a token appearance from the president-elect. Then a few tasks – both official and personal – followed by putting last-minute touches on the final draft of her inaugural address. Madam President would do a dry run of the speech before heading over to the Capitol to examine the platform. Her first presidential oath was in the Oval Office after her predecessor had resigned for his part in the debacle that was the abduction of former President Weston by Saudi operative Fadi Al-Majeed. This time would be different, filled with every possible bit of pageantry, every conceivable item of pomp that her political party could imagine.

And President Sandra Hendrickson intended to relish every second of it.

Josh was still lying on the bed when Maggie emerged from the bathroom wearing her attire for her first day in the West Wing.

"So, what do you think? Too much? Not enough?"

Morgan surveyed Maggie up and down and said, "I always think it's not enough," as he rose and tried to pull her closer and kiss her neck.

Maggie playfully pushed him away and called him an asshole.

"You know what I mean. Too dressy? Too casual? I mean… Morgan, it's the White House!"

Taking the cue that this was no time for fooling around, Morgan said, "Honestly, Loughlin, I think it's perfect."

He assessed Maggie's navy-blue business suit of long skirt and jacket with an ivory blouse again. "I do, hon. I think it's just right."

Maggie's cheeks flushed slightly. She exaggerated her sigh for effect but the nervousness it conveyed was real.

"Wish me luck," she begged.

"Luck is the last thing you need. You're gonna be perfect." Josh gave Maggie a gentle kiss on the forehead and a warm embrace. He handed her the new briefcase he had given her when she got the news that she had been hired. Another embrace and she turned to leave. She was rewarded with a slap on her butt. Maggie never turned but wagged her right index finger backward toward her fiancé. She smiled.

✦

Ed Broussard and his four companions began to map their strategy. For them, strategizing was basically hashing out where to locate themselves and when. Complex planning wasn't their strength. Still, they had a firm goal in mind. It was enough to have a chick as president but the thought of that black bastard as VP. That was more than these good old boys could deal with. If there was one place the bitch and her "boy" were bound to be tomorrow morning, it was that yellow church near the White House. They could probably get as close there as anywhere else, but it might not be close enough to pull off what they'd planned for weeks.

The quintet talked softly though not as quietly as they thought. The four Louisianans and an Arkansan from the backwoods tended to be loud. They mapped their strategy on the back of a napkin and having talked it through, wadded it up just as the waitress served their biscuits and gravy, pancakes, and over-medium eggs. The round booth in the corner of the diner barely accommodated the mastermind and his minions. Hot coffee refilled their cups, which they held aloft in the sincerest of toasts, "To the south!"

"Hell, this is gonna be somethin'," a conspirator said. "Bitch gotta go, one way or 'nuther." Charlie poured a dash of cream in his cup, stirred the java with his finger, then licked the liquid off it. "But, all things considered, I wouldn't mind gettin' in her pants first."

"Damn, Charlie!" Eddie laughed, snorting some coffee through his nose. The entire table looked around nervously to see what attention they'd attracted. But not a soul in this diner in this D.C. suburb heard a word nor cared that the five southerners even existed. The good ol' boys exchanged glances and laughed again.

"Damn, Charlie," Eddie repeated with a shake of his head as he dug into his breakfast.

Margaret Loughlin, as identified by her ID badge, cleared through the gate into the White House grounds without delay or complication. Well, there was the scan with the metal detector. A dog sat nearby, sniffing her, Maggie supposed. A uniformed guard inspected her briefcase. Nope, no delays whatsoever.

Ms. Loughlin, as the guard who was her guide into the West Wing called her, followed the escort through double doors into the center of power for the free world, the West Wing. Maggie was afraid the gasp was audible rather than just in her mind. She had been here for interviews, but now she worked in the place. The guard led her past several cubicles. She was prepared to be directed into one at any moment. Instead her attendant walked her through the center aisle to an office – with a door. Small, but an office.

Maggie looked around and, sure enough, about the office sat the personal belongings she had sent ahead upon her appointment as the Principal Deputy Press Secretary.

"Will there be anything else, Deputy Secretary?"

Maggie almost giggled. "Uh, no. Nothing."

The attendant turned to walk back to his post. Maggie leaned out the door of her office and said to the retreating figure, "Thanks. Thank you."

She set down her satchel and the small cardboard box of belongings she had brought. She collapsed into her ergonomically advanced chair behind her desk – modest, but hers – and pressed "9" on her desk phone to make her first call as Principal Deputy Press Secretary of the President of the United States of America.

"Morgan!" she proclaimed to the call's recipient. "Jeez, sweetheart! This is incredible!"

President Sandra Hendrickson, if she were honest with herself, never truly felt like the real president. Yes, she conducted all the duties of the office – quite well, she thought – but the manner in which she ascended to the office... well, she felt like a bit of pretender. Being on the ticket as vice president was as much a marketing strategy as anything else. It was all about the electoral tally, after all, and the fact that she was from Ohio and had helped reel in her state's eighteen electors was no less important than her being a woman. But this time, this election, voters determined that they wanted Sandra Hendrickson to be their president – her specifically, her as a person. She hadn't been this excited since... well, she had never been this excited.

POTUS had made the final notes to her address slated for the following morning. She had practiced in her office and in front of the dais in the press briefing room. It was time to head to the Capitol steps. She wouldn't go through the entire speech, just a sort of march through the opening remarks and then a blah, blah, blah to get a sense of what she felt would be the experience of a lifetime. Even if she ran for reelection and won, there would be nothing like, as in many aspects of life, nothing like the first time.

This day would start with a luncheon and leadership conference, as previous newly elected chief executives had begun theirs. That evening, she would attend the gala that would commence the official inaugural festivities. The event would serve to welcome the attendees, both politicians and constituency, who would avail themselves of the opportunity to celebrate what they believed to be the hallmark of American democracy. There would be a concert with entertainers ranging from operatic to pop to hip-hop to country. In other words, the political advisors ensured there would be something for everyone.

Early the following morning, the day that was the crux of the two-day event would begin early. A church service at St. John's Episcopal Church would kick things off. Following the service, which served to unite the political nature of the office with the supposed spiritual ordination of the country's beginnings, she would be off at a hectic pace.

A couple of busy days, and the president was increasingly excited and even more determined to take it all in. President Hendrickson ate a sumptuous breakfast with her family and left the executive residence to start ticking off the items on her schedule.

Madam President decided to take a detour through the West Wing to visit briefly with Press Secretary Marie Ginnetti.

The tall, slender brunette rose at the sight of her boss and extended her hand cordially. The business part of their conversation went quickly and as the president was leaving her press secretary's office, she paused.

"Your new assistant starts Wednesday, right?"

"Loughlin? No. Turns out she came in today. I wasn't expecting her but was just about to go down to greet her. Why don't you come with me? I'm sure it would be a thrill."

✦

"No shit, Morgan. He called me 'Deputy Secretary.' It was so cool." As Maggie listened to her fiancé's reply, her concentration was interrupted by a knocking on her door, rapidly followed by its opening. President of the United States Sandra Hendrickson entered, followed immediately by Press Secretary Ginnetti.

"Good morning, Margaret," said the president.

Maggie stammered to nobody in particular. Then without saying a word, she placed the handset on its cradle and stood in much the same way as when she had been called to task as a child in private school.

"Madam President." She gulped intensely enough that she knew it was bound to be apparent. "Secretary Ginnetti." Her smile was undoubtedly as weak as her knees.

✦

Gennadiy Valeryevich Borzilov passed through the metal detector in the foyer of the Russian embassy. He had no real duties that needed his attention today, yet decorum required that he be at his desk for at least part of the day. Entering the not-much-larger-than-closet-sized area that constituted his office, he sat abruptly into his chair.

Situated at 2650 Wisconsin Avenue, the Embassy of the Russian Federation was only a short distance from all the festivities associated with the installment of the current/incoming President of the United States. Still, the certain crowds meant walking. And walking meant time. Gennadiy wasn't in the upper echelon of diplomatic staff, so consequently he had never been to the White House in an official capacity. Furthermore, he wasn't invited to any of the inaugural events to which diplomatic personnel were invited as a matter of protocol. Still, it wouldn't appear unusual for him to make the trek to environs around the presidential residence. He knew the area well, having spent the last few years in the District. But despite his time there, he'd never been present for this event. His tenure at the embassy for his real job in the employ of the SVR, the Russian Foreign Intelligence Service, hadn't overlapped the previous instance when the full spectrum of events of the transition of the American presidential cycle were observed.

The Americans prided themselves on this most consequential of events in their democratic process, the one that represented, as they called it, an orderly transfer of power. Of course, in this case it represented no such thing, in that the current American president was merely permitted to continue residing at 1600 Pennsylvania Avenue another four years.

Though a refresher with regard to the route wasn't essential, Gennadiy nevertheless accessed Google Maps and reviewed it for the following day. Next, he searched for and found the schedule of inaugural activities.

"Eight-thirty AM – church service at St. John's Episcopal Church. President and vice president elect to attend." This wasn't news to Borzilov but simply a confirmation of his schedule for the following day, too. It was the only part of the president's day he cared about.

With nothing more to do, the Russian agent accessed online services and news of home. Without a conscious thought, he lifted the portrait of his family, kissed it, and clutched it to his breast.

✦

Maggie Loughlin stared at POTUS, looked down, and looked up again. Embarrassed as she was, she intended to bluff her way through it.

President Sandra Hendrickson extended her right hand to Maggie.

"I've heard wonderful things about you from Secretary Ginnetti. She is confident, as am I, that you'll be a wonderful asset to this administration."

"Thank you, ma'am." At once, Maggie felt more at ease at the president's kind disposition. POTUS made small talk with the new deputy secretary for nearly ten minutes, enquiring about everything from her new employee's fiancé – though she already knew much – to Image Quest, Maggie's business back home, to Maggie's personal background and more. When President Hendrickson finished the visit, she took Maggie's hand again, this time with both of hers, and said goodbye.

"I know Marie has made sure you'll have a good seat at the ceremony tomorrow. And I'm looking forward to seeing you at the opening gala tonight."

She turned to leave but not before quietly saying to Maggie, "Please resume your phone call." The president had turned to leave so her smile wasn't apparent to Maggie. Maggie was sure her embarrassment was more than obvious. Still, as soon as the president and the press secretary were sufficiently down the hall, the new deputy secretary lifted the handset from its cradle and began to punch in the familiar digits.

"I've got to tell Morgan about this." While waiting for him to answer, she finally noticed the bouquet of flowers on the credenza along the wall.

"Oh, that's sweet," she thought.

Morgan answered, "Hi, sweetheart."

Maggie practically gushed, "Thank you so much, darling."

Without missing a beat, Josh answered, "You're welcome. I was rather good – no, great this morning – but you were amazing, too. Thank *you!*"

"Turd! I meant for the flowers."

"Uh, I'm sorry, Mag. I didn't send you flowers," Morgan said, while simultaneously realizing that he should have. He immediately followed up with, "I was going to send some Wednesday. You know, when I thought you were starting." He grimaced because he knew Maggie would see right through his attempted cover.

"Liar," Maggie said and looked at the card on the bouquet.

"Looking forward to a long association. Marie" Not "Marie Ginnetti." Not "Secretary Ginnetti." Not "The Secretary." Just "Marie."

She spoke into the phone. "Sweetie. I'm gonna like this."

✦

The remainder of the day was a blur for everyone else. For Maggie, it was an exercise in utter futility. Occupied with all things "inaugural," Secretary Ginnetti had no time for her. Perhaps that's one reason the Secretary was so willing to plan Maggie's start for the day after the inauguration. But the new-hire found a number of things to occupy her time. She found the Keurig coffee maker and made herself the strongest brew she could find. Just about the time she was thinking about breaking into her Tupperware filled with salad makings, her door opened without a knock.

"I'm Dick Klein. Ginnetti says I'm to show you around the online systems. I'll be gone at the end of the week so try to get it the first time through. Understood?"

"Wow! 'Dick' suits you," she observed to herself.

Dick spent the next thirty minutes speeding at Mach One through the antiquated computer applications that made up the West Wing press group's software. Her "mentor" spoke only the minimal amount necessary, apparently assuming she would get it through osmosis or perhaps figuring she had an eidetic memory. At any rate, the session was virtually lost on her and she determined quickly that trying to take notes was pointless.

When her guide rose to leave, he said only, "And that's it."

Maggie said, "Thank you." And after an extended pause, "Dick."

She figured Morgan was right. She would just have to "West Wing-it" for today.

Maggie had another cup of coffee and grazed on her rabbit food while struggling through the technical hierarchy of the press department's systems. Not nearly as sophisticated or technologically up-to-date as even the meager system she used at Image Quest, the applications were easy to navigate.

In the middle of the afternoon Secretary Ginnetti knocked politely and entered Maggie's office. She led her assistant to her office and handed her a stack of three-ring binders.

"These are all online but, you'll have to excuse me, I find it easier to get to the important stuff in the notebooks."

Maggie agreed, "I'm the same way."

The Secretary continued, "We'll go over this in more detail in a couple of days, but I just wanted to lead you through these policies and procedures. Anything you need to know…" Ginnetti thumbed the edges of the pages, "…you can find it in here."

A page tore loose from the metal rings.

"Maybe," she said with a smile, donning the reading glasses that hung perpetually around her neck on a soft nylon strap.

Maggie thought again, "I really am gonna like it here." And for the first time in several weeks, Maggie Loughlin felt completely at ease.

Back at the Xcalibur Motel, Eddie Broussard and his redneck friends were drinking beer on the tailgates of their pickup trucks.

Bobby said, "We gonna do this… or we gonna do this?"

"Hell, yeah!" confirmed Sam.

Billy and Charlie yelled their support. They clinked their glass beer bottles.

"Damn the bitch and her boy!"

"To hell with 'em both!"

"We're gonna be freakin' heroes back home!"

"Hell, yeah!" They were all in agreement… and loud.

✦

Maggie introduced Morgan to Secretary Ginnetti at the gala but otherwise the evening wasn't noteworthy. They listened to some wonderful entertainers, though not all appealed to them. They finally strolled hand in hand alongside the Reflecting Pool for a time after the event was done. Finally, the pair decided it was time to head home.

"Home," thought Morgan. He couldn't quite think of this place as "home."

But Maggie was here and that was pretty much all that mattered.

"You know, Josh…" Maggie's words showed a new enthusiasm he hadn't heard with regard to this move and her new job.

"I think," she continued," that this is going to be one heck of an adventure."

Still the descending volume of her voice convinced Morgan that the adrenaline that had sustained her for the last few weeks, the last couple of days in particular, was about to run out. Yes, it was time to take her home.

CHAPTER 4

Day 4 - Tuesday

Even with aides to awaken her at any hour she chose, or at any other hour that the world beckoned, the president still set her alarm every night to get her started at the appointed hour each day. It sounded at 4:30 AM in the executive residence, though this time it was hardly necessary. Sandra Hendrickson had barely slept. After all, it was January 20. She had a big day ahead of her.

✦

Throughout the city people rose to execute their respective duties. Wakeup calls sounded in hotels in every part of the District and in the surrounding areas. Restaurant personnel showed up at ungodly hours. Capitol Police Officers began their briefings. Special Agents from the FBI discussed operations and contingencies.

Even souvenir vendors rose early to man their carts in prescribed locations along the streets. With everything from Hendrickson/Logan buttons and pennants to gold leaf logoed shot glasses emblazoned with the presidential seal, there were an almost infinite number of ways to pluck dollars. Inaugurations weren't just about democracy; they were also about capitalism and entrepreneurship.

✦

In The Wharf development of D.C., another alarm clock sounded. Maggie didn't budge. It was the first night of sound sleep she had managed in quite some time. Morgan rose and slipped on his Georgetown sweatpants and Texas Longhorns t-shirt. He proceeded to the kitchen and started brewing some coffee. Neither he nor Maggie were big breakfast-eaters, so he took some bread out of the package to make some toast. He sliced avocados and tomatoes and set them on a plate.

Maggie walked into the kitchen in the oversized USC shirt she often slept in.

"My, aren't we a contradiction of collegiate loyalties?" Morgan mused.

He observed a smile on Maggie's face that hadn't been there much as of late. While she took out a cup for herself and poured for both of them, Morgan took the slices out of the toaster and topped each piece with avocado and tomatoes and applied a liberal sprinkling of freshly-ground pepper.

"So, what's the plan for today?" he asked.

"My credentials will get me – us – into the Capitol Building to wait around until a few minutes before the inaugural ceremony. Then we take our reserved seats on ground level just below the stage where the swearing-in will be done."

"Inside the Capitol? That's good."

"Yep! You're in prestigious company. I am definitely somebody now."

Maggie held out her hand for Morgan to kiss. It wouldn't bother her if he bowed, too. Instead he smirked and shook his head.

"That might be so, Your Highness, but I was talking about the weather. It'll be nice to be inside for as much of the morning as we can. Look outside."

With a cup in one hand and lifting her slice of avocado toast to her mouth with the other, Maggie moved to the window overlooking the scene below their fifth-floor apartment. She surveyed the landscape for a few seconds until Josh joined her.

"Wow," she remarked.

The sky was overcast. The flat lighting provided no shadows or relief on the nearly one foot of snow that blanketed everything from the grounds of their residential complex to as far as they could see.

"Yeah," Morgan said.

"It's still pretty. I mean, it would better with sun…"

"And mountains."

Maggie elbowed Josh in the side. "Yes. And mountains. Let's get ready."

✦

Eddie Broussard and his companions opened their respective motel room doors to the bleak sky and thick layer of snow. They were sluggish from the previous night's alcohol-centric party in Charlie's and Billy's room. The additional eight or so inches of white powder that had accumulated beyond what had lain on the ground when they went to bed was a shock. They weren't prepared for this type of cold. They each had either hunting jackets or Carhartt work coats and gloves. Their hunting boots would keep out the moisture sufficiently to keep their feet dry but the undergarments they had each brought wouldn't provide nearly the warmth they needed.

Perhaps a little antifreeze would help. Despite the early hour, a couple of the men pulled out flasks and passed them around. They piled into Ed's Ram truck and Billy's ten-year-old Chevy pickup. They were accustomed to getting up at obscene hours to go hunting ducks or deer, even after an overnight binge lasting until a couple of hours earlier.

Billy pulled a lever under the truck's dashboard, grabbed a plastic container from the back seat, and jumped back out of his red truck that had gray Bondo patches along the left side that covered repairs from crashes. He lifted the hood and topped off the radiator with the last of the antifreeze. He looked around and, seeing nobody nearby, tossed the empty yellow jug onto a snow bank. He looked at Eddie and his two companions in the Dodge and gave a quick thumbs-up before jumping back into the cab. Billy turned the key and the truck made a few whirring attempts at starting. The Louisianan pumped the accelerator three or four times and turned the key again. His pickup struggled before reluctantly coming to life. Another thumbs-up in the direction of the other truck and he pulled in behind it as they led the way.

The Xcalibur's night clerk watched the sputtering truck pull out of the parking lot. On the cab's rear window were all manner of stickers and decals. The most prominent of the lot stated, "Hunters Do It Early in the Morning." Another showed the outline of a hand with extended middle finger and the suggestion, "Kiss my Southern ass!" The clerk shook his head and lay it back on his folded arms on the counter.

✦

Throughout the city but particularly along the route that the inaugural parade would follow later in the day, workers were making final preparations and people were taking their places.

The first event open to the public would be the inauguration itself. The Constitution prescribed that the president began the new term at noon on January 20 following the election. The initial parts of the program would begin at 11:00 AM, but people would begin to gather on the Capitol grounds in the very early morning to get their preferred location on the west front of the building.

Preparations had been ongoing for some time ahead of the event. The Architect of the Capitol had overseen erection of the inaugural platform and worked with the Joint Congressional Committee on the inaugural ceremonies to make sure all the arrangements were completed on time. Crews set up fencing and seating.

On the platform, of course, the closer to the incoming president, the more important a person was. On the president's left would normally be the outgoing president and vice president. Because Mercer had officially left office for "health reasons," many speculated that he would be seated there. But because of the truth behind his departure, Madam President felt it would dishonor the constitutionally-mandated event simply for the sake of appearance. In a first, and again because President Hendrickson felt the country owed him much, she invited former President Trenton and First Lady Alicia Weston to occupy those seats. People generally assumed that Mercer was too ill to attend. He had disappeared from public view after his resignation and was indeed in failing health due to the strain of his last actions as chief executive. All but the most radically partisan applauded the selection of the Westons to take Mercer's place, seeing it as a nod to the elder statesman for the ordeal he had endured. In addition, many considered the inclusion of her predecessor's predecessor as an attempt at unity in a political environment that had been decidedly ununified and hostile for years.

Behind the Westons would sit the nine Supreme Court Justices, members of the incoming Cabinet, and other administration officials, while on the president's right while speaking and behind her when she was seated would be ranking members of Congress and other administration insiders. Other VIPs would sit at ground level in front of the platform.

The good old boys from the Xcalibur Motel finally found parking about two miles from their intended spot. Gathering their signs and plastic megaphones, they headed toward the location nearest St. John's Church that was available to the general public. With the crowd, the cold, and the restricted areas to navigate, it would take longer than expected to get there.

Eddie Broussard tucked his oversized smart phone in his camouflaged jacket's pocket. Along their route, they paused twice to take sips from the flasks they had brought. Each man held his cap alongside his head in an attempt to shield the silver containers from unwanted eyes. The five men were desperate to be near the church before the bitch and her lackeys got there. They picked up the pace. It was going to be close.

The president was excited. She couldn't wait to begin the day. But her schedule had been published some time ago so deviating from it would disappoint a great number of people from throughout the world, not to mention upsetting the media coverage of the day. So, she waited until the appropriate time to depart the White House for the church adjacent to Lafayette Square.

Becoming simply Sandy and Mom for a few more minutes, she enjoyed a light breakfast with her family. AJ and Adam seemed unfazed, but Noelle was every bit as excited as her mother.

"So, what happens today, Mom?"

"First, we go to the church," Mom answered. She noticed that AJ rolled his eyes. "Then we come back here for a while before heading to the Capitol. You and your brother will hang out with the Secret Service while your dad and I visit with a bunch a people." She noticed that it was her husband who appeared less than enthusiastic this time.

Then we sit on the Capitol steps while some people talk…"

"Too many people talk," her husband interjected.

The wife tilted her head and cut her eyes toward her husband while she continued. "…while some people talk. Then Vice President Logan gets sworn in. Then I get sworn in and give a speech."

"It's really gonna be cold," AJ said.

"They'll have heaters in front of us. They'll help. But be sure to dress warmly. And I want to see what you have on before we leave," she warned, delivering her "mom look" to each of her children. The last part sounded just like what every other mother who didn't live at 1600 Pennsylvania Avenue would require of her kids.

"Then we ride back here and watch the parade."

"Is it going to be warm in that glass box we sit in?" Noelle asked.

Mom answered, "Promise. Adam, would you make sure they start getting ready?"

She rose and patted her youngest on her head and, having stood, morphed once again into the Most Powerful Person in the World.

At exactly 7:30 AM, responding to an internal timer, a device sprang to life inside the rightmost of the center columns at St. John's Episcopal Church, where it has been placed during repairs to damage inflicted to the Historic Landmark by a van belonging to District Miracle Plumbers. In addition to the apparatus was a mobile phone and a separate battery pack that had kept it charged during its dormancy.

Maggie Loughlin sized up her guy in his suit.

"Yowzah!" she exclaimed. "Modeling for *GQ* now?"

Josh smiled. "You know, I never wear suits. Just for you, Your Highness."

"Well, if you're gonna wear one, at least look good. And you're a stud!" She walked over and gave Morgan another up and down survey. Her smile and arched eyebrows put the exclamation point on her approval.

Maggie already had her shin-length overcoat on. Morgan said, "So let's have a look"

His fiancée pulled open the as yet unbuttoned winter coat to reveal a gray wool skirt extending to just below the knees and light gray tunic length pullover sweater. Kneehigh black boots and black wool topcoat finished out the ensemble.

"You know you're not supposed to look better than the president, right? I mean, not only is it her day but ultimately, she's your boss."

The couple joined hands and headed out for what promised to be an eventful day.

✦

The Hendrickson family paused at the door leading from the White House to the snow-covered ground and temperatures in the upper twenties. The president took a deep sigh and in the manner of any wife, reflexively straightened her husband's tie. It would be just about the last private moment they would have as a family for the rest of the day. Of course, when you're the first family, privacy was a relative thing. In the foyer of the executive mansion, they stood among their White House staff. But once they opened the doors, or rather when they were opened for them, they were the focus of attention for the White House press corps. Beyond the fence around the compound, throughout the city, tens of thousands more were waiting for them, including well-wishers, protesters, the simply curious, and those toting their children through the frigid weather so that they could be a part of history.

"It's going to be great," Adam told Sandy.

"Have a wonderful day," a staffer told the president.

The Official Presidential Photographer snapped away and positioned himself directly behind the family as doors were opened and they stepped out to face the countless individuals who, in their own ways, required something of them that day.

POTUS had elected to walk to St. John's that day, a decision favored by nearly nobody else.

In a perfect world, the Secret Service would prefer that Spinnaker was never out in the open. Her code name referred to her lifelong love of sailing that dated to her childhood in Florida. Her family would've wished to avoid the cold, as would the press who followed like puppies waiting for a treat. Regardless, she had made her decision and would stand by it. Besides she rationalized, she would be just as cold as everyone else.

It was a relatively short walk. The only inconvenience was indeed the cold. The snow had mercifully ended around 3:30 that morning, permitting time enough to clear it from the drive, sidewalks, and surrounding streets. By noon and the president's swearing-in, the temperature was forecast to be around 34 degrees.

Secret Service agents closely surrounded President Hendrickson. Walking alongside her was Antoine Logan and his sister. A bachelor, Logan had a steady girlfriend he had been dating for eight months. He was crazy about Olivia and they saw each other as often as his office as vice president allowed. But despite his genuine feelings for Liv, he wasn't so serious about her that he wanted to create the sort of impression that would certainly occur if every newspaper in the universe and the entire scope of the Internet showed photos of her as his escort on this significant day. So, Logan had asked his twin sister to join him, a decision that had resulted in intense friction between him and his image-conscious significant other.

The group walked diagonally to the left across Pennsylvania Avenue. AJ wondered sarcastically if they would give his mom a ticket for jaywalking. From there they walked through the center of Lafayette Square. It always held a number of surveillance devices and was always monitored. On this January 20 though, owing to the president's stated intention to walk to church, the park received even more scrutiny.

At this point, the Secret Service agents riding in their cars piled out and closed ranks with their peers for the walk through the park. The presidential limousine, followed by the agents' vehicles, sped away to wait for the group to arrive on the far side of the Square at St. John's.

When the pedestrians reached H Street NW at the north boundary of the Square, it was a matter of mere yards to the fabled structure that every president since John Madison had visited.

The walk had invigorated POTUS. She paused on the south side of the street for the press to avail themselves of the limitless photo opportunities from every angle. Even AJ managed to smile, despite freezing his ass off.

Press Secretary Ginnetti said discreetly, "I believe that's long enough, Madam President."

The first gentleman remarked, "And just in time."

A light flurry began as the procession began the short walk across H Avenue NW. It occurred to POTUS that the Inaugural Committee might decide to move her ceremony inside. She hoped not.

CHAPTER 5

Eddie, Charlie, Billy, Sam, and Bobby made good time and were in place sooner than they'd expected. They were as cold as they had ever been. They'd certainly seen their share of twenty-eight-degree weather, considering the amount of time they spent outdoors in the winter. But they were always prepared for it. Even in the current sub-freezing temperature, their walk covering the nearly two miles had been brisk enough to generate a light sweat, which now chilled them further. The contents of the two flasks were long gone. They were icy.

Not many years past, people would have considered the signs the five friends held to be beyond the pale. But in the bitter climate of an evenly divided constituency, the public followed the lead of their elected representatives as they abandoned any semblance of esteem for anyone who disagreed with them. So now, instead of viewing the obscene rhetoric with scorn, the viewers' reactions were at best indifferent. Some even shouted their agreement.

The men began with unbridled enthusiasm, holding their signs aloft and shouting through the tiny plastic megaphones that sported the names of their hometowns' high school's team mascots. After a very few minutes, their vigor faded. The signs of two of them were dragging the ground. The other three had discarded theirs entirely. Eddie managed to keep his rancor at something close to fever pitch while Billy leaned against a pole with his collar pulled up and his hands in his pocket. Charlie sat on the curb talking on his cell. Sam had headed off to find coffee. Bobby was… well, the others had no clue where he went.

The group of men located themselves at the intersection of I Street NW and 16th Street NW. Their arrival time made it difficult, but they had managed to force their way into a position immediately alongside the barriers. Even Eddie finally decided to save his voice and energy for later. Other people continued to arrive at the site, despite the fact that it wasn't a prime location. It wasn't on the parade route. Nothing much would happen there, that is, except for very short windows of time. Those were when the first family arrived to enter St. John's Episcopal and when they returned into view after the service. It would be for the briefest of times and they would be surrounded by a crowd. Complicating their mission further was that the bitch president would be little more than a speck at that distance. But what they had in mind didn't require their proximity.

✦

Maggie's credentials got the two of them into the Capitol more easily than they had at the White House.

She and Josh stood in the rotunda amidst a sea of people, important and otherwise. Some were very recognizable, but she and Morgan knew none of them, so they stood visiting only with each other and people-watching.

A great number of the people busily texted on their various devices and a few even spoke on them.

✦

Eddie was suddenly energized when he saw the presidential limousine pull up near the church. He called his three remaining fellow protestors who had fallen back into the horde. They forcefully pushed their way through the crowd, getting cursed and cursing in return. They joined Eddie at the barricade only to see the limo stop well away from the front of the church. Looking down 16th past the church, they saw a procession moving across H NW. The cheers and increased activity in front of St. John's made it apparent that the president and her group had walked from the White House and were making their way to the church. The four conspirators immediately put their plan into action, which consisted of jumping the metal barrier, heaving their signs skyward, and screaming the foulest obscenities they could think of. They made it about ten yards before each of them was brutally tackled by security personnel.

✦

The commotion hardly mattered a block south, going completely unnoticed by President Hendrickson as she greeted parishioners, clergy, and other well-wishers. The leader of the free world and her group lingered long enough to throw them behind schedule.

Vice President Logan basked in the glow of the situation, even if he wasn't the main attraction. All in due time, he thought. He had his own plans but for now, he couldn't be happier than to be part of Hendrickson's administration. She was the right person for this time in the nation's long story of democracy. He watched her work the crowd with grace and a genuine appreciation for where she was and gratitude for all the people who worked with her.

A block north of St. John's Episcopal Church, a warmly-dressed man slid into the spot at the barricade that had, until a couple of minutes ago, been occupied by four obnoxious assholes. A brown leather glove covered his left hand, the one that held his mobile phone into which he had entered a number. The index finger of his ungloved right hand was at the ready to press "Send" when the moment arose.

The man watched anxiously, knowing that this act was his only recourse in the dilemma that had unfolded for him personally.

At the south end of the block, Press Secretary Ginnetti informed Madam President's chief of staff that it was time to proceed to the service. Noah Chandler relayed the request to his boss and POTUS prepared to lead the congregants through the giant pillars into the chapel. The president gathered her son and daughter and put her arm through her husband's and assumed a worshipful attitude as she moved along at the head of the procession.

Gazing over the barrier that prevented constituents from achieving inappropriately close proximity to their president, the man's stare was almost trancelike. He watched as it became certain the woman would indeed proceed into the sanctuary. He closed his eyes and steeled himself. Then he pressed the key that would initiate the call. A moment of mixed anticipation and dread and... nothing. In a panic, he depressed the button again. Still nothing. Another look at the phone's screen at the location where the bars should've been, he saw displayed, "No Service."

"*Dermo!*"

"Shit!" Gennadiy repeated, this time in English.

Josh and Maggie were getting updates via their iPhones about the progress of the day's events. They learned that the president had just entered the St.

John's chapel. Neither knew that use of their mobile devices would end once the president arrived at the Capitol.

Recent acts in which terrorists around the world used phone-detonated bombs to carry out their attacks had convinced the agencies tasked with protecting POTUS that additional precautions were necessary. For the last several months an aide had joined the presidential detail lugging a large briefcase in the same way another member of the entourage carried the "Nuclear Football." However, instead of carrying everything necessary to allow the President of the United States to authorize a nuclear strike from any location, this case contained technology that jammed all frequencies used by mobile communications devices. The technology itself wasn't new but the capability to pack the power of this one into such a small unit was groundbreaking. Except for those bands reserved for use by the president and the federal personnel involved with her security, every frequency was disabled for a radius of about three blocks.

✦

Gennadiy Valeryevich Borzilov was in a near panic. The cause of the failure was irrelevant now. Only a recovery mattered.

The Russian had a second transmitter in his possession that could've initiated the explosion by communicating with a second trigger connected to the C-4 buried inside the white column. However, its purpose was never to be a backup in case of the phone's failure. Instead the redundancy was an alternative to his phone if for some reason Borzilov was unable to secure an unobstructed view of his target. The second transmitter was built around new Russian technology that employed NLOS – or non-line-of-sight – propagation. The planners of the assassination, presently only an attempted one, viewed it as an inferior solution because, despite superior technology that removed visual obstructions as an impediment to communications, it presented the problem of a very limited range as compared to using the phone. Such devices' primary application had been to enable very short-range communication through walls, not to detonate bombs at moderate to long distances. Secondly, in addition to the minimal effectiveness in terms of distance, its very use implied that direct observation was impossible or imprudent. In this case, Borzilov preferred line of sight in that it allowed him to time detonation for maximum effect. Knowing the precise moment when the president was nearest the explosive device was key and the designers of this plan considered it highly unlikely that detonation without line of sight could assure the American president would die. And that was, after all, the only result that mattered.

Therefore, since the precision of direct observation provided a more certain likelihood that the president would be neutralized, the choice of phone-initiated detonation was the logical one. There would be a short delay while the phone call connected, but the Russian could allow for that, in essence "leading" his target.

While the Muscovite struggled to comprehend what had gone wrong and worked to retrieve the alternate transmitter from the pocket of his great coat, a man with the crazed appearance of a demoniac straight out of the New Testament violently forced his way through the crowd at the intersection of 16th Street NW and I Street NW. Bobby filled the cold air with unrelenting curses, some of which a majority of those around him had never heard.

"You gonna die, bitch! Your time is coming! Your sorry ass is history! You…"

The Capitol Police in the area had had enough and slammed Bobby violently to the pavement in the same manner they had his friends. They followed up his seizure by taking him to join them.

Then fearing additional trouble, security personnel directed the crowd to move away from the area. They led them two blocks farther away to ensure that any further actions wouldn't endanger the president and her companions when they exited the church.

So, the worst-case scenario seemed to be occurring for Gennadiy. The relocation removed the ability to time the explosion visually, which had failed anyhow. And it complicated Borzilov's mission further due to the extended distance from the church and therefore the plastic explosives' receiver. If he wasn't certain it would detonate the plastic explosives from one block away, how could he have any confidence that it would work from three times that distance?

And there was the matter of the phone. Success still depended on his ability to use it. The alternate needed to be a separate device because he would be using the phone for another purpose. Internet access was now the only way to determine when the president was departing the Christian structure. With no way of knowing about the jamming in the first place, the agent of the Russian Foreign Intelligence Service certainly couldn't have made the leap that he had at least possibly moved beyond its effective range of protective interference. Gennadiy saw that his phone's signal strength was fluctuating between one and two bars now. At least, he thought, one matter seemed to have improved.

Still, the Russian agent had absolutely zero confidence in completing his objective. Would his transmitter work over the increased distance to St. John's? Would his phone maintain sufficient signal strength for him to maintain the video feed? And even if both of those essential elements of the plan succeeded, could he now time the explosion for the desired outcome?

Zero confidence… but he had no other choice than to try.

"This is all fucked up," he muttered in Russian.

The Russian accessed the Internet and attempted to reach the news site that he knew carried live streaming of the American president's activities.

CHAPTER 6

"How 'bout we blow this joint?" Morgan suggested.

"Not a chance. The fun hasn't even started yet," Maggie said. "And, by the way, don't use the phrase 'blow this joint' here," she continued with a wry whisper.

Morgan watched his auburn-haired beauty brush her hair out of her eyes and smiled.

"What?" she demanded.

"You're hot!" he answered.

Maggie loved his come-on but slugged him in the arm anyhow.

Josh checked his phone for the time. Though he still wore his watch, he mostly reflexively used his phone.

"Nine o'clock. They should be leaving the church any time now. That is, if they're running on schedule."

The couple stood in silence a few seconds.

"I can't wait for the ball tonight," Maggie said, breaking the silence.

"Hello, sir."

Maggie was puzzled at Josh's odd response to her comment until she saw that he was looking past her. He followed up with, "Good morning, Mrs. Weston."

Maggie turned to face their friends. She, Morgan, and the former president and his wife greeted one another with hugs.

The foursome chatted a few moments. A hand touched Morgan politely on his shoulder. The ex-CIA officer turned to face a gentleman dressed in a three-piece pinstripe suit.

"Mr. Morgan?"

Josh was surprised not only that the man holding out his right hand knew him by name but that he spoke with a British accent.

Josh took his hand. "Yes? Have we met?"

"I'm sorry for the intrusion on your conversation. Albert McGinnis. And no, we've never met," said the about-sixty-year-old. "I'm at the embassy." Then he extended his hand toward the ex-chief executive of the U.S., who seized it with both hands and broke into an enormous grin.

"Sir Albert! How in the world have you been?"

"Trent. Alicia." Sir Albert embraced Alicia Weston warmly.

President Weston placed both hands on his British friend's shoulders, although he was speaking to Josh and Maggie. "This wonderful gentleman and I go way back." Then to Sir Albert, "You look terrific."

The small talk continued for only a couple of minutes before the Brit waved to another acquaintance on the other side of the rotunda.

"Wonderful to see you, Trent, Alicia." Then to Morgan and Maggie, "Again, my apologies for the intrusion."

"Not at all, sir," Maggie assured him.

"Our pleasure," agreed Morgan.

As he started across the room to greet his friend, he glanced over his shoulder and whispered to the ex-CIA operative, "Outstanding work on that thing with Blake and the Saudi." He waved to yet another acquaintance and moved to engage her. He glanced back over his shoulder and winked at Morgan.

"What did he whisper to you, Josh?"

"Nothing, Maggie. Nothing important. Just apologizing for the interruption again." He smiled and let his gaze follow the gentleman as he walked away briskly. Though puzzled at the man's recognition of him, he knew beyond a doubt that he and the man shared a similar background.

◆

Ivy Eccleston, the president's speechwriter, admired the sermon from Rev. Michael Severs, the St. John's rector. It was an occupational hazard, she supposed, to always assess what she heard on the basis of subject, structure, and a strong call to action, as well as other elements of a good speech, spiritual or otherwise. This man had it all. Eccleston raised her head from the concluding prayer and waited for the cue from her boss.

President Sandra Hendrickson rose from pew 54, the one reserved for the president when in attendance. The quietness of the chapel during the service gave way to a murmur that crescendoed into unrestrained conversation among the celebrants. POTUS spoke to a few of the parishioners while making her way to the exit. Her chief of staff, Noah Chandler, helped move the presidential party along in an effort to keep some semblance of adherence to the schedule. His efforts were in vain. His boss hadn't the heart to refuse to speak to each clergy or layman with whom she made eye contact.

Finally, the Secret Service intervened and insisted she move along. She neared the doors that led outside and to a continuation of her inaugural activities. Though packed with demands on her time, this day held little of the pressures of leading Western nations.

She stepped outside and pulled her scarf more tightly around her neck. The sky was gray, and the snow was falling even more now than when she entered the church, but things couldn't seem brighter for her. She was enjoying herself.

✦

"The Brit seemed nice. How do you think the Westons know him?"

"No idea. But, you know, President Weston's been around." He acted nonchalant about the encounter, but he was equally curious about the man. The gentleman with the salt and pepper hair and well-manicured moustache definitely had personal knowledge of things very few people knew about. "MI-6?" he wondered silently. Certainly more than just embassy, he knew.

✦

The signal was weak but Borzilov's screen managed to maintain the streaming video fairly consistently. There had been occasions of buffering when the image froze but those occurrences were infrequent and brief. His primary concern was whether the limited range of the non-line-of-sight transmitter would be adequate.

Without the ability to see the church, almost all of the people who had been relocated with him had left for better vantage points. He had remained and positioned himself at what he felt was the closest point to the church and the American leader that the security teams allowed people to stand.

The Russian stared at the device intently. Finally, on the screen, the doors to the church opened. A pair of robed clergy held them open as people began to emerge. First were what were obviously Secret Service. Two other agents who had remained outside during the service joined them. The scene on the Russian's phone changed from the door to show the presidential limousine awaiting its occupants on 16th Street NW.

"*Nyet, nyet!*" Borzilov said to the image. "Back to the doors," he begged. The streaming image returned to the doorway and... locked up.

"*Nyet!*" he shrieked again, this time aloud, drawing the attention of the few remaining men, women, and kids around him. He prepared to press the red button on the transmitter. He fleetingly wondered why such devices' buttons always seemed to be red.

Suddenly the video resumed and, more importantly, "caught up" to where it would have been without the interruption for buffering. Standing precisely between the centermost white pillars was President Sandra Hendrickson.

Gennadiy Valeryevich Borzilov pressed the transmitter's button.

The wait felt longer than it was. The barely one second that it had taken for the sound to travel the approximately 390 meters between St. John's Episcopal Church and Borzilov's location ended with a thunderous report that staggered the man. The sonic wave rattled windows and continued for some seconds as it echoed down the streets beyond. Pigeons, grackles, and assorted other birds flew from the ground and trees. A squirrel jumped straight up before scampering in no particular direction.

The Russian agent whispered, "*Spasibo*," though he really didn't know who he was thanking. He placed the transmitter in his coat pocket and put his glove back on his right hand.

Gennadiy Valeryevich Borzilov walked calmly away.

CHAPTER 7

Inside the U.S. Capitol the sound was more muted than it was immediately outside. However, it was still sufficiently powerful to startle everyone. And it was easily recognizable as an explosion.

The collective thought inside the home of the United States Congress was a frightened and desperate, "Oh, no!"

◆

On the western side of St. John's, debris showered down for seconds. Pieces of the towering column served as shrapnel, maiming anyone unfortunate to be in the blast radius. Bodies lay everywhere; many lifeless. Some twenty-five yards from the epicenter of the explosion, its energy threw President Hendrickson savagely to the pavestone blocks. The two Secret Service agents nearest her were likewise thrown down by the blast but those awaiting her by the Beast, the president's limousine, instinctively sprang into action and covered the short distance to their protectee. The first immediately fell atop her and surveyed the immediate area around them for any remaining threat.

Once other agents arrived, they lifted her to a somewhat vertical position and sped Spinnaker, feet dragging behind, to the Beast. Barely conscious, Sandy strained to look past the agents removing her to locate her family. She recognized the motionless body of her husband, who had been standing next to her when the explosion occurred. In her addled state, she couldn't locate AJ, who had been standing behind her, between his mother and the church, or Noelle, whom she thought had been ahead of her.

The president's wits were reeling and her only sense of anything at all, though she could barely hear, was the awareness of a door slamming behind her, of someone shouting, "Go! Go! Go!" and the sudden surge as the vehicle carrying her accelerated away from the scene. Nausea overtook her and then everything went dark.

The area between the yellow church and the street in front of it had the appearance of a battle zone. And perhaps it was. Pieces of the column flamed briefly before dying out. Secret Service personnel brandished all manner of lethal weaponry they had retrieved from inside coats and scrambled to protect those in their safekeeping while simultaneously efforting to secure the area and assess it for remaining potential assailants.

Capitol Police SWAT Teams were already nearby and were rushing to the scene in support. As always, medical personnel were in close proximity to the president though not in sufficient numbers to attend to all the needs here. Swarms of uniformed Capitol Police Officers appeared seemingly out of thin air and began to secure the surrounding buildings and streets. So many people were present for the inauguration that it was impossible to restrict them to the area so that they could be identified as witnesses or even suspects.

The Secret Service assigned specifically to the first family lost agents. Others that had surrounded St. John's dashed in to take their place. They attended to those for whom they had responsibility, disregarding the plight of their fellow team members. At the same instant that POTUS had been shoved into the limousine, agents were already beside their next highest priority, Vice President Logan, though the first one there saw immediately that he was beyond saving.

✦

It was chaos in the Capitol. Nobody knew what had caused the boom. There was no doubt among any of them that it had to be bad so, to a person the only questions they had were, "How bad?" and "Where?"

Morgan had instinctively covered Maggie though the explosion was obviously some distance away. He turned his attention to where President and Mrs. Weston had been standing but Agents Johnston and Coulter had already spirited them to a safe room in the Capitol.

Mobile phones were lighting up throughout the building. Ranking members of Congress who were present – some had been with the president – received calls. They and their aides rushed to their offices. Capitol Police quarantined the building, closing doors and preventing anyone from leaving until the nature of the emergency had been identified and analyzed.

Additional security officers descended on the building.

"Josh?" Maggie looked to him as if he might have an inkling of the circumstances unfolding though she knew he couldn't. What she saw was her fiancé's head shaking weakly as he stared straight ahead.

"Damnation," was all he said.

✦

In front of St. John's, the activity was an evolving mixture of Emergency Medical Technicians treating the wounded, Capitol Police and FBI personnel attempting to preserve the crime scene, and Federal and District officers initiating the investigation. It was a costly attack in terms of lives lost and injuries sustained.

Remarkably, President Sandra Hendrickson suffered relatively minor injuries. Motivated by the persistent reminders by her chief of staff that they had a schedule to keep, Spinnaker was almost to the street when the charge went off. She was thrown to the ground with some cuts. Her most serious injury was absorption of the sheer power of the sonic pressure from the explosion that left her disoriented and semi-conscious. Secret Service sped her to the hospital where the medical staff administered a concussion protocol. They tentatively cleared her but would hold her for observation.

Her husband was beside her at the time of the blast and endured some cuts from debris. Noelle suffered only a temporary loss of hearing from the intense sound, as did everyone else for quite some distance.

Unfortunately, Adam Jr. had fallen behind the rest of his family and was nearer the blast than they. He suffered extensive injuries, including a broken right leg and deep lacerations. The rips in his flesh along with the sheer power of the blast wave caused internal injuries.

The most noteworthy loss to the nation – although each decedent's family would dispute the notion that anyone else represented a more significant loss than their loved one – was Vice President Antoine Logan. He and his sister had lingered behind the president and her family and were standing next to the column hiding the C-4 when it exploded. Their deaths were instantaneous. Logan's head was ripped open and his sister's heart was virtually destroyed from shrapnel in the form of plaster from the column.

Rector Michael Severs survived largely uninjured. He had escorted the first family out of the service and was a fair distance from the column when it erupted. However, two members of the church's clergy died immediately where they stood by the doors bidding farewell to their parishioners.

Two Secret Service agents were also near the doors from the chapel awaiting Logan so they, too, perished. Another one just ahead of the procession was tragically hit in the neck by a single piece of debris that flew over the mass of people behind him, severing his carotid artery. Three other agents were injured, one seriously. The other two had relatively minor cuts. In fact, they had managed to continue their duties in spite of injuries.

Presidential Chief of Staff Chambers had moved to the limousine and was unhurt.

✦

News had spread of the explosion. People were on their phones gathering information, accurate or otherwise, and disseminating information to others, accurate or otherwise.

Being that she didn't officially start her new position as Principal Deputy Press Secretary until the next day, it hadn't occurred to Maggie to be surprised at not being in the loop yet on matters related to the president.

In fact, Maggie had forgotten that she had received her press department phone the day before when she stopped by to move in to her office. So, when it rang in her purse, muted though the sound was, she flinched so dramatically that Josh feared something was wrong. She hadn't received a call on it, nor had she made one. In fact, had she remembered even having it, she would've set it to "vibrate." Her nervousness in the aftermath of the explosion had left her jittery. The loud default "ring" of the device unnerved her.

Maggie gave Morgan a bewildered look, shrugged and arched her eyebrows. She retrieved the phone from her purse and touched the "answer" icon.

"Maggie Loughlin."

"Loughlin. Dick Klein."

Maggie's eyes widened as she turned her gaze toward Morgan. He mouthed the word, "What?" but the wave of her hand told him he would have to wait. The call was brief and after she had pressed the red icon to disconnect, Maggie's face paled and she stood in mute contemplation.

Taking her by both shoulders, Morgan turned her to face him and said, "What?" aloud this time.

"I… I, uh, have to go to work." She stuffed the phone back into her purse and headed for the door with Morgan falling in behind. As she neared the exit, a Capitol Police Officer moved to intercept her and held up a hand.

"I'm sorry but nobody…" he began.

Maggie flashed her new credentials and said, "I work at the White House…" That sounded peculiar and somewhat frightening. "… and I've been called to the office."

Not only did the officer not challenge her assertion, he got on his two-way and called one of the department's cars to transport her there. He eyed Morgan as he continued on behind his fiancée as though ready to prevent him from leaving with her but didn't.

An officer held the door for the pair as they entered the white car with the blue stripe and the words "Police United States Capitol" printed in gold letters.

The door shut and the driver confirmed, "White House?"

"Yes!" Morgan blurted on the White House staff member's behalf.

Maggie gave him an irritated look. "Yes," she answered and shot her fiancé another glance.

The officer turned on the lights of her car. She accelerated from the east front of the Capitol Building northward, where she turned onto Constitution Avenue.

Maggie's countenance was pale, and her voice quivered as she gave Morgan a quick summary of what had happened at the church. "The president is going to be fine, but Marie Ginnetti was injured critically in the explosion. There seems to be some question as to who's in charge of the press group. It might be me."

"That would be some first day," said Morgan, but the look of abject fear evident on Maggie's face made it clear she didn't share his mild humor.

"It will be fine. More than fine. You've got this." He held her hand and the pair sat in total silence for the remainder of the trip.

The patrol car quickly intersected Pennsylvania Avenue and the officer turned on her sirens and accelerated to an even higher speed as she moved her car and its passengers onto the fabled street. As she did, Maggie looked out the window to realize that they were following the route that the inaugural parade would have. Mostly empty metal bleachers sat in front of the many government offices and monuments they passed. A few people remained, possibly because they had nowhere else to go, and most of them were on their phones, no doubt learning what they could and passing on what they had heard.

The driver sped along Pennsylvania past the glass-fronted reviewing box constructed for President Hendrickson and Vice President Logan, their families and other guests. She reached the Northwest Appointment Gate and stopped at the guardhouse. Someone had apparently called ahead because the review of Margaret Loughlin's credentials was much quicker and entrance was granted for the car, less one occupant.

Particularly in light of the heightened state of security, nobody who didn't have credentials entered the White House complex, employee's spouse or not. Josh stepped out. He was about to reopen the door to give Maggie a kiss when the patrol car sped down the drive. Through the closing gate, he could see Maggie turning to look through the rear window. All Morgan could do was wave. And he did, weakly.

The snow was falling harder now, and it occurred to Morgan how little sense that made. The word "hard" should never be used to describe snowfall.

"At least I'm dressed for it," Morgan thought. "Sort of."

✦

Press Secretary Marie Ginnetti was a parishioner at St. John's. She had lagged a bit behind as the presidential procession exited after the service to say some parting words to people she knew. She was very near ground zero when the blast occurred, and it was likely that the only thing that spared her life – at least to this point – was that she was still inside the chapel and the walls afforded her some measure of protection. The wall where she was standing partially collapsed but it at least shielded her from the full brunt of the force. Still, she had a collapsed left lung, a broken left arm, major trauma to her left side, and a concussion. She was transported to the hospital where she was in serious but stable condition.

The president's speechwriter suffered far worse. A dear friend to Ginnetti, Ivy Eccleston was at the press secretary's side, between her and the wall that was thrust toward them. She experienced more of the bomb's force and lived only seconds before succumbing to her injuries.

✦

It had been a long day already even though it was only just past 11:00 AM. SVR Agent Gennadiy Valeryevich Borzilov thought it a productive one. On his way back to the embassy, he had ditched the burner phone that he had used for longer than he should have. The spy dropped it in a trash can some distance from where he had last used it to time the explosion at St. John's. He made one call with a second phone and likewise tossed it in a dumpster. Both were English language and locally purchased.

His official phone had rung scant moments after the event with the order to return to the Russian embassy. Things would be buzzing with activity, he knew.

The spy called his wife Larisa to ask if she had heard the news. It was early evening in Moscow. She told her husband that news outlets were just beginning to report that something had happened but that there were no details yet.

Larisa Antonovna Borzilova had only recently returned to Mother Russia from the United States. She had waited for six months after Gennadiy had moved to Washington to join him there. She had stayed for over two years until two months ago, and only five months after the birth of their daughter, her husband insisted she return home. SVR was going to reassign him to its Moscow headquarters soon and he had sent her ahead.

The agent wondered, if he hadn't initiated her move and she had still been in his company, would he be in the mess he was in?

They talked for a few more minutes. As was customary Larisa let their son Valeriy, named after Gennadiy's father, talk to his daddy. She held the phone up to Ulyana's ear to listen to her daddy's voice, too, but the infant was too young to understand the noise in the device.

Husband and wife ended the call as Gennadiy reached the embassy. He sat at his computer in his tiny office pouring over internal posts about the attack on the American leader, anticipating the news of her death.

The SVR agent froze upon reading one report. He leaned wide-eyed to his display and gasped aloud in utter bewilderment at what he saw. Unable to accept what he was reading, he clicked the link that opened the site of American news channel QNN. They had yet to report what his internal intelligence sources were saying.

Borzilov returned to his embassy reports and read again what had so dramatically surprised him. "American president expected to fully recover," read the post.

The Foreign Intelligence agent leaned back in his chair. He stroked his chin until, in disbelief, he ran both hands through his hair. Borzilov sat in stunned silence before leaning toward his display again. He clicked on every update, though they were being posted at a furious rate, expecting to see a correction. But none came. Finally, a single update shed more details on Hendrickson's condition, as Russian intelligence analysts believed it to be. It was a concise report: "stunned, minor injuries, under observation at hospital."

"*Nyevozmozhno*," he wanted to believe. But not only did it appear possible, it became increasingly likely that the woman had survived. Even the American press was beginning to report what Russian operatives had determined. The U.S. president would be fine.

Gennadiy slapped his phone from his desk in anguish. His face reddened with the anxious realization that he had indeed failed.

✦

"Serious but stable was the word," Dick Klein told the handful of staff present. Many had left their posts before the inauguration. A few more, including Klein, would leave at week's end. Despite that, he was acting with authority he was certain was legitimately his, Maggie thought. But she honestly didn't mind. He'd been around a while and though she was technically the second in command, she had just reported for duty.

Klein started to map out assignments and assured the others that he was preparing a press release and comments for the media.

Maggie sensed some resentment toward him on the part of a couple of others but again, she just got here. She was happy to be spared having to run the department. She had built a very successful boutique public relations company back home in Wyoming. But this? This was about as big time as it got.

The press staff began to brainstorm what would be needed and who would do what. Klein gave Maggie nothing of real import but dumped a lot on her that was really insignificant. She didn't mind in the least, but his attitude seemed to convey that her coming into the department in the number two spot seemed to be an affront to him personally. She didn't understand because the Dick had turned in his resignation before she hired on. He had certainly made that point crystal clear during the faux orientation he provided yesterday.

"Wow! Yesterday," she thought. "That already seems so long ago."

Maggie walked to her office to find that Klein had set up shop there and had moved some of her personal items and stacked them carelessly atop the credenza along the wall. Now she was mad. But she only had to deal with him through Friday, she told herself.

✦

Ambulances transported all the injured persons to George Washington University Hospital, a mere 1.2 miles away. All except the president. Once Secret Service assessed Spinnaker's condition and considered it to be non-life-threatening, they elected to take her directly to Walter Reed National Military Medical Center. A Secret Service SUV led the limousine across the Potomac and flew north on the George Washington Memorial Parkway. The drivers covered the twenty miles in sixteen minutes.

POTUS regained consciousness shortly after being hauled into the vehicle and her input and relative alertness contributed to their decision to go to Reed. She was frantic about her family and the agents provided updates as fast as they could get them by radio from their fellow team members still on the ground at the church. The agents were most concerned about her going into shock.

Once they reached the hospital, they informed the president of Logan's and Eccleston's deaths and Secretary Ginnetti's serious condition. They were as delicate about AJ's condition as they could be, but they made Spinnaker aware that his injuries were serious. President Hendrickson's attending physician at Walter Reed, Dr. Wayne Munroe, examined her and the Center admitted her. She demanded to go to be with her son. Dr. Munroe, though he was uncomfortable telling the President of the United States what she could or could not do, forbade it. Until she had been under observation for at least twenty-four hours, she couldn't leave.

Except for Secret Service, Sandra Hendrickson was alone in her room. Adam and Noelle were at the University Hospital with AJ. Her husband had called – his was the only non-official call she had been allowed – to say that their son was in serious condition. His broken leg had been set and splinted. A permanent cast would be applied after more evaluation and once other injuries had been addressed. Adam told his wife that the doctors had tried to describe the extent of the internal damage, but he hadn't quite understood. He said he didn't know if it was because he was still in an addled state himself or just that he was a dumbass. He tried to laugh at his attempt at humor but broke into a sob that his wife joined. The first gentleman promised to call with news as soon as he had some. The couple assured each other of their love and hung up.

After the call from her spouse, POTUS spoke with her chief of staff who gave her updated news about Ginnetti. Chandler also gave her the most recent info he had about other casualties. As his boss' husband had, he promised additional news as it developed.

◆

Borzilov was dismayed. He had continued to survey internal reports on his computer while watching news reports on his television, changing channels frequently between the major networks to see if one had information that the others didn't. He pushed his mouse away and shoved his chair back from the desk. He rubbed his eyes, then massaged the front of his neck with his left hand while leaning forward to his desk to get his cup of tea.

How could things have gone so miserably wrong? He had thought through everything that had transpired. It no longer mattered that the original effort with the phone had failed. That was, as the Americans said it, water under the bridge. He had considered the delay in his phone's streaming image due to buffering but that, as he recalled, seemed to have been brief, perhaps only a second or two. And when the image returned, the American leader was standing almost directly beside the column and the bomb that it held. Yet reports all indicated that she was actually some distance from it when it exploded. Because of that, she had survived with, apparently, only minor injuries.

The Russian stood and walked to the hallway outside his office. When he returned with a refill of hot water, he lifted the teabag from the saucer on his desk and swirled it around. The brown streaks began to emanate from the bag and momentarily he had another cup of tea. There was no room in his office for pacing or he would have done so. Instead he simply stared at the photo of him and his family on his desk. There had to be something he missed.

The television's screen splashed with the graphic, "Breaking News," although it didn't always mean it was "breaking" or that it was "news." Often it was just a colorful tool to get the viewers' attention. But this time, the report really contained things that he hadn't heard before – at least an updated version of events. It contained a revised casualty list. The death of the vice president was of little importance to him – the president was the target – and the news of the grave injuries to the press secretary mattered even less. The report of the president's son's injury bothered the Russian. He imagined briefly how he would feel if his son were the victim of some similar event. But the thought was fleeting. He couldn't allow himself such sentiments and quickly reacquired his professional detachment.

He turned his attention back to the monitor on his computer but heard QNN newswoman Cameron Neal tell her co-anchor, "Tracy, throughout Washington there is a deathly silence." Gennadiy supposed that the use of the word "deathly" was intended to be poignant.

Borzilov leaned onto his desk and, seizing his mouse, began to click on various lines of the embassy feeds to open them.

The talking head continued. "However, some are continuing the protests that they had planned for the day, undeterred by the events."

Tracy Adams picked up the account, shifting his gaze from his co-anchor to the camera.

"That's right, Cameron. These are live shots from the U.S. Navy Memorial Plaza on Pennsylvania Avenue…"

The channel's image changed to a street-side view.

"… about halfway between the Capitol and the White House along what would have been the route of the parade. Five to six individuals, perhaps seizing the opportunity to steal some time on-camera are shouting and waving signs demanding the Navy cease exercises in the Atlantic they say are detrimental to marine mammals in the region. So even on a day such as this, filled with tragedy, some people are intent on getting their issues…"

Suddenly, in the foreground, a man in his twenties threw down his handmade sign, turned his backside to the camera and dropped his pants. The exposure of his bare ass was interrupted by an abrupt change on the television screen to show the anchors, apparently unprepared for the return to the studio. Neal's face was buried in one hand until she looked up toward some unknown person off-camera. She stared ahead and fidgeted with a stack of papers.

Adams immediately turned to face the camera as it zoomed in on him.

"Disgusting," an unseen Cameron Neal muttered.

Tracy Adams regained his composure.

"Most viewers know that even our live broadcasts aren't really live…"

"Thank goodness," came the comment from the still off-camera but mic'd blonde.

"…but have a delay built in, partly to handle situations just like that. So, apparently unmoved by the tragedies of this day, some…"

Gennadiy Borzilov considered the words from QNN momentarily, threw back his head and slapped his forehead in the universal symbol of self-disgust.

✦

It was cold. Never mind that Morgan had spent the last few years in

Wyoming, experiencing winters filled with just this type of weather. It was very cold. Abandoned by his fiancée, the ex-CIA spook had made his way to Swing's Coffee, west of the White House complex across from the Old Executive Office Building. He had been there on occasion when he was in town to be at Langley. His friend Ben Reid had introduced him to the place and to its own outstanding Mesco Blend. In fact, he had stopped there on the day he first met then-President Weston. He had needed a cup to help steel him for what he thought was a looming ass-chewing in the Oval Office.

It was crowded, no doubt with other inauguration-goers whose plans had been shattered, but he had waited with a cup in hand until he landed a seat. He left his coat on long enough to get warm, nestling the cup between both palms for the same reason. But now he was comfortable and scanned his phone for news. When it rang, he looked at the display, hoping it was Maggie. It wasn't.

"Mr. President."

"One of these days you have to start calling me 'Trent.' I'd say we have enough of a history."

Up until now, Morgan had never felt quite right being that familiar with the man despite the fact that they definitely had a long and significant history together.

"Yes, sir," was all he could say.

"I – we – wanted to see how you and Maggie were. We were escorted out pretty quickly after things started happening."

"So were we. In fact, Maggie's at…"

"Work. Yes, we know."

"Do you know anything… have you heard anything?"

"Nothing I'm at liberty to tell you, son. Of course, they're talking to everyone. They have some persons of interest in custody, but I don't think they really believe they're involved. But like I say… talking to everyone."

"Yeah…"

"We'll keep in touch. And I'll let you know anything I can. Give our best to Maggie."

"Thank you, sir."

"Hmmm… persons of interest. Wonder who?"

◆

Ed Broussard sat in an interrogation room across the table from a Special Agent of the FBI. He was determined not to say anything. Hell, he didn't *know* anything.

"You know it's just a matter of time until we nail you for this," Special Agent Miles Russell bluffed. "You weren't exactly subtle in your threats."

He couldn't conceive how this buffoon could have masterminded this but that didn't mean he couldn't be involved.

"Listen. Tell me what you know. Maybe I can help you. If not, then…"

Ordinarily given to bravado, Eddie knew this was not the time. Besides he really didn't know anything.

"What 'threats?'" he asked.

FBI pulled prints of photos from a folder. He spread them in front of the Louisianan. Eddie looked at images of the signs he and his four companions had carried. The Special Agent pointed at one that said, "Time's up, bitch."

"Just words."

"Pretty clear." He pointed at another photo of a sign that requested Hendrickson perform an act on the male part of his anatomy.

"People say that kind of shit every day."

"Yeah? Well, they don't try to blow up the president every day. And the vice president is dead. You understand that, don't you, Broussard?

"And one of your running buddies was heard screaming, 'You're going to die,' in the direction of the church moments before the explosion."

That was indeed news to Broussard. He and three of his pals were long gone before Bobby returned to the fray.

"I want a lawyer," he said meekly, fearing he was about to soil his pants.

In another room. Bobby blurted out, "Yeah, we did it! Hell, the fuckin' bitch had it coming. U.S. has become a shithole while she's been in office. And that buck she had with her. Country's better off now. So, fuck, yeah! We offed her!"

Special Agent Juan Esquivel kept his poker face, just barely. But he was stunned. Did he just get a confession? The president had survived but maybe this guy didn't know that. But there had indeed been an assassination; the veep was dead.

Interrogating this moron seemed like a colossal waste of his and the Bureau's time. Esquivel wasn't sure he believed this ass. He was sure he couldn't have pulled it off. But the Special Agent held the same view as his counterpart in the other room did, that even stupid people could be involved in profound events.

"Write down everything you know!" He pushed a legal pad to the confessed assassin.

Esquivel turned to the one-way glass behind him. He dared not shrug in front of the suspect but his expression to the two observers and camera/sound operator behind the glass conveyed pretty much the same impression. The two other Special Agents observing the grilling were as astonished as their fellow agent in the interrogation room. The pair looked at each other.

"Crap!" exclaimed one.

"Holy crap!" said the other.

✦

Dr. Munroe returned to his patient's room. He had made some calls and began to relay to the president what he had learned more understandably than her husband had been able to.

Her son's injuries were serious, he said, and he explained which of them posed the greatest threats.

The president's eyes glazed over at the news and began to mist. But the woman seemed to gather herself, the doctor observed, and listened intently as he spoke.

Finally, he concluded, "The next twelve to eighteen hours will tell us a lot."

The president pulled the oxygen sensor off her finger and removed the cuff that monitored her vitals.

"Get my clothes, please," she said to the Secret Service agent. Though she said "please," it really wasn't a request.

The agent looked at the doctor while POTUS looked at her.

"Ma'am. Of course." Agent Joy Griffith decided she should obey her boss and her boss was Sandra Hendrickson, President of the United States of America.

"But Ma'am," Griffith continued, "I'm afraid your clothes… well, they're a mess."

"Then get me some scrubs… anything."

Joy Griffith looked at the doctor once more, who smiled and looked at his patient.

"It's against my professional judgement. As a doctor, I recommend against it."

The president began to object but Dr. Munroe stopped her with a raised hand.

"But…," he said, "but, as a father, I understand. I'll see that you get something to wear."

✦

Gennadiy looked at the time. It was 2:00 PM. He knew it mattered little at this point, but he was now sure what had happened. He looked at his Google results, found a likely link, and clicked on it.

The built-in delay for live television was seven seconds, he read, at least for a broadcast channel. Borzilov clicked the "back" arrow on his browser and returned to the search hits. He clicked another link that he hoped would be more pertinent. He scrolled down to scan the article as rapidly as possible to find his answer. Gennadiy learned that the term for what concerned him was latency, though he didn't care. He also saw the terms HTTP-based protocol and non-HTTP-based, which meant nothing to him but apparently mattered in the number he was looking for.

"Image capture, encoding, transmission, and…

"'Jitter buffer?' I don't care what 'jitter buffer' is," he lashed out to the writer of the article, as if it had been written solely for his consumption. His expletive was aloud and audible enough that one of the embassy staff that happened to be passing his doorway stopped and stared in for a second.

The SVR agent rose abruptly and slammed the door. He continued scanning.

"Finally! In Internet streaming, latency for non-HTTP is usually in the range of five to ten seconds and it's typically fifteen to forty-five seconds for the other one – HTTP.

"Fuck!" – in English.

The image Borzilov saw on his phone to time the explosion wasn't real-time.

"Likely ten or fifteen seconds," he said aloud. He grabbed a tissue and wiped his brow. "Why didn't I know that? Why didn't the people I'm about to answer to tell me that?"

It occurred to him that if the transmission delay had been at the high end of the range in the article he read – say forty-five to fifty seconds – he could've missed almost everyone in the president's group.

SVR Agent Gennadiy Borzilov was enraged… and terrified.

CHAPTER 8

Sandra Hendrickson donned the green top and bottom she had been given. She looked down past the two-piece uniform at her shoes. They were the ones she had started the day with and were decidedly too dressy for the scrubs. She looked at her reflected appearance in the mirror, only out of curiosity. She couldn't care less how she looked. With some attempt at humor she really didn't possess, she said to herself softly, "Pretty incognito. Could probably get out without escorts and not be recognized in this getup."

The past handful of minutes while she was dressing had been a rare occasion. Outside the White House, and even in most places inside the executive mansion, she was hardly ever alone. There were generally staff or other personnel with her. And Secret Service were always lurking nearby, even in the security of the People's House.

But now, for a brief few minutes, she had indeed been entirely alone. Secret Service Agent Griffith had waited politely outside the door, standing with other Service detail. Of course, other team members were everywhere throughout the hospital and on its grounds. For security's sake, the president had been assigned an interior private room so that she could not be exposed to any peril through a window. Moving every other patient off her floor had been impossible, but at least hospital staff working with the protection detail had been able to clear the nearest rooms to Spinnaker's. And having done that, analysts and techies in Service offices were speedily performing background checks on George Washington University Hospital patients and personnel, prioritizing the ones who remained on the president's floor and moving out from there. The necessity of those checks was about to end.

President Hendrickson stepped to the door and knocked without exiting. She knew better. Agent Griffith entered and managed to stifle a smile that almost emerged on her face at Spinnaker's appearance.

"Someone to see you, ma'am."

Hendrickson was puzzled but nodded. Her guard opened the door and in walked Chief of Staff Chandler and Supreme Court Chief Justice Bartholomew Richter.

"I beg your pardon, Madam President. I can't tell you how sorry I am for this intrusion and more importantly, for the tragedy of this day. Having said that, we have some overdue but necessary business to attend to," Chief Justice Richter said.

Sandra Hendrickson had imagined this day differently. When she pictured it, Adam Sr. held a Bible upon which she rested her left hand. Adam Jr. and Noelle beside her, she would lift her right and repeat the oath of office, only thirty-five words in length.

But she knew the Constitutional necessity of this. She insisted on inviting Dr. Munroe and a few of the medical staff. POTUS even demanded, over Chandler's objections, that he include any patients on the same floor who were physically able to join the "ceremony." Phones were confiscated for the duration of the swearing-in. And the guests would all have to understand that the president couldn't linger afterward. But Hendrickson had always appreciated the fact that the office of president might be loaned out for periods of time to women and men who honored the position to greater or lesser degrees, but it belonged to the People.

While other agents stood alertly by, Joy Griffith was temporarily assigned the position of inaugural photographer and, using Spinnaker's own phone, captured the occasion – video during the actual oath and a handful of still images before and after.

So, with no husband, no AJ, and no Noelle, and with Noah Chandler holding a Gideon's Bible from the hospital room, Sandra Hendrickson held up her right hand and repeated after Chief Justice Richter:

I do solemnly swear that I will faithfully execute the Office of President of the United States, and will to the best of my ability, preserve, protect and defend the Constitution of the United States.

Chief Justice Richter shook the president's hand gently and said in a low enough voice that only she could hear, "In most cases I would conclude my part with a 'congratulations' but in this case, I think it more appropriate to say, I'm sorry. God bless you. I'm certainly praying for you as president and personally."

Then he leaned very close to her and added in an even lower voice, "Please don't tell anyone I said that whole 'praying for you' part. That 'separation' thing, you know.

"And so you'll know, just before coming here, I administered the oath to Vice President Bauer in his office at the Capitol."

In an odd twist that the Constitution allows, POTUS and her new veep were of different political parties. Because the conservative party had barely maintained their majority in the House of Representatives, the Speaker, Aiden Bauer, was from the opposition party and by law, he ascended to the role of vice president. The potential conflicts the scenario might present constituted only a fleeting thought in the mind of the president before she turned her attention back to Chief Justice Richter.

"I'm grateful, Justice Richter."

"You're welcome."

With that, the man smiled a very warm and sincere, encouraging smile and the president smiled back. And without regard to appearances or protocol, she leaned in and hugged the man and said simply, "Thank you."

With that, POTUS took her phone from Agent Griffith and said, "Get me to my family."

Noah Chandler told her, "You know, I have to say I'm against this."

His boss stared at him without speaking. Her chief of staff looked at her, then moved his gaze to Secret Service Joy Griffith and said, "You heard the president. Get her to her family."

POTUS wouldn't be restrained by the moderate pace the agents wanted to maintain. The aide with the Football and the one with the jammer fell in behind her as did the others charged with her safekeeping.

Her chief of staff's eyes followed her purposeful strides down the hall. He laid the Gideon King James Bible on the counter at the nurse's station briefly but, thinking better of it, retrieved it and put it with the other items he had kept to mark the occasion. Whether jubilant or somber, it was history.

It was 11:00 PM in Moscow and Larisa had uncharacteristically been in bed for two hours when the bell to her *kvartira* sounded. The apartment was a communal flat, small by even local standards. She jumped at the sound of the buzz. Normally it was the sound of Ulyana's restless stirring that awoke her at any time during the night so, regardless of the sound, her daughter was what immediately sprang to mind. She strained her eyes and saw that her infant girl lay safely and quietly in her crib. Quietly, that is, until the buzzer rang a second time.

This time it was the thought that something had happened to Gennadiy that pierced the cobwebs that hadn't yet cleared. She looked about for her robe until she realized she still had it on. When Valeriy had fallen asleep, Larisa had lain on her bed intending to rest a moment before returning to the kitchen to clean up. But the clock beside her bed said 11:03. Again, she thought of her husband. It would be in the middle of the afternoon for him and...

This time, pounding on the door replaced the buzz and that brought her baby's crying to full volume.

"*Da! Da!*" she shouted. She opened the door and two men and a woman pushed their way past her into the flat.

✦

As POTUS walked into her son's hospital room, she suddenly became just Sandy again. She looked at AJ and the assortment of cables and tubes attached to him and the clear liquid of the drip bag. The lights that changed to update his blood pressure and heart rate glowed brightly in the dimness of the private room. As she watched the monitor, the line peaked at regular intervals with an accompanying audible signal that his heart was beating.

Adam Hendrickson moved beside her and took her hand. She watched the rise and fall of AJ's chest as he breathed. After about three more beeps of the monitor, his mom lost her composure and fell into his dad's arms sobbing.

After what he felt was an appropriate time, her husband reported, "It's still touch and go."

He paused again, trying to maintain his own composure. He cleared his throat.

"I'm so glad... I, uh, I don't know what I..." His efforts stalled and he joined Sandy's crying.

✦

FBI Special Agent Miles Russell gave Ed Broussard the news that he had himself just received.

"You're in beaucoup trouble. Your buddy just sold you all out."

Broussard seemed genuinely astonished.

"Here's your last chance to get ahead of this thing. Tell me what you know, Eddie."

Broussard was literally shaking.

"I, I need that lawyer. I need a lawyer."

He lay his head face down on his folded arms on the table in the interrogation room. Agent Russell thought the man was crying.

The Special Agent left Broussard and joined the other agents peering through the one-way glass into the second interrogation room where Special Agent Esquivel sat at a table with Bobby Taylor.

Esquivel stood and paced a couple of steps before turning to face his associates on the other side of the glass. He was saying something to his suspect, but they couldn't hear him. They had momentarily turned down the volume to the speaker in their observation room while they talked. But it was obvious that he was pissed off at the man who had confessed to the attempted assassination of the president and to the successful assassination of the vice president. They knew he wouldn't reveal that frustration to Taylor; it was only for their eyes.

"He's making this up," reported Supervisory Special Agent Annchi Liu. "Taylor didn't write a thing for the first minutes after Esquivel first gave him the note pad."

"Not unusual," countered Russell. Suspects often hesitated before committing their confession to paper as they considered whether they really wanted to put that declaration in writing.

"Yes," conceded Annie, the Americanized version she had chosen for her Chinese first name. "Then came the hurried scribbling, almost frenzied – again like we often see. Like he was achieving some sort of catharsis."

Special Agent Phil Jeffries spoke next. "After about ten minutes, he quit writing. Esquivel started to take the pad, but the a-hole said he wasn't through."

"Juan told him to take his time and took a seat across from him," added Liu.

Jeffries continued. "So, he writes a little more; couldn't have been more than a few words."

"Juan waits," said Supervisor Liu. "Taylor doesn't put his pen down. Juan waits some more. Finally, we hear him ask if he's finished. Taylor pulls the pen back like Juan was going to take it away from him."

"He hadn't even reached for it," Jeffries said.

Liu resumed her narrative. "Juan tells him to take his time. Tells him not to worry about details. Just write what he knows."

"He scribbles a little more; pauses; resumes; pauses; resumes."

"Having to think about it," concluded Russell. "Yep. Making it up."

The words didn't get completely out of his mouth when, through the glass, he saw Supervisory Agent Liu burst into the interrogation room.

Jeffries hurried to turn the speaker's volume back up.

Liu got right in Taylor's face and wagged a finger not two inches from his nose. Bobby Joe Taylor recoiled.

"Listen, you little shit..."

In the observation room Jeffries and Russell smiled at each other. Jeffries was pretty new to the District FBI offices and didn't know his supervisor well. Never had he heard his boss swear; well, not at a suspect.

"Here's what you're up against. You did the thing? You write it down."

She stood up and turned her back to Taylor to affect a bit of drama. When she did, she winked at the window. The agents on the other side laughed. Annie reacquired her "enraged" demeanor and turned back to face the confessor. She slammed her fist on the table.

"But, swear to God, if you're lying to us, for whatever reason that makes sense in that small mind of yours, we'll bury you – either for multiple counts of murder *anyhow* or, if you're lying, for interfering with a federal investigation."

Liu lowered her voice and got close to Taylor again.

"You got that?" It was almost a whisper.

Taylor grabbed the yellow legal pad and tried – unsuccessfully – to rip it apart. So, he shoved it across the table. He began to spill his guts. This time it was the truth.

"She always like this?" Jeffries asked.

Russell gave a wry smile and put his hand on his associate's shoulder.

"You have no idea!" The Special Agent chuckled a bit and headed for the door. "C'mon. Appears we still have a terrorist to catch."

CHAPTER 9

Dick Klein had called his group together and was holding forth on the importance of his team doing a good job during this crisis. He actually referred to the group as "his." Secretary Ginnetti would expect nothing less, he said.

Maggie felt that this meeting was a waste of time, just another opportunity for the Dick to grandstand. Her nickname from their first meeting had stuck in her mind and she couldn't help but think of him that way. Besides, she thought, it fit.

The Dick was in mid-sentence, "In preparing my statement..." when the door opened, and Chief of Staff Chandler walked in briskly.

Maggie felt herself sit up a little straighter at the sight of the president's right-hand man. He surveyed the group and complimented them.

"This is what I like to see; people being proactive and taking the initiative."

Klein stood. "I called my group together so I could get them out ahead of this crisis." Klein's chest practically strained at his buttons.

Chandler hesitated before taking The Dick's hand, apparently seizing on the man's characterization of the group as his.

"And... you are?"

"Klein, sir. Richard Klein. Call me Dick, Noah."

The expression on Chandler's face told Maggie that Dick had just swung and missed. Strike one. Chandler ticked up a notch in her assessment. She wanted to smile but didn't.

"So, Noah," Klein said," I suspect the president is a little... well, distracted right now. Oh, don't get me wrong. It's understandable. *Absolutely* understandable. I've prepared a statement of my remarks for the White House press corps."

Klein handed the chief of staff a sheet of printer paper

Chandler never looked at the paper. Rather he stared quizzically at the thirty-something year-old man trying so hard to impress.

"I'm sorry… your name again?"

Strike two, Maggie thought. Suddenly she was beginning to like Chandler.

Gennadiy Borzilov set his latest burner phone on his desk. The call had been brief and straightforward. He would complete his mission or, as threatened, the consequences would be dire.

Larisa Antonovna Borzilova and her two kids didn't even get the chance to gather belongings before the three visitors forced them out of her flat. Now at 1:30 AM, she cradled Ulyana in her arms and held Valeriy against her tightly in the back of the black sedan. She wanted to call her husband, but not only wasn't it permitted, her escorts hadn't let her get her phone when they shepherded her family out.

The two men and one woman initially said they had a message from Gennadiy, but none was offered. And they now seemed very dismissive when Larisa asked about it. They never spoke to her nor answered her questions. The man and woman in the front stared straight ahead the entire time. The man in the back seat with Mrs. Borzilova and her kids was likewise silent.

Chief of Staff Chandler went around the group, asking each for a quick introduction and a statement of their position in the department.

"Maggie – Margaret Loughlin, uh, Principal Deputy Secretary." She started to sit back down but Chandler walked to where she stood.

"Principal Deputy? Then who are you again?"

Maggie thought it an odd question since she had just introduced herself. Still, she thought it best to simply repeat herself.

"Marg…"

Chandler held his hand up and turned to point at Klein. "You. Who are *you?*"

The Dick appeared a bit uncertain of the body language posed by the chief of staff. He pointed to himself and leaned his head forward as if to say, "Who? Me?"

Instead he only said, "Klein, sir. Dick Klein." His reintroduction was almost a question, as though he was now uncertain of his own identity.

"And why are you leading this meeting?"

"I'm the senior member here."

"Senior member? What's that mean?"

Klein stiffened as a surge of resentment coursed through him at the seeming challenge to his authority.

But just as suddenly, his confidence waned and he stammered, "I've, uh, been here the longest... sir."

"'Been here the longest.' Hmmph."

Chandler stared at him a moment. He folded his arms and sat on the corner of a desk. Finally, he said, "Next," and pointed to the young man to Maggie's left.

The young man and the remaining two in the group introduced themselves. The chief of staff looked at Klein and simply said, "Proceed."

Dick Klein seemed intimidated but undeterred in marking his territory, much like a dog does. He never asked for input from the group. He only laid out his plan to personally address the nation, asserting again that Madam President was too "distracted" to do so. He compared the circumstances to when Captain Kirk, in one of the Star Trek movies, had declared Spock "emotionally compromised" and therefore unfit to serve.

Chandler rose from the desk and walked to him.

"Dick..." He paused. "There's been an assassination attempt on the president. Vice President Logan is dead, along with countless others, and you're quoting movies? Exactly what are your feelings about this administration?"

"I'm sorry. I don't understand the question."

"What are your feelings about the president? Why are you here?"

"Well..." Klein looked at his co-workers, as if seeking some moral support. None was forthcoming.

"Well, technically, this Friday was to be my last day."

"'Technically?' 'Was to be?'"

"I've turned in my resignation... sir."

The chief of staff seemed confused. He waited before asking, "May I ask why?"

"Uh, I..."

"Exactly why did you resign?"

Klein smiled nervously and again looked around the assembled team.

"Sir, you must know that a lot of us were sorry to see President Mercer resign. He had a lot of admirers in his administration..."

"Uh-oh," Maggie thought.

Chief Chandler returned to his previous question. "So, if you're leaving – because you're such an admirer of the previous president..." – the man placed significance on the word "previous" – "...again... why are you leading this meeting?"

"I'm needed, Noah. I'm sure we both agree that this is a chance to get things back on track…"

"'Needed!?' 'Back on track?'" Despite the somewhat muted volume of the remark, it carried the impact of a roar. Klein sat and leaned back.

"Let me tell you what I see." Chandler's volume was increasing. "What I see is an opportunistic son of a bitch who cares nothing for this president or her administration. 'Needed?' Hell, none of us is needed. We're all just pieces of the whole. Each of us is merely a cog in the wheel and, at any level in the hierarchy, we all serve at the pleasure of the president. Do you understand?"

"Uh, uh, I…"

"Never mind. You want out? Why wait till Friday?"

"Sir?"

Chandler drew closer to Klein.

"Are you… firing me, Noah?"

Chandler's quiet rage increased. "Firing you? You resigned, you little shit. I'm just accepting your resignation, effective now!"

Klein said, "How will you get by?"

Despite her disdain for Klein, Maggie sort of wondered the same thing.

Chandler addressed Maggie directly, "You're second in charge. What do you think this group's task is right now?"

Klein stepped almost between Chandler and Maggie and demanded, "Why in hell are you asking the newcomer? What the hell is going on here? I've got this covered, Chandler!"

Maybe this whole scene was a case of emotions boiling over, specifically for the chief of staff who was famously intolerant of anyone whose first loyalty wasn't with his boss, but Maggie felt that, without his even knowing it, Dick Klein had just struck out.

Klein was dumbfounded. He didn't move.

"Do I need to call security?" Chandler barked. His face was beet red. He stepped toward Klein. Everybody in the room looked down and shifted in their seats.

Dick Klein summoned enough resolve to start to say something and raised his right index finger. But when Chandler inched even closer, he thought better. He only said, "I'll get my things."

"We'll get them to you," Chandler said.

And with that, Klein walked out of the press department's room and out of the West Wing.

"You. Come here. What was your name?"

Maggie looked up to see Noah Chandler looking directly at her.

"Maggie, sir. Maggie Loughlin."

"Well, Maggie Loughlin, are you up to this?"

Though every fiber of her being objected and the voice in her head insisted "no," the Principal Deputy Press Secretary pronounced, "I am, sir."

It was a good thing she was already seated because her knees went weak. "Then what's our first priority, as you see it?"

"To remain calm. And to communicate calm from the White House as we go about our work."

Chandler smiled.

CHAPTER 10

Morgan had called Uber and was back in his and Maggie's apartment. He reflexively turned on the television. It was 7:30 PM and he was finishing the chicken fajita wrap he had made for himself and was sipping a beer. Maggie hadn't called, but he wasn't surprised. She was undoubtedly immersed in doing whatever tasks she'd been assigned.

QNN's Tracy Adams finished reading the latest casualty list. Two additional parishioners had passed.

Adams paused to glance at his iPad's screen and cocked his head slightly as he listened to the voice in his earpiece.

The "Breaking News" banner splashed across the TV screen and this time it really was. He reported, "Quantum News Network has just learned from an anonymous source inside the White House that President Hendrickson has joined her family at George Washington University Hospital, where her son, Adam Hendrickson Jr. is being treated. The news about the young man isn't good. We learned from GWU Hospital PR Director Latonya Spencer that AJ, as he is called, remains in an induced coma and is classified as critical but stable.

"As for the president, we still have no details about her condition beyond what we reported earlier when we covered the brief announcement by Dr. Wayne Munroe. Dr. Munroe, who is treating the president, stated that her injuries were not life-threatening and that she was resting comfortably. That seems to no longer be the case – that she is 'resting comfortably' – and that she is, in fact, with her son. That would seem to indicate she is fine and that is certainly remarkable and great news."

The news anchor's head tilted again. "Pardon me, we're getting more details," he informed the viewers. "Uh-huh. Okay," he said to the disembodied voice in his ear.

"Our source is saying Dr. Munroe had advised the president that she should remain under observation for a while longer but that she, against that advice, had left and was with her son at George Washington University Hospital. So, in the midst of the tragic death of Vice President Antoine Logan and others, it's nice to have some good news to report."

"Bet the Secret Service isn't happy that they're announcing POTUS' location," Morgan thought as he rose to get another beer. He turned back to the TV when he heard the ascending synthesized notes that proclaimed even more "Breaking News."

Adams' co-anchor Cameron Neal broke in as the colorful graphic once again appeared and faded.

"Tracy, we now have news along a different front. QNN has just learned that the FBI has four persons of interest in their custody. Our source says the suspects are from Arkansas and were in the area of St. John's when the blast occurred..."

The source had a few details wrong – specifically the number of suspects and their home state – but what was really in error was that the FBI had already ruled out these men as suspects beyond anything more than their conduct a block from the church.

Morgan went into the bedroom and changed into his sweats and t-shirt. He knew he was bound to doze off on the couch. As interested as he was in the developments, it had been a really long day. Especially after the second beer, he wasn't going to last much longer.

He returned to the couch and pressed the button that reclined him into a more comfortable position. He thought about Maggie, knowing that she was undoubtedly overwhelmed. He wished he could call her but, if she had time to talk, she would call him.

As Morgan began to nod off, he wondered, since Press Secretary Ginnetti was out of action, how was her staff dividing the work load? Who was leading the effort? The answer came sooner than he could've anticipated and in an unlikely way.

"Cameron, the White House has just announced that incoming Deputy Press Secretary Margaret Loughlin will hold a news conference at 9:00 PM Eastern Time."

Morgan's eyes popped open. He tried to sit up but was prevented by the extended lower section of his reclining couch. He pushed the button with more force than needed as though that would speed up returning his section of the leather sofa to an upright position.

"We were wondering," Tracy Adams continued, "when we would get official comments from the administration. Outside of a few comments from Chief of Staff Noah Chandler throughout the afternoon, there has been no word directly from any of President Hendrickson's staff..."

Maggie didn't have an official portrait yet so the photo on the screen was from her Image Quest website. In fact, their narrative about her consisted of reading directly from her company site's bio, though they didn't attribute it as their source. Behind the scenes, QNN researchers were busily building a biography and putting together whatever pieces of info they could. Principal Deputy Press Secretary hadn't ranked high enough on the administration roster to merit a profile. Today's events changed that.

Network staffers were searching the web and dialing their phones furiously to contact anyone who knew Margaret Loughlin.

Morgan's phone rang. He didn't recognize the number. Until he got the job as visiting professor at Georgetown, he wouldn't have answered unknown callers. But having missed some calls from University staff, he'd had to change his practice.

"Josh Morgan," he announced. The caller was speaking so quickly that about all he heard was "CNN" and the woman ask if he was the Josh Morgan engaged to Margaret Loughlin. Without really thinking, he answered in the affirmative.

"Yes, Maggie and I are engaged." Other questions were flying at him so quickly, he really wasn't being given time to answer. He occasionally grunted a "yes" or "no" and somewhere in the course of the call, he heard the beep indicating that another call was waiting. This caller was identified.

"QNN?" he saw. "Holy cow!"

He interrupted the woman on the other end of his current call – it took a couple of tries before she stopped speaking. It seemed like she was only reading stuff she'd found out about Maggie online and trying to get his confirmation so that she could attach a name to it.

"I'm sorry, but I think all of these questions are things you should take up with… Margaret."

The voice persisted.

"I'm sorry…please… could you stop talking for a min…" Morgan finally disconnected, hoping it wouldn't somehow reflect badly on his fiancée.

The phone rang again immediately. It was from NBC. He didn't answer. Calls continued to beg his attention endlessly. He thought about just turning his phone off, but he was afraid Maggie would call.

"Man, I wish I could talk to her."

✦

The FBI labs were analyzing every bit of evidence they had and, considering they had collected everything from pieces of plaster to scraps of paper to bits of clothing, it was a lot. In other locations, autopsies were continuing on victims. Causes of death would all be essentially the same, except for the specific locations of the fatal trauma on the different corpses. The bodies were themselves evidence as was every piece of shrapnel taken from them.

Investigators still remained at the site of the explosion searching for everything that might have been missed that could add to the growing profile of the event. They had already collected obvious items, of course, but thoroughness was key. A single seemingly insignificant piece of evidence could unlock an avenue of investigation that could solve the who and why of this terrorist act.

As in all such situations, pieces of the device were of unmatched importance but, obviously, they were scattered furthest in sometimes microscopic sizes. Their very function placed them at the epicenter of the explosion and exposed them to the brunt of the destructive force. Yet despite the difficulties these facts posed, the FBI technicians were the world's best in piecing together – literally – the tiniest parts of puzzles.

After only a few hours, one fact was already undeniable. The components of the device were Russian-made. That didn't indicate whether the bomber simply used Russian parts or was himself (the profiling of these terrorists always suggested a male) Russian. If he was indeed a Russian, then the conclusion was terrifying beyond any other possibility: The United States' adversary over so many decades had launched an attack on the president on U.S. soil. If that came to be the consensus of federal investigators, the chain reaction of events that resulted from it could lead to the worst of all possible scenarios.

The Department of Homeland Security was involved at every step of the investigation, as were the Central Intelligence Agency, National Security Agency, and every other alphabet organization that could help or would be impacted by the conclusions produced from the investigation. All were either taking actions or monitoring what the FBI was doing.

Everyone was keenly aware of the ongoing situation of the president and attempted to be as respectful of her as a mother experiencing a personal crisis as they could. Therefore, as information developed, a small group of individuals in her administration filtered it to determine what was urgent and what could wait. The group decided what to tell POTUS and what others under her authority could handle on her behalf. The positive identification of the fragments as Russian was of such incontestable importance that POTUS had to know and she had to know now.

✦

The collection of protection and support personnel outside the room where Adam Hendrickson Jr. lay in critical condition was no different than if his mom, the President of the United States, were having dinner at a local restaurant. The environment around POTUS, when she was outside the White House, never changed. Her responsibilities transcended all personal matters, even one as delicate as this. The call from Gabriel Austin, Director of the Federal Bureau of Investigation went to the National Security Advisor. Senior staff had selected Edgar Templeton to be the buffer between Hendrickson and the outside world. Templeton listened for a few moments and his initial reply was simply, "Damn."

He knew he had to tell POTUS. "I'm assuming you've already informed DNI Donleavy. Perfect. And, if you haven't already, you certainly don't need to wait to inform everybody else who needs to know. Parnell at CIA, Larson at DHS... You have? Good."

Templeton pondered who else should be on the list for immediate contact. He listened to a question from Director Austin.

"Good question. You know, let's get the president's orders concerning which members of Congress," he concluded. He dreaded this but...

✦

"Yes," answered President Hendrickson to the knock on the hospital room door. That was Secret Service Agent Griffith's cue to step aside and let Templeton enter.

"Madam President, I'm so sorry for the intrusion but..."

"Not at all, Ed. Please come in."

Of course, the "interruption" meant the first gentleman had to leave the room. He understood but resented it. That was his son on the bed. Still, he left without objection.

Her National Security Advisor filled her in on the details that pointed to a possible – he emphasized "possible" – Russian connection to the bombing.

POTUS almost smiled, "I can't believe that. It's so implausible as to be..." The smile left her face. "That would be an act of war."

"Yes, ma'am."

Hendrickson ran her hands through her hair and rose. She stood by her son's bed and likewise ran her fingers through the boy's hair.

"All right. As unimaginable as Russian involvement is, we should proceed per procedure. I should call the Chairman of the Joint Chiefs and have him tell them."

"Shall I call him for you?"

"Please, Ed, if you don't mind."

"What about Congressional leaders?"

"I suppose they have to know but then this will get out. Leaks spring up from that group almost the moment they hear something. I'll have Noah call them. He's at the White House taking care of things there." As an afterthought she said, "And would you mind giving President Weston a call and filling him in? Nobody knows how much I've relied on him. He's been a great friend."

"Sandra, you okay?" Templeton and Hendrickson had known each other since college. They had even dated a couple of times but decided they were better pals than couple. He was delighted when Wendell Mercer named her as his running mate and absolutely thrilled when she became president, though he hated the reason. But he was still one of only four or five people in government who called her by her given name. He certainly never did so in public.

"No, Ed. I'm not."

They hugged like friends do.

"Whatever you or your family need, Sandy."

"I know, Ed."

Templeton was dialing his phone before he ever made it out the door.

Morgan wasn't surprised that the press briefing was running almost an hour behind. But it was driving him nuts. He was wide awake and ready to hear his Maggie make her debut.

His phone had continued to chirp that calls were coming in rapid-fire succession. He had ignored all of them except two whose names he was happy to see on Caller ID.

Becky Reid called to say she had heard on the television that Maggie would be leading the press conference. Becky was his friend Ben's wife – he never could say "widow." He knew Ben from CIA. Ben had tipped him off about the truth behind the situation with Trenton Weston and ultimately was murdered because he had.

When Becky commented that she had no idea that Maggie's new job called for that, Josh laughed and said that she didn't either.

The second call was from Curtis Jones. Curtis was Maggie's assistant at Image Quest and was the only one she considered to run things during her time in Washington. Like Morgan, Curtis had been smothered with calls all evening from reporters who wanted to know everything they could about his former boss. He had quit answering his phone, too. It was so constant, in fact, Curtis told Josh that when he pressed the phone to call him, he had inadvertently connected himself to someone from ABC who had been calling at the same time.

Curtis and Morgan each worried how nervous Maggie might be, but both agreed she was up to the task.

Once he had hung up with Curtis, Morgan turned up the volume of the TV. He had backed off the beer to coffee now to ensure he would be awake for Maggie's debut.

"More 'breaking news,'" he saw and heard. He was disappointed to see that, instead of the beginning of the press briefing, there was more info about the men in custody. The only new news was that they had adjusted the number of persons of interest to six – still incorrect – and added Louisiana to the list of their home states – their source got this right.

Finally, the moment Morgan had been waiting for. Deputy Press Secretary Margaret Loughlin was already behind the podium when coverage began.

"What? No grand entrance? The president always makes one." Josh laughed though his stomach was churning for Maggie.

"She must be a wreck."

✦

Maggie was supposed to keep things simple. Her guidelines were exactly what she would have advised Image Quest clients.

Read the prepared statement. Don't try to speak from memory. Or paraphrase.

Take only a handful of questions. Don't really answer them. Dodge and defer. And when you can, say something you want to say, whether it really answers the question that was asked or not.

There were other guidelines but another one that really mattered was, no smiling. If you have to smile, make it small, appear forced, and brief. This was a tragedy and a national crisis.

"Hello, ladies and gentlemen. The events of today are certainly a national tragedy. President Hendrickson wants to first convey her deepest sympathies to the family of Antoine Logan and his sister Jennais Logan. The double tragedy that this family has suffered is unimaginable. The vice president will be remembered personally for his cheerful personality and the honor with which he lived his life. As a public servant, he displayed an unmatched commitment and tenacity in pursuing equality and prosperity for all Americans.

"Secretary Ginnetti remains in guarded condition. She has stabilized.

"Of course, we have lost many today."

Maggie read a list of every person who died that day.

"The president has endured her own heartbreak. She wishes to thank everyone for their thoughts and prayers and extends her own thoughts and prayers to those who have lost loved ones today and others whose friends or family have been injured. She understands the anguish of waiting, unable to do anything for them, but encourages you to have hope that God is in heaven.

"The president wants you to know of her unwavering belief that we are one nation, under God, and indivisible. While we mourn individually, we also mourn together. But alongside our sorrow we must embrace a courage and a resolve to emerge on the other side of this trial as we always have; stronger, freer, and more committed to justice in the world.

"And justice is at the very heart of President Hendrickson's promise to the American people. She pledges to you that the perpetrators of this horrific attack will not prevail. There will be no safe place for them.

"Finally, President Hendrickson has these words for the monsters who made the unfortunate choice to attack our great nation. You have made the biggest mistake of your lives. The world isn't large enough to hide you. The night will never be dark enough to shield you. The president assures you that every resource of the United States will hunt you down. We will find you; and we will catch you or we will kill you. Your fate now depends on new choices you must make.

"You have been warned."

Maggie looked up with enormous relief. But she knew the real challenge for her lay ahead.

"We only have time for a couple of questions."

Hands shot up everywhere. How to pick? None of the questions was unexpected.

Who's behind this?

"The FBI is leading the investigation, joined by the Secret Service, DHS, and others. It's ongoing, so we can't comment, of course. But we have the finest investigatory agencies in the world. The president is absolutely confident they will identify the party or parties behind this and bring them to justice."

What will happen when they're apprehended?

"We are in the initial stages of the investigation so obviously we can't comment on that."

The condition of Adam Jr.?

"Unfortunately, we can't comment on the condition of the president's son. The president wishes to convey her sincerest thanks for your asking and, as mentioned in the opening statement, she extends her sincerest condolences to those who experienced losses and her prayers for those with injured loved ones."

The six men in custody?

"We can't comment on an ongoing investigation, but officials are following every lead."

The progress of the investigation?

"We can't comment on an ongoing investigation. Officials will follow it wherever it leads."

Why didn't our intelligence agencies have any warning of this?

Maggie paused for the only time in the briefing. (Good question, she thought.) "We can't comment on that."

And Maggie was done. After a quick thank you and a promise to update the press as new details emerged, she walked through the doors from the briefing room. Chief of Staff Noah Chandler met her immediately. He put his hands on both her shoulders, which might have been inappropriate – she didn't know or care. She was just glad to be done.

"How do you feel?"

"I really can't comment on that," she said.

The man had a puzzled look at first and then smiled. "I think Secretary Ginnetti made a good choice – a great choice. We're going to enjoy having you around."

Chandler rushed away, making a phone call as he did.

✦

Josh Morgan was beaming. "Maggie Loughlin, you done good, sweetheart."

No sooner had he said that, his phone rang.

"For crying out loud," he complained but then he looked at the Caller ID. He pressed the icon and blurted out, "Maggie, honey, you were great. You were meant for this."

"I love you, Morgan. And thanks. I didn't seem nervous? I was scared shitless."

"No, no, you were really great…"

The two lovebirds talked for the few minutes Maggie had and hung up. She would be home if she could, but it would be late.

Josh lay down in his and Maggie's bed. The two hadn't spent a night apart since he got back from tracking Fadi Al-Majeed around Mexico and Texas all those months ago.

The bed felt too big, so Morgan returned to the couch. The television was still on, but he was soon fast asleep.

✦

The snow was almost a foot deep and still falling. Regardless, the Russian was where he often went to sort things out, along the reflecting pool walking from one military monument to the next. Day or night, this area was his personal monument to contemplation. The SVR agent always felt alone here, regardless of the crowds.

The white stuff shone tonight in the reflected footlights along the Wall and the hazy silhouettes of Korean War Soldiers. Borzilov knew from historical accounts that the soldiers there actually hiked through much deeper accumulations during the actual conflict. He always thought the Americans knew how to memorialize their heroes and their history. On this night, however, once again it was the Lincoln memorial that occupied his thoughts. Perhaps it was because he needed someone to emancipate him from the circumstances that enslaved him. Or perhaps it was because Lincoln was an assassinated president.

Borzilov took the bottle of Russian Standard Vodka from his coat pocket and offered The Great Emancipator a toast.

"Vechnaya pamyat! To your everlasting memory, Mr. Lincoln."

CHAPTER 11

Day 5 – Wednesday

The gentle kiss on his neck caused Morgan to smile even in his sleep.

"Who is that?" he teased.

"Turkey. Come on." Maggie pulled at his arm until he adjusted his recliner and got up. She led him to their bed. She shed her clothes and the two of them settled in under the covers that hadn't been made up from the night before.

As he rolled over to snuggle with Maggie, he saw that it was 3:45 AM. She was in such a great mood. He was happy for her. Her improved attitude over the last few days, despite the events of today, was already worthwhile. In less than three minutes, Morgan heard her soft, steady breathing. He kissed Maggie on the back of her neck and was soon asleep, too.

Most people would've been shocked at the thought of the president sleeping all night in a rollaway bed in a hospital room, perhaps even appearing undignified in pale green hospital scrubs that she still wore from the day before. Yet change the mental image to a mother staying with her injured son and the vision transforms into one deserving of great admiration.

Sandy Hendrickson awoke numerous times aghast at the horror the president had experienced the prior day. Each time she did, she prayed that it had been a dream but each time it tumbled into the reality it was. And each time she was crushed to see her son lying across the room from her, still attached to the myriad of medical devices that were sustaining him. And with the realization that everything had indeed happened, she rose enough to assure herself that AJ was still breathing.

This time, when she stirred from her fitful attempts at slumber, the clock on the wall said 5:30 AM. There would be no going back to sleep. Adam had slept in the waiting room with the attendant Secret Service agents watching over him. Noelle was back at the White House with the Secret Service protector assigned to her who was also her *de facto* governess.

Agent Griffith cracked the door and peeked in. Perhaps that's what had awakened her, Sandy thought. Seeing Spinnaker awake she handed her the clothes that staff had brought from the White House along with the assorted toiletries they had gathered for their boss.

"Good morning, ma'am. How's your son?"

The pair talked, POTUS thanked her, and the agent stepped out to allow Spinnaker some privacy. Momentarily the first gentleman came in. Sandy finished dressing and the couple silently hugged beside AJ's bed. Adam Sr. was just about to speak when he was preempted by the loud squeal of a single, steady tone. The parents panicked at the realization that their baby boy was crashing. Agent Griffith yanked the door open and sized up the development that was unfolding. She shouted down the hallway for help that was already on their way.

President or not, the ICU nurses and doctor pushed Hendrickson aside and began to shout instructions to one another about injections, pulling back the child's gown, and prepping for action. The worst possible scenario was materializing.

"This can't be. It can't be happening," Mom cried, burying her head in Dad's chest. Scant seconds elapsed before the parents heard an electrical whine, its pitch increasing as it persisted.

"Clear!" shouted the doctor, and there was a loud pop as the electrical device discharged. AJ's torso lurched upward. The loud, steady tone returned.

"Clear!" came the command for a second time. The crack of electricity repeated. Sandy watched her son's chest pitch upward yet again.

The doctor seemed to delay his command a millisecond this time, thought Mom, but he shouted it again.

"Clear!" The defibrillator paddles discharged their nearly 1,500 volts a third time and finally there came the steady, intermittent beep that all had hoped to hear. Every person in the room turned their attention to the monitor and, with each beep, a blip rose from the previously flat line as Adam Hendrickson Jr's sinus rhythm returned to normal.

Mom sobbed. So did Dad, who said, "Thank you, God."

✦

Josh rolled over to check the clock. Six o'clock, read the digital display. Maggie came out of the bathroom, opened the closet door and looked at her choices. She made her selection and, seeing her fiancé awake, smiled past the toothbrush in her mouth.

She looked happy, Morgan thought. Less than three hours of sleep, yet wide awake and in a good mood.

"Amazing," he said aloud.

"What?" Maggie asked from the bathroom

"Good morning," Josh said. He rose to go prepare a light breakfast. "Bagel okay?"

"Something bigger."

Morgan couldn't help smiling. "Hungry, huh?"

"Famished. Didn't eat dinner last night."

"Nothing at all?"

Noah Chandler had the White House staff bring over sandwiches. I ate half of one."

"So, what's up for today?"

"Chandler will meet with what's left of the press department. Then I'll introduce him at the next press briefing scheduled for 9:00."

Maggie ate the omelet Morgan prepared for her and was out the door.

Georgetown had announced that classes would be closed for at least two weeks, so Morgan had that time to prepare some lessons and do some unpacking that he had put off from the move from Wyoming.

✦

The FBI labs were always staffed twenty-four/seven, but a number of normally daytime personnel pulled all-nighters along with the regular night shift.

The quantity of items brought in was incredible. From nearly microscopic to large chunks of the church itself, articles ranged from basically worthless as evidence to things that could probably communicate volumes. Some of the things were found large distances from the scene of the explosion. A huge area of several square blocks was canvassed. Some of the material spread out in the huge collection rooms were quite literally garbage, having been gathered from dumpsters and trash cans lining the streets surrounding the gigantic crime scene. Almost none would be related, but investigators still had to catalogue and examine each item. Some were curious enough finds that technicians held hope that they might yield some pertinent information.

One such find was a cell phone found in a garbage can five blocks from the site of the attack. It was dusted for prints. Strangely, it was completely clean on the body where it would have been in the palm of the user's hand. Only the keys had fingerprints. No single key had a complete enough print to provide any value. However, expedited analysis of the digital images made from each of the keys successfully generated a stitched composite of a single fingerprint. It was obvious that the phone's owner had entered phone numbers with a single finger, possibly an index finger.

A mobile phone was rarely thrown away unless the owner wanted to achieve some separation from it. This phone was typical of a burner phone. It was inexpensive and purchased with prepaid minutes for temporary use. Since there was no contract, there would be no owner registered with any mobile carrier.

It was possible sometimes to associate a phone's serial number with the store where it was shipped and subsequently bought. A security camera in the store might have recorded the purchase. A stroke of luck might allow investigators to pair the sale with its date. The difficulty, if such a recording existed, would be in pinpointing the specific transaction out of many captured. And even if – and it would be a very big "if" – investigators somehow had the extraordinarily good fortune to identify an individual in this way and, again, if he turned out to be a bad guy, he might not be *their* bad guy. If he was stupid enough to allow himself to be imaged during the purchase, he probably wasn't smart enough to have been involved in the church bombing. The analysis of the incident was already building a profile of someone extremely intelligent with very sophisticated skills.

So, even in the highly unlikely event the phone was a tool in this plot, it would most likely not yield any useful info.

The perp also had to have help. Undoubtedly the driver of the District Miracle Plumbers van who drove it into the church was involved. And at least some of the crew who made the repairs were involved.

That branch of the investigation was already underway. In fact, it began minutes after the bombing.

In one of the many interrogation rooms at the FBI sat Tom Morley, driver of the van that had damaged St. John's, thereby creating the opportunity for implantation of the bomb. Not only was Morley the driver, he was the owner and sole employee of District Miracle Plumbers. Interrogators decided that he was an unwitting dupe.

Supervisory Agent Liu huddled with Special Agents Russell and Jeffries.

"Yes, ma'am. We're confident. No involvement beyond just a hired driver. He was contacted by phone and the caller told him that he had a business opportunity for him. All he had to do was crash his van into the church. $25,000 cash," Russell said. "Morley was sitting in his truck in a park when we found him. Said he knew we'd be coming, and he was trying to decide whether to turn himself in or eat his gun. The BOLO located him, and Capitol Police got to him before he decided."

"Did he ever meet the guy – the one who hired him?" asked Liu.

Jeffries spoke up "Yes. The guy brought cash to the initial meet. Guy wore sunglasses and a cap. Morley got 5K at the first meeting and the rest at a second meeting. We've got a sketch artist in with Morley now, but we don't expect much."

"Sketch" was a misnomer as the "sketching" was all done with computers now.

Liu asked, "And he didn't wonder why the guy wanted the church wrecked?"

"The plumber figured he just hated Christians or something. Said for that much money, he wasn't going to ask questions," Russell answered.

Jeffries added, "One thing of interest was the guy's voice. Morley said it sounded 'off.' Not exactly an accent he could identify; just 'off.' Like maybe he was of foreign nationality but spoke nearly perfect English."

Russell continued the narrative. "We have Morley's truck and there's at least some potential there. The guy told Morley to wait at a park and he would find him. Same park where we found Morley. The guy got in the truck while they talked. By the looks of it, the plumber doesn't clean out his truck too much. Maybe we'll snag a print or something."

"And the money's all gone, I'm sure?" Liu was certain it was.

Russell shook his head. "Nope. None of it. Morley says he only did this to help pay for his eleven-year-old kid's college down the road. Still has it all and, get this; he buried it. We have some guys on their way to dig it up now."

"Well, maybe there's something to be gleaned from the truck and the money. We have a lot we can charge him with. He's an accomplice whether he meant to be or not. I don't think he'll see his kid graduate from college. Keep me posted."

✦

Morgan kept the television on while he began to develop lesson plans for his journalism courses at Georgetown. He always looked up whenever the "Breaking News" graphic popped up although it was rarely significant. This time it was.

"QNN has Breaking News. A source close to the White House speaking…:

"Only under condition of anonymity," Morgan said in unison with the morning news anchor.

"…has told QNN that investigators are strongly suspecting a Russian connection with yesterday's bombing at St. John's Episcopal Church in which Vice President Logan and others were killed. The source tells us that the components used to make the device were of definite Russian origin. Whether this implicates Russian authorities remains to be seen…"

Morgan was in full analytical mode now. "They're not. They wouldn't use something that so obviously ties them to this thing. Someone's just using Russian bomb making stuff."

In a conference room near the ICU of George Washington University Hospital, another interested party watched the television but had a different concern.

"Damned leaks," POTUS said to Edgar Templeton and CIA Director Elizabeth Parnell. Her tone wasn't one of surprise, merely exasperation. "Seems these days nobody in Washington can keep their mouths or their zippers shut."

President Hendrickson was receiving her daily intelligence briefing, though from a smaller group than usual; only her National Security Advisor and Parnell. The hospital had prepared this room for POTUS' use while she stayed with her son.

She shook her head at the conclusion of the television talking head's remarks about the possible Russian connection. "Wonder how far the speculation will take everyone."

She placed a call to her chief of staff.

"Noah, you heard? Okay. Better get the Russian ambassador in to talk with him. Tell him that, yes, the report is accurate but no, we don't suspect they're involved. But see what he knows. See if they have any intelligence they can share.

"I can't believe they know anything. Even with current tensions, surely they would've told us." She hung up.

POTUS wanted to ream Betsy Parnell for the failure of U.S. Intelligence on this thing but it wouldn't be fair, she decided. Parnell would just be a target of opportunity because she was sitting right here. None of the U.S. agencies had seen this coming.

The door cracked and Agent Griffith peeked in.

"Ma'am, the doctor would like to see you in your son's room."

Mom dropped all her papers on the conference room table and sped out the door with her Secret Service agent trying to keep up. She pushed the door open and looked immediately to her son.

AJ's eyes were open, not terribly alert, and he turned his head to his mother. His smile was subtle, but it was the most beautiful thing his mom had ever seen. Adam Sr. stood on the far side of the bed.

A doctor smiled at the mother as she entered the room. "We noticed that his brain activity had shown a change, so we decided to bring him partially out of the induced coma. Surprising, given this morning. He's not completely out of the woods but I think it's safe to say, things are looking pretty good."

His left hand still had the IV attached and the index finger sported the oxygen sensor, but Adam Hendrickson Jr. gave his mom and dad a very weak thumbs-up.

✦

Maggie's morning was stressful but not overwhelming. She supposed getting her first foray into the public eye had served in getting that off her checklist of job duties. She had expected it to come much later and under far different circumstances. At Image Quest she had coached many of her clients, even some politicians, to do just what she had done last night. And even though she had been interviewed on radio and TV many times, never had she done a press briefing like that.

As she sat at her desk anticipating the next such briefing that was scheduled for fifteen minutes from now, her phone rang and an unidentified voice announced, "Please hold for the president."

Acting Press Secretary Margaret Loughlin gulped and stood up, as though POTUS had entered the room.

"Margaret, this is President Hendrickson. But you go by Maggie, don't you?" Before Maggie could confirm that, her boss continued.

"Maggie, I just wanted to call and thank you personally for how you've stepped up at this critical time. I can't tell you how proud I am of your performance at the briefing last night. And I know that Secretary Ginnetti would be, too. It's a great comfort to me personally to know the department is in such capable hands. Chief Chandler filled me in on all the drama with Klein yesterday. Marie always felt he was never really looking out for the interests of this administration. She never liked him."

Even though she wanted to agree, Maggie held her tongue. Still, she thought that to be an oddly personal and frank remark. She simply answered, "It's my honor, Madam President." And she meant it.

"How is your son, ma'am?"

"This isn't for public consumption, Maggie, but he's better. The doctors just told us they think he'll make a full recovery now. There was a close call very early this morning, but things turned around and they brought him out of his coma. The last few hours have been remarkable. Thank you for asking."

"Yes, ma'am. I'm happy for your good news."

"I'll be coming back to the House in a few minutes. Don't imagine Noah has had time to tell you. I just got off the phone with him. I want to handle this morning's briefing myself. You don't need to prepare anything. I already know what I want to say. Just inform the press pool that the briefing will be delayed. Don't say why. Thank you again, Maggie."

"You're very…" The line went silent.

Maggie sat down and reflected on what a thoughtful thing the president had just done. She really didn't have time, Maggie knew, so the gesture was even more meaningful.

The acting press secretary walked into the briefing room where White

House correspondents for every media outlet imaginable were already gathered and announced the delay without explanation.

✦

Gennadiy Borzilov sat at his desk. It had been a restless night with little sleep. He wanted desperately to speak with Larisa but was certain that couldn't happen. Regardless of the outcome of his undeveloped plan, he might never see her or the children again. The agent realized his survival was irrelevant now. The failure of the bomb to achieve its objective was apparent enough. The American leader still lived. Gennadiy had hoped the mere act itself coupled with the death of the vice president would suffice, but his handlers were unsatisfied.

He turned up the volume on his office television to hear that the five men held since yesterday had been cleared of any involvement in the bombing. They were still being held on unspecified and unrelated charges.

The American journalists were certainly doing all they could to help the Russian. The ability of the American press to report whatever they wanted, mostly unfettered by government restrictions, was something he never understood. In Russia people knew that their government conducted much that they would never know, nor did they have a right to know.

But in spite of his attempt on Hendrickson's life, or maybe because of it, the press was obsessed with every moment of the woman's day. Thanks to their reporting, the SVR agent always – well, almost always – knew where she was.

He had to find a course of action to finish what he had been commanded to do. He wouldn't have the support he had been given for the original attempt. No, he was completely on his own now. He knew he had to have foreknowledge of where the president would be. And he had to construct a plan flexible enough that it would work anywhere and at a moment's notice.

Borzilov's orders had nothing to do with his position as an agent of the SVR. It would make more sense if the directives had come from there, based on national interests. And had they originated there, his family wouldn't be in danger.

✦

This had come together pretty fast, even considering the urgency commensurate with an attack on the president and Russell couldn't wait to report it. He knocked on Supervisory Agent Liu's door and opened it without waiting for an invitation. She didn't mind.

"We might have something. Well, not really anything in itself but at least something that gives us some direction."

The Special Agent handed his boss a report but summarized it for her before she could read it.

"We got some matching fingerprints from the bag that held the money we dug up from Morley's yard and his truck."

"So?" responded a so far unimpressed Annie Liu. It had been a long twenty-plus hours and the pressure and the sleep-deprivation were starting to take their toll.

"That's what we would expect, isn't it?"

"Yes… well, I mean, no. You're right. We'd expect some matching prints on those objects. And no, we haven't ID'd anyone yet. But get this, remember the phone we found in the trash can five or six blocks from the church? And remember, our tech guys stitched together a bunch of partials on its keys? Those guys are amazing, by the way. Well, their composite of a single print is a match. It's a perfect match to a right index finger on the money, the plastic bag, and the truck."

Liu looked over the report, but it said exactly what her agent had.

"That's good work!"

"That's great work! Like I said, those guys are amazing. Of course, there's luck thrown in. Morley spends the money or even just unwraps it and throws away the wrapper and the bag, any prints in the truck are useless. No way to connect any of them to someone that we know is the bomber – or at least involved. And without th…"

"Without that," Liu finished the deduction, "we don't know the phone belonged to someone involved."

Liu rolled her chair back from her desk, "Wow!'

"Yes, ma'am. The phone will be a tough nut to crack. But we know it's his so if we get anything from it – anything at all – it's helpful! As you'd expect, we've got guys all over this."

The supervisor lifted the handset. "I'll let the Assistant Director know. He'll tell Director Austin. And I'm sure he'll let the White House know."

Liu was in a much better mood than when her agent had arrived.

The White House press corps had all gotten wind that the president was in the building and hoped that the reason for the delayed start to the briefing was because she would be present.

Shortly, the doors to the press briefing room opened and Maggie Loughlin announced, "The President of the United States."

Sandra Hendrickson had always been something of a darling to the press. They uncharacteristically broke into applause upon her entrance. Regardless of political allegiance, anyone without admiration for this woman who had been injured in an assassination attempt some twenty-four hours earlier, who had lost her vice president and friend in the attack, and whose son even now lay in the hospital with serious injuries wasn't paying attention.

She took her place behind the lectern displaying a very slight, not-quite smile that had just the right combination of warmth with a hint of sadness while her posture carried the appearance of strength, resolve, and defiance.

"Thank you all. Thank you for your kindness and for your concern for me and my family over the last day. Let me say first how much I appreciate the tremendous help Maggie Loughlin has been. She stepped in for my friend and press secretary, Marie Ginnetti, under the most trying of circumstances and has done a wonderful job. Thank you, Maggie."

The president turned to Maggie. Her smile brightened slightly.

"The last twenty-four hours have seen extraordinary events that have no precedent in the history of our nation. We have lost good men and women. Vice President Logan was a friend, a confidant, and I will miss him. Our nation will miss him.

"The audacity of anyone presuming to attack our people and our nation is matched only by its recklessness. The brazenness to carry out such a wanton act of cowardice at a place with historic significance as a symbol of the religious and moral foundation of our nation is surpassed only by its treachery.

"The soul of the United States is its people. Where some are struck down, others rise to take their place. The heart of our nation is found in our kindness and our devotion to freedom. Sometimes the inevitable manifestation of that freedom is in our disputes with one another, much like the bickering that might be found within families.

"But make no mistake, we are one nation and one family. And when that family is threatened, when our safety and peace, in fact our very lives are endangered, our kindness is supplanted with a ferocity that has no equal. We will defend our lives and our safety.

"To the evildoers who did this, let me say this: You have unleashed a power unlike any other on Earth. It is the power of the American people; the power of right. This is our promise. You will never be safe. When we find you – and we *will* find you – you'll wish you'd never been born."

President Hendrickson turned and walked to the door, followed by shouts of unacknowledged questions from the reporters.

Maggie stood briefly behind the podium, just long enough to end the briefing with a simple, "Thank you." As she made her exit and with the president already gone, the reporters directed their questions to acting Press Secretary Loughlin, who likewise ignored them. Passing through the doors she considered how the correspondents would report the transformation of Hendrickson's words from lofty rhetoric to blunt, direct promise of justice.

"That'll give 'em something to chew on," she thought.

✦

POTUS entered the Oval Office. Director of National Intelligence Chris Donleavy, Director of Homeland Security Anson Larson, CIA Director Betsy Parnell, National Security Advisor Ed Templeton, and NSA Director Paul MacMillan awaited her. A moment after Hendrickson greeted her visitors and took her seat, a Secret Service agent escorted FBI Director Gabe Austin into the room.

"Sorry I'm late. I was on the phone with Deputy Director Drake." Anthony Drake was serving as point man for the investigation into the bombing.

Austin filled the group in on the developments he had learned about earlier that morning surrounding the fingerprints and the burner phone.

"But my call with Drake just now concerned an even more recent development."

Austin began his report on the Bureau's conclusions from interviews with management and workers from the company that had performed the repairs on the church. The discussions had begun at just after noon following the bombing and had lasted through the night. It was no surprise that the repairs were on the up-and-up, so identifying the company involved was simply a matter of contacting the church's Director for Operations, who was more than eager to help.

"It's remarkable how this all worked through typical channels. Plumber Morley crashes his van into the columns. He provides his insurance information. His total coverage amounted to nearly two million dollars. The church files a claim on his professional liability insurance and his automobile coverage. That was the plan all along, we're convinced. One unintended consequence that Morley wasn't smart enough to anticipate was that his insurance providers dropped his coverage. Not only that, due to the nature of the claim they're suing him for personal liability."

"He's got bigger problems than that," remarked the president.

"The church and the insurance company agreed on a contractor for the repair: Patriot Historical Restoration and Construction. Doing this sort of work on historically significant structures is their specialty."

"And they're legitimate?" asked National Security Advisor Templeton.

"Entirely. That's the beauty of this thing – at least from the perspective of whoever's behind it."

POTUS asked, "So how'd the bomb get there? I'm assuming Patriot didn't do it."

"Correct. They didn't. Not long before Patriot closed up the hole in the column, a man shows up claiming he's representing the insurance company.

His credentials identify him as a structural consultant. His job, he says is to take measurements of the load on the column, an entirely reasonable requirement that the insurers would want their own guy there, so nobody gave it a second thought. He had 'specialized equipment' and worked by himself while Patriot's crew was at lunch. None of them suspected anything so they didn't compare notes with each other. But when we pressed them, none of them remembered him leaving with his equipment."

CIA Director Parnell concludes, "And that was the bomb."

"Yes. Had to be."

The president was skeptical but said anyhow, "Tell me we got pictures."

"Not good ones but Drake says we did. We already had video from the traffic cams but didn't know what to look for. The guy wore a cap and sunglasses, even though it was cloudy, and did a pretty good job of keeping his face away from one camera but apparently got careless. For one brief instant, something gets his attention and he turns squarely toward the camera."

"Holy cow!" exclaimed Donleavy.

Austin continued, "Our squints have already created some variations of the bastard's face as it might look without the glasses and the cap. We've transmitted copies to every agency with the capability to work on it. Let's keep our fingers crossed that facial recognition will come up with a match for one of those speculative images."

"Anything else, Gabe?" Hendrickson enquired.

"Yes, Madam President. One more thing. And this is probably something none of us want to hear because of where it might lead. The phony structural guy seemed to have a slight accent. The two guys from Patriot who talked to him couldn't identify it; just said he sounded 'different.' This is in line with what Morley said. But… and this is the unsettling element to this… the guy takes a call and turns away from the Patriot supervisor standing there for privacy. In doing so he exposed the face of his phone to the supervisor who saw all sorts of weird characters. He said they looked like Russian letters. Our interviewers showed him some samples of the Russian alphabet. He said he couldn't be sure but thought they looked like what he saw."

That was the last thing the president wanted to hear – another hint at possible Russian involvement.

"Shit."

CHAPTER 12

"Maggie," Josh said. "I'm glad you could call. I wasn't sure when you'd have time. How's everything in the West Wing?"

His fiancée spent a few minutes catching Morgan up on an uneventful morning – at least as far as she was involved.

Morgan never said a word. She was so excited that he just let her ramble. Finally, he asked hopefully, "Got time for me to take you to lunch?"

"Oh, Josh. I can't."

Despite expecting that answer, he was still disappointed. "I understand."

"But you can come here!" Maggie said. Her voice had the lilt it often did when she was excited.

"Seriously? How?"

"My background checks involved additional checks on everyone I know. Well, you know that. They interviewed you. But part of my onboarding was to arrange clearances for my immediate family. With restrictions, of course. Yours flew through. The early part of your life was already on file because of the background checks when you applied to CIA. They essentially gave you a pass on the Terrador thing because of your role in the Blake/Saudi nightmare. Everyone close to the president knows about you. And I think you might've gotten help from your former president friend."

"Again."

"Yep."

"That's wonderful news."

✦

The president requested that Noah Chandler meet with the ambassador from the Russian Federation in light of the leak that the components on the bomb were Russian-made. The conversation possessed a whole new perspective now.

The chief of staff and Ambassador Valentin Nikitovich Listunov had developed a cordial relationship that was in contrast to the tensions between their respective nations. They weren't quite friends but often used first names. Chandler felt he had a pretty good read on the Russian while being able to keep things from him. Of course, the ambassador felt exactly the same way about the chief of staff.

"Valya, I wanted to say, first of all, that we have no reason to believe your nation was involved in this terrible act." That was no longer entirely true, but his instructions were clear. Proceed as if they had never uncovered the recent clues of a possible Russian on the site where the blast occurred.

"I'm pleased to hear that, Noah. Even if the information is true that the device was Russian, that doesn't mean that we were involved. As I've told you many times, my friend, your free press is often too free... in my opinion. What have you learned about this incident?"

Noah thought it unusual that a diplomat would blow right past any expressions of condolence or matters of courtesy to get straight to a discussion of facts.

"We had some men in custody we thought at first might be involved. We learned rather quickly that they were not, but we still hoped they might prove to be valuable witnesses. They were very near the site of the blast. But that was untrue, as well."

"Unfortunately, Valya, we have almost no leads," he lied. "One of the reasons I wanted to speak to you in person was that the president hoped that perhaps your intelligence personnel had discovered something – anything that might be useful to us."

"Alas, we have nothing. But President Tatarov has offered our assistance to you. We will help in any way we can. He has authorized us to share any intelligence we develop. And, of course, he extends his sympathy and his outrage at yesterday's events."

The discussion ended not long afterward.

Ambassador Listunov left relieved that the Americans had no information that might implicate his country with the attack.

The chief of staff was certain that the Russian diplomat had some knowledge concerning the bombing. Knowledge didn't necessarily connect them, but it troubled Chandler anyhow.

Listunov left for his embassy. Chandler headed straight for the Oval Office.

✦

After passing through a metal detector and still being subjected to a scan with a hand wand, Morgan was permitted to go with Maggie into the West

Wing.

She showed Josh her office, followed by a visit to Secretary Ginnetti's office, which was right next to hers. Chandler had insisted she work from there while acting in her place. It was over four times the size so there was more room for meetings with the rest of the White House Press Department. The Secretary's office also had an extra computer, a larger television screen than hers, and four more smaller ones. She had already moved anything that Josh shouldn't see to her desk drawers. Next, she showed him the press briefing room.

Morgan had hoped to meet some of the administration officials though he would never ask and knew that Maggie would never presume to ask.

She took him down the West Colonnade where he could hurriedly catch a glimpse of the Rose Garden. On the way back to Maggie's office, at the point where the West Colonnade intersected the hallway that led to the Cabinet Room and the Oval Office, Morgan saw a familiar face.

Elizabeth Parnell recognized Morgan, too. They had met at a memorial for his friend Ben Reid, who had worked for Parnell at CIA before she had promoted from Deputy Director of Intelligence to CIA Director. They spoke little then of the whole affair surrounding the kidnapping of ex-President Weston, preferring to talk about Ben.

"Josh Morgan, you do get around."

They shook hands. Morgan said, "Maggie, this is CIA Director Elizabeth Parnell. This is my fiancée…"

"Maggie Loughlin," Parnell continued for him. "I saw your press briefing last night. Remarkable job, especially in light of your having just started here."

"Thank you."

The director hadn't time for small talk so quickly excused herself. As she walked away, she looked back over her shoulder, her arched eyebrows punctuating a threatening look.

"Don't go sticking your nose in my business again, Morgan."

The message was clear to Morgan and Maggie, although it was thoroughly lost on the aide accompanying Parnell.

"I'll try, ma'am." He smiled.

The director looked at the ex-CIA spook a moment longer, wagged a finger at him, and finally smiled back.

"Great seeing you. Nice meeting you, Ms. Loughlin."

"Thank you, director. You, too."

The pair had a very quick lunch in Maggie's office and started back to the lobby for Morgan's exit.

A voice from across the lobby said, "Who's that scoundrel following you around, Ms. Loughlin? Should I call security?" Former President Weston was cutting through the lobby from the late vice president's office to the Oval Office when he caught sight of the pair. Foregoing handshakes, he hugged both Maggie and Morgan.

"Gee, Morgan," said the acting press secretary, "you know as many people here as I do."

With Weston was Sir Albert McGinnis, the British "diplomat" Maggie and Morgan had met at the Capitol while waiting for the swearing-in that never happened – at least not there.

"You remember Sir Albert."

"Yes, sir. Pleasure seeing you again."

Without another word, except to say, "I'm sorry. We have to go," Weston exited the lobby with the Brit in tow.

"Ms. Loughlin. Mr. Morgan," said the Englishman with a slight bow.

"Sir Albert," they both replied.

Maggie didn't give the encounter a second thought, but Morgan's antennas were up.

"Hmm. Wonder why he's here?" he said to himself.

◆

"President Weston. Sir Albert," greeted the president.

"Madam President," her two guests said in unison.

"Thank you for your time, Madam President."

"It is I who thanks you for your time. We can never overstate the importance of the bond we have with the United Kingdom and our friends at MI-6. And thank you for meeting first with President Weston. He has been kind enough to help the administration. Things are unsettled and there are few people I trust to help sort through the noise and to assist in prioritizing matters."

"Not at all, ma'am. He's an old friend and it's always a pleasure to see him, even despite these circumstances."

The president's time was at more of a premium than usual. Sir Albert understood. She motioned them to the love seat in front of her desk as she took a seat in a chair across from them.

"President Weston says you have information for me."

◆

Ambassador Valentin Nikitovich Listunov sat in his office at the Russian embassy with SVR *Rezident* Maksim Vladimirovich Shikhov. On the phone with them in Moscow was Shikhov's boss, Pavel Semyonovich Orlov, director of the Foreign Intelligence Service.

"The Americans have dismissed the idea that we were responsible for the attempt on the life of their president," said the ambassador.

Rezident Shikhov added, "We are using all available assets to determine if they know anything at all. It could be that our easiest means of getting the full scope of the event is to get it from the Americans themselves."

Director Orlov was curt. "And who did this thing, do you think?"

The two men in Washington looked at each other. It was the SVR station chief who gave the answer.

"Director, it is conceivable that some other branch of our intelligence agencies was responsible. GRU, perhaps. We each know that our Military Intelligence Agency often conducts its own operations without informing us. And it has sometimes been done with the full knowledge of the Federal Assembly, indeed under direct orders from Comrade President. That is, by far, the worst of the possibilities.

"Equally troubling is the thought that we might have a rogue agent who operated independently – or rather a group. It seems too complex for a single man. But currently there is no basis for suspecting involvement by anyone of our nation."

"I want every agent working this matter until we have discovered the truth of it," demanded Director Orlov. "If there is involvement, it must be covered up even if it puts us in conflict with others of our government. In either situation – another agency or rogue group – the impact is far beyond any reparations to the Americans. It quite possibly puts us on the path…"

"To war," agreed the ambassador.

✦

QNN anchor Tracy Adams was in his usual chair. As with any high-profile news event, the senior anchor wouldn't yield the role as primary voice to the nation to anyone else. He was happy to share the limelight with his relatively new co-anchor, Cameron Neal. QNN had given Neal an anchor role in non-primetime broadcasts after her extraordinary work on *El Aguila de la Amistad,* the train that played such a central role in the kidnapping of ex-President Trenton Weston. Recently Neal had been brought alongside Adams when his broadcast partner left for a similar role at another network.

"So, Cameron, the White House has released some pretty remarkable images."

"Absolutely, Tracy."

Maggie looked up from the desk at the huge TV screen on the wall of Secretary Ginnetti's office. She had not only seen the photos and video, she had been the one to distribute them to journalists in the press corps offices down the West Colonnade from where she worked. Maggie wouldn't make that mistake again. She had completely underestimated what an enormous story she had become among them. Immediately upon entering the first of the two rooms, she was besieged by reporters who launched a barrage of questions about herself.

The acting Secretary had neither the time nor the inclination to become the interviewee – certainly not during the current crisis.

She took the remote and turned the volume up as Neal said, "These photos were made with the president's own phone as she was sworn in. The video shows her reciting the oath of office as it was administered yesterday by Chief Justice Bartholomew Richter in the room where the president was being held for observation. As you can see, President Hendrickson is dressed in hospital scrubs."

Maggie sighed at the realization that the government must go on irrespective of whatever crisis it might find itself in. She turned down the volume and resumed work.

✦

POTUS rose and walked behind her desk. She folded her left arm across her chest while resting her head in her right hand.

"How confident?"

"Our confidence level is quite high, Madam President. The texts we intercepted were of a nature that only after the bombing occurred did we understand them. The content, after the fact, seems indisputable."

"And at the risk of sounding disrespectful and skeptical, you're quite certain of the locations of the communicators?"

"Yes, ma'am. Washington and Moscow."

✦

Larisa Borzilova couldn't sleep. She didn't know what time it was but guessed it was around 5:00 AM. Fortunately, she saw, her children were sound asleep.

She, Valeriy, and Ulyana had been locked together in the small room for several hours. The room was sparse but clean. There was no television or radio and Larisa had been allowed no phone calls. None of the three captors had said a word to the mother and her children but neither had they mistreated them in any way. The fact that they were being held against their will terrified Larisa, but their "hosts" had provided them with food, including baby formula, milk for the baby, and bathroom breaks.

The Russian woman didn't know why they were being held. All she knew was that they had mentioned her husband by name when they first arrived to take her and the children. At the beginning of the car ride to wherever it was that they had taken her, they hadn't blindfolded her or otherwise restricted her view. But the woman of the three had told her in a very severe voice that she wasn't to look outside. The Russian captive complied. The drive had been about one hour's duration, so she knew they weren't far from Moscow. All the woman knew was that she was terrified for herself, Valeriy, Ulyana – and Gennadiy.

✦

"I can't believe this is where we've arrived," said POTUS to her chief of staff shortly after President Weston and Sir Albert McGinnis had left her office. She and Chandler were waiting for Weston to return from escorting the MI-6 operative out of the West Wing. Hendrickson had also asked her secretary to get her NSA Director on the phone.

POTUS' phone buzzed, and her secretary announced that Director McClintock was on the line.

"Paul," the president said as her door opened, and Secret Service allowed the ex-president in. Hendrickson motioned Weston to a chair beside Chandler.

"Paul," she began again, "I know you've been looking back at communications intercepts…" By "you've" she meant the entire National Security Agency. "…But we've had some developments that should help you narrow your focus. MI-6 Station Chief Albert McGinnis brought over some collections from the GCHQ."

She summarized the info from the UK's Government Communications Headquarters, their equivalent to McClintock's agency.

"I'm already having the entire document sent over to you but wanted to give you the basics. Right."

Hendrickson hung up and turned her attention to the two men in the Oval Office. She sat on the corner of her desk and rubbed at the bandage on her neck. It was the only visible injury from the bombing.

Both of her guests sat patiently while their host rose and walked to the window behind her desk. She massaged her temples.

"This is unbelievable." And repeating her earlier words, "I can't believe this is where we've arrived."

POTUS seated herself across from Chandler and Weston.

"I think there's little choice but to expand our preparedness to include…" She paused to take a deep breath. "…To include military options."

Such options were always on the table after national emergencies like the bombing – well, there had been no parallel to this attack – but they were generally options to covertly strike at a terrorist camp or other limited targets. But the president was referring to an expansion of the catalog of operational contingencies to attack a nation-state.

"Do you concur? It has to be considered."

Both Weston and Chandler had the gravest of countenances. They nodded.

"Noah, get everyone over here ASAP. Cabinet, Joint Chiefs."

Noah Chandler and Trenton Weston stood to leave.

"President Weston, could you stay a moment?"

Once Chandler had exited, "Trent, you've sat behind this desk. You're the only one who has done so that I can trust to both understand and to advise me if I'm doing the right thing."

The former POTUS returned to his seat. "Sandy, right now 'doing' simply means preparing. You have no other alternative to what you're doing right now. You know far too little to take us to war. You know far too much to not prepare for it. I think it's a matter of some urgency to start planning. I think you're responding the only way you can – measured, appropriate, and all-encompassing. So, yes. You're doing the right thing. It's precisely what I'd do.

"I don't presume to tell you how to proceed but am happy to be a sounding board when you need it," Weston concluded.

"Thanks for that, Trent. I'd like you to attend this meeting. Speaker Bauer… rather, Vice President Bauer…" That was the first time she had said those words. "…Will move into his office tomorrow. He should be far enough along in his own transition with the Congressional leadership to assume his new role. We've had a couple of phone conversations but nothing of any substance so he's not in on the nitty-gritty of this thing. He'll certainly be at this planning meeting, but I'd really value your presence."

"Thank you, Sandy, but I think I should stay mostly invisible. I'm happy to do whatever you ask, and if you insist, I'll be there, but I'd ask you to consider that the friction that might arise could outweigh any benefit.

"If I may, I'll go back to the vice president's office. I'll make any phone calls you wish. I'll receive them. I'll help filter and prioritize any visitors, as I did with Albert. But I think I should remain largely behind the scenes, publicly and with regard to members of your administration."

POTUS always appreciated Weston's ability to provide counsel with such humility. The difference in their ages and the fact that they were, after all, from different political parties notwithstanding, the former president was the only mentor she had.

Hendrickson simply nodded and Weston took his leave.

Mom decided to call her son.

✦

With the start of classes being postponed until further notice, Josh Morgan had no place he had to be. He had completed all the course outlines for the two topics he would teach at Georgetown. The first was "Photo and Video Storytelling II." Though he had done little video in his career as a photojournalist, which was really a cover for his real job as a CIA officer, the elements of presentation were very similar to a photo spread. This course didn't deal so much with equipment and technology, nor editing. It was intended to augment the Level I course that dealt with such topics. This course's goal was to deal with the composition of the story from an aesthetic point to project impact to the viewer by conveying personality or drama as it related to the subject.

His second course assignment was "Sourcing & Interview Techniques." It had little to do with his actual expertise in photography but rather focused on finding subjects and securing interviews with people who could provide the background to the images that would attract viewers. Though Morgan had developed a well-deserved reputation for his photographic skills, CIA needed him in his role to make contact with people the Agency deemed important enough to be of value as assets. And Morgan had an even greater skill in doing just that.

The Company had any number of patrons in the world of journalism who assured that the young man got great assignments in the locales they needed him and that the assignments carried the certainty of publication in well-known outlets. These created the visibility that accelerated the process of his becoming a respected photojournalist.

His value to CIA wasn't in his photographs. It was in his ability to create assets. Of course, in his cover, he had to come through as a photographer to fulfill that role.

Fortunately, Maggie's day allowed her to call Morgan a couple of times, but it was still certain she would have to remain at her desk until after midnight. Looked like another lonely night with the television.

◆

The entire Cabinet was there, even those whose duties were in no way connected to affecting counter-terrorism ops or war plans. They were, after all, advisors to the president and their management experience was valuable in all areas of governmental decisions. The Defense Secretary and Director of Homeland Security – or Secretary of Homeland Security, his title in the context of the president's Cabinet – were among them and their departments would have responsibilities and direct involvement in managing the contingencies. The Director of National Intelligence and the CIA director were also Cabinet members who would be critical to what they would be discussing. Rounding out the primary players were the Secretary of State and Ambassador to the United Nations. One additional non-Cabinet member attendee was the Chairman of the Joint Chiefs of Staff.

Finally, in the chair immediately across from the president, the one formerly occupied by Vice President Antoine Logan, sat newly sworn-in VP Bauer. Despite his substantial political pedigree, the sixty-eight-year-old former Oklahoma Governor had a "deer in the headlights" look. He shifted in his seat frequently and showed a reluctance to speak that was at odds with his reputation.

After acknowledging her new veep, the president began.

"The matters we are here to discuss are perhaps the gravest we could be facing," the president began.

She went through in detail each of the items that, when considered *in toto*, seemed to indicate that the Russian Federation might be the entity behind the attempt on her life and the deaths of Vice President Logan and a number of others.

When POTUS got to the texts that were intercepted by the British GCHQ and passed on to her by Sir Albert McGinnis, she turned to NSA Director McClintock and asked, "Director McClintock, would you please pass on the information you shared with me by telephone just before you headed over to this meeting?"

McClintock spoke without passion, very matter-of-factly conveying the expedited findings of his agency after the prompt from POTUS.

"It seems very clear that the texts disclosed to us by our British friends did indeed concern the attack on our country. Furthermore, in addition to the text messages, there were at least three voice calls between the same two devices."

There was an instantaneous buzz among the Cabinet members and others in the room.

The NSA director bristled because he knew what they were discussing, and it was – though justifiably – an affront to his organization's competence.

"You are no doubt wondering how we missed such a critical communication. And while I agree with you that it's a disastrous intelligence failure, there are some crucial specifics you should know. First, there weren't sufficient keywords to trigger a flag on the communications by 'The Program,'" referring to the President's Surveillance Program.

"Secondly, the individual on the domestic side of the conversation was apparently not an individual known to U.S. agencies or we would have had surveillance on him specifically. We do have one more piece of information, Madam President… Director Austin."

Borzilov was indeed known to intelligence agencies, both as a low-level diplomat and as a suspected spy, but he had somehow avoided detection during his planning for the bombing.

"Madam President, after you called Director McClintock, he called me to compare notes. The phone used on this end of the communications was clearly the one the Bureau has in evidence. For those of you who don't know, immediately after the bombing our investigators discovered a burner phone in a trash can not far from St. John's Church. We thought the odds that it had any relation to the bomber were pretty long, but we pursued it, of course, and without going into detail about the process, we were able to lift a single fingerprint from it.

"We've tied that print to an individual known to be at the church during the time when repairs were being made to the church's columns and we know that was when the device was planted. We have a photograph of the suspect, a poor one but we've had facial recognition churning on it since earlier today."

The president picked up the narrative with a summation of her understanding.

"So, let's see if I've got this right. We now have a photo of a suspect..."

"A poor one," reminded Director Austin.

"A poor photo," POTUS corrected, "...a fingerprint, intercepted texts and calls, and one of the phones known to have been involved in those calls?"

"Correct," verified the FBI director.

"And they point to Russian involvement?"

"I'm afraid so, ma'am," the NSA director affirmed. He knew the gravity of that last bit of evidence.

Everyone in the room waited.

Finally, President Hendrickson broke the silence.

"Let's get to work."

By midnight, she and her team had worked out their respective assignments. The goal? To construct a plan for war with Russia.

CHAPTER 13

Day 6 - Thursday

Russian embassies were never immune from gossip, hearsay, or speculation. Leaks to the public or open criticism of the government might've been treated harshly, certainly more than in the United States, but plain old watercooler chinwag? The Russians were no different in that regard than any of the other humans on the planet.

Russian SVR Agent Gennadiy Borzilov was hearing the rumors and they were creating a mild panic in him. The *Rezident* was concerned, to say the least, about the reports in the American media of Russian involvement in the attack on the U.S. president. The embassy station chief was a severe man in his own right, but he took his marching orders from the Foreign Intelligence Service's Headquarters in the Yasenevo District of Moscow. And that meant that ultimately the man behind this enquiry was Director Pavel Semyonovich Orlov himself.

Borzilov knew when he undertook the mission to assassinate the American leader that his time as assistant station chief was over. The initiative for the plan didn't rest with the SVR and the plot had successfully remained secret from everyone in the organization, top to bottom. Furthermore, Russian agencies were exactly the same as their U.S. equivalents in that they were notorious for often withholding information from one another, whether domestic or foreign in nature.

What he was hearing was that the ambassador was deeply concerned about his nation's alleged involvement in the bombing. Borzilov understood that Listunov knew that, even as the leader of the diplomatic mission to Russia's primary adversary, he might be – as Americans say – kept out of the loop in even the most momentous operation. Moscow generally felt their ambassadors rarely needed to know of intelligence activities, unless it was discovered. Then it would be Posol Listunov's job to clean up after it, in terms of providing an explanation, or more precisely a denial, to the American White House.

So Borzilov knew that the ambassador's trepidation existed along divergent possibilities. First was that an agency of his country that was out of his purview had once again executed an operation without his knowledge. If so, he would have to explain it to the American president. The other possibility was that Russia had nothing to do with it and he would still have to explain it to the American president.

But SVR Agent Gennadiy Borzilov held no concern for Listunov's dilemma. His distress lay only in the fact that he would soon be asked to comment on his knowledge, or lack of it, with respect to the attack.

His handlers wouldn't be understanding if his role were discovered prematurely. Gennadiy looked at his clock – 1:30 AM. He tried to dismiss the impending conversation with his *rezident* and get some sleep, but he knew it would not happen.

✦

POTUS was in her bed at the White House. She had spoken with her husband and learned that their son had made remarkable progress. It was astounding, particularly given the near-catastrophe of that morning. Seeing her son so near death was beyond her ability to comprehend. She wished she could be there, but the late hour of her Cabinet meeting made it impractical. Mom's only comfort was in the person lying next to her.

Noelle was a vision of perfection in the eyes of her mother. To have come through the blast virtually without injury was a miracle beyond understanding.

As a mother, Sandy was blessed. As the president, not so much. Her thoughts returned to the dilemma facing the United States and her as its leader.

Sleep was often elusive for her. It would be tonight.

✦

Carl Smith was scouring over the images on his monitor in the lab at the FBI. He was a day shift technician but like many at the Bureau right now, he was working long hours. He had come in at 5:00 AM so he had been at work only ten minutes when he heard the ping on the other computer. It had been churning data nonstop for almost twenty hours, using the program's most sophisticated algorithms with one purpose.

"Smitty" was so engrossed with the screen before him that he jumped at the intrusion of the sound. It took only a nanosecond for him to swivel around in his chair.

"Oh, my god!" He pushed against the desk where he'd been working to send the chair rolling on its casters to the second table. It was waist-high so Smitty stood, straightened his glasses, and leaned toward the display.

"Oh... my... god!" he repeated. He lifted the phone from its switch-hook and started pressing the keypad.

✦

Her sigh was prolonged. She looked at the digital display on her bedside clock and... 5:45 AM. The gently rapping on her door resumed. President Hendrickson looked at her still-sleeping daughter beside her in the bed.

"I envy you, sweetheart," she whispered.

POTUS donned her robe and walked to the door. The Secret Service agent politely whispered to avoid waking the first daughter.

"Ma'am, the chief of staff would like to see you."

"Why didn't he just call?" she wondered. Chandler was one of only a small number of people who had authorization to call her direct line at any time, day or night.

"Tell him I'll be right there." She closed the door to the family quarters and leaned her head against it. The sudden recollection of the national crisis came roaring back into her consciousness, and she became instantly wide awake.

A short time later, President Hendrickson emerged from the residence into the West Hall where a staff member handed her a cup of coffee. The agent escorted his charge down the stairs that marked the boundary between home and work.

Entering the Oval Office, she was only slightly surprised to see FBI Director Austin with Chandler.

"Good morning, Noah – Gabe."

"Good morning, ma'am."

She sat on one of the chairs beside the coffee table in the center of the room, where a fresh cup of brew and a light breakfast of a small omelet and toast awaited her. She took a piece of toast and bit at one corner before turning to Chandler, who simply nodded to Austin.

The Bureau director handed POTUS a photograph. "This is the guy," he said with some urgency.

✦

He knew it would be pointless but Gennadiy tried again to call Larisa. It was about two-thirty in the afternoon back home, which was the agreed-upon time for the husband and wife to talk each day. But as it had the evening before, his call went straight to voicemail. The Russian knew that leaving a message would be futile. His wife would never hear it. He was confident that no harm had befallen her – yet. His family was the leverage that had forced him into his current circumstances.

Borzilov nearly dropped the phone when it rang. He pressed the icon to connect the call.

"*Da?*"

He listened for the terse summons he knew the call would entail and simply acknowledged with another, "*Da.*"

✦

POTUS pushed away her plate of uneaten breakfast and leaned back.

"Who is he?" She braced herself for the answer with another drink of the hot, black coffee.

"Gennadiy Valeryevich Borzilov. Assistant *Rezident* at the Russian embassy."

Gabe Austin paused for a follow-up but, when there was none, he proceeded.

"His cover is 'Associate Diplomat' but we've known for some time he is SVR. He was formerly *Spetsial'nyy Otryad Bystrogo Reagirovaniya*. Might still be. The *Russkiye* are known to spy on each other; one agency placing an agent in another to get information that isn't readily shared. SOBR was the Russian rapid response unit. It's been renamed the *Otrjad Milizii Spetsialnogo Naznachenija*, or OMSN. It's primarily tasked with anti-terrorism. They were heavily involved in the 2014 invasion of Crimea."

Austin took a sip of his coffee and proceeded.

"So Borzilov might even now be SOBR or OMSN. But whether he still is or not, the fact that he ever was means he's one elite son of a bitch."

"So, he's well-trained in SpecOps and is the Assistant SVR Station Chief. And he's our mystery man. This just gets better and better." Hendrickson finally took an unenthusiastic bite of her omelet, which had gotten cold. She took the piece of toast again.

"'Associate Diplomat?' What is that? Or rather, the question is, is his position high enough to have full diplomatic immunity?"

"Probably. But we don't know yet," Chandler said. "Maybe only functional immunity. We would need to get State's opinion on that."

"So, what's next?" asked POTUS. "Do we confront the ambassador?"

Chief Chandler opined, "I think we wait. If he does have full immunity and it's a government op, they might just get him out of the country, albeit with a promise to look into it. If he's acting alone on this, they might be willing to waive his immunity like they did in '97 when their number two diplomat in the Georgian Republic was driving drunk and killed that teenager. But we're going to have to have some leverage to get them to do that."

"And we're going to have to grab him ourselves. They get a whiff of this, even if he's rogue, they'll snatch him and deal with it themselves," Austin added.

Hendrickson thought for a moment. Finally, she nodded.

"Agreed. I know I don't have to tell you this, but I want everything on this guy. I want it personally. You guys surveil him; do your thing. But I want to personally know everything from his family to his favorite fast food. When I finally talk to Listunov, I want to know this bastard cover to cover.

"Thank you, gentlemen," she said, though she really wasn't thankful for this development.

As they were leaving, she called Trent Weston.

"I need a sounding board."

✦

Borzilov sat in front of his SVR boss and his cover story boss, the ambassador. Live bullets, rebels, traitors, and the like had never unnerved him like this.

His superiors' questions carried no hint of suspicion – at least not yet. They asked his opinions about whether there really could be a connection to the Motherland. Did he suspect another Russian agency could be involved?

"To hell with them, if they are!" threatened Listunov. "I have been caught in the middle of such lunacy before and I will not allow it any longer." He knew that he had no power over such situations but was terrified of the possibility of such a truth; what it would mean for the Russian Federation; what it would mean for him personally.

"Lunacy!" he thundered again.

The conference – it felt more like an interrogation – ended with Listunov demanding answers, and Shikhov and Borzilov promising them.

✦

The Federal Bureau of Investigation's Counterintelligence Division was the primary owner of surveillance of foreign embassies. From direct visual to electronic signals intercepts, the group attempted to monitor every aspect of the lives of diplomatic corps. The higher up the embassy ladder, the more resources were devoted to them.

The Russian and Chinese Embassies commanded a huge amount of attention, along with the Korean complex. As much detail as possible was gathered during the construction of the structures and ongoing scrutiny was carried out on the ground from nearby buildings and above by helicopters, drones, and even satellite. Although they had residences within the compound, it was known that some diplomats maintained off-premises private apartments. The surveillance was no less intense there.

Borzilov had warranted a lot of attention because of his dual positions as Associate Diplomat and Assistant Station Chief. As with the other staff, his personal *kvartira* was known and watched. He was tailed every time he left either the embassy or his apartment. But his lofty position as number two to the SVR station chief also meant that he was an expert in tradecraft. So, on the days he was planning the bombing, the times he carried out meetings with surrogates, posed as a structural engineer at St. John's, and activated the bomb, he often had extensive gaps in his surveillance. That was due to his talent for "dry-cleaning;" that is, identifying and eluding his tails. He never felt he justified more than one, so as soon as he recognized one, he felt he was in the clear.

Gennadiy was more diligent when he began the activities leading up to the bombing. During that time, he realized that if he was under suspicion, he would merit more surveillance and the chances of uncovering all of his tails, expert that he was, was more unlikely. He understood that he wouldn't know he had failed to locate one until he was in custody. But he had never uncovered more than one, so if he discovered that follower, he felt safe enough that he could continue with whatever covert plans he had for the day.

Leaving the embassy today, the SVR operative would have to be exceptionally cautious. In the wake of the bombing, surveillance would be heightened. Considering the reported leaks advanced the possibility of a connection to his country, everyone in the city with a Russian surname might be the object of attention by U.S. counterintelligence.

Gennadiy turned south onto Wisconsin Avenue. He made a few turns here and there, watching in his rear-view mirror. He made a couple of blocks and zigzagged, looking for anyone duplicating his unusual path. A black sedan did.

"Too easy," he figured as he easily shook them off. Soon they rejoined the hunt, moving in behind him a bit further back. The Russian made a couple of evasive moves, losing the tail. This time they didn't return.

Borzilov turned south on 35th Street, NW. He knew his success had been for show; that they had deliberately given the impression that he had evaded them. The plan was to throw him off the second car that the Russian now was certain was there. The agent sped up, slowed down. Nothing apparent. He accelerated to a speed just above the posted limit. He made a few more turns at high speed and made his way to the Francis Scott Key Bridge and across the Potomac.

Speeding ever faster, he turned right onto US 29 and soon merged onto I-66 W.

"Almost there," the Russian said aloud. He believed he had uncovered another pursuer. Soon he would know.

On the Interstate, he slowed to slightly below the speed limit and drove patiently. His driving companion in the mirror likewise slowed. Approaching Exit 71, he decelerated dramatically and engaged his emergency flashers.

Behind the SVR agent, two Special Agents of the FBI had a dilemma. The white Toyota Avalon they had been tailing, the one driven by suspected bomber Gennadiy Borzilov, had turned on his flashers and pulled onto the shoulder of the Interstate. To all others, it would appear he perhaps had car trouble. The agents knew better. And that presented them with a choice. If they, too, stopped, the jig was up. If they continued past him and took the exit ahead, Exit 71 toward Glebe Road, Borzilov would speed ahead on I-66. But if they continued on I-66, he would take the exit.

The agents discussed their options and decided to continue past the now-stationary vehicle on the interstate, find a place ahead to pull off, a place with a good vantage point of I-66 and an easy way to get back on it. Maybe their Russian would make his way back to the interstate also and they could slip back in behind him and continue the chase.

Gennadiy watched as the black sedan continued past him. He immediately turned off the flashers and exited the interstate. He had no intention of returning to the national highway.

About a mile past Exit 71, the Special Agents sat in their car on the frontage road waiting for the white Toyota to reappear so they could proceed down the onramp and resume their tail. It never showed up. The driver slammed his hand on the top of the steering wheel. The passenger called headquarters to report their failure.

CHAPTER 14

The Russian ambassador to the United States and the SVR *rezident* were well past simply losing patience. Their mutual subordinate was fifteen minutes overdue for their meeting. The trio would discuss what the approach should be with respect to their fear that some element of the Russian government or possibly a rogue operative from one of the nation's agencies had executed the bombing at the church near the White House.

The tardiness was unlike Borzilov. In addition to his lateness, he wasn't answering his phone. An aide to the ambassador entered the conference room with his findings.

"We cannot locate him."

The ability to determine the wayward agent's location by his phone far surpassed that of the simplistic "where's my mobile phone" applications available with the devices. The SIGINT technology in the Foreign Intelligence Service's operations center inside the embassy was among the best in the world. In fact, its capabilities were advanced enough that there was only one circumstance in which a device would not be found.

"The phone has been destroyed," Ambassador Listunov realized.

"*Da,*" agreed the SVR *rezident*.

The ambassador feared, "Something terrible must have happened to Gennadiy."

Shikhov had another theory.

✦

Deputy Director, FBI, Tony Drake was livid but screaming at his agent wouldn't improve the state of affairs. How it had happened was even irrelevant.

He simply said, "Lost him? You are shitting me!"

He disconnected the call with his field agent and called Director Austin.

✦

SVR Agent Gennadiy Borzilov had taken his embassy-issued mobile phone apart as soon as he had successfully ditched the men following him and had destroyed each component separately. The parts were scattered individually along his route as he threw them one-by-one out of the moving car.

The Muscovite drove to an abandoned warehouse and left his auto. He knew it would be located by the tracking device the Russian Federation's embassy placed in their own cars. It was buried so deeply in the auto's structure that it would take so long to retrieve it that embassy staff would arrive before he succeeded. He cut through vacant lots he had scouted for just such an occasion. However, he presumed when he created the plan that he would be attempting to elude someone other than his own comrades. Slogging through the foot of snow was uncomfortable and slowed him considerably but he was in top physical condition. He knew Shikhov would already have someone on the way to the Toyota so every meter of distance he covered was critical.

He used one of the several burner phones he had purchased personally to hail an Uber. He dropped the phone in the snow when his ride arrived to take him to a storage unit he had rented under a false identity. He had another personally-purchased vehicle at the facility. In it were additional clothes for all sorts of weather conditions, and a go-bag replete with multiple IDs and fake passports, again purchased independently of his nation's embassy.

By 1:00 PM, he was driving northwestward from the city toward Rockville, Maryland, about an hour away. He had booked a motel room before leaving the storage unit. As he expected, there were rooms available. Most of the people who had been in the District for the inauguration had gone home, in light of the events.

The motel clerk greeted his customer who indicated he was checking in. "Mr. Williams, could I see a photo ID and a credit card?" He began the check-in process.

"Were you in town for the inauguration? Wasn't that something? Sure hit us hard. I mean, not that it is important under the circumstances. But people cut their stays short and headed home."

The desk clerk asked a couple of questions of Mr. Williams, who answered briefly and without so much as a hint of an accent.

By 1:40 PM, "Marvin Williams" was in Room 108 of the smallish motel. He had brought enough food and snacks to sustain him. He wouldn't leave his room for any reason. Borzilov was contemplating his next move.

✦

If it had been any other crime, the president considered, they could just make Borzilov's photo available to the news outlets and ask for the public's help. But that wouldn't work here. First, Borzilov was extremely dangerous. But even more than that, she simply couldn't disclose the fact that the administration's position now was that Russia was behind the bombing. She would be thrilled to be proven wrong, that this was some sort of rogue operation, but she couldn't assume that.

✦

As press secretary, Maggie didn't need to know the nuts and bolts of every issue. Details weren't in her arena. She did, however, need to know enough to answer questions in a way that was consistent with the official narrative. Because of that, she had been briefed sufficiently to do her job but nothing more.

But the parts that the president and her chief of staff decided Maggie needed to know – well, they horrified her. What also terrified her was that she couldn't *appear* terrified when correspondents asked questions about the possibility of Russian involvement.

Standing before the White House press corps was no longer the panic-inciting experience it had been the first time. But neither was it old hat. She no longer felt uncomfortable with the prepared comments before all these people. It wasn't even the question and non-answer period afterward. She had taught others how to handle that. No, it was the possibility that her demeanor would give away some knowledge she possessed but wasn't allowed to share. Everyone familiar with these briefings on the opposite side of the podium from Maggie knew she was always holding back. But if she indeed gave the appearance that she was withholding details in regard to a specific line of questioning, the press might read into it – possibly correctly – some subtle nondisclosed aspect. Speculation would be rampant.

Chief of Staff Chandler had told her to open up some; to reveal a bit of her personality.

The acting press secretary began her remarks.

"Good afternoon, ladies and gentlemen. The president thought we might begin with something a little off-topic from the real news; some good news, for a change. Because so many of you have been nice enough to enquire, she has asked that I let you know that AJ is doing very well. He has improved such that he is out of the danger, out of the ICU, and, too frequently, out of snacks in his hospital room."

The room erupted in applause at the report of the first son's improved condition.

"President Hendrickson thanks you sincerely for the well-wishes. Her son will be moved to Walter Reed soon..."

The rest of her prepared remarks were important but not at all the matters of greatest interest among her audience, both in the room and through the various media.

Maggie shared news that Press Secretary Marie Ginnetti was improving but still not out of danger She also said that details regarding the funeral for Vice President Logan were nearly finalized and would be forthcoming.

Then her body screamed for a deep breath when she opened up the briefing for questions.

Any more details on the Russian connection to the bombing?

"First of all, let me state again that there is no known Russian connection and any conjecture along those lines is unwarranted."

We've been told that you have a suspect who is Russian.

Maggie's first thought was to wonder how the correspondent knew that. That leak was as yet unknown to the president though she wouldn't be surprised to learn of it. Maggie said to the collective media, "You believe everything you hear in the media?"

Everyone laughed while the Principal Assistant Press Secretary continued, "I believe I just answered that. I will go on to say that no avenue of investigation is being left unpursued, but we have no credible knowledge that there is any kind of involvement on the part of the Russian Federation."

The next reporter persisted. "What course of action will the president take if she learns the Russians are involved?"

Maggie wanted to scream, not just at the singlemindedness of the questioners but because there was the same question floating around in her own mind. "Any plans on the part of the president as to a specific response would be premature without facts in evidence to support a conclusion to justify them. I can say that nothing can be ruled out when nothing has been confirmed."

She concluded, "That's all for now."

"Shit!" Maggie said to herself. "That was an unforced error." Despite all the denials that there was any evidence linking Russia to the attack, she had just stated that "nothing has been confirmed." That was just the kind of open door to start theories of what might be known but unconfirmed. Outside the press briefing room, as she was heading to her office, she came face to face with Noah Chandler. The chief of staff didn't look happy.

Maggie waited for the verbal onslaught that the man had a reputation for. Finally, the stern look on his face softened somewhat. The two stood there silently for what seemed to Maggie to be an interminably long time. Desperate to break the standoff, she was about to acknowledge her mistake when Chandler beat her to it.

"Nice job… for a rookie. Try to be a tad more careful, will you?"

"Yes, sir." And that was that.

"I'm going home tonight," she told herself. There was no urgency to the tasks she had before her and she needed some time with Josh.

When she got back to her office the "rookie" called Morgan to tell him she would be home in three hours or so.

✦

In Room 108 in a small motel outside Rockville, Maryland, Marvin Williams was grateful for the information he had just received from the broadcast of the White House press briefing. He hadn't been able to come up with ideas about how to proceed. Now he had two.

"*Spasibo*," he said to Maggie Loughlin, though he'd never met her.

✦

Josh Morgan wondered if he would ever tire of seeing Maggie on TV. He was proud of her and impressed beyond words. He noticed the little mistake at the end. His work as a spy had trained him to be very alert to unintentional slips of the tongue and to seize upon them.

But it was a minor gaffe, he believed. Only thing was, the inadvertent comment made *him* wonder if there was more to the Russia thing than the White House was saying. He knew others would speculate, too. There was always more to things than they let on. You just never knew what things.

Of course, Morgan expressed nothing of this to Maggie. He did promise to have her a nice glass of wine waiting when she got home and that he would cook a nice dinner for her.

"Sweetheart, instead of cooking, why don't you have something delivered? I want all of your time to myself. I need to snuggle up with you on the couch for a while. And maybe I have some plans for you after that."

The reply was instantaneous, "Delivery it is."

They both chuckled softly.

"Love you, Mag."

"Love you, too, Josh."

Morgan began to sort through some delivery options when the phone rang again. Without looking at the ID, he picked it up and said, "Forget something?"

Ryan Crenshaw had been many things to Morgan – his Russian professor at The University of Texas, a close friend, and ultimately the man who recruited Josh to the Central Intelligence Agency. He had been a Company man himself, stationed in Moscow for several years, and only began teaching Russian at UT when he retired from the Agency.

"Josh, son, how are you?"

Morgan sat up a little straighter and smiled, despite the fact that the reason for the excitement couldn't see it.

"Ryan, what a great surprise. I'm great – well, dismayed along with everyone else about the happenings of late, but really great. How are you? Wow. It's been six or seven months."

"Almost nine."

The two chatted for some time, catching up on personal matters and about the recent news. Finally, Crenshaw said, "I was surprised when I got your email a few weeks ago saying you two were moving to D.C. I've seen Maggie on TV a couple of times. Looks like she's fitting right in."

"What can I say? She's brilliant. I'm a lucky man."

"Yes, you are, Josh. Say, I'm going to be in Washington for a few days. Think you could spare some time for your old professor?"

"Of course, I can. It'll be great seeing you. What's bringing you to town?"

"I'll fill you in when I see you. I arrive tomorrow just before noon. I'll call you when I'm settled in."

"Nonsense! You're staying right here with us."

"Oh, I…"

"I'm not taking 'no' from you. All right?"

Crenshaw hesitated before taking his former student up on his offer. Truth was he really expected the offer and hadn't booked a room.

✦

It was 8:30 PM before Maggie got home. But at least she was home. She gave Morgan a tired, long hug. She rested the side of her head on his chest and sighed.

"Hi, Josh."

"Glad you're home. Rough day?"

"Not especially. Just some things wearing on me. I think being thrown right into this role didn't give me time to toughen up. Some of the things I hear are overwhelming. I'm sure over time you get some separation from the things going on behind the scene. You know, a little desensitized."

"What's going on?" He pushed her gently away with hands on her shoulders so he could look into her eyes.

"I can't tell you…. but it's got me a little scared."

The couple snuggled on the sofa, no TV and very little conversation, and munched on the Thai food Josh had ordered. A glass of red wine had softened Maggie's mood. Morgan thought she needed a hug, a bunch of them and had decided almost the moment she walked through the door that romance wasn't in the cards for tonight. He was just fine with that and it was good that he was. By a little before ten o'clock, Maggie was asleep.

Josh carried her into the bedroom and lay her on the bed. He covered her with the comforter, which she instinctively pulled around her and continued her sleep.

✦

At 11:30 PM the SVR station chief was alone in one of the secured phone rooms in the embassy. On the other end was Pavel Orlov. It was seven-thirty in the morning in his Moscow office. After his last conversation with Ambassador Listunov and *Rezident* Shikhov earlier in the day, the SVR director had spoken with members of other agencies and even Russian President Boris Yaroslavovich Tatarov. To a person they had offered denial after denial of knowledge of a plot against the American president. Yet President Tatarov had sounded sufficiently vague so as to cause Orlov to question if his denials were covering some awareness of a plot. Certainly, an operation of this magnitude could never have been authorized by anyone short of the Russian leader.

The Director of the Foreign Intelligence Service was privy to almost all the activities of his government and the intelligence gathered by every agency in addition to his own. But the emphasis was in the word *almost*. With the risk of cross-agency interference in conflicting, or at best competing operations, his people still carried the age-old suspicion of one another. And that distrust carried all the way into the upper echelons of government administration.

Tensions had been ebbing and flowing with the Americans since Russia annexed Crimea in 2014. Orlov never understood the Americans' inability to appreciate that the act to do so and to crush the Ukrainian separatists had been the only practical response to George W. Bush's administration's pursuit of NATO membership for Ukraine and Georgia.

The current rift between the two superpowers represented the most extreme crack in their fragile accommodation in years. But an assassination attempt? To what end?

It was ironic that Orlov was speaking with his subordinate demanding the same level of secrecy that he had marveled at between governmental bureaus.

"So, we are clear?"

"*Da, Tovarishch Direktor.*"

Rezident Shikhov understood. He would not communicate the plan to the ambassador. Listunov would get his marching orders from his bosses who would get theirs from President Tatarov.

The Foreign Intelligence Service would determine its own course of action. First among the goals they established was to find Agent Borzilov.

CHAPTER 15

Day 7 - Friday

Maggie Loughlin awoke with a jolt. She had slept soundly and without waking. Falling asleep on the couch as she had, she hadn't set an alarm. She couldn't imagine being late to the White House. She sat bolt upright. On the edge of the bed was her fiancé

"Don't be 'alarmed.'" He laughed at his own pun as he often did. Maggie's smirk told him it was too early for the wisecracks, so he continued, "I set an alarm. You're right on schedule." He handed her a cup.

Maggie smiled as she took her coffee. Suddenly, the real world, the one that existed beyond her and Morgan, was firmly in her consciousness. It unsettled her.

"What's going on?" implored Morgan.

"I can't tell you, sweetheart. You know that"

"I know. You just seem really anxious. I'm only trying to help."

"Josh, you were a spy. You of all people should understand my position."

"You're right," he finally surrendered.

Maggie got dressed and ate the bagel Morgan had topped with avocado and tomato slices. The pair made small talk while Maggie made sure she had everything. Morgan informed her that Crenshaw was coming and would be staying with them.

She poked him in the stomach.

"Okay, but you're on your own cleaning the house and making sure we have groceries."

She grabbed her purse and another cup of coffee in her travel mug. As she reached the door, she paused before turning to face Morgan.

She blurted out, "There's more to the Russian possibility than the White House has been admitting to."

Then she wheeled around without a word and left.

"Wow!" Morgan thought. But his gut had already told him as much.

✦

The assembly in the Cabinet Room consisted of the same ones who had been present Wednesday night.

Everyone stood as the president entered the room with Chief of Staff Chandler following close behind.

She took her seat and got right to business.

"Thank you for your tireless efforts and completing the draft of our plan so quickly. When we met night before last, the consensus was that it was only prudent to develop a plan…" She could hardly speak the words. "… A war plan against the Russian Federation."

Each head in the room was nodding assent.

Every department and agency had worked nonstop to create its portion of the plan. Political, military, police, and security each had a role and the pieces must mesh seamlessly for it to work.

"The primary piece of this puzzle is to find Gennadiy Borzilov. What is the progress domestically, Director Austin?"

His report took longer than it should have because it basically affirmed that the Federal Bureau of Investigation had no clue where the SVR agent was, hadn't linked him to the Russian government, hadn't uncovered a possible motive – essentially nothing.

"What of our international efforts to locate him?"

CIA Parnell shared the same lack of success that the FBI director had but was much briefer.

"Madam President, we cannot confirm that he's still in the country, but we have found no evidence that he has left."

The president rarely displayed displeasure openly and it never had an angry component when she did. But the stakes were as high here as they could possibly be.

"People, we're looking at the possibility of launching a strike against the Russian Federation; looking it square in the face. Finding Borzilov might prevent that. If we can determine with a high degree of certainty that he acted alone, or at least independently of his country, we may eliminate the need for this operation!"

The president lowered her voice and looked at NSA Director McClintock, who really wished he had gone first. He reported no progress beyond the determination of a reasonably precise location for the Russian end of the mobile texts and voice calls. Unfortunately, it appeared to be in Red Square and the openness of the locale offered no clue as to the caller's identification.

"The Agency is collating calls and texts that occurred around the same time period from areas in the U.S. and Russia near where the callers had been during their communications. We've foregone computer filtering of the calls. It's slower without using it but we believe it's prudent because keywords failed to flag the communications we have knowledge of. Real people listening to our recordings might peg something because we know the context of what they should be listening for."

POTUS tapped her pen on the table and leaned back.

"Damn."

The next agenda item was to discuss how to approach this thing diplomatically. Oddly, Russian Ambassador Listunov had himself requested another meeting with the president. He didn't specify what it would be about except to say, "current events." The president's staff was working on anticipated questions or remarks and would offer suggestions for her responses. They were busily developing talking points for her, as well, from two perspectives. First, if the ambassador broached the subject of Russian complicity, either confirming or denying it, how should Hendrickson respond? But if he didn't bring up the speculation, the president had decided she would. She had to decide exactly how close she would get to an accusation.

The remaining items before the president were the strategic and tactical plans the military had devised in the event Borzilov remained unfound and if diplomacy failed. The plans were in the early stages, but the general framework of each branch was in place and the Joint Chiefs were having their staffs examine them for cohesion.

The plans looked good. The prospects for not using them did not.

✦

Back in her office President Hendrickson spent the next while returning calls from leaders around the world who had contacted her to express sympathy for the deaths of the VP and others. They each offered assistance, if needed. She hadn't time for this, but it was important enough to make time, she knew.

POTUS left it to Brianna Washington, her secretary from her first day as vice president to Mercer, to handle any written or electronic expressions in the name of the president.

Vice President Bauer took care of returning calls that came from anyone other than heads of state. It was his first official task in his new role.

Once Hendrickson had completed the highest priority replies, she and Chief of Staff Chandler returned to the more urgent matter of preparing for the meeting with Ambassador Listunov. SecState Gerard Lively had been reviewing the draft of the talking points in the sitting area of the Oval Office while POTUS had made calls.

Replacing the phone to its cradle, the president replaced her right earring and stretched. She buzzed for Ms. Washington.

"Brianna, I hate to bother you… would you bring me a cup of coffee? And…" POTUS pointed to Chandler and Lively. One acknowledged with a raised index finger. The other nodded."

"Make that three, please."

Hendrickson joined her two advisors around the coffee table.

"What do you think, Gerry?"

"I've made a couple of suggestions. But I don't see the need for any changes in approach."

POTUS and her chief pulled up the shared document on their respective iPads and began perusing the scribbling in the margins.

Over the next forty-five minutes the trio discussed the document and their strategy for the meeting until they felt that every "i" was dotted and every "t" crossed. They were confident that they had anticipated every line of discussion that Listunov might bring up. Finally, having completed an outline for the president that included responses and points she wished to initiate, they adjourned for a brief lunch.

✦

United Express Flight 6028 arrived at Dulles at almost straight up noon, about thirty minutes late. Not bad considering the weather. Josh Morgan had texted his friend and mentor that he would pick him up at the airport.

He had kept up with the flight's status on his phone, so it wasn't a surprise when its number showed up on the monitor at the baggage carousel.

Another twenty minutes later, Dr. Ryan Crenshaw appeared through the glass of one of the revolving doors. He was smiling before he emerged.

"Hello, Josh."

"Hello, sir."

The two shook hands warmly.

"Any bags?"

"Nope. This is it." Crenshaw had a computer bag slung over his shoulders. He extended the handle of a small suitcase to pull it along. Josh took the computer bag.

"How was the flight?"

"Good. But getting up early enough to be at Bergstrom for a 7:30 flight… I'm retired. I'm rarely out of bed at 7:30."

The two friends made their way to the short-term parking area, gabbing back and forth. The former spy turned professor and his former student advisor turned spy reminisced about their times at The University of Texas, particularly the evenings on the front porch of Dr. Crenshaw's home near Dripping Springs, a short distance from Austin.

Crenshaw said, "You know, I still come to D.C. once in a while. I'm always amazed at how it's changed each time."

"What brings you here?"

"Oh, I occasionally get called in on Company stuff. You know, you never really leave the Agency."

"Unless you've been a bad boy and get fired."

Crenshaw didn't know if Morgan's comment was light-hearted or not. The younger man's face didn't give it away.

He finally said, "Well, you're in the clear for all that now. I know Director Parnell thinks highly of you."

Josh's look was a mixture of surprise and skepticism.

"Really?" he asked. "Parnell does?"

"Don't sound so sarcastic. That's what she told me."

"You know her? I thought you were way before her time."

"Wow. That makes me sound ancient. Well, she spent time at the Moscow Station. Her first year there overlapped with this dinosaur's last one."

Crenshaw filled Josh in on his time supervising the young case officer Parnell.

He wound up the flashback by saying, "She was as headstrong as another young case officer I knew. I never worked with him but that's what I heard."

"I think that's highly overstated," Josh countered with a smirk. "Regardless, he was one fine officer. And devilishly handsome, too, don't you agree?" He winked at himself in the mirror and blew a kiss toward the image for emphasis.

Crenshaw let out a hoot.

"I really gave her a hard time sometime. As cool as she was in the field, she sure couldn't take teasing. You know how everybody calls her 'Betsy' now? I started that, I think. She hated it so, of course, that's all I ever called her. But Betsy came to like it. Or maybe she just came to accept it."

Another chuckle from the older ex-spy.

Morgan turned his SUV into his assigned space at his and Maggie's apartment.

Once he had settled into the guest room, Crenshaw headed to the den and looked out the window over a snow-covered Washington, D.C.

"Really great place, son. Nice view, too."

Trenton Weston and Ryan Crenshaw were the only ones to call Josh "son" – at least the only ones that he didn't mind doing so.

Crenshaw wandered to the kitchen where his host was holding up a bottle of Jacky Navarre Vieille Reserve Grande Champagne Cognac.

"For after dinner," he said with a wry expression.

"Good lord, Josh. That's two hundred dollars a bottle."

"Well, I've got light beer, if you prefer. Or water."

Crenshaw waved both hands to reject the suggestion.

"No. No, this will do nicely."

"I thought so. Besides, Maggie stole it from the White House."

Crenshaw did a double take. Even after all these years, he'd never quite gotten past being caught off-guard by his young protégé's humor.

"Funny. So, I've got to head over to Langley. Give me a ride?"

"Of course," Morgan obliged, but the thought of going anywhere near CIA Headquarters gave him a sudden wrenching in his stomach.

✦

The Russian ambassador looked at his watch again. At 2:15 PM, the president had kept him waiting fifteen minutes past their meeting time. Listunov knew Hendrickson had to be very busy. But more likely, he suspected, she was simply making him wait.

He tried to project patience and nonchalance while he sat in a chair in the corridor just a few steps from the Oval Office, but he suspected he was failing. He never liked waiting. Listunov's rank meant that everyone adapted to his schedule; everyone except the President of the United States, he was learning. Additionally, he was on edge. He felt unprepared for this meeting and the wait was making him nervous, seasoned diplomat that he was. He suspected that was precisely the American leader's objective.

He was correct.

✦

POTUS recommended to her chief of staff, "I think he's stewed long enough. Don't you?"

Chandler's laugh indicated his agreement and a fair amount of satisfaction.

Ms. Washington stepped out of her office into the corridor and announced to the Russian, "The president will see you now."

The ambassador rose, gave the secretary a rather irritated smile, and started toward the president's office. Chandler emerged from the doorway to escort him. Visitors never just walked into the Oval Office, even when expected.

Listunov was surprised to see that the chief of staff remained in the office as he closed the door behind himself. In addition, Secretary of State Gerard Lively was in the office, too. He and Chandler sat off to the side. The Russian diplomat felt as though he was on display. He and the American leader shook hands, greeted one another, and she motioned him to take a seat.

His chair was in front of the president's desk and the nearness left him feeling awkward. The only other time he had met with President Hendrickson in her office, they had talked in the sitting area in the center of the room and away from her desk. It had felt decidedly more amiable. This day, he felt like a schoolboy called before his headmaster to answer for some wrongdoing. He subtly moved the chair away to give himself some personal space.

Chandler and Lively exchanged a bemused glance, unseen by the Oval Office visitor, and mutually thought that POTUS was already ahead on points.

The ambassador began the parley, "Thank you, Madam President, for accommodating my request. It must seem unusual."

"It's unusual?"

"Well, it is short notice and you must have an incredible amount on your mind, and on your agenda..."

POTUS smiled through her intentional interruption, "I do. So, what can I do for you?"

The diplomat's annoyance was obvious. He opened with a denial of Russian involvement in the blast, an assertion that made it difficult for the president to disguise her anger – and even more, her contempt. He then spent the next ten minutes asking questions. They were general, vague, and disjointed, and appeared to have as a goal the elicitation of information from his host.

"A fishing expedition," Hendrickson thought. Finally, she went on offense.

"Mr. Ambassador, we have direct evidence with an enormously high level of confidence that a Russian agent of the SVR, one of your own, perpetrated the bombing that killed a number of Americans, including our vice president, and injured countless more."

The ambassador's discomfort appeared genuine, though perhaps he didn't seem as surprised as he should have been.

All three Americans realized at that moment that the ambassador was aware of the Russian agent's action and that his foreknowledge didn't bode well for the ongoing debate concerning his nation's involvement.

"But Madam President, you have said publicly – and privately, I might add – that you did not suspect *Rossya* was involved. It appeared..."

Hendrickson seized the initiative again.

"Valya..."

Hendrickson had never called the ambassador by his first name and certainly not by the diminutive form. Her desired effect was immediately visible on the man's face. The flash of red at the breach of protocol left no doubt that POTUS had hit the man where it hurt most – his pride of position.

✦

Morgan and Crenshaw continued catching up during the thirty-five-minute drive. When Morgan asked his friend why he was going to CIA Headquarters, Ryan only said, "Just dropping in on some old friends."

Morgan suspected there was more to it but dropped it.

He turned off of Virginia 123, or Dolly Madison Boulevard, onto the long driveway into the complex housing the Company. He stopped at the visitors' gate to turn the vehicle over to his house guest.

"Here ya go, Ryan. Guess I just wait out here, huh?"

"No. Drive on up to the main gate."

Morgan's furrowed brow attested to his puzzlement. Crenshaw insisted with a tilt of his head toward the gate.

"Josh."

The younger ex-spy shrugged and shifted the stick back to "D" and rolled forward slowly.

The guard at the gate checked Dr. Ryan Crenshaw's Agency credentials – his *current* credentials, Morgan saw.

Crenshaw looked at the man in the driver seat. "What? I gotta have *some* secrets, kiddo."

Morgan let out a small snort and shook his head. His mentor turned back to the guard.

"This is Joshua Morgan. I believe you'll find he's cleared to go with me."

Morgan's head turned to Crenshaw and his mouth opened.

✦

"Madam President, I must protest…"

"Valya, we know the identity of the primary in this and we're closing in on the three that helped him" This was a bluff Hendrickson hoped would pay dividends. He was rattled and off his game so when she saw surprise in his eyes, it was at the moment she mentioned coconspirators.

"So, he's aware of the op but stunned when I mentioned collaborators," she surmised. She analyzed the possibilities silently, "Either he's surprised that we know, or… there aren't any? How could one man pull this off, even with some logistical support from embassy personnel or others?"

POTUS resumed her stream of proclamations of what they "knew." She never specified the details that they truly had but instead moved forward with generalities and ambiguous speculation that Listunov might accept as fact or know to be incorrect. Hendrickson, Chandler, and Lively were alert for any giveaways that would indicate recognition that would affirm or refute the president's "facts" as she was laying them forth. Diplomats didn't have many tells.

Hendrickson felt no misgivings at the severity of her tone with Ambassador Listunov. She felt she had confirmation that Russia was behind the bombing and that this son of a bitch knew all about it.

Russia had committed an act of war against the United States of America. They had attempted the assassination of a U.S. president. Hendrickson didn't know what her country's response would be and dreaded making the decisions that would be hers to make, but she knew she would make them. The electorate had put their confidence in her to make the tough choices and she would summon the resolve to do so.

POTUS asked the Russian representative to the United States to excuse her. She and her two team members left for the Cabinet Room. Two Secret Service agents assumed positions deliberately close to Listunov.

Hendrickson, Chandler, and Lively huddled together. They agreed that their guest's reactions, verbal and body language, left little room for doubt that the Russian Federation had chosen to undertake this evil act, though they couldn't begin to understand why. Perhaps to create chaos to provide strategic opportunities for them throughout the world. With the United States off their game, well…

Only one thing remained. The American leadership broke up their confab and POTUS returned to her office with her Secretary of State close behind. The chief of staff headed to his office to begin calling the Cabinet to the White House. His first call was for the acting press secretary.

"Maggie, please come to my office."

✦

The dial tone came rather abruptly. Usually, she thought, Chief Chandler said a "goodbye" or "thanks" or something, but not this time. But instead of being disappointed or annoyed by the sudden disconnect, she smiled. She collected a legal pad and her iPad.

"The new must be wearing off," she decided.

Principal Deputy Press Secretary Margaret Loughlin started for the office of the chief of staff. She had no idea what awaited her.

CHAPTER 16

Josh Morgan looked at the CIA badge hanging from his shirt. It read "Visitor" but it was an Agency badge. It had been years since he had been in the George Bush Center for Intelligence, the official name for the headquarters complex. He was, in fact, welcome the last time he was on-the premises. After the events transpired that ended with his dismissal, he never set foot in the place.

Morgan remembered that last trip to Langley had included some time with his late fiend, Ben Reid. But with as many great memories as he had about the place, it was impossible to separate it from the events that left him in fear for his life and propelled his life into its years-long downward spiral.

The ex-officer observed his friend Ryan Crenshaw examining the Atrium Sculpture Wall, though he had seen it countless times before. He had often mentioned the pieces of art to Morgan; that he liked the mustangs of "The Day the Wall Came Down," and "Windwalker," the 48-inch bronze American Bald Eagle named after a Cherokee medicine woman. But his favorite, he had told Morgan, was "Intrepid." Intrepid was the code name of Sir William Stephenson, a Canadian who led the New York Office of British Security Coordination. It was he who lobbied Franklin Roosevelt to appoint William J. "Wild Bill" Donovan to a new position to oversee the intelligence activities of the FBI and the military.

But just as Crenshaw did, Morgan preferred the Original Headquarters Building, which was connected to the newer building by a tunnel. The Main Entrance to the building was the one familiar to most fans of spy movies. The features of the entrance had appeared in many. Especially recognizable was the sixteen-foot diameter granite CIA Seal on the floor. Often mistakenly assumed to be the Agency Motto, a Bible verse was on one wall. From John 8:32, it read: "And Ye Shall Know the Truth and the Truth Shall Make You Free." But the most significant feature to anyone who had ever worked for the Company was the northern Memorial Wall. Its stars were engraved posthumously to represent CIA officers who died serving in intelligence. The inscription above the stars read: "In honor of those members of the Central Intelligence Agency who gave their lives in the service of their country."

Morgan's trip down memory lane was interrupted. "Sirs, come with me."

Not long afterward, an astonished Josh Morgan sat in the office of the Director of Central Intelligence.

Momentarily the DCI rushed through the door.

"Ryan Crenshaw! Who let you in?"

Her joy at seeing her old friend was evident and mutual. They embraced with obvious affection. Morgan stood respectfully by with his hands folded in front of him.

"Betsy, it's been way too long. I can't tell you how proud I am of you. I was thrilled at your appointment as DCI. Amelia sends her love."

Director Parnell's excitement lessened a little as she turned to Morgan. It caused him to wonder if he was welcome. Maybe his reception at CIA was as cold as ever.

"Morgan. Welcome. Good to see you again." She shook his hand firmly.

Ryan and Betsy shared a few moments of conversation. Morgan thought he should've waited at the visitors' gate. Maybe toured the museum.

When the DCI returned her attention to him, her tone became not exactly unfriendly, just businesslike.

"Josh... can I call you Josh?"

"Sure. I mean, yes, ma'am." He noticed he instinctively stiffened.

The DCI smiled. A little.

"I wanted to get you in here to talk with you."

Morgan's tension increased. His impulse was to gulp but he managed to stifle it. So, *he* was the reason for this meeting!

"I thought having Ryan here would make it an easier visit. President Weston could've provided valuable input and even though he's a former DCI himself... well, I just thought Ryan a better choice. A mutual friend to us, you know."

Morgan pondered the nature of being called to CIA Headquarters. It couldn't be good, he decided. "Input about what?"

✦

Leaving Chief Chandler's office, Maggie was shaken. She was trembling slightly and without benefit of a mirror, she was certain her face was ashen. She wasn't prepared for what she just heard. She couldn't possibly have been.

Personal trepidation aside, this turn of events would test her professionally. The acting press secretary wasn't sure her poker face would be good enough to face the press with this knowledge, especially given that the news wasn't going to be made public for an indefinite amount of time. Even when it was, it would require her to perform the most delicate dance she had ever been required to do.

The deputy secretary had just started to experience real confidence in her ability to fill in until Secretary Ginnetti was back on the job. She wished she could consult with her but her superior – that word just took on a more definite precision – wasn't able to have visitors or phone calls yet.

Maggie wouldn't be able to talk to her best friend. Josh wasn't cleared. Her pronouncement to him about Russian complicity that morning was more than she should've said.

"Shit," she realized, "there are people way above my pay grade who aren't even cleared for this information." The chief of staff made it clear that individuals throughout the administration would be read in incrementally as they needed to know. She was only told of the current state of affairs because she would be better able to answer questions if she had some familiarity with what the hell was going on.

Ironic, Maggie thought, that, in her position, she would be better able to keep a secret if she knew it. Sheesh.

She sat at her desk; correction: Secretary Ginnetti's desk – and how she wished the actual press secretary were sitting at it – and put her face in her hands. Chief Chandler said that even President Hendrickson knew this would get out long before she wanted. And the chief told Maggie that the responsibility for containing it lay partially with her.

She wished she and Josh were back home in Jackson Hole. But they weren't. So, she'd better get busy prepping for the onslaught.

✦

"NSA Deputy Director Everson Blake…"

Morgan was immediately on-guard. So that's why I'm here. His pulse raced. He wasn't prepared for this.

He cast a glance over at Dr. Crenshaw. Why hadn't he given him a heads-up? But his friend's countenance suggested he had no idea what the DCI was talking about. Morgan realized that there was no way Ryan could have his back on this. Morgan had never told him the truth of what happened on that pier at Gulf Mariner's Marina eighteen months ago. The only one who did know was the only other person who was there – Trent Weston. Parnell had mentioned that she had considered bringing him in.

Where was the DCI going with this? He found out in the next instant.

"NSA Deputy Director Everson Blake didn't really shoot himself. Did he?"

Morgan was in near-panic mode now.

✦

It was 2:00 AM in Moscow. Nevertheless, Russian Federation Ambassador to the United States Valentin Listunov had no choice but to call his superior.

Foreign Minister Jaromir Grigorievich Davydov's voice was brusque.

"Unthinkable," he screamed at his subordinate. "Why would Russia do such a thing? Has the American president gone mad?"

"She is certain. She gave me facts." Listunov delineated step by step what the woman knew about Borzilov. "The American's facts corroborated what we knew at the embassy."

"Valentin Nikitovich, why did you not inform me as soon as you knew this thing?"

"We were uncertain. But now Hendrickson said there would be consequences."

"What consequences?"

"What do you think they will be!?" It was the ambassador who was yelling this time.

After another twenty minutes of discussion, the two diplomats of the Russian Federation's Foreign Ministry tried to decide what Russian agency had concocted such an operation. Both were outraged that such a thing would be done without first preparing the Foreign Ministry for the fallout.

With the dread becoming apparent in his voice, Foreign Minister Davydov informed his U.S. representative that he would have to awaken the Russian president to inform him and to demand answers. Both knew that Davydov wouldn't "demand" anything of their leader but, under the circumstances, the rhetoric seemed appropriate.

The American president had demanded answers. Davydov would try to get them.

✦

"What are you implying?" the ex-CIA operative asked the current CIA director.

"It's a simple enough question," Parnell countered, leaning forward on her desk, tapping her fingers on it.

"Why do you doubt that that's what happened?" Morgan questioned.

Elizabeth Parnell stood and walked around her desk and sat on the corner closest to Morgan. She folded her arms.

"Morgan, are you just gonna keep responding to my questions with questions? Again, it's a very simple question. What really happened on that dock?"

Morgan felt Ryan Crenshaw's eyes boring into him, too. The man only knew the official narrative of Blake's death; that resigned to facing prison or even execution and being exposed as a hypocrite when he was hailed as a hero among Christian conservatives, he had put a bullet in his chest. Did even this old friend suspect now that there was more to the story, that Morgan was guilty of something?

Morgan wondered why Parnell was bringing it up. And why she even cared. He calmed himself and decided he was going to control where this thing went.

✦

President Sandra Hendrickson was having an argument with her husband Adam. He was irate at her not being at the hospital. He was normally understanding about the demands of being president. But these weren't ordinary circumstances. Especially now that AJ was doing better, he was aware his mother wasn't there. He was putting on a brave front, but Adam Sr. could see through it.

The father was yelling. "What kind of mother are you?" he barked.

The mother's tone showed more control, but her heart was breaking. Her husband was right. These weren't ordinary circumstances. Just not in the way he thought. And she couldn't tell him. Not this. Not yet.

She asked if they could talk about it later.

"Later? Your son needs you now!" Her husband hung up.

Sandy Hendrickson wanted to sit in her office and cry. But President Hendrickson was preparing a speech, in fact two or three of them; one for each of the possible outcomes for the crisis her country was in. Hendrickson was expecting to hear from the Russian president in the morning.

She called to her secretary, "Brianna, would you have Chief Chandler and Secretary Lively come back into my office now? Thanks. Oh, and after you do that, I think I can get by without you for the evening. Thanks again."

POTUS folded her arms on the desk in front of her and lay her head on them. Then she pounded her fist on the surface.

Brianna Washington buzzed that the two gentlemen were there.

"Give me just a moment. Say 'hi' to your family and enjoy yourself tonight."

Hendrickson walked to the lavatory off her office. She splashed her face with water, brushed her hair. She touched up her makeup and straightened her dress. With all that done, a determined POTUS returned to her desk and pressed the intercom button.

"Brianna, please send them in."

✦

127

Gennadiy Borzilov sat on the bed in his motel room. He looked at maps. He looked at news sites. He tried to determine which of the two possible events might be best. Finally, he determined he would avail himself of whichever opportunity came first. If he failed, he would try again. The difficulty facing him – well, one of them – was that he wasn't uncovering any information about either possibility. One would likely not be publicized. The other would receive much attention but the American president would be virtually impossible to reach.

The Russian family man called Larisa again but, like the other times he had tried, no answer. He likewise called her captors, but they never answered. His only communication was when they had called him twice.

✦

"So Morgan, here are the problems I have with your story. First, who tries to kill himself by shooting himself in the chest. Blake was an ops guy. A shot to the head would be more certain."

"Back to 'Morgan' now," the name's owner observed silently.

"Secondly, the entry wound's angle was wrong. And no powder burns."

How she got this info was a puzzle to the ex-spy. But she was Director of the CIA, after all. And the issue that bothered him now was the same one that bothered him earlier. Why, all of a sudden, did Parnell give a shit?

"Finally, how'd you get the drop on Blake. He had the only gun on the scene when police arrived. You said you dropped yours in the water?"

"Yeah," Morgan thought, "I realized that was pretty stupid as soon as I said it way back then."

"There are other things but those will do for now."

Morgan recognized that she had built a formidable enough case against him that denying it would be impossible. His only option was to keep his mouth shut. But he had to know.

"Director Parnell, why are you doing this? Why do you care now?"

✦

Maggie finished a draft of talking points based on the outline Noah Chandler had given her. With her speechwriter dying in the bomb blast, the president was relying on her chief of staff and he on Maggie to help with things Ms. Eccleston would've done. Maggie had recovered her professional detachment and was able to work through any personal distraction from the national security quagmire that was about to manifest itself on an already nervous, mostly unsuspecting public.

Chandler finished his review of the shared document on his iPad.

"Spectacular, Maggie. Just brilliant. I don't think you fully realize what an asset you've been to the administration and to POTUS and me personally. I shudder to think what a mess this department would've been without you in Marie's office."

"Thank you, Chief Chandler. How is Secretary Ginnetti?"

"First, out of the public eye, you can call me Noah. Secondly, Marie's much improved. The docs are still keeping her heavily sedated but she's improving. She won't be back for an indefinite length of time. So, don't get your hopes up. You're not off the hook yet."

Noah and Maggie both laughed.

"Come with me."

"Sir?"

"Let's get this in front of the president. I think she'll be very happy with it."

Maggie sat in disbelief at the prospect. She'd had private, brief interactions with POTUS but had never briefed her on her own work before.

"Well, don't hold things up. Snap to it, rookie."

"Yes, Chief... uh, Noah."

"I just left the Oval Office. We were working on this thing from the president's perspective when I got your message that you had finished the draft. Secretary Lively is still there."

Another momentary look of discomfort flashed across Maggie's face. Chandler turned to face her directly.

"I don't know if the apprehension I just saw was because you're personally explaining your work to the president or if it's because of the same knot you have in your gut as I do about what's happening. You're capable and confident so I don't expect it's the former. Just let me assure you that our republic keeps on rolling despite all the challenges we face. Always has; always will. And when some of the pieces are missing – like Logan and Ginnetti – others jump in to take over their roles.

"Trent Weston has been invaluable to the president in Logan's place. And you have been an anchor for this department – for *your* department. I think you should consider it as such, temporary though it is. So, let's go let you do your job."

With that, Chandler was off at such a pace, Maggie had to hurry to keep up.

✦

DCI Parnell wove her fingers through her mostly gray hair.

"Josh..."

He smiled. Back to first name again, are we? Morgan; Josh – Josh; Morgan. He didn't know if the director was having trouble keeping it straight or if she was engaging in some attempt at one-woman "good cop/bad cop" but suddenly he felt energized and confident.

Elizabeth Parnell continued. "Josh, you might not believe this, but this is for your benefit. I'm on your side here."

"Good cop," Morgan recognized silently.

Ryan Crenshaw made his first comment in the back and forth between his two friends.

"Son, I have no earthly idea what's going on here," he interjected, "but I know you trust me. And I trust the director. If Betsy says she's trying to help, you can believe her."

Morgan bit at his lip and stared at Crenshaw with mild contempt for his having brought him here for this. He wondered if his friend was being a bit naïve. Perhaps his friendship with Parnell was getting in the way of objectivity.

"Time to come clean about all this, Josh," recommended his friend.

At that moment Morgan decided he had to choose whether or not to trust Elizabeth Parnell. The woman had helped him in his showdown with Blake, after all, but he hardly knew her. And why was she just now interrogating him about the endgame? No, he couldn't be sure he should trust her, but he did trust the man sitting in the chair beside him in spite of a mild sense of betrayal by his older friend for thrusting him into this situation unaware.

He was about to begin his tale when the DCI, sensing a change in the mood of her guest, interrupted.

"No, Ryan. Josh asked me a fair question that I think deserves an answer."

"Fine work, Maggie. Now go home. I know it's late..." POTUS glanced at her watch. "Six-thirty. That's not as late as usual, so go home to Josh. Try to be here around eight tomorrow. The waters are going to get choppy but no use getting here at the crack of dawn. Thanks, Maggie. I mean it. Nice work... and not just on this."

"Thank you, Madam President. It's an honor to serve."

Maggie knew she had a ton of work she could do but decided to take POTUS up on her offer. She locked Secretary Ginnetti's office and headed out of the West Wing.

"Good night, Secretary Loughlin."

"Night, Oliver," she said to the guard with a smile.

She saw that a car was already waiting for her. It was a perk that Noah Chandler had decided she deserved, and he had no doubt called ahead from the Oval Office to inform the driver to come to the exit.

Once in the warm interior of the sedan, Maggie texted Morgan to let him know she was on her way home. He didn't reply and that miffed her somewhat. But she realized that Dr. Crenshaw was with him and they were no doubt caught up in some old tales and likely some brandy.

✦

In almost the blink of an eye the DCI's demeanor and her tenor mellowed significantly

"Josh, my harsh approach was intentional…"

"Thanks," Josh said.

"I wanted to try to rattle your cage some to see what popped out about the events involving Blake, Weston, and Al-Majeed. Nothing came of it – which, by the way, impresses me – but I wanted to get some unguarded answers, if I could. Just in case you didn't want to volunteer your account."

Director Parnell handed Morgan and Crenshaw folders that each contained a three-page document.

Morgan opened his and looked at the memo. It wasn't on letterhead and was without the usual "To," "From," and "Subject" lines. His transitory scan of the document indicated what appeared to be legal references. Parnell was still speaking so the two men respectfully returned their attention to her.

"This is completely off the record. I put that together myself so excuse me if it's a bit unpolished."

Ex-CIA case officer nodded his agreement. His gut correctly told him this wasn't going to be good. Still, he was more at ease since Parnell was going to lay her cards on the table.

"I've had several conversations with my predecessor Chris Donleavy about your time with the Agency. And becoming DCI has given me access to the entire timeline about the op in Terrador. Like President Weston apparently does, I believe your involvement was unwitting. His intervention for you on many fronts through the years, including this ridiculous story about the culmination of his kidnapping, helped soften your punishment.

"You know, that story would've never held up without a former POTUS backing you. Given everything he had just gone through, he was given *carte blanche* to frame the narrative any way he wanted. Here's the bottom line, Josh, the resolve of the remaining people that your actions in Terrador screwed around has resurfaced."

"How so, director?"

"Oh, heck. Call me 'Betsy.'"

She smiled at Crenshaw who turned to Morgan and said, "See?"

"The mishmash of legal jargon on the document I gave you is essentially their game plan. I know, rather everybody who knows you were even involved in Weston's rescue – and that's only a handful of people – knows you shot Blake. Nobody cared. In fact, most applauded you. But in the time since Blake's been gone, a few of his cronies have resumed using their knowledge of global intelligence to conduct illicit activities. Call it caution or preemption. Call it anything you want. I think it's plain old payback. But they've put a target on your back."

"Again," stated Morgan. "I should've known things were looking way too good for me." He laughed from a genuine realization of the irony.

"So, what's the legal mumbo-jumbo, Betsy?" That felt awkward.

"Before we get into that, what happened at the marina?"

Morgan had already decided he would "confess" so he didn't pause for a deep breath. He just launched into the facts of what transpired before and after he killed Blake.

Morgan thought back to the final moments with Blake, struggling to keep his composure in the presence of the DCI. Blake had pursued former President Weston after Saudi Operative Fadi Al-Majeed had kidnapped him. But rather than rescuing Weston, Blake intended to make sure he died in order to settle an old score.

Josh had caught up with the Arab and killed him. Then he caught Blake and was preparing to take him into custody. The NSA Deputy Director threatened Maggie's life and made it clear that his story would cast suspicion on Weston as being in league with the Saudis. None of it made sense but Blake had already gotten by with so much over the years that Morgan believed he would indeed fulfill his threats. So, Morgan had shot him in cold blood.

When authorities arrived at the marina, Morgan was prepared to confess to everything. But President Weston interceded and told the police and later federal investigators that Blake had committed suicide, giving birth to the official narrative.

Weston made sure that investigators friendly to him took the lead in sorting through the whole affair. And because Mercer had been involved in enabling both the Saudis' plot and Blake's intentions, the matter simply went away.

His confession lasted a few minutes.

"And that's it," he concluded. "I think the bastard had the power behind him to survive this fiasco, if for no other reason than to hush it up. And if he skated, I had no doubt he would indeed do the things he threatened for Maggie and the Westons. And me," he added as an afterthought.

CHAPTER 17

Whatever catharsis one might have thought Josh Morgan would get from baring his soul to the CIA director didn't materialize. The man had long since come to terms with his decision that day. He and President Weston would sometimes allude to his abduction and rescue, but they never discussed details, only referred to it offhandedly. And the demise of Everson Blake never, ever came up.

Morgan raised the folder. "So, what's in the paper?"

"First, I'll address the elephant in the room. As you are no doubt aware, there is no statute of limitations for murder."

Morgan never so much as shifted in his seat.

✦

Her driver dropped Maggie off at the apartment. The snow was falling again, adding to the one foot of accumulation on the ground. A groundskeeper for the complex was shoveling the new powder while another sprinkled ice-melt behind him.

"Morgan," she called as she opened the door. She called again before concluding he wasn't there. She peered into their guest room and saw Ryan Crenshaw's belongings, so she figured they were out catching up. She was surprised that he had left no note or texted. But that caused her to believe he would be home soon. She was disappointed but not angry. She poured a glass of wine and reclined her side of the sofa. She turned on the television, which crackled to life on the Quantum News Network, where her news junkie fiancé had left it.

"I don't think so," the acting press secretary said aloud. She put her wine on the end table and switched to a classic movie channel. The old Patrick Swayze, Demi Moore movie "Ghost" was on.

"I always liked that movie," Maggie informed the TV. And then she was asleep.

✦

SVR Agent Borzilov had two contingencies for another attempt on the president. Dates weren't available yet, but some preliminary details were starting to emerge for the state funeral for Vice President Logan.

"More than just difficult," the Russian said to his computer display. "It will be virtually impossible to get near enough to the woman for a reasonable chance for success. He thought of the worst scenario – getting captured or killed. Then there would be no hope for Larisa and their kids, as his handlers made clear before Borzilov even undertook this operation. He knew that, should he prove unsuccessful and out of the picture, they would murder his family out of pure spite.

If his first opportunity turned out to not be viable, he would stand down and hope that his second option would be. But there was no guarantee that Hendrickson would even be there, despite the personal nature of the occasion.

Despite the promise he had made to himself to not leave his motel room, Gennadiy walked to a liquor store only a quarter mile from his lodging to get a bottle of vodka. He liked the snowfall. And momentarily he was able to shut off his mind to his dilemma and enjoy the scenery. The white landscape reminded him of the Motherland.

He made his selection from the inventory of Russian products and walked to the counter.

Staring at him from the television behind the cashier was a picture of... himself.

The White House had finally released a photograph of the bombing suspect. The press release provided no details: no name, no nationality, nothing. The extent of the disclosure was a single photo, a statement that he was a "person of interest" in the attack in Washington, and a plea to the public for help in finding him.

The suspect was shocked. And he had a problem. He could set the bottle down and walk calmly away but that might arouse suspicion. Besides, the cashier had already seen Gennadiy when he asked where the vodka was. He turned away from the counter while the clerk completed the transaction of the only person ahead of the Russian.

"Next."

Gennadiy kept his face slightly downward but carried on a conversation in his American accent in the hopes that it would prevent the man from looking at the television mounted above him. The volume was muted. By pretending to fidget in his pocket for something, he might keep the cashier from getting a good look at him.

Gennadiy took his change from the cash payment, bid the man a great evening, and turned to the door.

Arriving at the motel, Borzilov packed his sparse belongings. He had been careful to limit the things he touched in Room 108 but wiped down the room anyhow. He collected his belongings and started for his car, intending to bypass the office altogether.

Unfortunately for the Russian, the desk clerk was walking out to his car to get something and saw Borzilov leaving. He told him he might as well stay. It was snowing harder and he was paid through the night, but Marvin Williams regretted that something had arisen that required him to leave immediately.

Agent Borzilov had already planned for this possibility and started his car toward the next motel, where "Max Elliott" would check in with corresponding identification and, this time, a disguise.

✦

Josh Morgan had no visible reaction to the DCI's comment about murder having no statute of limitations. He just said, "I've known since it happened that might be a possibility, though I've largely pushed it out of my mind."

"No," the DCI said. "They're not pinning their hopes on a murder conviction. They'll try but it's a longshot with President Weston backing you up."

"I guess all these references on the document will divulge their strategy?" He was shocked when he looked at the paper again and the first word that jumped out at him was "treason."

Director Parnell walked him through the particulars of the laws the notes referred to. He was overwhelmed at the possibilities but remained outwardly stoic.

"All this for little old me?"

Both Parnell and Crenshaw appreciated his ability to appear unfazed.

"They'll throw enough crap on the wall to see what sticks. And they might not even have to be involved. They may just identify a friendly prosecutor and send the information as an anonymous whistleblower. That would be difficult, though."

"Some of them have to be at CIA. Others at NSA, perhaps DEA."

"So just like old times, huh? But with a different cast of characters. They're picking up where Blake left off. Maybe they won't be out to kill me, though."

Morgan smiled but, for the first time, a crack appeared in his bearing.

"Josh, you have to believe me. I'm trying to head this off, but…"

"Yeah, I know, Betsy. The way things are compartmentalized here, people can keep even evil secrets. Unless you know where to look and what you're looking for, even as DCI, it'll be hard to track down."

The CIA director rose from behind her desk and extended her hand. The meeting was over.

Josh shook her hand. He was certain she was a friend to him.

"Thank you, Betsy. I mean it."

"I'm just sorry this thing has reared its head again. Blake had it coming, but even that asshole had friends loyal to him. I'll keep you posted."

She hugged Crenshaw and said, "Always good to see you. Thanks for bringing Josh in and for providing some moral support. Give my best to Amelia."

"I will."

✦

The two friends reversed roles on the ride home. While Ryan drove, Josh looked over Betsy's documents. They were mostly silent, especially since the older ex-CIA officer was having to concentrate intensely on his driving. The white stuff was coming down at a rate that made it hard to see far into it. And it was packing up on the highways and streets pretty quickly.

"I don't see snow like this in Austin. Hardly any at all. It's usually ice, if anything. And it's infrequent enough that it's silly for cities to spend the money on the equipment to deal with it. I just stay at home when we have an ice storm. I haven't driven in stuff like this since my days in Moscow."

The SUV slid mildly to the right. Crenshaw gripped the wheel tighter but didn't overreact and the vehicle's orientation to the road was righted.

"Sure you don't want to drive?"

Morgan never glanced up as he said without emotion, "You're doing fine." He wanted to discuss this at greater length with Crenshaw. A bar would be nice but no privacy, especially in Washington where eavesdropping was second in popularity only to the Redskins.

So, the native Texan determined they would just talk at his apartment. Maggie wouldn't be home yet anyhow.

"Maggie! Crap!" He looked at the text she had sent much earlier saying she was going home. She would want to visit with Ryan so it would be a while before the two men could discuss Parnell's disclosures.

They pulled into Morgan's reserved parking spot. Crenshaw exhaled loudly and handed Morgan the keys. "Dang, Josh. Here. And I don't want them back. Until June maybe."

The men opened the door to the apartment without considering the need to be quiet, that is, until they saw the woman of the house snoozing on the sofa with an almost untouched glass of red wine on the end table, and the TV showing the beginning of Tom Hanks and Meg Ryan in "Sleepless in

Seattle." The men exchanged a smile.

"I'll wake her. She'll want to see you."

Ryan put his hand on Josh's forearm and shook his head.

"No, there'll be plenty of time to visit. I'm here a couple of days. Let's talk about our visit with Betsy. And I could use a drink," Crenshaw said with an impish grin. "But not the good stuff. Let's save that."

Josh nodded and retrieved a bottle of inexpensive brandy from the liquor cabinet.

"How 'bout this?" The two men agreed.

"This is what I drink when I'm on my own. I'm gonna disguise it as a better brand by using these nice snifters, though."

Josh left the TV at the volume Maggie had it, supposing it would provide some cover for his conversation with Ryan.

They clinked glasses and Morgan began.

"So, this is how I see it. Tell me if I'm wrong. They'll try for murder but are unlikely to get it."

"Because of Weston."

"Right."

"But then they're going for treason; or something related to it? And that's worse!" Ryan was incredulous.

"Yes. The way I understood it from Betsy is that it's all based on my knowing what the Saudi was doing and what Blake was up to, but not telling anyone."

"That's so thin as to be absurd! It's borderline insanity. Officials of our government – even President Mercer, according to you and Betsy – knew the story and did nothing. And they're going to try to set up somebody to come after you? Damn!"

In spite of his remaining connections to CIA, Ryan Crenshaw had never heard any of this story until today.

"Yeah, but you get some overzealous, politically bent lawyer and, well, who knows? Especially if that legal warrior has some ties to Mercer."

"What? You think he's connected to this somehow?"

"Well, he certainly wasn't happy to leave the White House. Plus, we saw throughout that whole affair what he was capable of. On the other hand, I'm not sure what kind of clout he has now."

"Your defense can be that Mercer knew what was going on, as did Blake. CIA knew but were told to stand down from pursuing it. Surely that'll fly."

"Here's the problem with the 'everybody else knew, too,' defense. There's no record of any of 'em knowing anything. Mercer was basically blackmailed out of office by Weston with the threat of going public with his actions."

"Weston can still testify to that."

"Yes, but the fact he didn't say anything for so long will surely diminish his credibility."

"And Blake and his pal Sanders? Well, they're obviously both dead. So, I'm the only one still around. And Trev O'Bannon, the CIA officer that Parnell sent to help me; he was unconscious and almost dead from his injuries. He has no idea what transpired on that dock. An additional problem with him is that, as you well know, the Agency is forbidden by law from conducting operations on home soil. But there he was. His involvement was a crime. Betsy can't attest to my motivation. She would, I think, but she really doesn't have any info that would help."

Both men sighed almost simultaneously. They sat in silence with their drinks.

Finally, Morgan resumed his combination of recollection mixed with an attempt to develop some sort of strategy.

"There are very few people who know what I did. And even they can't say why. While you were driving, I read over very carefully what the director prepared for me. Here are some definitions. Parnell got 'em right off Cornell University's Legal Information Institute website. Treason is betraying one's country, 'especially by attempting to kill the sovereign or overthrow the government.' Nobody was trying to kill Mercer. Does an ex-president count? I don't know.

"But again, with the right legal eagles and the right jury, they could make a case that I knew what both Al-Majeed and Blake were doing. And that brings me to the next point. Misprision of treason means 'the deliberate concealment of one's knowledge of a treasonable act or a felony.' So even if I wasn't personally committing treason, a case could be made that Blake was and I knew and didn't inform anyone."

Morgan began to feel he could convict himself.

"Josh Morgan, you stopped an evil thing, something horrible beyond comprehension. You acted honorably and you acted alone when no government agency was willing – or allowed – to find Weston and rescue him."

"I know, Ryan. In my heart I know all that. But the problem is whether I can prove it. I read all this legal shit and there's a possibility some might stick. 'U.S. Code: Title 18 – Crimes and Criminal Procedure.' This law is the nation's main criminal code of the U.S. when it comes to dealing with federal crimes.

"Ryan, one of the things Blake said right before I… well, at the end, was he bragged he could turn the tables on me about the Saudi/Weston thing and him. After all, I had a history of attempting to assassinate the leader of a country. And he was right – in Terrador. He threatened to implicate Weston and now, he's lied for me. You know, Blake's threats have outlived him."

Crenshaw was becoming increasingly worried about his young friend.

"The worst thing about all this," and Morgan stopped to laugh, "I could lose my pension if I'm convicted of treason." His observation dripped with sarcasm.

"Treason? What are you two talking about?" Maggie asked from the doorway into the kitchen from the den.

Morgan and Crenshaw were both unaware that she was there, and each wondered how much she had heard.

✦

All twenty-four-hour news networks repeated the same stuff over and over. Otherwise they'd never be able to broadcast around the clock. Sometimes though, re-airing news items had value. Inside Buzz's Liquor Store near the edge of Rockville, Maryland, a counter clerk finally had a lull between customers long enough to allow him to eat a snack and drink a power drink.

Carl was mostly immune to the images and sound of the television behind the counter where he worked taking people's payments for their beverages and sacking up their purchases. He leaned backward against the counter and turned up the volume to an audible level.

He froze in mid-bite of his power bar when one particular image came on.

The QNN reporter said, "We have no information about this man. When the White House released his photograph, they would say only that he was a person of interest in the bombing at St. John's. In most cases when we have an actual photo versus an artist's sketch, there is also more information, such as a name or description such as height, weight…"

Carl set his snack down on the counter beside his drink. A customer arrived to pay for her purchase at the same moment he was taking his phone out of his pocket. He waved her off with one hand and said tersely, "Uh. I gotta make a call. Be right back. Sorry."

The clerk walked through the doorway into the back room beside the counter, pushed the "home" button on his phone and said quietly, "Find the nearest FBI office."

His phone replied, "The nearest FBI office is located at 935 Pennsylvania Ave NW in Washington, D.C. I can call that location or get directions."

"Call," Carl ordered, looking around to see if anyone had followed him into the back room.

"Hello? Yes. Hey, I think I've got some information about the bombing thing."

CHAPTER 18

Day 8 – Saturday

It was 1:30 AM. All things considered, Carl wished he would've waited until in the morning – the real "in the morning," as in after he got up – to call the FBI. But he knew he had done the right thing.

"You're sure it was this man?" FBI Special Agent Phil Jeffries showed the liquor store cashier the picture of Gennadiy Valeryevich Borzilov.

"No. Like I told you on the phone, or whoever it was I talked to, I'm pretty sure."

"But not positive?"

"Right. Not positive. The guy was in earlier. We talked a bit. He acted a little squirrely when he was checking out. He was fidgety. You know, wouldn't look up."

"He paid cash?"

"Yeah."

"I need all your cash from the day's business."

"Seriously?"

"Seriously. To examine for evidence. You'll get a receipt."

FBI Special Agent Miles Russell returned from examining the recordings from the security cameras. There were two. One behind the counter beside the television. The other was above the entrance facing the interior of the store.

Russell reported, "The guy's good. Never looked at the cameras but, yeah, it's him. Never would've made an ID from the tape without already knowing who we're looking at. Very confident SOB."

Additional agents were arriving by the minute. The earliest there were developing a strategy to canvas the area.

Jeffries turned his attention to Carl, who was fading fast.

"Did you get a license plate?"

"Nah."

"What about the type of car?"

"Nope."

"So, he pulls in and you can't tell us anything about the car?"

"No."

Jeffries was grateful for the lead but was thinking he couldn't have gotten a worse witness. He was scribbling notes.

"He walked here."

"What'd you say?"

"He walked here. From that direction." Carl pointed the way.

Jeffries flew to the door. When he looked up the street in the direction his witness pointed, through the falling snow he saw the neon lights of the Rockville Deluxe Motor Inn.

Jeffries summoned Russell to their car and shouted a command to another agent to take over at the liquor store.

Some minutes later, the motel's desk clerk arrived back at the motel where his boss had summoned him. He was nodding.

"Yeah, that's him. Marvin Williams. Room 108."

The agents pulled their weapons and started toward the door.

"But he's not there. I saw him in the parking lot earlier and he was leaving. He was in a hurry. Some sort of personal emergency, he said."

Special Agents Jeffries and Russell holstered their weapons.

"Dammit!" Russell said.

"Yep."

Throughout the night the FBI personnel did their respective things.

Surveillance video was examined. Both the lobby camera's and the parking lot cameras' images of their suspect were of little use. Borzilov was apparently aware of the devices' locations and kept his face turned away from them as much as possible to avoid providing a direct view. That hardly mattered as the authorities already knew who they were after. The recordings confirmed that, at least for the time being, he wasn't accompanied by anyone.

The Bureau's crime scene investigators came up with a couple of fingerprints. The SVR agent had obviously wiped the room but had missed a couple. A quick inspection indicated that one was a match of his that they had already obtained from evidence of his visit to the church when he posed as a structural engineer and from the plastic bag that plumber Morley had buried the cash in for his role. They speculated that the remaining print was from another guest in Room 108, but an image was transmitted to the lab to see if it matched anyone in their various databases.

Their suspect had even been cautious enough to park his car in the corner of the lot farthest from the cameras placed there. It was a Toyota Camry, one of the most common cars on the road in the U.S., probably a 2013 or 2014 model – white. The recording was of moderate quality and would be taken to the lab for analysis, but the Special Agents' initial look showed no identifying characteristics on the vehicle.

So, the possibly big break in the case turned out to be not much of one. At least the results of the on-scene scrutiny didn't yield anything of real value so far. The investigators fanned out to canvas every store or facility in the area to collect any other footage they could find. They interviewed everyone else who might have unknowingly seen the Russian bomber.

The entire West Wing staff was in their places by 8:30 AM. Some arrived much earlier.

Maggie Loughlin released the details about the vice president's memorial to the press corps and to the major news outlets. Logan's body would lie in state in the Capitol, beginning this afternoon and continuing through Monday morning.

A service would be held in the National Cathedral Monday afternoon, following which the man's casket would be returned to his home state of Wisconsin for a private funeral on Tuesday morning. President Hendrickson would attend along with other high-ranking officials within her administration. Further information would be forthcoming, the release said.

POTUS' secretary informed her of the arrival of Russian Ambassador Listunov. The ensuing meeting was brief. The diplomat handed a letter from President Tatarov. The nation's top diplomat summarized the content for Hendrickson.

"The Russian Federation, while expressing sincere sympathy for the United States over the tragic events of this week, nevertheless strenuously denies that our country is responsible, either directly or indirectly, for those egregious acts. Moreover, we vigorously object in the strongest possible language to any suggestion, publicly or privately, that any agent or private citizen of the Russian Federation had any involvement in or knowledge of, no matter how tangentially, the unfortunate incident."

Listunov paused to gauge the reaction to his discourse. To his surprise, the American leader remained perfectly relaxed with her arms folded serenely on her desk in front of her. Behind her benign poker face, POTUS was boiling.

Receiving no interruption, the ambassador continued.

"Should your administration elect to make these accusations public, our

Federation will react with utmost urgency to hold the United States responsible. Our response will be powerful and wide-reaching to ensure that the consequences of your lies prevent you from such foolishness again."

Listunov handed the letter to the American president, placed his hands in his lap, and waited for her rejoinder. Hendrickson was completely unprepared for the aggressive nature of the Russian answer to the previous day's demands for answers.

She allowed the interval between the diplomat's words and her own to extend to several seconds. She lowered her head. Listunov couldn't decide if she was speechless or was simply choosing her words carefully. When she raised her head, he saw a woman's eyes painted with intensity. Nevertheless, her words were measured and concise.

"Thank you for the letter and for the direct manner of your communication." Then POTUS turned to her Secretary of State and her chief of staff and requested, "Gentlemen, would you take our guest out of here. Explain to him the meaning of the American term 'riot act.'"

As she dismissed her guest, President Hendrickson reached for a briefing report on her desk, opened it and began reading to convey disinterest to her departing visitor.

"That will be all."

SecState Lively and Chief Chandler stood near the Russian ambassador's chair. Listunov's gaze alternated between the two and the president, whose attention had turned to other matters. He realized he'd just been kicked out of the Oval Office.

Immediately upon the three men's exit, Hendrickson shoved her reading material to the side and reached for the phone. She pressed the button to speed-dial her acting press secretary.

"Damn!" The threatening tone and the content of the response had been unexpected, but it didn't change anything.

As soon as she heard "Yes, ma'am," she commanded, "Maggie, come to my office!"

✦

FBI Special Agent Miles Russell and Phil Jeffries were on their way back to headquarters, leaving a substantial team of Special Agents and crime scene investigators behind to continue their quest for clues.

Jeffries was updating Supervisory Agent Annie Liu on his phone when Russell's phone chimed. The driver checked the Caller ID and saw "Esquivel." The call lasted mere seconds after which he made an abrupt U-turn to return to Rockville.

Jeffries looked at Russell and said to Liu on the phone, "Hang on." Then to Russell, "Got something?"

"Hell, yeah. Put me on speaker."

Jeffries pressed the icon on his phone's display and from a little distance from the device said, "You there?"

His mobile phone replied, "I'm here," in Supervisor Liu's voice.

"The muffler shop across from the motel…" The Special Agent sounded almost giddy. "They have a security camera facing out from the building that's angled a little high of their parking lot. We have a license plate number!"

"Get that, Annie?" said Jeffries with equal enthusiasm.

"I did! I'll get a BOLO issued."

What none of them knew was that the trained spy was already changing cars.

✦

"Maggie, this is the one." POTUS handed her one of the three contingent press releases they had discussed the night before.

Maggie looked at the sheet of paper. Her eyes widened as she looked up to her boss.

Reading her expression, the president acknowledged, "Yes. It went that badly."

Maggie left for her office to prepare for the briefing. She leaned back against a wall in the hallway to catch her breath.

"I really wish I didn't know about all this."

✦

Gennadiy Borzilov had selected St. John's Episcopal as the site for the bombing for several reasons. First, he knew, based on inaugural tradition it was a specific location where the American leader would be, and when. Secondly, he could plant the device well in advance of the intended detonation at a time when there would be no need to defeat the extra precautions that would be in place when the president was really present. Next, the president would be exposed. She wouldn't be wrapped in the metal cocoon that was her armored limousine. Lastly, the church was a very public place for an execution. It would create the most visual and emotional impact.

But the plan had failed and all that mattered now was atonement. And the urgency prevented the time for planning far enough in advance to be selective about time, place, and method. Furthermore, there was no longer the element of surprise. That detail alone meant that gaining proximity to the woman would be nearly impossible. But the lives of his family depended on Hendrickson's death.

The SVR agent had determined that there were only two places where he was certain the president would be. One was the vice president's memorial service at the National Cathedral. There were advantages with that site. He could know within a short window when Hendrickson would be there. She most likely would be exposed at least for a couple of seconds for a rifle shot. On the other hand, the obstacles were formidable. Borzilov was a good marksman but it wasn't his forte. Another challenge was that locating a suitable sniper's nest would be impossible. The area around the U.S. president, wherever that happened to be at a given time, was the most secure place in the world. More so, if her location was publicized in advance, as the memorial was.

The second possibility was when the president's son was transferred from his current hospital to Walter Reed National Military Medical Center, as had been announced would be done – unwisely, thought Borzilov. Knowledge of the precise time Hendrickson would be there would be very difficult to determine. Even whether she would be there was uncertain but, as a parent himself, the Russian couldn't imagine that she wouldn't accompany her son.

A bomb might be an option and that was definitely Gennadiy's operational strength. Even a suicide bombing would be acceptable now. He would gladly give his life to save Larisa's and the children's. But the bubble of protection that was perpetually surrounding the American… how would he penetrate it? And while his target's location would certainly be obvious, the amount of protection afforded by the vehicle itself was formidable.

The first problem to solve was whether he might be fortunate enough to predict a slot of time when the limousine would be at a specific point along a stretch of street, assuming he could correctly guess the route.

Throwing himself against the rear window of the limousine might allow an explosive vest to penetrate the glass. But he knew he wouldn't make it more than a few steps in the direction of the president before he was dropped by Secret Service – either a sniper or someone in the motorcade detail.

Gennadiy was frantic. He couldn't see a solution.

✦

Acting Press Secretary Margaret Loughlin stood before the White House Press Corps at the hastily called conference.

"Good morning. As I am reading this, per Article 9 of the 1961 Vienna Treaty on Diplomatic Relations, United States Secretary of State Gerard Lively is delivering a letter to Russian Ambassador Valentin Listunov addressed to President Tatarov notifying him of President Hendrickson's decision to expel all Russian diplomats from the United States. With the exception of Ambassador Listunov and a small working staff to be determined by negotiations between the ambassador and the United States Department of Justice, we are demanding all personnel to leave."

"Article 9 states that we may, at any time and without having to explain our decision, declare any member of the diplomatic staff of the mission *persona non grata*. We are requiring that the Russian Federation recall the personnel concerned or terminate their functions with the mission.

"Russia has seventy-two hours to initiate compliance with our decision by reducing diplomatic staff in the embassy and all consulates within our borders.

"The president will address the nation later today to provide rationale for her decision."

In contrast to most pronouncements in the room, this one was met with stunned silence that lasted a few seconds before the customary verbal sparring began among all the correspondents to move their question to the head of the queue. The scrambling for attention didn't matter. Immediately upon concluding her remarks, Secretary Loughlin gathered her notes and moved toward the exit.

As soon as it became certain that she would not accept questions, the audience members began the physical scrambling to get their faces before their respective network's camera to explain what just happened. Problem was, none of them knew.

✦

The entire Cabinet along with the heads of every major agency and bureau had been informed of this decision and the group was almost unanimous in its support.

Perhaps the prospects for a war with Russia had never seemed real. But it was equally unthinkable that the United States' Cold War adversary would cross the line into a direct strike. Since the end of World War II, the battle for world supremacy had been mostly ideological with any actual armed conflict carried out by surrogates in third locations.

But cross the line they had, and no amount of diplomacy could alter that fact.

Simultaneously with Maggie breaking the news to the world, albeit without specifics that the Russians were behind the attempted assassination of POTUS and the successful killing of the vice president, others were undertaking the things necessary to proceed to a reckoning. The first was the SecState notifying the Russian ambassador of the expulsion of virtually his entire embassy. The second occurred in the Cabinet Room in the West Wing, where the president gathered with the Joint Chiefs to finalize the initiation of operations against the Russian Federation.

"I have instructed NORAD to raise our Defense Condition status from 'Double Take' to 'Round House.' I think we can anticipate further elevation of DEFCON to 'Fast Pace,'" POTUS affirmed to the collection of military levels.

Raising DEFCON from a not-unusual status of "4," or "above normal readiness" to "3," which prescribed an order making the "Air Force ready to mobilize in fifteen minutes," was significant. A further increase in readiness to making "Armed Forces ready to deploy and engage in less than six hours," was used briefly in the 1962 Cuban Missile Crisis. That time was also in response to Russian aggression, and that time they stayed ninety miles away from our border.

One of the benefits of the DEFCON system was that it served as a method of communications, warning enemies where the U.S. line in the sand was currently drawn.

"The Russians' aggressive posture was underscored by their President Tatarov's letter delivered by the Russian ambassador. They will escalate their military actions and claim it's in response to ours. But we have to assume they prepared for this escalation long before St. John's. When we go to 'Fast Pace,'…"

The realization of having said "when" rather than "if" caused an inward shudder in the president, wife, and mother.

"…it will mandate our military to be ready for deployment in six hours, but according to your team's plans, General, our special operations forces are already preparing for deployment."

General Dwight Richards was a doppelganger of every movie's commanding general. Short-ish, barrel-chested, and perpetually chomping on a usually unlit cigar, at least when not in the Cabinet Room with the president.

"Yes, ma'am. Ironically, we've taken a page out of our old Cold War playbook, a tactical approach known then as a 'Green Light Team.'"

The room's enormous OLED screen lit up with graphics supporting the four-star general's explanation.

General Richards continued.

"Post-World War Two, many in our military establishment and the government were uncertain as to how our conventional forces might stand up against those of the Soviets. Mutually assured nuclear destruction became a strategy that arose when you had no real strategy for victory, only a strategy for a standoff.

"To set the stage for a look at our initial incursion, let me give you a summary of the Cold War program that we've built on in recent years."

The general's aide advanced to the next "slide" which was an image of two cylindrical containers with canvas covers.

"Special operators, primarily Army Special Forces, were trained to infiltrate to positions behind enemy lines with the B-54 Special Atomic Demolition Munition (SADM), pictured here. These were what we called backpack nukes that were later more generally referred to by analysts and journalists as suitcase nukes. Two-man units, referred to as Green Light

Teams were trained to deploy with the low-yield devices to strategic locations – by parachute, generally, though other options were possible.

"The advantage was that of surprise. Once in place, the Green Light Team merely waited. Detonation could be accomplished at various durations of delay after the insertion of the Green Light Team. Or not at all.

"The program died because of the disadvantages. First, a plane or missile was more effective for almost every target than Green Light deployment. It also became apparent that these weapons didn't eliminate the potential for escalation simply because they were small nukes."

General Richards continued for some time offering a more than necessary amount of detail about the abandoned program. He finally got to the crux of why the background info was important.

"The new iteration of the Green Light Team is the SPecial Immediate Reaction Infiltration Team, or 'SPIRIT.'"

The image on the giant TV screen changed again.

"Like their forerunners, SPIRITs position covertly behind enemy lines for the express purpose of deploying a variety of strategic armaments, including the B-54B SNAP. The Special Nuclear Armament Package is an evolution of the original SADM B-54. In addition to small nuclear bombs, there is an inventory of non-nuclear options in SPIRIT inventory.

"And like the Green Light Teams, there are a couple of variations for execution. One is a Positive Response Solution. Unless the Team receives the specific order to execute, they merely wait. An alternative is the Negative Response Solution. The Team has a prescribed execution order to engage the device at a particular time. Absent a wave-off order, they proceed. The SPIRIT Team is the tip of the spear for the comprehensive plan we have developed."

The general proceeded through the rest of the war plan. He and other Chiefs of Staff detailed all the elements of the blueprint for almost two hours, from SPIRIT deployment to the endgame.

"Our consensus is that this is the best solution. With your orders, we will pre-position a six-man SPIRIT Team so that they'll be in place pending the vote from Congress. SPIRITs from the 10th Special Forces Group are standing by in Stuttgart, Germany, and will take off as soon as they receive your go-ahead."

President Hendrickson looked about the room. To a person, each military officer watched expectantly for her verdict. She understood that this was one of those moments that defined a presidency. But from a personal perspective, knowing the course of action she was endorsing – no, the correct word was initiating – she wondered at the effect it would have on her state of mind. At what point in her future would she know if she had made the right, the morally defensible decision.

Fortunately, POTUS understood, she wasn't in this thing alone. This group of men and women before her had fashioned a plan to accomplish the goals that she had set with them. Still, they were *her* orders that put them into action. Nor could she lay the commencement of hostilities off on Congress. Their approval of a Resolution of War was an endorsement of *her* appeal to do so. It was *her* work, *her* signature that would authorize war on Russia.

Army General and Chairman of the Joint Chiefs of Staff Dwight Richards held out a pen and opened a folder before his commander in chief. "Madam President…"

President Sandra Hendrickson took the writing instrument and scribbled her name on the orders.

"May God help me," she mumbled quietly enough that nobody heard.

Then aloud, "You are so-ordered."

✦

Stunned. The two ex-CIA Officers were dumbfounded at the revelation they'd just heard Maggie make on the televised press conference. The follow-up comments by the correspondents and their anchors were more rambling than any that Morgan and Crenshaw had ever heard. But that was understandable. Every news network in the universe was caught as off-guard as anyone else. Their research departments were good, but they likely had no "just-in-case" content prepped for this situation.

"I can't see this. Either side. Russia wouldn't attack the president. And on our side, it's premature for this kind of nonsense." Crenshaw tapped his fingers on the end table.

Morgan turned the volume down to a barely audible level and simply listened to his friend.

CHAPTER 19

Morgan and his mentor moved to the kitchen and refilled their glasses with a splash of brandy.

"When I was in Moscow, I met a number of members of the Foreign Ministry." Crenshaw applied air quotes to the words Foreign Ministry with his fingers.

"They were as genuinely a part of the ambassadorial organization as I was. When I met him, Pavel Semyonovich Orlov was a relatively low-ranking member of the SVR; a far cry from director. Friendship is far too strong a word. I guess you'd say we were professional associates. Each of us knew exactly what the other was. When we met, and that was rare, it was almost always in an official capacity. Only occasionally did we see each other in a social setting.

"When we did, there was a more transparent window into the soul of the person you were looking at."

The two men sat at the kitchen table and clinked a toast.

"To sanity prevailing," remarked the older man.

"To sanity," agreed Morgan.

Neither of the friends spoke as Crenshaw reflected on his time in Moscow and Morgan waited.

Finally, the older of the former spies proceeded.

"The Orlov I knew, while dedicated, was a thoughtful man. He was always aware of the potential consequences of actions. He was never shy about following orders or taking initiative. But the inevitable reactions to whatever ops were on the table were never far from his calculations.

"Don't get me wrong, he could be ruthless. That is, as long as he believed he was in the right. He just played the spy game like it was chess. Always thinking several moves ahead with the endgame in mind."

"So, what are you saying?"

"Just that this whole thing…" Dr. Crenshaw took a sip of his brandy. "You know, Josh, this doesn't taste cheap."

His smile was obviously unfelt as he continued. "It doesn't feel like Orlov. Not something he would initiate. And an op he would put the kibosh on if he knew about it."

"What if he couldn't?" Josh proposed. "Or he didn't know about it?"

"That's a possibility, son. But Orlov, as much as anything else was the most intuitive and the most connected man I've ever been around. I can't conceive of a scenario where he would be unaware of such an ambitious plot."

✦

"Max Elliott" sat in his motel in Oakton, Virginia. Rest was beyond his grasp, but he lay on his bed with his eyes closed. Each time he started using a new burner phone, he placed a call to his handlers in Russia for the primary purpose of communicating his new number. Each time his attempt to reach them went unanswered. Borzilov had resigned himself to a recognition that he wouldn't hear from them nor reach them until news of his success or failure became known worldwide. So accustomed to the isolation was he that, when his phone rang, he sat up with a start.

"*Da?*"

"Gennadiy?" The sound of his wife's voice brought moisture to the hardened spy's eyes.

"Larisa!" he exclaimed.

"They said they want to keep you motivated. To remind you what is at stake. What does that mean, Zhenya?"

"It's nothing, *lyubov moya*. Really, my love, it is nothing at all."

The two of the three handlers who were with Gennadiy's family allowed the conversation to continue for a little over five minutes. Gennadiy knew it would mean burning his current phone and replacing it with yet another. But that was of no concern. Speaking with his wife and son Valeriy and listening to the barely-understandable rambling of Ulyana had indeed reinvigorated the agent of the SVR. What happened to him no longer mattered. His only hope was that he could exchange the life of the American president for those of his family.

Though he felt reenergized to complete his operation, the renewal came with an intense impatience for its completion. A shudder overtook him as the fact returned to him that he had no control over the timing of his next attempt.

Gennadiy unscrewed the lid of his vodka and allowed himself a sip of the clear liquid. He always planned his operations with unforgiving precision. He left nothing to chance. He mitigated obstacles with multiple contingencies. But after his failed first effort at assassinating Hendrickson, the Russian had no such luxury. When news was broadcast of his opportunity, he would move.

Success was a longshot.

He turned up the volume of the television to an audible level to provide himself some distraction from his scattered thoughts. The news anchor for the cable network wrapped up coverage of the latest news about the unprecedented expulsion of almost the entire Russian embassy.

The speaker said, "Certainly of less global significance than our breaking news, we nevertheless have a bit of good news to share.

"Adam Hendrickson Jr., son of the president, has improved sufficiently to allow moving him to the Walter Reed Medical complex. We reported the expectation that he would be transported there but had not received confirmation. We now have that confirmation as well as a time. First thing tomorrow morning AJ, as the young man is known, will travel the short distance by ambulance to Walter Reed."

The co-anchor speculated, "Bob, do you think the move was hastened because of the current tensions with Russia? The Military Hospital is deemed more secure so perhaps, out of an abundance of caution, the president felt more urgency to move him."

"Possibly, Spencer. I would suspect, though, that President Hendrickson will miss accompanying her son. With everything going on, I'm sure she will remain at the White House, her attention solely on matters at hand."

Turning to another camera, the anchor shuffled a small stack of papers and got back to the weightier news, "Now back to our top story; the Hendrickson administration has expelled almost the entire Russian diplomatic corps in protest of…"

Borzilov-slash-Elliott lowered the volume. He knew that his opportunity was approaching.

"That news might be a less significant event to the Americans but it's not to me. And you are wrong, Mr. Reporter. The president will be with her son. Mothers are the same everywhere. She is his mother first and everything else comes afterward."

Borzilov polished off the remaining liquor that served him as both confidence and sedative. Perhaps it was the alcohol or maybe it was the catharsis of the news that his chance for redemption was almost at hand, but whatever allowed it, Gennadiy Valeryevich Borzilov nodded off to sleep.

✦

"I'm not sure what you're saying, Ryan. Are you saying the Russians had nothing to do with this? Or you're saying it was a rogue element? What?"

"I'm not even sure what I'm saying, Josh. Remember, I've been drinking your brandy all night." Crenshaw raised his glass for another clink with his host's and sipped at it again.

"Don't forget, I'm a Cold War veteran – one of the relics left over from the days of the Soviet Union versus the West. And while there were times where things got out of hand, mostly from miscalculations, generally people were working pretty damned hard to keep us off the brink."

Morgan offered a refill to his house guest, who declined with a wave of the hand.

"If this is Russia's play, it exceeds the Cuban Missile Crisis in terms of aggression. The Soviets parked those things there simply because they thought they could. The value to them was that the things had the *possibility* of launch. An assassination of the President of the United States – or fortunately an *attempted* assassination – is a different story. The missiles were a threat. This? Well, it's a completed act.

"We very nearly went to war over those damned missiles. This *is* going to lead to war. It's about reciprocity, son. It's always been about a balance of threats. Now one side has gone beyond a mere threat. Consequently, the other side has to act."

Dr. Crenshaw stood and placed a hand on his young friend's shoulder as he started to the guest bedroom.

"Good night, my friend."

Morgan simply smiled and raised his glass in the direction of the man.

At the door to his room, Crenshaw paused. Without turning he said, as much to himself as to Josh, "I'm saying that this feels wrong. Where are the cooler heads that threatened but ultimately knew where the lines were?"

When he finally turned to face Morgan, "Oh, both sides crossed the lines. Just never so far that we couldn't step back over it. Good night."

At the same time Ryan Crenshaw walked out one door, Maggie Loughlin walked in another. Neither she nor Josh spoke. She set her overcoat and briefcase on the coffee table and herself on the sofa. Josh sat beside her.

No kisses or hugs for greetings this time. Maggie just leaned her head on Morgan's shoulder. He put his arm around her. After some time of silence, Josh enquired, "Want a glass of wine?"

Maggie tapped her finger on her fiancé's snifter of brandy.

"One of those."

CHAPTER 20

Day 9 – Sunday

It was 7:00 AM and AJ Hendrickson felt well enough to act like a typical teenager. He pushed his hospital breakfast away and turned up his nose.

"Son, you might not believe this, but hospital food's come a long way. It's a lot better than it used to be," insisted his dad.

Adam Sr. took a bite of the eggs and likewise pushed the small plate away. "It's not White House food, is it?"

AJ upped the ante. "Not even McDonald's."

The son nibbled at the triangular slice of toast.

"Why can't I just go home?"

"Son, you're better – a *lot* better. And we're grateful for that. But you're not quite well enough to go home."

The teenager huffed his displeasure. He reached for the juice, which was just out of reach.

His dad handed the cup to him.

"You don't know how worried we've been, AJ. The last few days have…"

"Dad, are we going to war with Russia?"

The query caught Dad completely off guard.

"Why do you ask?"

The son griped, "Why do you always do what you tell me not to – answer a question with a question? Just tell me."

"It, uh, doesn't look good, AJ." The first gentleman and his wife, the president, had tried to keep their children isolated from the news of the last few days. "Your mom's doing everything she can but she's worried. How'd you hear about it? Text?"

"Yeah. Judd asked me."

"I knew we shouldn't have given your phone back to you," the dad lamented with some humor. "What'd you tell him?"

"I said that I didn't think so but that I didn't really know. And I told him that I couldn't talk about it if I did."

AJ's dad gave a doubtful look.

"Give me some credit, Dad. I'm not some dumbass kid anymore. I know Mom can't tell me things, but I overhear a little bit. And I don't repeat it. Swear! I'm not stupid."

For one of his first times as a father, Adam Hendrickson Sr. appreciated the fact that his son was indeed no longer a child. Not quite a grownup but certainly not a kid.

"Son, I'll tell you what I can. It's all stuff that's been on TV anyhow."

And the man summarized the details to the extent that he knew them of likely Russian culpability of the bombing that had nearly killed him, had succeeded in murdering several others, had attempted to assassinate his mother, and injured many more. He explained the expulsion of the Russian diplomats and what an extraordinary act that was. But he also reminded his young man what he had told him a few minutes earlier.

"Your mom's doing all she can. She has a great team around her and if there's any way out of this, she'll find it."

AJ felt a bit relieved at knowing everything. He felt even better at the fact that his dad had talked to him like an adult instead of a child.

◆

The team Adam Hendrickson spoke of, or at least a part of them, sat in the Cabinet Room at that very moment. The broad-brush plan was taking on fine strokes. Action plans were giving way to timelines and names of specific battalions, ships, and locales.

POTUS and a subset of her war team had been at the conference table since five-thirty, primarily for one reason: to finish up. President Mom had to get to her son.

◆

Gennadiy Borzilov had already studied the online maps a number of times and had committed the route to memory. His plan was firm, if improbable, but it was the best chance he felt he had to kill Hendrickson. He had decided that success was most likely at either end of the motorcade between the hospitals. Some intermediate point along the way held the worst chance that he would accomplish his goal, though the Russian operative knew that "best chance" and "worst chance" were relative terms. He held little hope at all that he could save his family.

The SVR operative went over his plan step by step, checking each item that was a part of it as he went. A black leather satchel held the primary plastic explosives wired with a single channel detonator linked to a transmitter that he placed in one of his trench coat's pockets. He placed three hand grenades in the other. With the grenades, Borzilov placed his MP-443 Grach PYa 9x19mm handgun. His BlackHawk S.T.R.I.K.E. Cutaway Tactical Vest that another of his aliases had ordered from an online store a year ago went under his gray sweater. In one of his trousers' front pockets, he placed a very small flash bang charge and, in the other front pocket, the transmitter that would set it off.

The last act before leaving his motel room was to become Max Elliott again. He carefully attached the beard to his face and put on the fake glasses, the same items he had worn when checking into his present motel. Certain he had been identified at the liquor store, he no longer had the luxury of Max Elliott looking like Gennadiy Borzilov, or like Marvin Williams. He had donned the disguise after leaving Rockville. And he had exchanged the car for another one that he had positioned in a paid parking garage outside of Washington two days before Inauguration Day.

Inside that vehicle had been the disguise kit and the explosives he would use today. He carried all his necessities to his white sedan and set out.

The Russian's scheme had a number of flaws. Would the presidential limousine follow the route he had guessed it would? Would pedestrians even be allowed on the actual route, given the previous attempt on the president's life? Would the woman really go to be with her son, or was she president before mother? All of his guesses had to turn out to be right.

A number of flaws, indeed. And Max Elliott knew this would be his last chance. Even if he lived to make this attempt, he held no illusions that he would survive it. So, to ensure that the deed, even if ineffective, would be attributed to the Motherland, the Russian Foreign Intelligence Service agent provided evidence to that effect. Inside the interior breast pocket of his jacket were his authentic embassy credentials and passport, the ones that identified him as Gennadiy Valeryevich Borzilov.

Morgan awoke to the smell of sizzling bacon. Maggie wasn't in the bed, so he expected she was making breakfast. Then he remembered – vaguely – that she had arisen and left for the West Wing much earlier. Part of his recollection was that he felt guilty not getting up with her. But it had been, oh, so early.

So, when he walked into the kitchen in his sweats and t-shirt, the cook couldn't have been anyone other than his friend, Ryan Crenshaw.

"Sit down, Josh. You're just in time."

Morgan sat at the table at the same time Crenshaw was setting a plate of thick-sliced bacon, fried eggs, and toast in front of him. Jelly, honey, and juice were already in place. Crenshaw set his own portions at the table and poured two cups of coffee.

"I hope you don't mind. I sorta took some liberties in your kitchen."

"Mind? Heck… you can move in."

"Maggie was off early?"

Morgan nodded. "A fact of life right now. I don't know if it's unusual because of the circumstances and will improve when Secretary Ginnetti is back at her desk. Or if this is just how it's gonna be the whole time Mag's here. She had her own business, so she's used to the responsibility and the early hours. I think she might miss the flexibility of being her own boss. We'll see."

There was talk of days past and also the current crisis with Russia while the pair wolfed down their morning meal. Finally, Crenshaw changed the subject.

"Would you mind me sticking around another day or two?"

"Not at all. Enjoy having you. Any particular reason? Or do you just love my company?"

"Love hanging out with you, my boy, but you're not Amelia. Was wondering if you'd fancy another trip out to Langley."

With all the news of the last twenty-four hours, Morgan had pushed his own resurrected troubles to the back of his mind.

"I don't know, Ryan. Is this about me again?"

"No, I can assure you it's not. I've got a couple of things to follow up on and I could use the company – and a driver."

Morgan pushed his cleaned plate away and got up to refresh their coffee.

"The roads are clear, so you'd be fine. But sure, I'll drive you."

◆

At George Washington University Hospital, Secret Service personnel swarmed the ambulance that was backed up to the door that normally received deliveries for the medical facility. The agents provided a show of force in the exposed weaponry they carried, as opposed to the concealment they usually maintained. The deliberately menacing display of the officers was echoed by the gaudy spectacle of their vehicles.

Radios crackled the location of the presidential limousine. The Special Agents shouted orders to each other and the procession of black armored SUVs, with a hospital ambulance embedded in the line, began to pull away. Lights flashed on all the vehicles, which spared no haste as they raced to and then rendezvoused with the president's procession. The combined caravan sped toward the Walter Reed National Military Medical Center.

Shortly, the pack of motor vehicles reached Interstate 66 West and ultimately, I-495 N, where they opened things up.

They finally took exit 34 to merge onto MD-355 S/Rockville Pike.

◆

A very short distance from the speeding caravan, Max Elliott, aka Gennadiy Borzilov lay in wait. Though he knew that the confined areas at each hospital were easier places to guard, he had determined that open parts of parkways and interstates presented some insurmountable obstacles. First was inaccessibility. Getting close to the limo would be impossible. Secondly, even if he could, its speed would make acquisition just as impossible. Lastly, and of no real consequence because of the first two, the Beast, or presidential limousine would have other vehicles surrounding it.

There was only one location on Google Maps that presented the remotest possibility of success. Borzilov had arrived before daylight and parked in one of the parking lots at Walter Reed Hospital. Gathering all of the items he needed, he walked to his chosen spot, holding a mobile phone to his ear to create the appearance of distraction with an imaginary conversation.

There were indeed a number of what had to be Secret Service agents positioned about, stationary and walking. None appeared to be proactively interviewing others in the area. There were few people there because, despite the clear skies, it was cold. Most moved as quickly as they could from their parked cars to the hospital entrance.

Borzilov continued ambling, apparently oblivious to the cold and the other people. He put the hand not holding the cellphone into one of his trousers pockets, strategically holding one side of his unbuttoned overcoat open to display a white lab jacket. The doctor's coat was consistent in appearance with the black doctor's satchel resting on the ground behind him. At one point during his "phone conversation" the "doctor" meandered aimlessly a short distance east of the intersection of Rockville Pike with Wilson Drive. The "physician" discreetly dropped a small item among the leafless trees on the northeast corner of the intersection before moving back across Rockville Pike to the spot he needed to be, southwest of the intersection.

◆

FBI Agents Esquivel, Jeffries, and Russell stood some distance away from the target behind parked cars watching FBI SWAT Team members move into position beside the door of an Oakton, Virginia motel room.

When the most wanted man in the world had exchanged cars and taken on the identity of Max Elliott, he had been observed by a parking garage security guard while making the move from one auto to another. To avoid suspicion – or at least in an attempt to – the SVR agent had parked the car he abandoned two floors lower than where he would retrieve its replacement. He knew if anyone saw him move from one vehicle to another directly next to it, it would appear unusual. But despite his caution, a bored employee of the garage sat watching the few people come and go at the not-so-busy parking structure on the video feeds.

The security guard had seen the man depart his original Toyota. He coincidentally moved his attention to the feed originating from the camera nearest the man's replacement auto.

While it seemed peculiar that a person would park two vehicles in the same garage, the guard originally passed it off as some horny guy trying to cover up his infidelity. In that light he thought it was funny enough that he showed it to a fellow guard and then to other eyes until someone thought, given the current environment after the bombing, that maybe they should let authorities see it. One observant soul made a connection with the face from the news.

The video found its way to the FBI, whose analysts confirmed the man as Borzilov. With the man's new ride identified, the BOLO found him, although it took longer than the officers would've liked or expected.

Now as the three Special Agents watched their SWAT Team prepare to crash Max Elliott's motel room door, their expectations were already low, given the absence of his car in the parking lot. Somehow Borzilov had managed to drive past the D.C. police staking out the place.

However, when the cries of "FBI" and "Federal Agents" pierced the air and a flimsy wooden door flew from its frame and armed, violent men streamed into the room of Gennadiy Borzilov, it wasn't as anticlimactic as the Special Agents had feared.

The reemergence of a single Tactical Officer to the doorway waving frantically for the plain clothes agents to hurry provoked a sprint.

Russell was the first through the door. "Jesus Christ, we've got a problem. Get Liu on the phone."

Agent Esquivel stepped out to make the call while Jeffries moved around him into the room. To his horror, scattered on the surfaces of the dresser, nightstand, and lavatory counter were the various components used in making bombs. The cause for the panic was that there was no bomb – and no bombmaker.

"Not a good thing to see all the ingredients of the recipe with the cake gone," said Jeffries.

"And the cook," added a SWAT Team member.

✦

Supervisory Special Agent Annie Liu ended the call she had received in a flash and called her boss, who in turn called his, who made his call to the head of the Secret Service.

The presidential limousine was the third car in the motorcade and was flanked by Secret Service SUVs. Other Secret Service vehicles came next, followed by the ambulance, itself bordered by vehicles. Bringing up the rear were three more black SUVs. Travelling south on Rockville Pike, the procession was nearing its destination.

Even from his distance, through the very dark glass in the rear section of the Beast, Borzilov saw the silhouette in the seat always occupied by the President of the United States.

As the string of vehicles arrived at the intersection with Wilson Drive, the cars began to spread out, virtually transforming into a single file line to make the tight U-turn back northward toward the entrance to the Medical Center.

Radios started to communicate the warning into the earpieces of every agent in the caravan.

✦

Josh Morgan and Ryan Crenshaw had just taken seats in DCI Betsy Parnell's office when her phone rang. She held up a hand and excused herself. Walking into an adjacent conference room, Parnell heard the disturbing notification that was making its way to every head of every law enforcement or intelligence agency in the District.

✦

As the cars made their ways individually through the bottom of the U-turn, they became individual objects instead of a single conglomeration of rolling stock. Just as the black limo reached the point to make its turn, a small smoky explosion sounded among the dormant trees on the east side of the street. Though fairly benign sounding, the charge got the attention of every agent in the area. From around the snow-covered lawn, armed agents raced toward the smoke while others turned their attention to the Beast.

At the same moment as he detonated the flash bang charge, Borzilov began a frantic sprint toward the president's car. Bullets from every angle flew toward the desperate Russian. Several slammed into his armor. One ripped part of his left ear off but he continued.

As soon he was close enough, the SVR operator sent his black bag sliding across the pavement. Immediately he felt the burn of a bullet creasing the crown of his head. The pain caused him to lose his balance, and he fell face-first onto the street. As his slide carried him toward the Beast, he covered his head – just in time.

The blast was catastrophic in its intensity. The limousine's acceleration had moved it ahead and far enough into the U-turn that the satchel exploded just under its edge and toward its rear. Still, the energy lifted the rear of the vehicle skyward and sent it leaning away from the Russian attacker. The vehicle's armored plating prevented substantial damage, but the impact stalled the auto's progress. It landed violently on its side with the bottom exposed. Though formidable, the metal plating was curled where it had peeled away. There were a few holes in the metal underside. Most were insignificant. A few were several inches wide.

Gennadiy Borzilov, despite his wounds from gunfire and shrapnel from the damaged limo, continued to crawl toward the Beast. With a pin pulled on a grenade, he shoved it through a gash in the underside of the black presidential vehicle into its rear interior. The explosion on the inside of the vehicle didn't penetrate the outer body. However, it expanded the shell in the same way a microwave popcorn pan's aluminum foil swelled when heated.

The Russian spy had three bullets in his left leg, two in his right, and a single one in his waist where the body armor had lifted up. A lower ear was missing, and blood poured from the bullet wound in his scalp. But as he watched protection personnel scramble toward the presidential automobile, he felt a wave of satisfaction and peace wash through him. He knew his family was safe.

The last things the man heard before passing out from his injuries were the voices of some of the president's detail shouting instructions to not move and placing him under arrest.

✦

DCI Parnell was absent from her office for several minutes. The two ex-spy friends passed the time with more speculation about the motive and culprits behind the attempted assassination of POTUS and deaths and injuries to numerous more.

Crenshaw expressed his doubts about Russian involvement, at least not at the state level. Morgan was beginning to have doubts, if only because of the convictions of his friend.

When Parnell finally returned, she informed the two visitors of the latest news.

"There's been another bombing; an attempt on the president."

✦

Sirens wailed. The activity was frantic. Throughout the scene, the horror of a second attempt on the life of Sandra Hendrickson was tangible. The area was cordoned off in no time. The faces of the governmental personnel and bystanders who were gathering ran the gamut from expressionless disbelief to flowing tears.

EMTs reluctantly treated Gennadiy Borzilov and placed him on a stretcher. He was critical and passed in and out of semi-consciousness.

As the medics were rolling him toward the waiting ambulance, the Russian fixed his eyes on the sight of the upturned Beast. The rear door was opened upward allowing Secret Service agents to enter the black vehicle. From inside, one agent handed something to another who was standing on the skyward-facing side. He lifted the figure upward by its two legs with some difficulty before tossing it thoughtlessly to the ground.

Gennadiy was mildly bothered by the treatment of the American president's corpse until he realized that what he'd seen deposited so harshly was a mannequin.

The bloodied terrorist's pulse suddenly raced before stopping entirely. An EMT's voice yelled to her associates.

"He's crashing!" The medics continued rolling the man into the ambulance. Outside personnel slammed the door to and the ambulance raced away with its siren screaming even though it only had a minimal distance to travel.

Around the block from the scene of the bombing, a laundry truck sat with its back facing a loading dock. With the walls of the building muffling the sound of sirens a block away, two nurses received the gurney from the EMTs inside the laundry truck. Following the patient onto the concrete dock were four heavily armed Secret Service agents and President Sandra Hendrickson and husband Adam Sr.

POTUS and the first gentleman stepped forward to take the hand of AJ and escort him to his new room at the Walter Reed National Military Medical Center. Bringing up the rear of the procession from the truck was the chief of staff, receiving the latest update from the scene of the second attempt on the life of his boss.

CIA Director Elizabeth Parnell received another call that she also took in the conference room. This call was briefer. When she returned her smile was one of obvious relief. She summarized the call for her visitors.

"So, it's still tragic. POTUS' driver was ripped apart by the grenade that the assailant somehow got inside the limo..." Parnell didn't have the full story yet. "… But the president is fine.

"You wouldn't call it a sting; just a precaution. The Secret Service admits it was risky, but the FBI had all this evidence that the unsub was hanging around. Why wouldn't he get out of town unless he was going to try again? With the exception of the Secret Service agent driving the limo, it worked. It drew out the suspect. They just never envisioned he would get this far. They never even remotely considered that he would get to anyone inside the vehicle."

The two men in her office were dumbfounded.

"Who knew about this?" asked Crenshaw.

"Only the Secret Service." Parnell shook her head. "How they kept this quiet in this town is beyond me. Not the FBI. Not the Agency. I think maybe DHS Secretary Larson might've known. And I'd be shocked if National Security Advisor Templeton was in the dark. But… whew."

Josh Morgan spoke next. "Remarkable. What about the assassin? Dead?"

"Not yet. He's been shot and pretty close to blown apart but, as of now, the bastard's alive. He crashed right before they carted him off, but they revived him. Emotionally, everybody wishes he was dead, but…"

"He could answer a lot of questions," Josh interjected.

"Yep."

Crenshaw pushed his receding gray hair back. "Well, I hope he does provide some answers. And I hope they stop a war."

Betsy nodded. "Well, I'm sure you'll understand but I'm going to have to ask your forgiveness. I need to reschedule our meeting. My availability just got canceled."

Parnell stood to escort her guests out. Morgan also rose but Crenshaw kept his seat.

"Betsy… director, please. It's important."

Parnell was irritated, even if Crenshaw was an old friend and mentor.

Finally, she sat and motioned Morgan back to his chair.

"Okay, Ryan. Ten minutes."

Crenshaw got right to the point. "What is your working relationship with SVR Director Orlov?"

CHAPTER 21

Acting Press Secretary Margaret Laughlin smiled at the news she received from her caller.

"Yes, Noah. I understand. Two o'clock. That's wonderful news." Maggie hung up and scribbled a few notes. Chief of Staff Chandler had given her a name – Gennadiy Valeryevich Borzilov. It wasn't for public disclosure, he had said, but she had worked hard, and he thought she should know. The press briefing would be at two o'clock. She would introduce Chandler; he would introduce Secret Service Director Keith Cortland. In the meantime, Maggie was to prepare an announcement to hand to the press pool. When she asked Chandler if he wanted to review it first, he said that he didn't. He told Maggie she knew what to say.

In short order the announcement was ready. Though Maggie knew it was good, she was anxious about putting out her first solo effort. Nevertheless, the explosion wasn't exactly a secret. News outlets were going to report details of their own if they had no other guidance. Maggie knew it was urgent to get something out now. She stood and walked the short distance to the press room.

✦

It seemed as if the release went straight from the room to live television.

"Tracy Adams. QNN has Breaking News from White House Press Secretary Margaret Loughlin."

Having read from a Teleprompter most of his adult life, the Quantum News Network anchor did so now as effortlessly as if he was rattling off his children's names.

"This morning a second attempt was made on the life of President Sandra

Hendrickson. The president is unharmed A bomb targeted the presidential limousine and while it did extensive damage, the president was not in the vehicle at the time.

"Regrettably, a Secret Service agent lost his life. His name is being withheld until such time as his family has had the opportunity to notify everyone it wishes.

"The perpetrator is in custody. He is the Russian male who has been the subject of the recent intensive manhunt. He was injured during the attack and is in the hospital in critical condition.

"The investigation is proceeding jointly by all governmental agencies, led by the Secret Service and FBI, with the assistance of local police.

"No other details are available at this time. A press briefing is scheduled for two o'clock Eastern Time."

Maggie turned down the volume of her office TV – rather Secretary Ginnetti's office TV – and called Morgan. No answer. She shrugged it off as his being out with Crenshaw.

✦

"I've known the man since I worked for you in Moscow, Ryan. Not as well as you did but I met him. Since then we've developed, shall we say, a tenuous working relationship. Now that we're both the director of our respective country's intelligence service, there's no longer any secret who we are or what we do.

"Normally any high-level communications are carried out by governmental leaders, not by us agency low-lifes. Honestly, Orlov and I have subordinates communicate, to the extent that any dialogue is necessary at all. Why do you ask, Ryan? What's this about?"

Morgan was a little uncomfortable at being present for this conversation between former colleagues and old friends.

Crenshaw expressed as succinctly as he could all the same questions and reservations that he had related to Morgan the night before.

"Ryan, I trust you. And you're practically famous for your instincts. Your gut is legendary. But what would you have me do?"

"Reach out to Orlov. In your official capacity, it would be completely appropriate."

"Ryan!? Are you kidding? It couldn't possibly be more *inappropriate*! What? I just pick up the phone and say, 'Pavel… comrade. Betsy. How ya doing?'"

"Come on, Betsy. A little less sarcasm…"

"Sorry, Ryan. But I can't. I'd lose my job. And rightfully so. Going outside channels."

"Channels, schmannels… It's within your purview."

"Now look who's being sarcastic! Ryan, I know you mean well. But I can't. Now, if you'll excuse me, I have to go."

Morgan and Betsy were starting to rise when Crenshaw spoke again.

"I told him you might call."

Morgan's head jerked toward his friend. Betsy collapsed in her chair. Morgan slumped into his. He spread his entire left hand to cover his face.

Betsy said, "I can't believe this. Un-tell him."

There was silence all around until Parnell stormed out.

"You told him? When? You've been at my place for a few days."

"I texted him. This morning. Before breakfast."

The DCI's office door opened, and a member of the security staff entered to escort them out.

President Hendrickson was distracted during the half hour she spent with her son. Mom was thrilled to have her son at Walter Reed and to be with him but POTUS was impatient to get back to the Oval Office and get details of the attack and, if available, the man who had tried to kill her – twice.

Sandy told her husband she had to go, and President of the United States Sandra Hendrickson walked out of the hospital room with Special Agent Joy Griffith. In the hall they joined six other Secret Service agents. They passed no less than twenty others in the hallway as they proceeded to a rear exit and a waiting, second Beast.

About ten steps from the exit, the president applied the brakes.

"Where is the son of a bitch?"

Chief of Staff Chandler asked for everyone, "Who, ma'am?"

"The bastard who tried to kill me. And who nearly killed my son and… Where the hell is he? I'm assuming he's being treated here."

Chandler tried to persuade his boss. "Madam President, I don't think that's a good idea."

"Noah, that wasn't a request."

In some cases, Chandler would've persisted, trying harder to convince POTUS, but he had long ago learned the moods and intonations of his boss. Pushing back on this would be pointless. He got on the phone and acquired the information.

"This way, ma'am."

He led the contingent down the hall toward the ICU where Gennadiy Valeryevich Borzilov was lying near death.

The ride back to Morgan's and Maggie's place was devoid of any conversation. Morgan entertained the notion that his friend was losing it.

When they pulled into Josh's parking spot at his apartment, he was about to get out when Crenshaw took his arm and held him from leaving the SUV.

"Son, I know you think I'm crazy. I'm not. I spent a good deal of my adult life playing the game. The Soviets were trying to dominate the world and we were trying to stop them. At least that was the story we subscribed to. But in the midst of it, there were a lot of people on both sides trying to keep us from blowing the damn thing apart.

"I told you earlier; we both crossed the line a lot. When it didn't work, we – what's the new buzz word? – walked it back. We never got so far into insanity that we couldn't dial it back. I'm just an old dinosaur. I admit it. But I didn't want to nuke the planet then. I don't want to see it happen now."

Dr. Ryan Crenshaw's eyes teared up. "I never had kids. You're the closest thing I have. And I hope to see some youngsters running around your house before long. We owe it to your kids to get this sorted out. I can't do it, but I can sure as hell try to push some people in the right direction."

Crenshaw opened his door. Having said his piece and making his defense, he walked toward the door of the apartment.

✦

At 4:30 PM local time at the Stuttgart Army Airfield in Filderstadt, Germany, just outside the larger city of Stuttgart, an MC-130J Commando II rose from the runway. In the rear, three SPIRIT Teams sat as calmly as if they were going on vacation. In a few moments, the six Army Green Berets would be asleep, waking after a short period to inspect the ordnance and other supplies.

✦

Gennadiy Valeryevich lay in bed with the myriad of cables, tubes, bandages, and other medical paraphernalia that you would expect to see on someone in the Intensive Care Unit. His status was "critical," and he was slipping in and out of consciousness. The medical team treating him recommended inducing a coma but in what can only be identified as threatening pressure from government officials, consented to withhold that option, at least for the time being. The other device the medical team had insisted on but was overruled was a ventilator. None of the doctors, it seemed, had the courage to resist the agents who demanded that the bomber/patient was left in a state where he could speak.

As President of the United States, Sandra Hendrickson's fury at the man was extreme but as AJ's mother, the rage was almost explosive. That this terrorist would receive the same quality of care as her son was unimaginable. But she understood the stakes. What the man said could greatly impact her future decisions, though operators had already begun to implement her course of actions.

POTUS stood immediately beside the Russian's bed.

"Has he said anything?"

A doctor began his reply until shushed by the Leader of the Free World.

"Oh," he said, stepping away from POTUS and deferring to the Secret Service agent who had been at the wounded man's side since he was brought in.

"No, ma'am. At least not anything useful. He's mentioned 'Larisa' a couple of times; his wife. But, no, nothing about his actions."

"What's the prognosis?"

The president waited impatiently for the doctor to realize she was speaking to him now.

"Oh." He stepped forward and back into the conversation. "Well, frankly, it's a miracle he's still breathing. We all admire his…"

The doctor slammed on his verbal brakes at the intense glare from the president at his use of the word "admire."

"What I mean to say is that, medically speaking, it's remarkable that he made it off the pavement and into the ambulance."

"Can I speak to the man?"

"Might as well try, I suppose. Hell, none of you are supposed to be in here anyhow."

The impudence of the thirty-five-year-old doctor earned him another stare from Hendrickson that persisted for several seconds.

"What would you have me say?" came a barely audible voice from the bed.

Multiple sets of eyes turned to the patient.

"Do you know who I am?"

"Of course. Surprised to see you – alive, at least," Borzilov said in perfect English before fading somewhat.

"What is your name?"

When the patient failed to answer, the president shook his arm. The doctor intervened but she persisted until the gaunt eyes reopened.

"Your name?"

"You know my name. Gennadiy Valeryevich Borzilov." The reply was weak. The man's monitor showed a marked increase in his pulse.

The doctor stepped in to try to intervene again when a burly Secret Service agent turned him away with both arms and led him from the room.

"Who sent you? Why did you do this?"

Borzilov's eyes drooped more noticeably and his voice diminished to a whisper.

"What do you want to know?" The SVR agent spoke in Russian now. The FBI translator in the room interpreted the content for POTUS. She leaned closer to the man as he continued, despite his tenuous condition, to relate the story his handlers had scripted for him in the event he was captured.

"All I do, I do for Mother Russia. My government renounces your treachery. SVR was tasked with making the move against..." The man's voice faded so the interpreter leaned in as closely as POTUS now to catch every word, relaying them as quickly as he could. The foreign agent's pulse elevated even further as he continued.

"Comrade President Tatarov ordered us to remove you... to kill you..."

The interpreter hesitated at hearing the words but dutifully passed them on.

Upon hearing the translation, POTUS said softly, with a mixture of fear and regret, "So it *was* Russia." The confirmation set in stone the plans that until now had still been tentative.

"Larisa..." the voice continued weakly.

"Why?" demanded the president. She shook the enemy's arm without response.

The Russian relaxed and upon losing consciousness, his pulse returned to a more or less steady rate.

President Hendrickson knew it was pointless to continue.

"Are you sure you got everything?"

The interpreter replied that he was confident he did. "But we'll review the recordings that we've been making since we got him," he assured, hooking his thumb at the twin video units with extended boom microphones. Hendrickson had been so focused on Borzilov that she had been oblivious to the redundant recording devices, including the smaller boom that was fixed to the rail of the hospital bed pointing a mic toward the occupant's face.

In possession of the knowledge she had come to get, President Sandra Hendrickson moved for the door. As she passed the sulking doctor outside the room, she ordered, "He has to live. Do you understand?"

The obstinate physician simply stared at the woman who would presume to order him around. When she stepped forward with raised eyebrows and a hardened expression, he reconsidered his tone.

"Yes, Madam President. We'll do everything we can."

Resuming her exit, she said to Chief of Staff Chandler. "I want the best medical team in the country on this. He can't die."

"Yes, ma'am." Chandler began to consult with the doctors.

✦

At the George Bush Center for Intelligence in Langley, Virginia, Director of Central Intelligence Parnell flicked at her private mobile phone on her desktop, spinning it about until it stopped and then she would start it again. Her Agency phone remained safely in her desk drawer. She gathered her personal device and carried it with her to the window overlooking the snow-covered complex before her.

As if to complete the action before her resolve faded, the CIA director selected a name from her Contacts and waited.

"Betsy," came the answer from the other end of the call. The greeting by the receiver didn't disclose any trace of surprise.

"So, Ryan, I suppose you have a way to reach the man we talked about earlier, a personal number."

Ryan Crenshaw, her former boss, recited the personal phone number of Russian SVR Director Pavel Semyonovich Orlov.

Without another word, Parnell ended the call.

She sat at her desk and began to tap numbers on the digital keypad of her disposable phone before she could change her mind.

A voice thousands of miles away answered.

"*Da?*"

"This is CIA Director Parnell," said the caller in perfect Russian. "I apologize for the lateness."

"Not at all," assured her Russian counterpart. "Our mutual friend said you might call."

◆

In Josh and Maggie's apartment, a self-satisfied and relieved Ryan Crenshaw placed his phone back in his pocket and returned to the sofa in front of the TV to await the press briefing with his younger friend.

The pair finished off their late lunches and sat silently for fifteen minutes until the LED screen changed to a view of the podium in the White House press room. Momentarily, Josh's fiancée walked to the area behind the lectern, followed by Secret Service Director Keith Cortland, FBI Director Gabriel Austin, and presidential Chief of Staff Noah Chandler.

Maggie stepped to the dais.

"Good afternoon and thank you for coming." The press secretary always said that although, in truth, where else would these people be. It was their jobs and moreover, the White House was the official source for administration information, even if the communications were somewhat obtuse and incomplete.

"The events of the last several days have been some of the most cataclysmic in our nation's history. To bring you up to date, Chief of Staff Noah Chandler."

"Thank you, Secretary Loughlin. These events underscore the peril of being a strong voice for freedom in a world where opposing elements often resort to violent means to achieve their ends. In the two attacks, we have witnessed the extent to which evildoers will go to interfere with our leadership in the world.

"Before turning things over to Director Cortland, let me pass along President Hendrickson's own assurances that she is fine. She was not in the limousine at the time that today's attempt on her life was made. She thanks you for your concern and passes along her condolences to the family of her driver, Agent Mark Simpson, who lost his life in the attack.

"After the first attempt on the president's life at St. John's Episcopal Church on Inauguration Day, precautions were put into place. The need for the efforts was reinforced by evidence that the terrorist behind the bombing was still in the area. That fact suggested that a second attempt might be in the offing.

'To explain those precautions, here is Secret Service Director Keith Cortland."

The head of the department that, among other things, carried out the protective services for the president spoke for about fifteen minutes. He provided a general overview of the use of stand-ins and mannequins on the occasions that POTUS would be out of the White House. The president, he disclosed, was never in a position where she would be visible to anyone since she returned from the hospital after the church bombing.

Cortland really provided no details; only the general narrative that they had made the decision to keep the president entirely out of the public view.

Following the Secret Service head, the FBI director provided a not-so-helpful update on the investigation that had led to Borzilov, though he didn't reveal his name, and the nature of ongoing information-gathering and follow-up on leads.

Following the two directors, Chandler returned to the podium.

"We'll take a few questions now. Yes?"

In the chaotic thrust of arms into the air and the shouts for attention, QNN's Chief White House Correspondent Emery Sorensen got the first question, as he often did.

"We know that the subject of the massive manhunt was a Russian male; a QNN source has identified that man as a junior Russian embassy diplomat named Gennadiy Valeryevich Borzilov. Can you confirm that?"

Maggie and the three gentlemen on the platform maintained their passive expressions. Perfect poker faces were a job requirement for anyone who wished to rise to their positions. But to each, the unspoken question was the same: "How the hell did they get that?"

Sorensen had received the scoop from a junior colleague who had a source inside the Russian embassy. It went without saying that the junior reporter had a promising future at the network.

FBI Director Austin leaned in from his place behind the chief of staff and said only, "We can't comment on the specifics of an ongoing investigation." But he and the others on the stage knew that they would have to go public with the name soon. Doing so would confirm his position in the embassy and lead to wild speculation about the extent to which the Russian Federation was involved in the bombing. The pursuit of sources and scoops would be manic and that always led to a mix of fiction with truth.

Other hands shot up and voices competed for attention. Most were assuming the identification of Borzilov as the perpetrator to now be fact, if only because of the absence of an outright denial. The shouts included questions about what his role was at the embassy. Was he considered to be a spy? Was he acting on behalf of the Russian government? And each "no comment" or "we can't confirm or deny that" added more credibility to the ID.

It was difficult to regain control of the briefing, especially without more self-inflicted damage by way of refusing to answer questions directly.

After the briefing, the chief of staff called his boss. She had watched the conference from her office and agreed that a statement confirming Borzilov as the suspect was necessary. She asked the chief to huddle with agencies' directors and the acting press secretary to prepare a press release to that effect. A spoken announcement would be better, but it would only open the door for more questions. A written release controlled the situation somewhat because it was one-sided.

◆

Interested parties watched the briefing around the world. Among those were Russian President Boris Tatarov, SVR Director Pavel Orlov, and Russian Foreign Minister Jaromir Davydov. Like the men in Washington, they, too, had to prepare a response to the disclosure of what they already knew. The decision that was most critical was whether to deny the account or to acknowledge Borzilov as the actor while denying any involvement of the Russian Federation and branding him as a lunatic who acted alone. The first option, denial, would be difficult since their agent was in the custody of the Americans. However, the Russians had never shied from assertions that conflicted with the truth. The second explanation, positioning their agent as a lone wolf would not only be simpler but had the added benefit of being the truth, each man believed.

Independently, their investigations had uncovered no hint that any agency had gone rogue and acted on its own to launch an attack on the American leader on American soil. One fact they would not disclose but supported the single rogue agent story was that his wife and children had disappeared. The SVR director had sent operatives to their flat to question them but they were not to be found and had not shown up in the time since then. The search for Larisa Borzilova and the boy and girl continued.

◆

Not very far from where the Russian officials watched the press briefing, another trio did the same. They raged at the second failure of their proxy to kill the American president. And the fact that Borzilov was in custody made it impossible for him to try again.

One of the two men in the group pulled his handgun from his pocket.

"What are you doing?" asked the second.

"What we said we would do if the imbecile failed. He has failed twice."

The woman agreed with a simple nod of her head.

The second man contended, "There will be enough time for that. Perhaps he will yet prove useful to us."

The woman understood, "I see. You are saying that our goal was the death of the American leader. But there were other pieces of the puzzle that might still come to be."

The first man argued, "And what if they do? Will the end result change? And it would not be because of Borzilov anyhow. We have kept the woman and his children alive only for leverage, have we not?"

His partners both nodded.

"Then we must separate ourselves from this situation now."

The other man reluctantly agreed. The woman cast her vote with only another nod of her head and followed the first into where the three prisoners were as he attached the cylindrical accessory to his gun.

Larisa Antonovna Borzilova, young Valeriy, and the youngest, Ulyana, had been treated relatively kindly during their captivity in the country cottage. And their end would be merciful now.

Outside the bedroom, the second of the two men who had reluctantly agreed to this final resolution heard it in the form of muffled metallic clacks and the almost inaudible accompanying pops.

The pair was emotionless when they returned to the central room where their partner was already gathering their belongings. They would perform a cursory wipe-down though a thorough cleaning of their prints would be impossible. They had been in the house for several days, cooking, building fires, while watching the television feed on their phones for news of their operation. They had, in essence, inhabited the dwelling as if it had been home. So, leaving behind a few prints would be unavoidable.

Bringing very little along with them when they transported their abductees to the hideout, they had very little to take with them as they left. Within thirty minutes of disposing of their hostages, the trio was on their way.

✦

At the conclusion of the television-watching meeting with his compatriots, SVR Director Orlov reflected on his clandestine phone conversation with the American Head Spy Parnell and wondered how he would be able to keep it unknown. Of course, he suspected she was in the same predicament.

✦

Director Parnell considered everything that SVR Head Orlov had told her. How much, if anything, was factual? The one thing that underpinned her desire to accept the conversation as true was her steadfast trust in Ryan Crenshaw. He was among the two or three most honorable men she had ever known. And his commitment to his country was unmatched.

She went into the anteroom of her office and dialed Crenshaw's number. The tone of his voice was expectant.

"Hi, Bets."

"Hi, Ryan. I don't know what to think. I've got all this information that, if true, tells me we're on the wrong track with this thing.

"Orlov was very forthcoming. But of course, we're all practiced at sounding helpful, aren't we? Anyhow, the *Direktor* insists that the Federation had zero to do with this – not officially or by way of some rogue agency. Everyone at the top there is firm in the belief that their guy acted alone. Or, if not alone, his support wasn't from any Russian bureau.

"Orlov gave me all sorts of information about Borzilov. I wrote as fast as I could but couldn't keep up. He certainly couldn't transmit it to me."

"Have him send it to me."

Parnell surprised Crenshaw. "I already arranged that."

"When he does, I'll get it to you somehow. I'll bring it out there."

"That's the thing, Ryan. I've heard all this background info, possible legends, history, ops he was involved in. An entire file on Borzilov is probably coming. And yet…"

"You can't do anything with it."

"Exactly. I don't even want it in my possession."

"So, what do you want me to do with it? Why'd you even have Orlov send it if you didn't want it?"

"Don't ask me, pal." His former protégé's sigh was apparent even on the phone. "Keep it, Ryan. I can't believe I said that. But keep it and use it however you can. But be careful. Just having that information could be construed as treason."

"I'll be careful. The risk is worth it."

"And Ryan, share with your friend there. He's resourceful and has connections. If he's willing, that is, read him in."

"Was already planning on it. Thanks Betsy."

Crenshaw was about to touch the icon to disconnect when he heard his former subordinate in the U.S. embassy in Moscow speak again.

"And one more thing. I think you're right. I think this is looking more and more, at least to me, like we're about to go to war for no reason. Just wanted you to know, I'm with you. You were right."

Parnell disconnected her call. She had an enormous workload ahead of her for today – really, indefinitely – or she would take the day off and go home and drink. In a matter of minutes her immediate reports would come in to discuss their findings about this crisis. Intelligence failures were many. Nobody had seen any of this coming, so they were starting from ground zero.

Parnell would direct the intel collection and analysis with a presumption that the Russians were innocent of involvement. But selling that position might prove impossible. Everybody in the administration was certain that the Russian Federation had attempted to assassinate the chief executive and that it was incumbent on our sovereignty to respond reciprocally.

She felt like the Lone Ranger. Actually, she decided, she felt like Tonto. Ryan Crenshaw was now the Lone Ranger. Or was Josh Morgan Tonto?

"God. Get a grip, Bets," she demanded to herself.

✦

It was 4:30 PM at the apartment. Josh and Ryan were drinking flavored water and snacking on assorted bags of munchies, though they were giving thought to moving on to the brandy from last night.

Crenshaw had just completed filling Morgan in on his conversation with the CIA Chief when his cell phone dinged to announce new email. He opened the mail and the accompanying attachment and held up the device to show Morgan a very ordinary, very postcard-like picture of the Eiffel Tower. He arched his eyebrows up and down several times. Morgan couldn't interpret the impish smile his friend had.

"Uh, nice." The younger man was trying to be polite, but his lack of understanding was getting in the way.

Crenshaw gave the very recognizable and accepted "come with me" signal with his left index finger. Morgan watched while Crenshaw went into the guest bedroom to retrieve his laptop and returned to the dining table where he opened it and turned it on.

Momentarily the welcome screen appeared, and the former Russian professor typed in his password. In short order, he opened the same picture from Paris that he had shown his former Russian language student on his phone.

The email recipient's delight was obvious.

Morgan could only muster, "Okay…"

"Just watch," came the plea.

Crenshaw launched an app on his computer. He dragged the icon for the Eiffel Tower file into an empty frame. With a click of the decrypt "button" the man repeated, "Just watch."

The image enlarged and changed in appearance so that it was very pixelized. Several pixels at a time flipped vertically or rotated and then "flew" off the image of the Parisian landmark. As the Tower disappeared, pixel by pixel, another image, unrecognizable at first, began to emerge.

Morgan understood.

Finally, an image of a single file folder replaced the photograph. Another window asked, "Extract?" Crenshaw clicked, "Yes." A flurry of activity resumed on the display, much more rapidly than the first. Additional icon representations of file folders flew into a newly opened window where they neatly stacked "behind" one another until the process was complete.

The new prompt asked, "Decrypt another?" Crenshaw answered "no" with a mouse click and the app closed.

Before the two sets of eyes was the entire SVR personnel file of Gennadiy Valeryevich Borzilov. They opened random folders and the files they contained and were surprised to find that none of the text was redacted.

Both former professor and former student – and both former CIA case officers – were perfectly fluent in Russian so they flew through mounds of data. They had scarcely made a dent in the information after an hour of reading.

Finally, Morgan asked, "What're we gonna do with this?"

His mentor's eyes never strayed from the screen. "I don't know. I hoped you'd come up with something."

✦

Noah Chandler, Gabe Austin, Keith Cortland, and Maggie Loughlin had huddled for almost four hours debating the construction of what would finally result in a terse, matter of fact press release that would serve to confirm what all the networks were already reporting; that Borzilov was the culprit behind the bombings. The wording was as important as anything, but paramount was that the content had to reveal something that the QNN reporter hadn't already made known. Unfortunately for the three individuals driving the wording for the release, there wasn't anything they wanted to make public at this juncture.

Maggie suggested, "If we can't disclose anything new, then let's shift the goal. What we should suggest is this: The White House is being completely transparent, and the administration is out in front of this thing."

All agreed in the direction, but the three officials insisted on wording that Maggie disagreed with. Being the newbie, she was reluctant to challenge them.

So, the chief and the two directors nibbled at the food that the White House kitchen staff brought into the Cabinet Room and waited on the acting press secretary as she typed, retyped, composed, and reworded. They talked quietly among themselves until Maggie rewarded them with her composition. It consisted solely of the men's words, so she felt like she was merely transcribing dictation.

Each opened the shared draft on their respective tablets and read silently.

"The White House acknowledges that the man arrested by agents of the Secret Service has been identified as Russian national Gennadiy Valeryevich Borzilov. Borzilov is in critical condition at Walter Reed National Military Medical Center from wounds suffered during his attack on the presidential limousine.

"Borzilov was a low-level diplomat at the Russian embassy though it is not known if other individuals or the Russian government were involved. The FBI had identified Borzilov as the primary suspect in the St. John's bombing and he had been the subject of an intense manhunt and had been under surveillance for a short period.

"Every resource of the administration, the Secret Service, the FBI, and every arm of the intelligence and law enforcement communities are working around the clock. We are investigating every lead and will release information as we can."

The three men looked at each other with satisfaction, practically imparting verbal pats on their backs for a job well done, and prepared to leave. Maggie, on the other hand, decided she had to speak up.

"Excuse me, Chief Chandler, gentlemen." Maggie's words interrupted their departure. "May I run another draft by you? I'm sorry to keep you but I think there are some minor changes we can make to improve on this."

Chandler was the only one who seemed eager to listen. The two agency directors showed some disdain for a presumptuous, self-absorbed flunky who was only in her job because of the misfortune of someone else.

"Go ahead, Maggie. I know the president will welcome your contributions."

Maggie felt a little more confident because of the show of support the chief of staff had just provided merely through his willingness to hear her out and, more powerfully, by invoking POTUS' name.

The other two men returned to their chairs.

Maggie dropped her draft in the shared folder so the other team members could assess it.

The new version – her version – read:

"The White House has identified the man arrested by agents of the Secret Service as Russian National Gennadiy Valeryevich Borzilov. Borzilov is in 'critical' condition at Walter Reed National Military Medical Center from wounds sustained during his attack on the presidential limousine.

"Borzilov was a low-level employee at the Russian embassy though it is not known if other individuals or the Russian government were involved. The FBI had identified Borzilov as the primary suspect in the St. John's bombing and had made him the subject of an intensive manhunt. The Bureau and the Secret Service had developed preemptive tactics that successfully ensured the safety of the president.

"The Secret Service, the FBI, and every arm of the intelligence and law enforcement communities are working around the clock. We are investigating every lead and will release information when we can be sure that doing so will not jeopardize the investigation."

Austin spoke first. "There are quite a few changes here."

Cortland rebutted," Frankly, I don't see the difference."

Maggie tried to be gracious.

"'Acknowledges' implied QNN knew about Borzilov before you did. They didn't. You simply hadn't announced his name. Don't defer to them about something that's untrue. Next, I don't think we should ascribe his condition as 'suffering.' He brought this on himself.

"Also, I think identifying him as a 'diplomat,' true or not, elevated his status. 'Low-level employee' marginalizes him to a degree. It may serve to disassociate him from the Russian government.

"And, pardon my directness, gentlemen. I know you wanted to highlight your investigative successes and that you were closing in on Borzilov. But if he was 'under surveillance,' how'd he get so close to the president, or at least her limo? Instead, take credit for the remarkable thing you did do. You protected – heck, likely saved the president's life.

"Lastly, explain why there is sometimes a delay in providing information. You aren't just being secretive. You're continuing your investigation. By god, you're going to get to the bottom of this and if that means withholding information for a little while, then that's what you'll do. Most people will understand if you just tell them why."

Maggie was a little uncomfortable atop the soapbox she found herself on and wasn't sure how she got there.

"Agreed!" came the stamp of approval from the president's chief.

The others took longer to come around and their approval wasn't as enthusiastic as Chandler's but when they did, their consent was no less sincere.

"I see your point, Maggie," Austin finally admitted.

"Yes. Well done. Thank you, Maggie," offered Cortland.

Chandler wrapped up the session. "Get one of your team to type that up, Maggie, and ask them to distribute it to the press corps. Thank you, Gabe; Keith."

Upon adjourning the meeting, Noah Chandler gave Maggie a smile and a thumbs up. He only mouthed the words, "Nice job!"

✦

Maggie arrived home to see Josh and Ryan Crenshaw engrossed so completely in whatever was on the guest's computer that they never noticed her until she was upon them.

"Hi, guys!"

The "deer in the headlights look" on the men's faces was instantaneous and identical. Crenshaw sheepishly lowered the laptop's lid like a schoolboy caught with a "Playboy."

"Watching porn?"

Josh jumped up from his chair a little too enthusiastically, Maggie thought, but she didn't doubt he was glad to see her.

"Hi, sweetheart."

"Hey, Morgan." She peeked around her fiancé's hug and waved at their house guest. "Hi, Ryan."

"Hello, Maggie. I guess there's a sigh of relief around the office."

"You have no idea. There's still the bigger problem of the tension with Russia but at least this animal is off the street."

"Any evidence he had help?" asked Morgan.

Maggie had to think through what she could and couldn't say. "What I can say, Morgan, is that at least one other person was involved but it was unwitting. So far, there aren't any known co-conspirators."

"Spoken like a true press secretary, honey. What do you say we all go out to eat?"

"I'm gonna beg off but you guys go ahead. I've got to try to get some sleep."

Morgan looked at Ryan, who nodded. They grabbed their coats and gloves and were out the door.

"Have fun, you two."

Maggie hit the sack.

Morgan and Crenshaw found a sports grill and ordered burgers and beer.

"So, what do we do first?"

Ryan Crenshaw had no clue, but he knew there was one prerequisite. "We have to wait to see if Borzilov gives up any information that clears Russia of any role in this. If he acted alone or at some other entity's behest, all this goes away."

"Right. But what if he confesses to be an agent of the Russian Federation?"

The men cut off the conversation while the waiter brought their drinks. A smile; a thank you; and quick toast and the two were back on point.

"If he acted under orders from the Kremlin, and I'm wrong, then…" Crenshaw took a long drink of his ale, "…God help us all."

"Yeah."

"You know, Morgan, when I asked you to go see Betsy with me, Borzilov wasn't in custody yet. That changed everything. Or at least, has the potential to."

"So, we have some leeway in regard to time."

"Exactly. We can just wait."

✦

At 9:30 PM President Hendrickson's phone rang. It was General Richards.

"Nemesis is at Preamble. Operation Retribution is in the Foyer."

"Thank you, General. Good night."

CHAPTER 22

Day 10 – Monday

Russia's annexation of the Ukrainian peninsula of Crimea enflamed tensions between that nation and the West. The Kremlin's support for separatists in eastern Ukraine also made other Baltic nations more nervous and suspicious of Russian intensions for the region.

One result was that it opened doors for the United States and other Western governments. To bolster the confidence of NATO allies in U.S. support and reassure them of its ongoing commitment, in 2014 Washington initiated Operation Atlantic Resolve. Consequently, previously resistant nations became receptive to joint training exercises and other forms of cooperation. The United States increased its submarine presence in the Baltic Sea and provided more generous forms of logistical support.

One part of Operation Atlantic Resolve was a joint training mission of the United States and Finland. The U.S. deployed six jets from the 173rd Fighter Wing at Kingsley Field Air National Guard Base in Oregon to train alongside the Finnish Air Force.

So, it wasn't without precedent when a United States MC-130J Commando II landed in Kuopio, Finland, about 100 miles west of the border with Russia. The massive plane completed its rollout and made its way to a hangar. Doors closed behind it to shield it from curious eyes. There was really no way to guarantee people wouldn't know of its presence but landing at 2:30 AM definitely helped.

✦

The night passed quickly for Sandra Hendrickson. The days were passing quickly, too. "Seven o'clock here, so…" she muttered.

POTUS tapped an icon on her smart phone and looked at the "reference card" that opened on the display.

"So, Finland," she continued, "two in the afternoon. Three o'clock in Moscow."

She sipped the coffee that her staff had brought her. "In the planning meeting, General Richards called the SPIRIT Teams the 'tip of the spear,'" she recalled. "Let's hope they're as good as he says. Or this thing's over before it starts."

Sandy called her husband at the hospital. "Darling, I can't tell you how much I love you and how much I appreciate you. You've been remarkable, a rock. You've been with AJ day and night. And I've... been... it's just... I've..."

"Sandy... sweetheart, don't say that. You've been a rock, too. I'm sorry I was angry with you the other day. To be honest, I resented you. I believed you should've been here. But the way things have turned out... with the possibility that Russia did it... you were right. You've got the whole damn country to think about. And things look pretty bleak. I wish I could be there with you. This whole thing's been a nightmare."

"I know, Adam." She cleared her throat. "But you're right where you need to be."

The husband and wife hung up.

Mom desperately wanted to be just that. Just Mom. And just plain old Sandy. Not the president. Not the "Most Powerful Woman in the World" or the "Leader of the Free World." She'd give anything to go back a few years and make a different decision and never enter politics.

"But here I am."

She forced herself to eat her breakfast. Then she dressed for what promised to be another eventful day.

✦

FBI analysts and technicians were going through the latest trove of items that agents had gathered as evidence from Borzilov's most recent motel room the previous day.

FBI Lab Technician Carl "Smitty" Smith said aloud, "The guy got sloppy. Guess he figured he was untouchable. Or maybe he knew the endgame was at hand. At any rate..."

The tech looked at the two plastic evidence bags he held. Each contained a burner phone, more precisely a used burner phone. Each had phone numbers from previous calls. "These," Smitty knew, "should've been 'burned,' thrown away. And somewhere far away from his motel room."

The bomb-making materials were consistent with those used at St. John's. Definitely Russian. Very sophisticated. Beyond state of the art. These would set the standard for years to come. You didn't just pick these up on the Black

Market.

"So that supports the notion that the guy is a Russian with the highest-level skills," the techie concluded. But elsewhere at FBI headquarters, agents were considering evidence that made their prisoner seem like a rookie.

Supervisory Special Agent Annie Liu was reviewing digital recordings of Gennadiy Borzilov's confession to POTUS that he was acting "for the Motherland."

Deputy Director Tony Drake "rewound" the digital file to see and hear it again and stated, "I agree with you, Annie. He gave it up pretty fast and under no duress whatsoever."

Annie stretched and stood to walk around. It had been a long few days. "Granted, he was on morphine but the SVR, FSB, GRU – they're all just like the old KGB. Their operatives are all trained to withstand torture, drugging, the works and they'll hold out a long time before they say anything. This bastard blurts it out like he's dying to tell somebody."

Drake continued her line of thought. "He acted more like some al-Qaeda terrorist about to cut off somebody's head online or blow himself up in a crowded area and shouts 'Allahu Akbar' to make sure everyone knows his allegiance."

Liu picked it up again. "Russian agents will do whatever they must to keep from giving up any useful info. They'll protect Mother Russia with their lives. Certainly, they'll resist as long as they can. I'm Russia, the last thing I want is to be uncovered as the bad guy."

"I'm Russia," Drake counters, "I don't do this thing in the first place. There're all sorts of ways to attack us if you have some agenda. But killing our president? No backing down from that. It'll be war."

"And what do they gain from that?" Liu concluded.

The pair silently considered everything they had as evidence for a while.

"It all points to the Kremlin. What if we're overthinking this, Annie?"

"If it walks like a duck, etc.?"

"Yeah. I get that. Maybe Borzilov was just addled. I don't know."

"I'm sure I don't either, Tony. But we don't have long to figure it out."

The pair watched the recording several more times.

"I need more coffee," Drake said with a yawn.

"I need a vacation." Annie folded her arms on the table in front of her and rested her head on them. "Shit."

✦

President Hendrickson and her war team were in the Cabinet Room, as they had been several times recently.

The Navy Chief of Staff detailed the deployment of two additional submarines to the Baltic to supplement the ones already there. The Sixth Fleet was being deployed behind its flagship, the USS Mount Whitney, to the Eastern Mediterranean.

He reported that the nuclear-powered aircraft carrier U.S.S. Harry S. Truman had set sail from Norfolk last night with a strike group of five escort warships. He continued for another five minutes to describe the largest Naval deployment of all time.

The Air Force Chief described a similar level of air readiness with strike forces deploying in Germany, Poland, Turkey, the Czech Republic, Finland, and other nations. Sweden and Romania had refused to allow an expanded U.S. presence but generally speaking, most nations were receptive to cooperating in light of the apparent Russian attempt on the American president.

The remaining Chiefs reported similar preparedness.

Chief of Staff Chandler looked up from his phone and interrupted the presentations.

"Excuse me, Madam President. Russian Foreign Minister Davydov is making a statement."

POTUS nodded and an aide turned on the room's television.

The screen transformed from documents explaining some part of the war plan to a live picture of the man who represented the nation that the war plans concerned. Minister Davydov's voice was audible, though muted, while the interpreter's words took the lead. Davydov had a severe expression as he voiced his country's rebuttal to the American accusations.

"While the Russian Federation remains sympathetic to the tragedy in the United States, we must again protest the vile and outlandish suggestion that we are in any way responsible for it.

"The American government has interfered in the affairs of the Russian Federation and our allies throughout the world for decades and has been responsible for untold deaths. But the Russian people have never engaged in such immoral acts…"

The chief of staff whispered to the person next to him, "I'm sure everyone believes that."

"The American president has taken the unprecedented and provocative act of expelling our national representatives from our embassy. She has further accused us of the horrible act of assassination. The man in custody is indeed a Russian citizen and was in the employ of our delegation as a low-ranking diplomat and nothing more. He has no association with our intelligence agencies and, if proven to be responsible for this despicable act, he did so without the authorization, support, or knowledge of the Russian Federation.

"In a short time, our ambassador to the United Nations will file a formal complaint to the international community, who we are certain will join us in our objection to the reprehensible allegation. Around the Russian borders the United States is amassing unprecedented military forces, an unmistakable provocation that can only be a prelude to war.

"While we are hopeful that an apology will be forthcoming and the accusation withdrawn, be certain that Russia will defend ourselves against this unwarranted aggression."

In the Cabinet Room, heads were shaking. Anger was apparent on the faces of everyone. The president punctuated the prevailing sentiment with an uncharacteristic and decidedly unladylike, "Go to hell!"

Murmurs of agreement were evidence of the support for the president. She spoke again, this time to SecState.

"Secretary Lively, I have no doubt your team is already on this but have them go over that statement meticulously and prepare a response. Make sure the bastards know we're serious."

POTUS sat momentarily in silence, tapping her lips with her index finger. Then she moved her hand and her tapping to the paper pad on the table's surface. She took a deep breath and joined both hands together with her chin resting on her extended index fingers. Then with a decision apparently reached, she turned to the Chairman of the Joint Chiefs of Staff.

"General Richards, please give the order to raise our threat level to DEFCON 2."

The general's aide pressed a speed dial number on the phone and handed it to his superior, who rose to head for the door.

Though regarded as the last step before nuclear war, the second highest Defense Condition, code named "Fast Pace," had a technical definition that ordered U.S. Armed Forces to make ready to deploy and engage in less than 6 hours. In reality, the US military's preparation was well beyond that anyhow. While nobody in the room believed engagement to be that imminent, it was nevertheless a necessary step and would send a clear signal to the Russian Federation of the willingness to hold them accountable for their deplorable acts against the United States.

✦

Gennadiy Borzilov lay in his hospital bed. The entire medical team treating him marveled at his progress. The bomber's condition was upgraded to "serious but stable." From their perspective as doctors and nurses, they felt some measure of relief and even accomplishment at the improved health of their patient. It was remarkable that he had some possibility of surviving, as the president's order to them demanded.

The Secret Service and FBI agents hovering outside the Russian's room couldn't care less about his survival chances. Their only concerns were, could he talk, and how soon?

Interrogators had forced their way into his room a couple of times, only to be frustrated by the prisoner's inability to remain awake. And whenever he stirred briefly, he was unwilling to answer questions. It seemed that he was only prepared – or able – to speak with his intended target, the president.

Finally, around ten o'clock his alertness improved to a point where questioning might be productive.

FBI Special Agents Russell and Jeffries stood on each side of his bed.

"Can you answer some questions?" asked Jeffries.

"I want a lawyer."

"Miles, the man wants a lawyer," Russell said to his partner. "Do you think he should get a lawyer?"

"I don't think he should get one, Phil. And we're not required to provide one." Miles Jeffries directed his words to the injured man. "You see, Gennadiy, you're a terrorist so we don't have to allow you to speak with an attorney."

In truth, there was an ongoing debate within the FBI about the man's status and his right to an attorney. The legality was uncertain enough that one was even then in the waiting room down the hall. For the time being, the decision had been made to proceed with questions. Even if the interrogation was thrown out in its entirety because the man had been denied legal counsel, any information he provided could move the investigation further along.

Even without anything he might divulge at this point, if it were to be thrown out, the case against him remained ironclad. An enormous pool of witnesses had observed him at the hospital when he attacked the motorcade. He was even recorded on security cameras. His conviction was a lock so the risk of any information being deemed inadmissible was worth taking.

Both agents waited for a reply.

"I have diplomatic immunity," came Borzilov's assertion.

This, too, had been a topic of discussion among the FBI's legal team. Though they felt he wasn't entitled to the claim, the fact was that the Russian ambassador, perhaps unwittingly, had virtually nullified the status with his briefing this morning. A number of counselors had anticipated that Russia might initiate the immunity claim to enable their representatives to place guards with their spy to protect him from interrogation. Even if he had gone rogue, Bureau lawyers thought that would've been the smart play. But it looked as if the Russian was on his own.

"Sorry, comrade. Your country has sold you out. You're all alone, it appears."

Just as the Special Agents prepared to begin questioning the man, the door to his room opened. A consensus had been reached about his right to an attorney and it was that the government should err on the side of caution. So, the court-appointed attorney arrived. A translator was also provided out of an abundance of caution. Though they knew the Russian agent spoke perfect English, the FBI legal team deemed having an advocate fluent in his native language a necessary accommodation.

"Agents, I'd like to speak with my client."

Special Agents Jeffries and Russell were livid. They believed the man had no right to anything in the way of assistance. Nevertheless, they prepared to oblige the attorney.

Before they left the room, Borzilov's new attorney made a second demand. "Please turn off the recordings."

Even more furious, Russell walked to the console managing the cameras, microphones and other devices and, with the flip of a single master switch, powered down all of the electronics.

◆

In the United Nations building in New York City a confrontation was brewing unlike any seen in a meeting of the General Assembly since U.S. Ambassador Adlai Stevenson stared down Valerian Alexandrovich Zorin, the Soviet representative to the UN, during the Cuban Missile Crisis. Stevenson famously demanded an answer regarding the presence of Soviet missiles in Cuba by asking, "Do you, Ambassador Zorin, deny that the U.S.S.R. has placed, and is placing, medium- and intermediate-range missiles and sites in Cuba? Yes or no -- don't wait for the translation -- yes or no?"

In a remarkable moment before the international body, current UN Ambassador Kathleen Schroder, by design, channeled Stevenson to her adversary, Russian Ambassador Zhenka Vitaliyevich Bazhanov.

"Do you, Ambassador Bazhanov, deny that the Russian Federation dispatched SVR Agent Gennadiy Valeryevich Borzilov to assassinate President Sandra Hendrickson? Yes or no -- don't wait for the translation -- yes or no?"

Bazhanov was appalled at the impudence to try to embarrass him with the words from the Cold War. Unlike Zorin in October of 1962, the current ambassador had explicit instructions from the Kremlin. He squirmed, nonetheless.

The Russian diplomat was about to speak when Ambassador Schroder deliberately preempted him, "Let me help you out, ambassador." On the two large screens at the front of the General Assembly Hall of the United Nations Headquarters, a crystal-clear image with accompanying high-quality audio showed Gennadiy Borzilov confessing to trying to kill the American leader under orders from his homeland.

Despite Bazhanov's protestations and denials, his attempts to label Borzilov as a liar and a rogue agent, the damage had been done. The United States of America, on the world stage, had justified its intentions to go to war with Russia.

✦

Borzilov didn't trust the lawyer who was there to represent him. His request was simply a means to buy time.

The attorney asked about his family. That information was acquired easily enough because his profile, as a diplomat at the embassy, would have been provided as a matter of law to the American State Department, which would disseminate it throughout the various U.S. agencies. Most of the biography, however, would've been fiction, crafted to paint the picture of a low-level diplomat and nothing more.

However, as the Russian listened to the man, his thoughts turned to his family and those thoughts were altering his perspective on his actions. His mind began to reel with the possible events that would result. The ones he considered now were broader in scope than the narrower subject of the fate of his family, although it was his family's situation that provoked the change in his thinking. His mind was still filled with cobwebs, but it was clear enough that some objectivity began to penetrate the fog.

If his original attempt on the life of the American leader had succeeded, he would have been safely out of the United States and would've taken his family from Moscow to the third country that would've been their new home. But the fact was that he had failed. He knew before his second effort that the likelihood of getting out of the country, or even surviving, was almost nil.

His handlers had threatened Larisa and the children to force him into this operation. They had kept them alive as ongoing leverage. He failed the second time, too. But even if had succeeded, he would never have made it back to Russia alive, let alone the new home promised his family.

His stomach knotted as he let himself contemplate that his family was dead. What reason would there to be to spare them?

The results of his actions were supposed to be and would certainly be war. To what end? The politics of escalating tensions between America and Russia had not mattered to him but the thought of possibly millions of people dying under the ensuing mushroom clouds had come to bother him tremendously.

So even as Borzilov concluded that his family was most certainly dead, he wouldn't allow himself the time or distraction of weeping. He had to think through his options. The one that gnawed at him the most was this: Why would he continue to support the story of his handlers, whom he now considered as the murderers they were?

So, in a dramatic change of direction, Gennadiy Borzilov interrupted whatever drivel his lawyer was saying.

"I need to tell you something."

CHAPTER 23

It was 2:00 PM and Josh Morgan and Ryan Crenshaw were in their accustomed places in front of the television. Already dismayed at seeing the engagement between the U.S. and Russian ambassadors at the UN and understanding how significantly it had escalated the intensity of the crisis, they were aghast at what they were hearing now from the president.

"And so, in light of the threatening posture assumed by the Russian Federation, as made clear by the provocative words delivered by their Foreign Minister this morning, I, along with my advisors, have found it necessary to elevate our Defense Condition status to DEFCON 2.

"I encourage all of you to go about your usual business but to remain informed of developments as they occur. In due course, and possibly very soon, it might become unavoidable to enforce travel bans. We are not declaring martial law or enforcing any significant restrictions to your routines at this time. We are still hopeful for a peaceful resolution to the tensions that have arisen as a result of the bombings and the subsequent aggressive position of the Russian Federation."

In the background behind the president, Josh could see Maggie staring directly ahead with no visible reaction. His heart broke for her in being right in the middle of all the preparations for war that were without a doubt being made by the Hendrickson administration.

The president rambled on for another minute or so, but Morgan and Crenshaw tuned her out.

Morgan said, "This may really happen."

"And it might not even be the Russians behind it," observed his friend.

✦

Gennadiy Borzilov's court-appointed attorney motioned the Special Agents in with some urgency.

"My client has a different story to tell. Now he says that he did not act under orders from his government. At least, not that he's aware of."

Special Agent Miles Russell flinched at the confusion he felt upon hearing that statement. "What the hell does that mean – that he's aware of?"

Borzilov tried to explain. "Someone threatened to kill my family unless I followed orders to kill your president."

"So, there *were* orders," concluded Agent Jeffries.

"Yes... no... well, not from my agency."

"Then who?" asked Russell.

The Russian lowered his head. "I don't know."

"So," Jeffries continued, "those orders could be from your government... but you don't know?"

"Yes. But no. No. Why would they threaten my family? They wouldn't have to. I, uh, I work for the SVR." It was unusual to him to so freely admit that.

"SVR? We suspected as much," Russell confirmed. "Has your agency ever used coercion to, let's say, *persuade* you to conduct an operation you might have found questionable? I guess what I'm saying is, isn't it generally a practice of the Foreign Intelligence Service to instill a sense that your life is generally theirs? And that everything you own, all that you do, your entire family are subject to your job and their needs."

Borzilov didn't answer.

"Answer my partner, Gennadiy."

"They can be... I think your term is *heavy-handed*. They are demanding and require absolute obedience."

"So, it really could be your operation? Rather the SVR's?" Jeffries voice was raised.

"My family is likely dead!" The Russian husband and father held a quiet rage. He quivered as he spoke. "Why won't you believe me?"

And with that, the room started to spin, and the Russian passed out again.

✦

The Special Agents spoke outside in their Bureau car for privacy. Supervisory Agent Liu and Deputy Director Drake were on speaker.

Liu summarized the revelation. "So, initially he tells POTUS that he did all for country, which is the last thing we'd expect an SVR agent to admit. Now he says he was acting on his own... well, under duress... and that Mother Russia isn't involved?"

"Pretty much," said Russell.

"This story is what we would've expected in the first place from an actual agent who got caught," followed Jeffries.

"No," corrected Drake, "we would've expected silence from a trained Russian agent. Nothing for a long, long time."

"This makes no sense." Annie Liu spoke for all of them.

✦

It would be a relatively short hop for this type of mission. Two hours after takeoff, the MC-130J would make a looping turn over the Baltic Sea to return to the United States' Amari Air Base in Estonia, minus its human cargo. The Commando II would remain there for the duration of the looming conflict.

The four Rolls-Royce AE 2100D3 Turboprops mounted on the 132-foot wings of the Lockheed Martin Commando II began to move it forward. It would use up well over three thousand feet of the runway at Kuopio, Finland. In short order the almost one hundred-foot long aircraft would bank eastward and climb to its cruising altitude of twenty-eight thousand feet at a speed something less than its maximum of three-hundred sixty-two knots true air speed. Once at altitude, the Commando II would bank gently to due south and turn off its transponder and operate under what U.S. aviation calls MARSA, or Military Assumes Responsibility for Separation of Aircraft. Military aircraft weren't exempt from civilian rules for airborne conduct, so in disengaging their receiver/transmitters, the two pilots and Combat Systems Officer assumed the obligation to maintain a safe distance from other airplanes.

The scant snow on the runway showed itself as flakes spun up in spirals as the craft made its way down the runway. In the cargo area, two Loadmasters watched the six-man "tip of the spear" settle in for a short nap. By all appearances the SPIRITs were less nervous than the Loadmasters were.

✦

At about 3:30 PM, POTUS received a phone call. Hanging up, she turned her attention, or at least her face, toward her guest. Her mind was about forty-three hundred miles away with the six operators who would initiate Operation Retribution.

DCI Parnell waited respectfully for the president to reengage their conversation. Finally, Hendrickson put on her glasses and said, "I'm sorry, director. Now, where were we?"

America's head spy replied, "Not at all, Madam President."

Momentarily, before her advisor could continue her briefing, the president placed her glasses on the stack of briefing papers on her desk.

"Betsy, I know you're aware of the general timelines for each of the steps and, of course, you'll receive the flash broadcast momentarily but since you're sitting right here, I'll go ahead and tell you. That call was from General Richards. Operation Retribution has begun. Operation Nemesis, the initial phase, is underway. Our SPIRITs are airborne." And providing no more details, she resumed her meeting with the CIA chief.

Most, though not all of the topics concerned the ongoing crisis. This conference was different than most such briefings. A number of individuals normally attended the daily intelligence briefing each morning. At a minimum, National Security Advisor Ed Templeton, Director of National Intelligence Chris Donleavy, one or more experienced professional briefers, a CIA case officer, the vice president, and Parnell were present, along with subject matter experts, as needed. The faceoff with Russia was warranting additional individual sit-downs such as this one.

Director Parnell was becoming somewhat distracted herself. Finally, she removed her own eyeglasses and sat them in her lap.

"Well, Bets," she warned herself, "get ready to kiss your career goodbye. Or worse."

"Madam President, I want to fill you in on a conversation I had with Russian SVR Director Orlov."

President of the United States Sandra Hendrickson's jaw dropped. POTUS' poker face failed her miserably this time. Her bewildered countenance was so instantaneous, so intense that Elizabeth Parnell already regretted her decision to confess to the outreach to her Russian counterpart.

✦

A little less than two hours into the Commando II's flight, one of the plane's Loadmasters declared over the communications system, "Stand."

The six Green Berets did so. They had already checked and re-checked their assortment of equipment and had a few minutes earlier donned the aggregation of the items they would need for their mission. But it was time for a last rundown.

Their first order of business before beginning the routine of double- and triple-checking equipment a last time was to disconnect from the MC-130J's oxygen system. Upon switching over to their individual oxygen, the Army Special Forces operators inspected the connections and bottle pressure. It was essential to watch for symptoms and signs of hypoxia. When tissues failed to receive enough oxygen for the body's needs, damage to the brain, liver, and other organs could occur in mere minutes.

Confusion, coughing and wheezing, a rapid, or conversely, a slow heart rate, shortness of breath, or rapid breathing are all symptoms of the dangerous condition. In this situation, hypoxia in any one of the SPIRITS could endanger their mission. With none of the operators showing signs, they moved on with their final preparations.

✦

Brianna Washington, the president's secretary, continued her work totally oblivious to the dressing down that had erupted inside her boss' office. Any other office not likewise soundproofed would not have been able to withstand the volume of the language and would have permitted Ms. Washington to hear all manner of expletives.

POTUS was uninterested in the content of the CIA director's conversation with Orlov. She cared even less about Parnell's conclusions and was entirely dismissive of the DCI's reservations about proceeding with Operation Retribution until more intelligence was available. Though Parnell wasn't surprised, she was disappointed.

What concerned POTUS was that her CIA director had made overtures to the Russian spy chief at all. She had unilaterally made the decision to have a private conversation with Russia's highest intelligence official. She had conducted the conference outside of channels and off the record. It was insubordinate. It was inappropriate. It was potentially calamitous.

About all those things, Parnell knew, the president was right.

"What the hell were you thinking, Parnell?"

The director wasn't sure if that was rhetorical or not, but it didn't matter. The president continued before she could answer.

"What prompted you to do such a thing?"

The hands on the hip, the intense glare, and the proximity of the chief executive made it clear that she expected an answer to this enquiry.

Parnell was determined to maintain eye contact, but she wasn't able. She looked slightly to the side and shook her head.

"It was my own idea, ma'am." She had no intention of involving – or blaming – Ryan Crenshaw.

"I met Orlov when I was under Official Cover in our Moscow embassy. And I've talked to him another time or two. I thought…"

"So, this was like a personal call? You just picked up the phone and said, 'Pavel, buddy. How's it going?"

Betsy recalled saying almost those exact words to Crenshaw when he broached the idea of the call.

"No, ma'am."

The tongue lashing ensued a few more minutes until the president apparently ran out of steam. She sat at her desk, leaned back, and ran her fingers through her hair. She reached behind her head and massaged her neck. The silence lingered. It was uncomfortable and while uncertainty gripped her, Elizabeth Parnell was convinced she had done the correct thing. At the very least she was as certain as ever that there was more that needed to be learned before going to war.

✦

The MC-130J was flying at 28,000 feet above sea level, a reference that was especially descriptive and accurate since they were indeed over the Baltic Sea. The aircraft had gone wet near Ravijoki, Finland. Once over the Baltic the pilots had turned east-southeast. The flight path had brought them nearer and nearer Finland's border with Russia but their latest change in course had them flying directly toward Russia's Baltic coastline. They would maintain that path for only a short time before turning southwest on a direct line to the Amari Air Base that would become their home for the indefinite future.

Russian fighters had been patrolling the skies along the Russian border with Estonia since tensions between the U.S. and Russia had reached near critical mass. The U.S. military had begun staging increasing numbers of aircraft at the Amari Air Base. Planes of all types were arriving there hourly. Everything from B1B Lancer Bombers, A-10C Thunderbolt II tank killers, B-2A Spirit Stealth Bombers, F-15s, F-16s, F-22A Raptors, and all other flying war machines, along with C-130s and every other type of support aircraft arrived at the Estonian base for the impending war. Helicopters abounded – Black Hawks, Apaches, Chinooks, and more.

In addition to the aircraft, every available type of ground materiel was on its way to Estonia. The length of time to get the armored vehicles and other machines and fighting and support personnel there was of significantly longer duration than that of the planes. Winding through Europe with the requisite attention to friendly versus enemy borders complicated routes. And moving by sea – well, it was just a longer distance.

So, aircraft represented the bulk of the early arrivers and gave cause for concern to the Kremlin. Regular flights of every iteration of MIG from the -29 upward filled the Estonian border.

A single aircraft flying south toward Estonia didn't appear to represent a serious threat, but at the moment the Commando II made its turn toward the Russian coastline, two Mikoyan MiG-35s set a course from where they patrolled and headed north.

✦

In the Oval Office, President Hendrickson concluded her consideration of her course of action.

"Director Parnell, you've said that you and Direktor Orlov spoke in generalities and that no substantive information was exchanged between you two."

"That's correct, ma'am."

Silently she thought, "At least not between him and me." Beyond not mentioning Crenshaw, there was no way in hell that she would tell POTUS that she had suggested that Orlov send information to him – classified, foreign information.

"I hope that's true."

"It is."

"Nevertheless, I feel I can no longer trust you. Your behavior was beyond reproach. It borders on treason. Your judgement, your very lack of support for this administration… Well, as I said, I've lost any faith in you."

"I understand, ma'am."

"I can't afford the hint of a scandal right now, so my hands are tied in doing anything publicly with regard to your betrayal."

Director Parnell thought "betrayal" was too strong a word.

"For the time being, you're to refrain from any duties other than those that are purely administrative. You will delegate everything of substance. You will sit quietly without comment in our briefings. A simple smile and nod are all I expect. Am I clear?"

"Yes, ma'am."

"Am I clear?" POTUS repeated.

"Completely." The DCI wasn't really completely clear as to how she was going to do her job, but she accepted the president's authority to proceed however she wished.

The president looked the Director of the Central Intelligence Agency squarely in the eyes and let the hammer drop.

"Once we have navigated this crisis, I'll expect your resignation. And until that time, you may sit at your desk, you may receive your salary… Hell, you can even go to the company picnic. As long as you understand that, when it comes to any real decision-making, you're to behave as though you're already gone."

Elizabeth Parnell, though she hadn't let herself believe it would really happen, had considered that this was at least a possibility.

"That's all."

✦

The MC-130J Commando II slowed to a speed of 130 knots while still at an altitude of twenty-eight thousand feed. The SPIRITs all gave thumbs-up to their checks of night vision equipment, helmets, and GPS instruments. Each of the six operators wore stockings over their heads and faces, UF Pro Delta Ace sweaters, and Double Zipper Thermal Insulated Jumpsuits to make the exit temperature of minus thirty degrees Fahrenheit at least tolerable. Their Special Operations Vector SOV3 Jumpers high glide ratio parachutes (HGRP) passed the multiple inspections. They likewise accounted for the necessities for surviving on the ground for an indefinite period of time. And, of course, the lethal ordnance was ready for their exit.

At about 1:00 AM local time or 5:00 PM Eastern Time in the U.S., the call came through the Green Berets' headsets.

"Five minutes out."

"Acknowledge, Loadmaster."

The six SPIRITs walked toward the rear of the aircraft where the door was already open. The cylindrical packages containing the weapons to be carried by three of the paratroopers were staged nearest the yawning exit from the cargo area. The remaining three men were responsible for the packs that contained their other miscellaneous weapons and survival gear.

"Two minutes out."

"Acknowledge, Loadmaster."

The six operators began to stretch and prepare physically for their jump. They exchanged fist bumps and turned to give thumbs-ups to the Loadmaster.

Ninety seconds passed and then, "Thirty seconds out."

"Acknowledge, Loadmaster," came the response and each man clipped his long tether to the gear for which he was responsible.

Adrenaline was increasing but not to the extent it would have in mere mortals when the Army Special Forces warriors heard, "Five seconds." The countdown brought their immediate responsibilities into crisp focus.

"Four – three – two – one."

In succession the SPIRITs trotted across the dropped door of the MC-130J, moving toward and out of the exit into the sub-freezing open air. The first five men somersaulted forward in succession, descending with their backs down for about seven seconds before rotating facedown and letting their canopies fly. The final warrior dropped face down and deployed his parachute. As each man fell into the dark, cold night, his pack dropped before him to the end of its tether.

On board the aircraft came the acknowledgement from one of the two Loadmasters to the pilots and the Combat Systems Officer.

"Load clear; six jumpers."

The second Loadmaster added, "Red light."

The door of the cargo area began to slowly shut. The transport had completed its part of Operation Nemesis, the first stage of Operation Retribution, and turned toward its new destination, increasing to its cruising speed.

✦

Still some distance away two MIG-35s received word that the aircraft was turning away from the Russian coast and assuming a southwesterly path.

They banked to port to intercept the unknown plane and accompany them a while, just to make their presence known to them.

✦

Immediately upon exiting the Commando II, with chutes opened, the six SPIRITs formed up for the descent to their target. They were nearly fifty kilometers from the Russian beach where they would land after flying by parachute some twenty-five minutes. A vehicle was already making its way from St. Petersburg to their insertion point.

Over the last two days, U.S. diplomats throughout Russia had packed belongings, shredded files, removed hard drives, and prepared for their departures. Their expulsions were in retaliation for the eviction of their Russian equivalents in the Russian embassy and consulates throughout the United States.

One of the critical actions was to communicate with all the assets they had developed within the Russian government and military. Developing means to maintain contact received much attention. In St. Petersburg the CIA station chief had assigned one last task to *Stárshiy Leytenánt* Dmitri Larionovich Nezhdanov. Senior Lieutenant Nezhdanov was an attaché to the current district commander of the Western Military District, one of the Russian Armed Forces' five such districts. Colonel-General Jaroslav Borisovich Yarmolnik's aide had provided information to the U.S. St. Petersburg CIA station chief for three years. Most of it was of no real value but that wasn't always the case. This was the first time his handler had required him to perform any type of operational or logistical support.

Senior Lieutenant Nezhdanov was driving a six-year-old UAZ Combi. Affectionately called *Bukhanka* because of its shape's similarity to a loaf of bread, many compared it to a Volkswagen bus in appearance. The 4X4 had room for six passengers in addition to the driver. The dark green utility van had a passenger seat next to the driver. In the area just behind, it had two rear-facing seats and three forward-facing. The rear cargo area had a load capacity of four hundred-fifty kilograms, or just about one thousand pounds.

✦

Even with all the protective layers, the cold was still uncomfortable to the six operators gliding beneath their canopies in controlled descent toward their insertion point. Through their night-vision goggles, they could clearly see the shore's edge as they passed over it. Their GPS units directed them the short remaining distance inland where they stalled their parachutes for landing. Each soldier's tethered pack landed first with the owner trotting in slowly behind as his feet reached the ground. The three pairs of SPIRITs made contact with earth within fifty meters of one another about one mile north of the town of St. Ozerki.

The six efficiently gathered their gear, rolled their chutes into not much more that wads of material, and attached them to their packs with bungee cords. They proceeded eastward through densely forested land. Once sufficiently concealed in the trees, each removed his camouflaged thermal suit, and donned clothing typical of Russian workers.

The greenish image in their goggles made it clear that the trees were becoming less dense. The edge of the small forest appeared with a small isolated road a short distance beyond.

The SPIRITS kneeled behind adequate cover. To a man, they worried that their ride might not show. The plan was for Nezhdanov to arrive in the area about thirty minutes after the American soldiers' anticipated touchdown. He would park at the appointed spot on the road and wait only two minutes before driving away to repeat the process every ten minutes until his passengers emerged from the woods. The planners of the op feared that if he remained parked upon his first arrival, he might attract attention. There was the off chance some wayward *politsiya* looking for an out-of-the-way place to nap through his shift might happen by. If a police officer or anyone else ran off the transportation, it might not doom the initial stage of the operation, but it would make it categorically more difficult.

The six soldiers had sat for barely five minutes when a dark green van stopped on the edge of the road. The lights went dim, then flashed twice in succession. Sergeant First Class Tom Lechler recalled the words of Colonel Hannibal Smith on reruns of the television show "The A-Team."

"I love it when a plan comes together."

The six "Russian workers" sprinted toward the van with their collection of U.S. military equipment. Inside of ninety seconds, everything was stowed, and they were rolling toward the small highway that would take them toward St. Petersburg.

Master Sergeant Lechler took the front seat and made a single comment over the radio connecting his team with the overwatch team.

"Backstage."

The sergeant then spoke with the Senior Lieutenant in Russian.

Lechler kept the conversation on topic. Had the Russian Army Officer told anyone of his trip, even if he hadn't spilled the beans about what he was doing? Had anyone acted suspiciously toward him recently? The interrogation lasted a few minutes and the answers all came back with the desired answer or a "*Nyet*." The Team Leader was confident, at least as confident as he could be, that Nezhdanov hadn't sold them out.

The five other team members spoke very little. When they did, it was always very softly and among themselves. The first topic of conversation was about how cramped the seats were. They had been prepared for some discomfort but nothing like this.

The rear passengers settled in for some sleep. Lechler kept his eyes on the road and every vehicle that approached from in front of or behind. The planners would've preferred to travel during the daytime to mix in with other traffic, but the infiltration had to be done at night and the thought of having the men linger in the brutal cold of the middle of the winter in the area northwest of St. Petersburg seemed prohibitive. However, when they arrived at their final destination, they would camp in that very type of weather.

The team would feel exposed the entire one hundred kilometers of the night's drive. It would take about one and a half hours. So, every set of headlights on the Primorskoye Highway – though there weren't many at 2:00 AM – was a concern.

✦

It was an odd feeling to Director Parnell when she had stopped by Langley upon leaving the White House. Sitting at her desk, she felt like she was trespassing, given the fact that she'd just been fired. Rather she got the word that she *would* be fired at some undetermined point in the future. She had gathered the personal possessions that meant the most to her and brought them home. She feared Hendrickson might stew on her revelation about Orlov and decide she had to go now. That would mean she would be escorted from the building without the opportunity to collect her belongings. There were some things she didn't want to take a chance on losing.

As she sat on her couch at home, she was speeding through emotional stages. First, she grew angry at herself for ever calling Orlov. Her anger increased as she reflected on her decision to let POTUS know. But after further contemplation over a couple of glasses of wine, she redirected her consternation toward the president. It wasn't because she had reamed her out. It was that she was behaving so aggressively about the Russia thing. She was acting impatiently and that pissed Betsy off. But mostly she was worried. The long-predicted nuclear apocalypse might be just on the horizon.

Yet for all the criticism she had just leveled at the commander in chief for moving impulsively, Betsy Parnell knew she was about to do something very rash herself.

She picked up one of the burner phones she always kept and tapped in a number.

✦

"Hi, Betsy," greeted Crenshaw.

Morgan heard his friend's telephone greeting and walked a little closer. He figured that with as much as Crenshaw had gotten him into lately, he shouldn't mind some eavesdropping.

Morgan's mentor hung up and said, "Want to grab a beer?"

Again, considering the scenarios he'd been through with his former Russian professor, he dreaded the answer he was about to give.

"Sure. Let me get my coat."

✦

The drive took longer than expected – one hour and forty-five minutes – but was uneventful. Senior Lieutenant Nezhdanov was surprised that he was dropped off where he was, though in retrospect he realized he shouldn't have been. It would be about a mile walk to his apartment from the lonely side street in St. Petersburg, but he was dressed warmly enough for it. He watched in silence as the six men drove off in the green UAZ van toward the endpoint of the first leg of their mission, which was located at Furshtatskaya Ulitsa, 15.

✦

In the van Master Sergeant Lechler drove. Sergeant First Class Timothy "Fluff" Jones sat beside him. The move of Fluff to the front passenger seat freed up space for all the men. The four remaining in the back shuffled about in the extra room. The remainder of the SPIRITs' drive would be short, but they appreciated the ability to stretch their legs, nevertheless.

Four blocks from their destination a pair of headlights appeared in the exterior rear-view mirror. It hung back for the first block. Then, as if sensing the van's destination, it sped up to close the distance. It was too late, and the van and its occupants pulled through the opening gate at the St. Petersburg consulate. The Marines manning the position immediately closed the gate and took positions outside it.

The sedan slowed significantly while the driver and passenger stared at the sentries. Soon they sped off.

The Russian government had once ordered closure of the U.S. Consulate General, effective March 31, 2018. It had recently reopened only to be ordered closed again in response to the expulsion of Russian diplomats in the United States.

The six soldiers made their way to their assigned quarters inside the compound. Many of the consular personnel had already left for the United States. What remained of the diplomatic corps would drive to Moscow and depart the Russian Federation from there.

✦

"Fired!?" repeated Crenshaw. His tone was hushed but the words still conveyed the surprise and dismay the man felt for his former colleague. "I'm so sorry, Betsy. It's my fault. If I hadn't…"

"Oh, hush, Ryan. Don't flatter yourself. You don't have that much influence on me," Betsy Parnell declared with as jovial a tenor as she could muster.

"Shit, Betsy. I'm sorry, too. Fired?"

"Thanks, Morgan." Parnell thought about the story behind Josh Morgan's career with the Agency. "I guess you know how I feel, though."

Parnell raised her glass of beer toward Morgan, which he tapped with his own.

"You guys needn't feel responsible for this. Made my own bed." Parnell looked at her former mentor. "I just decided you were right, Ryan.

"And the worst of it is, Hendrickson dismissed my concerns – I guess you'd have to call it advice – completely out of hand. Most people, I'd say they were just being stubborn, obstinate. And I suppose she is. But I also know the woman well enough to know she's confident she's doing the right thing."

Morgan spoke up. "Doesn't change anything, though. Her certainty she's right is still carrying us to war with Russia. Hell, she may *be* right. But she should hit the pause button long enough to look into your apprehensions."

"Well, we tried," Crenshaw lamented.

"Tried, hell. We're not done yet. What did you learn about Borzilov from the information Orlov sent?"

The two men summarized everything the Russian spy chief had passed along. They felt it gave a clear sense of who the man was but that the data didn't provide any real value in developing a plan.

"So, Morgan, you're pretty good at sticking your nose where it doesn't belong. Up for another adventure?"

"No. Not really."

"Good. Glad you're in," the almost-former DCI said.

✦

Mom was in her bed in the executive residence with her daughter Noelle. It was far earlier than her normal time and she had no intention of going to sleep for quite a while. But with AJ still in the hospital and her husband staying with him, it felt lonely in the White House. It was hard on her daughter so for the past few nights she had allowed her to join her in the master bedroom. Once Noelle dozed off, Mom transformed into POTUS again and sat up in the bed reading the endless intelligence briefings and operational reports.

Not long before, she had received word that the Nemesis SPIRITs were safely in the consular compound in St. Petersburg. She marveled at the success of the initial stage but that's what these special operators did. She didn't fully understand the process. All she knew was that they had jumped out of an airplane over five miles above the earth and had glided laterally by parachute about forty miles to the Russian coastline.

"Remarkable," she whispered.

Her thoughts turned to the outrageous stunt that the CIA director had pulled. POTUS genuinely regretted dismissing the woman but what recourse did she have? She wondered again if Parnell's action indeed rose to the level of treason. She believed it did not, though it undermined the president's confidence of her support for the operations that were already underway. POTUS had always respected Parnell as something of a kindred spirit. Like Hendrickson herself she had overcome huge barriers to success in crashing through the glass ceiling that existed for anyone born with two "X" chromosomes.

Yes, it was regrettable having to fire her, but it was the right thing to do, the chief executive was certain.

The president considered who should know and decided that nobody, not even her chief of staff, needed the distraction.

"Damn," she muttered, and went back to her work.

✦

"We're going to need help," determined Crenshaw.

"More than is available to us," Morgan added. "Despite their not knowing your situation, Betsy, people are going to be reluctant to provide the type of support this thing will require." Morgan couldn't believe he was actually signing up for this misadventure.

"Who can we trust?" the DCI wondered.

"President Weston's a possibility. He was DCI when I was with the Company," Crenshaw suggested, "and we've become friends – well, friendly acquaintances over the years. He would probably get behind this. But you know him far better than I do, son."

Josh was already shaking his head and rolling his eyes before his friend spoke his name.

"No way. There's no way in hell I'll try to involve him in this."

"Just think about it, Josh," Parnell urged. "Don't ask him for help. Just tell him the background and see what he says. Then if his appears to be a like attitude to ours – you know, if the door seems open – walk through it."

Former CIA Officer Josh Morgan hated where this was going. But in a matter of minutes, he found himself dialing the number of former President of the United States Trenton Weston.

"Hello. Mr. President. This is Josh Morgan. I'm sorry for the lateness of the call. How are you?"

"So, we're back to the whole 'Mr. President' thing, are we?" He punctuated the remark with a soft chuckle.

"Sorry... Trent."

"That's better. We're great, son. How are you?"

Before Morgan could answer, Weston continued, "Oh, I have to tell you how proud we are of Maggie. We see her on the press briefings and she's just doing a wonderful job. And Noah Chandler thinks the world of her. Like I said, we're proud of her."

"Thank you, sir. I've, uh..." He glanced at the two sets of eyes fixed on him in the bar and grill.

"I've come into some information that I'd like to run by you. I know you're busy helping the president right now, but would you have some time tomorrow?"

"Sounds ominous. This information didn't come from Maggie, did it?"

Morgan knew the reason for the query. Weston would take a dim view of Maggie passing along information from her job to Josh, though he would understand that sometimes you just have to offload some of the burden. But if Josh was, in turn, sharing what she said with others, even an ex-president, that would be unacceptable to him – and disappointing. He wondered at what his friend's reaction would be at the disclosure, that it came from a sitting DCI and her counterpart in Russia.

"No, sir. I can assure you that it didn't. But it is of a sensitive nature, and I need your advice." He sighed. "And help," he didn't say.

"Actually, since the vice president is in his office now, the president hasn't needed me. So, of course I have time for you. We've been through hell together. Right?"

"Yes, sir." He gave a weak thumbs-up to his drinking pals.

"Do you need to come over tonight?"

"No. Tomorrow will be fine."

"How about breakfast then?"

"Perfect, Trent. Thank you."

They worked out the details and hung up.

✦

Maggie and Josh hadn't seen much of each other since Inauguration Day. They weren't used to it. In fact, they hadn't spent a night apart since Morgan returned from the debriefing about his intervention in the plot to transport Trent Weston to Saudi Arabia for trial as a war criminal. After the fact, Morgan started referring to the mess as "Operation What the Hell Was I Thinking." Of course, that was only in his own mind. Nobody outside of a handful of individuals in the Mercer and Hendrickson administrations knew what had transpired. Maggie knew very little of what her fiancé had accomplished, only what she had witnessed and the CliffsNotes version of what she hadn't.

But if the pair found it difficult having only a few hours from late night to very early morning, sleeping in bed, what Morgan was about to do would be impossible.

He walked into the bedroom where his fiancée lay sound asleep. Ordinarily each would wait on the other to go to bed when one arrived home late. But during the last period of a little over a week, Maggie was out as soon as her head hit the pillow, whether Morgan was home or not.

Morgan sat on the corner of the bed, struggling with whether he would tell her where he was going – if it worked out, that is – and what he was going to do. It wasn't like it was a real covert mission – okay, it would be covert, but not a mission. It was merely a factfinding effort. It was an investigation, not unlike what he did as a photojournalist. Of course, he had to remind himself, photojournalist was his cover and almost all of what he did was in the service of the Central Intelligence Agency. And that made all of CIA's resources and support available to him.

Josh slipped under the cover with his auburn-haired lover, who instinctively snuggled up against him without waking. He lay his arm over her waist and looked at her face close to his. The dim light brought into his mind just how beautiful she was. Everything he now had in life was wrapped up in his love for Maggie. He was torn. He wanted to keep her from worrying about him but the gnawing feeling that he would keep another secret from her was upsetting. When they first met, he could tell her nothing of his Clandestine Services career. When he finally told her all about his life, it unburdened him to a degree that he never knew he needed.

No. He had to tell her.

But he would sleep on it.

CHAPTER 24

Day 11 – Tuesday

At 7:00 AM in St. Petersburg, Russia, a string of vehicles rolled through the gates of the United States consulate. A truck carrying U.S. Marines led the way while another followed up. In the midst of the convoy moved a green van with six men now dressed in casual business attire to blend in with the consular personnel making their way from the compound.

The Green Berets had destroyed their parachutes along with every other item that was no longer needed.

The drive to Moscow would be around ten hours. The diplomats had all grumbled about having to make this drive when others had flown directly from the St. Petersburg airport. Only two knew that the purpose was to provide cover for a military operation that was already underway and, in fact, was being carried out in their midst.

As each vehicle emerged from the complex, agents of the Federal Security Service of the Russian Federation checked its description and license plates against a list of those registered to the consulate. The pair of FSB personnel noticed that the color of one Russian-made UAZ Combi didn't match the license plates that were on it. It was green instead of tan. They figured it was an error on the records and insignificant. In fact, the SPIRITs had exchanged their van's plates with those of a similar van registered to the State Department's facility. It had, as the Russians' records indicated, been tan but it had no cargo area, only passenger seats, and was unsuitable for the soldiers. The tan truck was left in the compound with other vehicles that were abandoned there. The operators brought the license plates that were originally on their truck with them to discard somewhere far away from St. Petersburg. If the Russians who would pour over the diplomatic structures after the Americans were gone discovered the plates, it might raise questions.

And the Green Berets had no idea where the Special Lieutenant had gotten the truck.

So, the FSB agents verified all the vehicles in the procession leaving the U.S. State Department facility matched their records, except for the one associated with "clerical error" on the observers' list.

Josh Morgan's alarm went off at 6:00 AM. He awoke without any recollection of the plans that he had made the previous night with Ryan Crenshaw and Elizabeth Parnell. It was those blissful few seconds before the real world pierced his woozy aftermath of sleep. When the reality of his actions finally penetrated the fog of just waking up, it was gut-wrenching.

Now fully awake, Morgan was again gripped with indecision about whether to inform Maggie of his likely trip out of the country. She was just coming out of the bathroom.

She gave him a quick kiss. Even with the intense pressure of her job and the crisis that existed for the United States, she felt good about her role. She felt like she fit.

"I'll wait until tonight; until after I've spoken with Trent," he chose.

"See ya tonight, hon," said Maggie. She hurried to the kitchen and grabbed a bagel that Ryan had prepared for her, thanked him, and started for the door. She spun around and stuck the bagel between her teeth to hold it while she grabbed her coffee mug.

She mumbled something Crenshaw assumed was some form of goodbye and she was gone.

Morgan rubbed his eyes as he walked into the kitchen.

"So, you going to tell her?"

"I'm going to get coffee." Morgan pulled the coffee pot from its maker and a cup from the rack where it hung and began to pour. He grabbed the bagel his house guest was preparing for himself and started back to the bedroom to get ready for his breakfast meeting with President Weston.

Crenshaw smiled and shrugged and placed another bagel in the toaster. Then he sat at the table and waited for his breakfast to pop up.

The procession of consulate vehicles with their U.S. Marine escorts was about an hour behind schedule. They had estimated that the snowy conditions would cause about a ninety-minute delay. It was an hour longer.

It was three in the afternoon in Russia. The caravan was about two hours from Moscow. A pair of sedans occupied by FSB agents had followed them the entire way. The diplomatic personnel in each of the State Department cars wondered if they would be pulled over at some point in the long trip. Certainly, under normal circumstances, the Russians wouldn't think of it. Vehicles were understood to be extensions of diplomatic property and therefore immune from search. But these were definitely not normal circumstances.

For the operators, their inclusion in the line of vehicles heading from St. Petersburg to the embassy in Moscow should provide the protection they needed.

They were counting on it.

✦

At 8:30 AM, Washington time, Josh Morgan walked into Seasons, the restaurant at The Four Seasons Hotel where President and Alicia Weston were staying. To his dismay, the former first lady was sitting at the table with her husband.

"Shit. No way to have this conversation with her there," he thought. But he smiled as though pleased to see her.

The power couple both rose to greet their friend. Alicia Weston hugged Josh and kissed him on the cheek.

"I just wanted to have a cup of coffee with Trent and stay long enough to say 'hi' to you. Love you, sweetie. Give my best to your Maggie."

Trent Weston greeted Morgan in his customary way, a strong handshake and a pat on the shoulder. Then he waved to his departing wife, who had turned to blow her husband a kiss. The ex-chief executive pretended to catch it and hold it next to his heart.

Irrespective of his frayed nerves and apprehension about the coming conversation, Morgan couldn't help but let out a little laugh. The former residents of 1600 Pennsylvania Avenue were completely without pretense.

"I hope Maggie and I are just like you two when..." Josh's words stalled.

"When you're old?" his friend finished for him.

Morgan's face reddened slightly. "When we're..." He tried to come up with something but now his mind would only let him hear the words, "when we're old."

So, he left the sentence incomplete and said instead, "Could I get some coffee?"

Trent Weston waived at the waiter, pointed to his own cup and then to the one Morgan was reaching for.

The sun of a cloudless morning shone brightly through the windows on either side of the corner table. The waiter poured the java. He returned once the two diners had made their decision, then retreated to place their orders.

Weston wasted no time getting to the point for his younger friend. He knew he would want to but would be too polite to jump right in. His face turned serious.

"So, what's bothering you?"

"I don't know where to start."

For the next forty-five minutes, Morgan provided his friend with every minute detail of what had happened to Betsy, her conversation with Orlov, and the personnel file on Borzilov that the Russian spy chief had sent to Ryan Crenshaw in the encrypted photo of the Eiffel Tower.

"And you're elected why?"

Josh had wondered about that himself from the moment Betsy Parnell had suggested it. But the rationale was unchanged from what she had told him when she asked.

"She can't send her own people, given her circumstances. First, there's no way to keep it quiet from others in the intelligence community. And second, she's in deep enough that anything more might be construed as treason."

Trent Weston leaned over the table toward the man who had once saved his life. His face had the earnestness of someone who loved someone and feared for him rather than what you would see from a superior giving his associate a warning.

"Josh, you know you would be flirting with treason yourself. Right?"

Morgan hung his head and nodded.

"Son, this isn't just chasing around Mexico and Texas trying to get me out of my jam. You'd be walking into a superpower on a level with us. And one we're about to go to war with."

"Sir... Trent, Crenshaw said something to me the other night. He didn't say it quite this way, but the essence was that sometimes we do things for our kids and their kids. We want some little Maggies and Morgans. Someday..."

At that, to lighten the mood, Trent Weston interjected, "Little Morgans? God help us."

Morgan didn't so much as smile or slow down in his remark. "...If this thing goes the way doomsayers have always said it would – and I believe it's more than hyperbole – then there might not be a world left for my children."

President Weston waved off the waiter who was approaching with the coffee pot and leaned back.

"Josh, let's carry this conversation up to my suite." The two men rose, and Weston thanked the waiter. His expression was so cheerful, so gracious that one would never imagine that he'd been talking about treason, nuclear war, and the end of the world.

✦

President Hendrickson rubbed her temples with the first two fingers of each hand. She had just received a report that the exodus of the Russian diplomats from their Washington embassy and the array of consulates around the United States was nearly complete. The decision had not been made to expel the remaining personnel from the foreign service posts, though Russia and the U.S. would each demand that very soon. The terms of the agreement that allowed Ambassador Listunov and a support staff to stay had been worked out in short order. When the administration finally expelled the remaining diplomats, as a matter of practicality, a token Russian delegation would take up residence in the D.C. embassy of one of their allies, perhaps Cuba.

POTUS was receiving regular updates about Operation Nemesis. At last report the Nemesis SPIRITs were nearing Moscow. President Hendrickson had wondered at the name *Nemesis* for the initial phase of Operation Retribution, having always understood the word to mean an archenemy. General Richards told her that the origin of the word was that it was the name of the Greek goddess of divine retribution or revenge.

At the Walter Reed Medical Center, Gennadiy Borzilov was making unexpected progress. The Russian SVR agent had made the decision to take out his own revenge on the handlers he was sure had killed his family by now by telling what he knew. Besides, he had decided, this whole operation was, as he believed the Americans called it, a fool's errand.

What made cooperating difficult was that he had no information about the men who had coerced him into his actions. He had never met them. The American FBI already had his phones. Two would have numbers he had called and from which he had received calls. Perhaps their National Security Agency could do something with the numbers.

The Muscovite no longer concerned himself with his own fate. He had no desire to attempt to bargain for leniency and, again, he could provide no real details about the men themselves.

Gennadiy gave his interrogators full and exact details about how he had carried out the bombings. He told them where he had kept his additional items, the cars, bombmaking materials, extra clothes.

Borzilov gave information about his private apartment, though officials had already searched it, even though there would be nothing of importance there. And lastly – and this was the thing that he felt true remorse about – he gave all the details he could about his family; remorse that he had done this thing that had undoubtedly cost them their lives.

But with all the information he had disclosed, the American questioners found themselves little better off than without it. The Russian spy knew he hadn't convinced them that his explicit orders had been to make sure the Russian Federation got the blame for the attacks. He had decided in his own mind that his Motherland wasn't involved and that embittered him at his own betrayal of his country and left him inconsolable at the path he had set his nation on.

But in truth, he couldn't say to a certainty that the men who had blackmailed him to do this thing weren't rogue operatives. If so, they were then, equally traitorous as himself.

So, at the end of the day, the Americans were left with little to persuade them that they were going to war against the wrong offender.

Borzilov found it astounding that the Americans hadn't believed him when he said Russia was the instigator, and now they didn't believe him when he said she wasn't.

✦

DCI Parnell was constantly amazed at her employer's capabilities and how quickly the Agency's experts could turn out perfect results. Fortunately, nobody had reason to question her request.

She had taken a photo of Josh Morgan with her phone at the bar last night. She needed to have an image that existed nowhere else in the world. The CIA director held two booklets in her hands. On one was the expressionless face of Alejandro Manuel Sanchez from Spain. On the other, Russian Aleksandr Ivanovich Sokolov stared back at her. The two men looked identical to one another. And they each looked identical to Josh Morgan.

The former spy would need the Spanish passport to get through whatever countries his route took him until he boarded a plane for the last leg. Once bound for the Russian Federation, he would switch to the Russian document. Each passport was complete with stamps from a variety of international destinations and the overnight preparation also included any other supporting documents that he might require.

The chosen names were deliberately commonplace in their respective nations. Should any customs agent at any entry point decide to conduct a name search, they assured that it would return tens, if not hundreds of hits. This particular Alejandro; this specific Aleksandr – well, they would both be lost in the crowd of Spaniards and Russians with exactly the same names.

In addition, Betsy had selected Morgan's legends with his skills in mind. He had learned Spanish growing up in Texas and was thoroughly fluent. He had studied Russian at The University of Texas under Dr. Ryan Crenshaw and likewise spoke that language flawlessly and without accent.

The one potential problem was with his Spanish dialect. The language Morgan picked up in his upbringing was Mexican Spanish. His Spanish identity should speak Iberian or Peninsular Spanish. There were significant differences from what he knew. Betsy hoped the gatekeepers to the ports of entry Morgan would pass through would be unfamiliar with the distinctions. That Spaniards were often light-skinned would play to his advantage so that his looks might influence the perception toward Spain as his country of origin and overshadow any flaws in his speech.

Parnell placed the passports and other documents in her purse and started the trek from her corner office to the building's exit.

◆

Former U.S. Commander in Chief Weston motioned Morgan to a chair. His face suddenly looked grim.

"Josh, I trust you more than I can say. Otherwise I would never share this information with you."

"I understand, Trent."

"Sir Albert McGinnis – you met him the other day – he's MI-6."

"I suspected as much."

"He called me yesterday. We had a meeting similar to the one you and I are having. This is very sensitive intelligence. He shared it with me because he has the same concerns that you do; that you, Parnell, and Crenshaw all have. He said that MI-6 has the same uncertainties that the Russians are behind this. Sir Albert can tell me things like that because I was president. But he's *comfortable* telling me because I'm his friend.

"He says Parliament is with us but they're nervous. Their intel is raising enough doubts in enough people's minds that they believe we're acting with undue haste. It's been what – a week? – and we're on the cusp of war with Russia."

Morgan felt vindicated for his qualms – his, Betsy's, and Ryan's.

"Yes, we are. With operators already on the ground in Russia, things are…"

"What's that?"

Betsy Parnell had passed along that bit of information. It didn't occur to Morgan that the former president wouldn't know. He explained the little bit he knew about the SPIRITs.

"Betsy felt that, if I was going to do this, I should know where things stood. I assumed you knew. Yes, I know she broke the law…"

"No. She was right in telling you but, damn, Josh. I just had no idea."

Morgan didn't know if he should apologize. He felt sorry for the man. It was obvious that he was hurt for being out of the loop.

For his part, Weston indeed felt slighted. When Hendrickson's predecessor was in office, he treated Weston with such disdain that the ex-chief executive thought that the reputed courtesies shown from previous presidents to their successors was largely apocryphal. He'd gotten used to it. That is, until the current president had brought him into the fold. But perhaps, he thought now, she was no different than Mercer after all.

"You should talk to Sir Albert. You're going to need help."

"I don't know, Trent."

"You came to me because you wanted my help. I don't know how I can, but I think the Brit can. You trust me. Trust him."

"Maybe Sir Albert can just tell the president."

"He already has, Josh. Shared the intel that seems to point to a small group rather than a nation."

"And?"

"Hendrickson thanked him but didn't suggest that it would impact her decisions. He had passed it along to DHS, CIA, and NSA. Son, you know they ran it up the chain to her. But also, to no effect."

The light bulb clicked on in Josh Morgan's head. Betsy Parnell decided to go along with Ryan Crenshaw's proposal to call Orlov because she'd already been read in on the information from British Intelligence. Then she spoke with POTUS to say she had second-sourced what MI-6 had provided.

"Damnation!" Morgan said.

Halfway around the world six Nemesis special operators arrived at the U.S. embassy in Moscow. They would lay low there for two nights before beginning their mission. As dangerous and critical as every step had been up until this point, they had all been solely to put them in the position to deploy.

"Where's your funding coming from? This isn't going to be cheap."

Morgan joked that they were considering crowdfunding before admitting that they hadn't quite got it all worked out. He simply shrugged and shook his head.

"Talk to Sir Albert. I'm sure he won't be able to provide any financial resources, but he might be able to help with some other support."

"Can you give me his number?"

"I'll do you one better."

Weston got on his phone. "Albert, what we talked about the other day. Think we could revisit it over lunch? Great. My hotel suite? Perfect. Thanks."

He set his phone on the table and turned to Morgan.

"Stay for lunch?"

Maggie Loughlin sifted through the demands for comment. She separated them into categories of true or false and then subcategories of those headings. She made lists of things that each request had in common. Then she passed them out to press department staff to research against what they knew they were about to release anyhow and things that they had been specifically ordered not to divulge. What made it difficult for the entire staff was that the press was asking questions about things they appeared to know but that the staff did not.

Maggie brushed her hair away and lay her head on her arms on her desk. As she was thinking of calling Morgan, her phone rang. She read the ID on the display.

"Josh, I was literally just thinking of calling you. Where are you?"

Morgan let her know he was with Trent Weston and let it go at that. No more details about his role in plans of a group that had grown in size from three to four during the morning and was perhaps about to expand to include another individual.

"So, what's up, sweetheart?" she asked.

"Just needed to talk to you. I wanted to see how you're doing."

"So, how's our favorite president and first lady?"

Morgan and Maggie talked a while longer before she knew she had to go.

"Lots going on, of course. I'm sure I'll be late tonight. You and Ryan stay out of trouble."

Josh choked up a little. "I love you, Maggie."

"What's going on, Josh? Something's wrong."

"No," he reassured. "Just checking in."

"Okay." Maggie didn't believe him. "I love you, too."

Maggie held the phone to her heart a moment.

✦

On the other end, Josh made his decision. He couldn't tell Maggie that he was off to Russia. She would worry if she knew. She would be distracted. But more than that, he was afraid someone in the West Wing would notice something was wrong with her and figure out he was gone. Knowing his history, they might start to look into things. It would be a longshot that they could piece things together about him, but they might put pressure on Maggie. She wouldn't tell but she didn't deserve the grief she might get.

The other thing that Morgan realized concerned some offhanded remarks he had made in justifying his decision to act on Betsy's plan. He had never really thought about kids that much but in the last day it was on his mind a lot. Maybe he really was doing this for his kids.

Morgan called Crenshaw to update him on his discussion with Weston and the coming conference with Sir Albert McGinnis.

Crenshaw had been pouring over the information his comrade Orlov had sent on Gennadiy Borzilov. He had compiled a cheat sheet of sorts for Morgan to memorize. He had organized it by category and included specifics about his family and known associates in Moscow. He organized a list of places in Moscow that Borzilov frequented along with addresses. He would give it to Morgan when he got home.

The most important thing was that Betsy had dropped off an envelope. Ryan didn't open it but his protégé told him the contents. He would let Morgan see it for himself rather than talk about it on the phone.

Morgan's attention turned to Secret Service Agent Jack Johnston as he leaned over to whisper to Trent Weston.

"Please have him come up, Jack," Weston instructed. And to Morgan, "Our guest is here."

CHAPTER 25

President Weston spoke first.

"I think it's important that we each realize – and I think we do – that at its most basic level, what we're doing can be construed as a betrayal of our respective countries. If anyone wants out, this is the time."

The three men looked around the table at each other without comment.

"Very well then. Sir Albert."

The MI-6 station chief dove right in.

"Mr. Morgan, you may or may not know that the GCHQ provided intercepts of phone calls and texts that prompted your NSA to look into the possibility of some level of involvement by individuals in Russia with the initial attack on President Hendrickson. Notice that I say 'individuals' because no conclusions were reached or intimated to the White House that the Russian Federation was behind the bombing. Our analysts did not rule it out. We just didn't have the confidence to make such an assertion. President Hendrickson was grateful, and I believe acted prudently on the shared intelligence.

"What you do not know is that we have shared with your government other signals intelligence identifying calls and texts as originating from Selyatino, a small town about fifty kilometers from Moscow; thirty or so of your miles. The intercepts from the same general location from multiple numbers suggest disposable phones. They went to several numbers in various locations around the District of Columbia. The content suggests they were to the same individual, who was also using throw-aways.

"While your intelligence agencies seemed appreciative, they were also less than enthusiastic about the shared intercepts. I would like to think that it was because your analysts came to a different conclusion than our GCHQ, as opposed to…"

Morgan understood his concern. "…as opposed to dismissing them because they were inconsistent with conclusions they'd already reached."

"Regrettably, yes." Sir Albert slid a small file folder across the table to Morgan. "Here is a list of the numbers, the content of the calls, and the locations – at least as close as we could determine. They're accurate to within approximately one hundred meters."

Morgan scanned the information

"This is interesting. You've identified two of the voices as female. Because of the words, I would assume 'Female 2' is the other caller's wife – or lover – and that 'Female 1' must be involved in an operational role."

"That is our assessment; yes. There was only one call with Female 2. The caller from this end called her 'Larisa' which we know to be the…"

"Name of Borzilov's wife," Morgan completed.

"Yes."

Weston interjected, "And he called her by name? Sloppy."

"Yes. And that call also had the man speaking with two children."

"Borzilov's kids." Morgan concluded.

Sir Albert clarified, "Yes. So, the confidence is 'near certainty' that this was Borzilov. And since it's him, the other people must be involved. Well, 'must' might be too strong a conclusion."

"I don't think it is," contradicted Morgan. "But I don't get the sense he's a willing partner in this. Though the parties stay away from specifics – no exact declarations, they're being careful – the content suggests some leverage. And why would his family be with them?"

Sir Albert continued the conjecture. "Precisely. And look at the conversation with his wife. It doesn't come through in the written text of the dialogue but Borzilov seems to have some emotion about the talk." He pointed at a couple of the Russian's remarks written on the transcript.

"I can see that."

Weston speculated about the scenario that seemed to be playing out on the written pages. "So, the family isn't *with* the operators. They're being *held* by them!"

Former CIA Officer Josh Morgan summarized. "They're coercing Borzilov and using his family as leverage. It doesn't mean the Russian government isn't involved in this. They've been known to play dirty, even with their own personnel. But I think it provides a reasonable doubt."

Morgan read another couple of minutes. Finally, placing the typed document on the table, he reconfirmed, "And our intelligence agencies have all this?"

Sir Albert nodded. "They do. They probably intercepted the same calls. But they seem to be relying solely on the confession by Borzilov – the one your UN ambassador played for the General Assembly – that he acted upon orders from superiors."

The three men sat silently. Finally, the British spy spoke.

"So, what precisely is your plan?"

Morgan rolled his eyes. "I'm going to Moscow and..." he read the name of the town on the MI-6 station chief's notes again. "... And Selyatino, I suppose, to try to get some facts."

Weston warned, "They may, in fact, support the president's people's interpretation of the plot, Josh."

"They might. But at least then we'll know. And if that's the case, it's a moot point that we know. President Hendrickson is acting completely within her authority. But if facts from our investigation contradict the ones driving the operation, she needs to know. And that's what I'll try to prove."

"What I fear," said the Brit, "is that emotion is too great a part of this. If it were a Royal, or our Prime Minister, we might lose some objectivity, as well, and be hell-bent on revenge. So perhaps a little detachment is permitting us a slightly different take."

✦

Inside the United States embassy in Moscow, Russia, six Army Special Forces operators, designated "SPIRITs" and codenamed "Operation Nemesis" were reviewing plans and about to get some shuteye.

They had inspected their ordnance to ensure it had survived the grueling insertion. Of course, packing such items for some abuse was a requirement. Their examination showed no signs that any damage had occurred. SFC Fluff Jones joked to his team leader, Master Sergeant Lechler, "Wouldn't these diplo-pukes shit a brick if they knew what we had here?"

Lechler and the other four men laughed their agreement.

Beside the beds in the dormitory style room that housed the operators sat a newly developed backpack drone and a non-nuclear electromagnetic pulse device, or E-bomb, also a new addition to the U.S. military arsenal.

But the device that the SPIRITs believed would cause anxiety among the diplomatic corps who were still in the compound was the B-54B SNAP. The Special Nuclear Armament Package was a new generation of the B-54 Special Atomic Demolition Munition. The first generation was developed in the early days of the Cold War and retired in 1989, in part because the notion that anyone in the military chain of command would ever authorize its use seemed absurd. In recent years, though, the idea of a limited nuclear engagement had crept back into the Pentagon's thinking. The most accepted use of a low-yield nuclear weapon was against non-nuclear nations or entities such as ISIS. In those applications the fear of retaliation and escalation on an equal scale was practically nonexistent.

Yet here the SPIRIT warriors sat with the weapon in a dormitory style room in the U.S. embassy in the heart of Moscow. And after two nights rest, they would move it into position and prepare for a potential execution.

✦

Sir Albert McGinnis heard the details of the plan developed by the three individuals Morgan described to him as, "soon-to-be-fired CIA Director Parnell, former Moscow station chief and rogue citizen Ryan Crenshaw, and disgraced former CIA Case Officer Joshua Morgan,"

The veteran British spy couldn't stifle a smile as he heard Morgan wrap up his portrayal with the question, "Have you ever heard of an unlikelier group of misfits being tasked with saving the world?"

Former President Weston chuckled himself. But having witnessed and been the beneficiary of Josh's resourcefulness, he believed the young man might just pull it off.

"If you get what you're after, Josh, if you discover hard evidence to discount the 'Russia-did-it' working theory, what will you do with it? How will you make anyone listen?"

"One step at a time, Trent. We really don't know."

McGinnis' comment was a mixture of hope and a warning. "I will help any way I can. But you have to understand, the assistance will be limited. And it will be – it must be – indirect and deniable. Support of a direct nature could have the potential of classifying you as an agent of a foreign country. And though that nation is the UK, America's closest ally, it would still be treason."

"I understand, Sir Albert. I accept the risk. Shit. If this doesn't work out, we're probably all going to disappear in a mushroom cloud anyhow. I'm grateful for any help at all."

"I can get you to London. No problem with that. If that will help," promised the Brit.

Morgan considered briefly what that could mean. "I think it might. Thank you."

The three men concluded their confab with a bit of brainstorming and went their separate ways.

✦

Morgan arrived home where Ryan Crenshaw gave him the package that Betsy Parnell had delivered. Inside it, Morgan found two passports and every other document he would need to support his two new identities. His one constant thought was, "I can't believe I'm really going to do this."

Having a legend to learn was new for him. In his non-official cover as a photojournalist, the former spy had always traveled as himself. And when he wanted to contact a potential asset, he simply walked up and introduced himself.

Betsy had outlined these covers. Neither had much detail and both were very simple. It wasn't as though he would be undercover for a long period of time. If all went well, he only needed to be Alejandro or Aleksandr long enough to get through customs in a handful of airports.

Getting out of his own country had been simplified greatly. Sir Albert had arranged for him to leave Andrews Air Force Base on a British military transport that had been in the United States for joint training.

Upon landing in RAF Brize Norton, a British air base about seventy-five miles west of London, an MI-6 car would transport him the one hour and forty-five-minute drive to London. From there Alejandro Manuel Sanchez would catch a flight out of Heathrow Airport to Paris, France. There Sokolov would board a flight to Moscow.

Ryan Crenshaw had spent the day collecting funds for the operation. He withdrew $3,000 from his personal savings. Morgan had collected $1,500 from his account on the way home from his meeting with Weston and McGinnis. Betsy Parnell had chipped in $5,400 in cash of her own money in the envelope she had left for Alejandro/Aleksandr. The total cash would keep him below the ten thousand euros or approximately US$11,300 limit for entry without declaration in Customs in France and below the US$10,000 limit in Moscow.

Josh took his passports and the $9,900 and went to a money exchange. "Alejandro" purchased a money card worth five-thousand-five-hundred in U.S. dollars and a second denominated in Rubles, valued at US$2,000. He kept the remaining $2,400 in cash. With his official passport Alejandro Sanchez completed his transactions without problems.

With the initial tasks completed and the overseas portion yet to come, Morgan knew that the most difficult one was to come later that night. He still had no clue as to what lie he would tell Maggie.

✦

Maggie was home uncharacteristically early. It was eight-thirty when she entered her apartment. Her smile was genuine though not as wide as it usually was when she saw Morgan at the end of the day. Her fiancé's smile, on the other hand, was completely manufactured. And Maggie knew it.

As soon as she pushed the door to and turned to face Morgan, she paused momentarily. Her own weak smile disappeared instantly. Maggie set her briefcase on the floor beside the door and draped her topcoat on it.

"What's wrong?"

Morgan had concocted a few different scenarios explaining his absence, from visiting friends in Europe to being offered a photojournalism assignment by one of the major print publications. The job would take him to Estonia to cover war preparations at the Amaris Air Base. That one made the most sense, given world events, and was the one he settled on.

"Sit down, sweetheart. I need to be out of town a few days."

Maggie sat and her furrowed brows begged for an explanation. Upon hearing Josh's fiction, she sat back fully on the sofa.

"Is it dangerous?" Her voice strained at the query. Her eyes lowered as she decided Morgan wouldn't tell her if it was.

"Oh, no, sweetheart. Not in the least. I'll be safely on the base, interviewing personnel and making the rounds taking photos of equipment and the business that goes along with making things ready for the engagement."

"But why you? You've been out of that for how many years? And besides, you weren't really a photojournalist?"

The ex-CIA spook took some offense at that.

"I *was* a 'real' photojournalist. And a damned good one. It was my cover, but I was in demand for my work…"

"You're lying to me."

The accusation caught Morgan by surprise. But he was glad it came. He stood and walked to the large window overlooking the cityscape. Maggie joined him there. Uncharacteristically there were no hugs, no kisses, and no eye contact.

The silence drew out to a few seconds.

"You're right. And I can't do it."

Maggie wasn't frightened by what she was going to hear. She didn't know why should be yet. She was only curious and disappointed that Josh had felt like he needed to lie to her. In a moment she understood.

"I'm going to Russia." The admission came out in a rush. A prolonged exhale followed.

Maggie was in surprised disbelief. Josh turned to face her. She continued to look at the snow-covered scene before her, unable to speak.

Morgan didn't know whether to proceed. He elected to give her a moment. His eyes followed her as she returned to the sofa and sat. When she finally made eye contact, the look was dazed and bordered on skepticism.

"Russia."

Morgan understood from her intonation that it was an acknowledgement and not a question.

For the next fifteen minutes, Morgan told Maggie everything. And for the second time in the brief time since she'd returned home, Maggie Loughlin asked the question:

"Why you?"

Initially Morgan could only say, "I have the same question."

Another period of silence.

Finally, Morgan provided the only answer to "why" that he had.

"Hendrickson has all the same information and is convinced that retaliation is the only acceptable response. She's acting rashly – or at least with undue haste. Betsy Parnell is willing to defy her. So is her Russian counterpart. They may be the only sane people in either country.

"She accepted Ryan's theory. In fact, she had the same feeling because of intelligence she'd received. She had the courage to reach out for answers. I can't do any less. I'm an outsider. I can fly under the radar. And we have to keep the group small."

Morgan didn't mention that Weston and Sir Albert were involved.

"And Parnell can't tell the president."

"She did. She even lost her job over it."

Maggie's eyes widened.

"Hendrickson fired her? For a difference of opinion?"

"For going behind her back to Orlov, the head of Russian intelligence operations."

In the years that she'd known Morgan, Maggie had never questioned his judgement. Even when he decided to go find Weston, she understood why he was doing it. And she accepted that he felt that nobody in the government was going to try to rescue him. But this was different. The government *was* doing something. He just disagreed with it.

"What will you do if you find out something that contradicts the basis for action against Russia?"

Morgan shook his head.

"None of us know."

"When do you leave?"

"I have to be on a plane at four in the morning."

"At Dulles?"

"At..." Josh reconsidered his answer. "Somewhere else."

Maggie propped her elbows on her knees and rested her head in her hands. Tears were on the verge of appearing, but she choked them back.

"What do I say at work?"

"I've thought about that. Tell them we're having some... well, difficulties at home."

Still in her cupped hands, Maggie turned her face toward him.

"And have them think we can't – *I can't* – do this job and handle things at home? No, thanks. I'll tell them you're sick." She wanted to add that she thought he *was* sick.

"That should explain why I'm distracted and worried."

"That's definitely better." Morgan leaned to put his arm around his fiancée. She pushed him away. He understood and watched her silently.

"I'm sorry, Mag."

Her eyes were moist, but the main thing Morgan got from them was the anger they communicated.

Finally, Maggie punched him in the arm and leaned her head against him. Morgan put one arm around her trembling shoulder and pulled her close with his other.

◆

Ryan Crenshaw had taken up residence at The Four Seasons where the former president was staying. Neither he nor Weston knew how they would monitor their friend's mission but felt it would be nice to be close in case of developments. It would also help to simply have someone each could talk to.

Ryan looked at his phone for the time.

"Eleven-twenty; so, seven-twenty," he calculated.

The former spy launched his encryption app. He typed the words, "Tourist coming. Would be nice to have a guide." He dragged the highlighted words over a JPEG file of the Great Wall of China. After some digital work, the file was ready, and he sent it off.

In only three minutes, Crenshaw received a text from the number to which he'd sent the photo.

"*Da.*"

CHAPTER 26

Day 12 – Wednesday

The alarm rang, though it was hardly necessary. Neither Morgan nor Maggie had slept. And the pair had spoken few words.

Morgan knew he would have plenty of time to catch some winks during the extended time he was about to endure in the air, if he was able. But Maggie? She was already sleep-deprived from the demands of her job and the stress of the knowledge she had because of it.

Morgan worried that he'd done her an injustice by putting this burden on top of the already enormous pressure she was under.

They said little. Finally, Morgan gathered up the small suitcase he had packed with clothes that he had selected to take. Nothing that looked too "American" was inside.

"Try to go back to sleep, Maggie."

"Back?" she answered without a hint of humor.

"Okay then," Morgan rephrased. "Try to get some sleep."

"I won't be sleeping. I'm just going to try to eat and then head to the office."

A moment lapsed before Morgan spoke.

"Well, I…"

Another moment passed.

"Yeah."

"It'll be okay, darling."

Maggie rested her head softly against Morgan's chest and hugged him.

Finally, the two separated. Morgan took Maggie's hand and they walked to the door.

Morgan lifted Maggie's chin and placed a small kiss on her lips.

"I'll see you in a few days." He had no idea what "a few" would mean. "I love you, Maggie Loughlin."

"I love you, too, Josh."

The door closed and the tears that Maggie had successfully held in began to trickle down her cheeks.

✦

At 11:00 AM in the embassy compound, four U.S. soldiers played cards. Another read a spy novel. The final SPIRIT listened to George Strait on his smart phone. They were passing the time as best they could. There was only so much reviewing and rechecking they could do. They would, of course, go over the plans again before leaving the complex in the morning but they had already covered everything they knew about contingencies and other operational elements. Preparation was only effective to a point. After that, it could only serve to provide a door for doubts to creep in.

None of them knew who first spoke it but each believed the admonition. "Plan your work and work your plan." They were confident in the plan and supremely confident in themselves. They were itching to get into the field. With their plan in play, they would be far less antsy than they were now, even though almost the entirety of the mission required sitting and waiting; just as they were doing now.

Once in place, the six-man team would lie in the elements. Right now, the elements meant just over a foot of snow on the ground and freezing temperatures but even that would be better than doing nothing. No amount of training prepared you for the wait before deployment.

Master Sergeant Lechler surveyed his men, the Army's "quiet professionals." The Green Beret motto was *de oppresso liber*, Latin for "to free the oppressed." Nobody needed freeing in this operation. It was about a reckoning. It was simply about retribution, as the overall operation codename made evident.

Even at half the size of the usual Green Beret team, he felt his Operational Detachment Alpha was about four men stronger than he would've preferred. The size and makeup of the typical A-Team was flexible but operational requirements placed certain limitations on how large or how small the ODA could be. The amount of equipment alone that was required for this mission demanded six men to haul it. And there had to be redundancies in personnel in case any were incapacitated. But the six-man size of the team made stealth more difficult in a semi-urban environment. The ability to remain undetected was everything in operations like this one.

The reduced detachment size required doubling up on team roles from the standard contingent of twelve.

Whereas A-Teams are usually led by a Captain, this team was comprised of six Sergeants. In the absence of an officer, the Master Sergeant served as the Detachment Commander. He also filled the role of Operational Sergeant, or "Team Daddy."

SFC Fluff Jones got his moniker from the huge moustache he'd had since he graduated high school. The walrus-style was so thick and long that hairs fluffed up with the puffs of air that accompanied his words. Fluff was the oldest of the SPIRITs and the Assistant Operations Sergeant, who directed the intelligence efforts of the group. However, that role was secondary to his other one as the Weapons Sergeant, responsible for the tactical security of the SPIRITs.

SFC Daquan Jackson was the unit's Medical Sergeant. "Jack" was the youngest of the group. Growing up with video games, particularly First-Person Shooters, he felt a bit removed from real action as this team's drone operator.

SFC Lucas Matheson had the role of Communications Sergeant for this op. "Cool Hand" Luke, or "Cooley," also owned the primary tactical role for this deployment as EMP Specialist.

SFC Angus Macduff was the SNAP Technical Sergeant. His primary duty was to deploy the 3.0 kiloton SADM B-54B SNAP, if matters came to that. "Bull" was also the backup medic.

SFC Abdal "Abe" Aboud, the Electronics Sergeant, was also the backup Comm Sergeant.

Lechler had hand-picked these men eight months earlier when the idea of a mission such as this first entered the minds of the strategists at the Pentagon. They had always thought the SNAP Program, like its predecessor, was lunacy and that the chances of ever deploying was a crock.

"But here we are," Master Sergeant said aloud. All of the men looked at him quizzically, except for Abe, who was singing out-of-key along to "Amarillo by Morning."

✦

Morgan had boarded the RAF A400M Atlas with little in the way of information. He didn't know why military personnel throughout the world had to do things at such ungodly hours. Maybe they were just showing off, he figured. He had shown his passport identifying him as Alejandro Manuel Sanchez, had been told, "Very good," and was led past a line of British military personnel on each side of the aircraft to a small jump seat at the rear of the plane. A few of the soldiers glanced at him as he walked by. Most paid him no mind.

Now two hours into the flight, his stomach was churning. He wondered what he thought he could really accomplish. "A little late now, Josh," he lamented to himself.

The Airbus-manufactured craft was enormous. It would carry twice as much as the C-130 Hercules fleet it replaced in the RAF years before. Speed-wise, it was no Concorde, but cruising at 485 MPH meant the craft could cover the approximately thirty-seven hundred miles across the Atlantic in about eight hours. Still, with the time zone differential, that put arrival time at 5:00 PM local time.

Morgan thought through what he was going to do next. Rather, he thought about what needed to happen next. He had no idea what he was really going to do.

Director of Central Intelligence Parnell had reserved his flights from London to Paris and then on to Moscow. He knew time was of the essence but feared she had cut things a little too close. Regardless of how urgent it was for him to get to Russia, the operation's timetable fell apart if he missed a flight.

Morgan wasn't even sure what was going to happen when he got to RAF Brize Norton. Sir Albert McGinnis had said, "Don't worry, lad. It's taken care of."

It always worried Morgan anytime someone said, "Don't worry." His mind raced to all sorts of crappy possibilities.

The jumbo transport landed right on time. A British officer ordered his troops to remain seated while he asked Señor Sanchez to step forward. None of the men looked very happy at the delay in getting off the plane.

"And any one of them could kill me," Morgan knew. He managed a weak smile as the officer escorted him forward. None of the other passengers smiled back.

The officer ushered his VIP to a sedan not far from the Atlas. The Lieutenant held the door open for the "Spaniard," who remembered to say, "Gracias," instead of "thank you" and "leftenant" rather than "lootenant." That was a courtesy that the junior officer would not have expected but he seemed to appreciate the acknowledgement, however his guest pronounced it.

There was a single person in the sedan, the driver. Morgan sat in the front alongside him. The driver introduced himself as Aldrich Ainsworth. Morgan almost laughed at how stereotypically British-sounding both the first and surname sounded. He wondered if it was really the man's name.

"There's an assortment of items in a bag in the rear seat. Chaplain thought you'd need a hand getting your necessaries in order." Sir Albert had alerted Morgan to his codename, so he wasn't caught off guard.

Traffic extended what should have been a one-hour trip by thirty minutes. Before driving into Heathrow, Aldrich pulled into a parking area to allow Morgan, aka Sanchez, the opportunity to look over the items that Chaplain had provided. Nothing of real significance was in the bag. But it was clear the items were there to avoid tearing apart his story of a Spaniard returning home from some time in London. Or a Russian national returning home from abroad. The clothing was very generic. A cap and gloves. On top of the bag lay a parka for a very, very cold climate. It was overkill for western Europe but exactly what Aleksandr Sokolov would need when he got home. All the clothes were Morgan's/Sanchez's/Sokolov's size.

"Nice touch, Chaplain," Morgan thought. Morgan left his own bag and picked up the one Sir Albert had provided. Aldrich drove the remaining distance to the departure area and the gate where Alejandro Sanchez would board his plane.

Sanchez had forty minutes, so he quickly thanked his driver and rushed to catch his flight. Fortunately, he cleared every stage of the check-in procedure with ease. At 8:10 PM Alejandro Sanchez boarded his plane. By 8:35 PM he was on an Air France flight bound for Charles de Gaulle Airport in Paris.

The trickiest part of all was making his flight in Paris. If he missed it, Morgan would have to get one out the following morning and that would cost him about six-and-a-half hours. He wasn't sure what the timeline for U.S. military action was, but things felt awfully urgent. All he knew was what Betsy told him: The U.S. had operators on the ground in Russia ready to deploy.

As the plane touched down in Paris, Morgan nervously looked at his watch.

"I'll never make it," he worried.

But once inside de Gaulle, his perspective changed.

"*Gracias a Dios*," said a grateful Alejandro Sanchez. His outbound flight to Vnukovo Airport in Moscow was running a half hour late.

Sanchez cleared Customs with no difficulty and walked toward the gate where he would board his Aeroflot flight for Russia. Halfway down the corridor, Sanchez went into a restroom where, in a stall, he exchanged his Spanish passport for the Russian one. He pulled out the papers showing he had successfully cleared Customs under his new identity.

"Thank you, Betsy," he thought.

When his change was complete, "Aleksandr Ivanovich Sokolov" walked out of the airport restroom. In spite of his renewed apprehension, Josh Morgan commented silently, "I feel like a new man."

But thinking better, he repeated, "я чувствую себя новым человеком." His attempt at settling himself with humor failed in both languages.

✦

Acting Press Secretary Maggie Loughlin's day was a mixed bag. In the moments between bursts of work, her mind flew through the possibilities that existed for Josh. She knew she wouldn't hear from him until… well, until this thing he was doing was over. In her worst moments, she feared she wouldn't hear from him again – ever.

Chief of Staff Noah Chandler had come by during one of those moments of panic. Noticing her different-than-usual demeanor, he stood momentarily outside her office door before knocking quietly.

"Maggie?"

"Oh, hi, Noah. Come in."

"You look distracted. All this getting to you?"

And here was her first occasion to lie to someone about what was going on with Morgan and his small group of… were they patriots, conspirators, traitors?

"No, no, not at all. Well, of course, it's tense and I've never been through anything like this. But I'm just thinking about Morgan. He's got the flu."

"Ah, I see. Stay away from him. We can't have you getting sick. We need you around here," Chandler said with a smile.

"Ha! Why do you think I came in so early? May have to sleep here to keep away from his germs."

"Well, give him my best. Hope he's better soon."

"Oh, it just has to run its course. He'll be laid up a few days. As long as he's got his Xbox, he'll be fine. Well, when he feels like getting out of bed."

"Ha! Boys and their toys!" Noah said as he walked away.

And that was it. Easier than she thought. That bothered Maggie a bit.

She looked at the time on her television. It was almost 4:00 PM. She was amazed at how light her workload had been for most of the day. Aside from the daily briefing, there was nothing of real consequence. That conference was the usual back-and-forth. Reporters asked variations of the same questions so they could get their voice recorded asking them and then play her reply. Many of the enquiries weren't questions at all. The correspondents threw out what they had heard or what they thought? Those were always followed up by, "Any comment?"

For her part, Maggie simply did the dance that she had learned as a public relations consultant and which she was perfecting here. Say something but don't provide any real answers that broke new ground or provided information that the administration wasn't prepared to announce.

Part of Maggie's job was to stay informed about what the various news outlets were saying about the current crisis. Members of the White House press department monitored the news on television and on the web and provided their acting boss with summaries.

So, all in all, things were relatively slow for her. Maggie marveled that so little had seemed to change for the people of the United States, considering the world might be on the verge of Armageddon. People were still eating out, going to movies, and doing whatever they would do in the course of a normal day.

Normally, when the Defense Condition was raised to "2," the government leaders provided accompanying instructions to the citizenry to change their routines so that they could stay informed. Such a warning hadn't been issued this time causing Maggie to momentarily think that maybe the DEFCON 2 status was more for show than of real substance. Maybe things weren't as bad as they seemed. But, no, she had seen enough and been briefed enough to know that this was really a nightmare.

Maggie could hardly manage the personal horror she felt at the prospect of nuclear war. And now Morgan was right in the middle of it. The relative slowness of the workday made it difficult not to think about him.

"Slow" was, of course, a comparative thing when it came to her duties in the West Wing. But they were indeed well below what her "normal" day would have been.

She decided that, when you were about to go to war, you didn't advertise it. But the sluggish pace of the day made it rough. She wanted to work late to occupy herself with anything other than what her fiancé was doing.

It wasn't working.

CHAPTER 27

Day 13 – Thursday

Former CIA Officer Josh Morgan knew that CIA Director Elizabeth Parnell had thought through his itinerary and made some important decisions based on matters he wouldn't have thought to anticipate.

With world tensions being at unbelievable levels and centered around the already intense and growing conflict between Russia and the United States, Russian Aleksandr Sokolov would've certainly received unusually heightened scrutiny at each airport through which he traveled. A Spanish national would pass through more easily.

Yet, Alejandro Sanchez would receive more attention upon arriving in Moscow than a son of Russia would in returning to the safety of the Motherland from the prejudices and dangers he would face abroad. Sokolov was going home. Furthermore, Parnell had made the judgement to fly Morgan through Paris because France had made no declaration of an alliance with either of the two superpowers that were preparing for war against one another. The French Parliament hadn't picked a side in the fight, but they hadn't declared neutrality. The stereotypical waffling of France made it the most benign choice to make a connecting flight to the Russian Federation.

Unable to sleep for even a few minutes, Morgan ran through scenarios for what Sokolov would do once he landed. And he was mostly drawing blanks. He wondered if his Russian would pass scrutiny. Often in foreign lands, hints of a foreign accent might be attributed by locals as simply an indication that the speaker possessed a dialect that resulted from living in another part of the country. That wasn't a possibility for Morgan. Sokolov's passport clearly identified him as a Muscovite. Fortunately, his Russian professor, Dr. Ryan Crenshaw, spoke dialectically as a resident of Moscow and had taught that way. Still, Morgan knew that if Sokolov's dialect betrayed him, this could be the shortest operation in history.

The unlikely once-again spy gazed absentmindedly out the window of the Airbus A319. There was nothing to see. Ordinarily he would've seen the lights of cities in Germany, Poland, or Belarus but clouds obscured any sign of life below him.

With just over two hours flight time left before arriving at Moscow's Vnukovo Airport, the American's anxieties surrendered to this body's needs and he fell mercifully asleep.

For the millionth time, Maggie checked the time on her phone. It was 9:20 PM. She wondered where Josh was. He didn't give her any details about his itinerary. "Itinerary," she thought. "Makes it sound like he's just on vacation somewhere."

She had arrived home around eight o'clock and tried to eat but couldn't. She settled onto the sofa – on Morgan's side – in front of the TV. She flipped channels to find anything other than news. Maggie settled on reruns of M*A*S*H.

The worried woman sipped at her wine. She would've liked to indulge in something stronger – she thought it would help her sleep – but there was work tomorrow.

Maggie looked at her phone again: 9:25. She knew time would pass this way the entire time Morgan was gone.

Wherever he was, it was already tomorrow, she concluded.

Hawkeye and BJ were up to their usual shenanigans, but Maggie didn't have a laugh anywhere in her.

The half-hour episode ended, and another began.

"9:32. Shit."

Morgan – rather Sokolov – awoke with a start. He moved his head around to relieve the stiffness in his neck. He stretched his arms to the extent that he could and not encroach on another passenger's personal space.

It dawned on the traveler that it was light outside. Well, sort of. The sun was just on the horizon from the Airbus' perspective, casting rays of light through the fluffy aggregation of water vapor. White and bright from above, the clouds would be dismal and gray once he stood on the ground in Moscow.

His plan was simple. He would get through Customs, hopefully without being arrested. That was it. That was the entirety of his plan at this point. Once safely somewhere other than a Russian Gulag, he hoped, he would sit and try to come up with Step 2.

As he predicted, Morgan saw a dreary gray Moscow. The clouds' ceiling was so low, it had deprived him of the sight of St. Basil's Cathedral, the Kremlin, Red Square, or whatever other sites might've been within view during the landing. Though by no means a tourist, he would've enjoyed seeing the city from the air. In his shortened stint as a photojournalist in the employ of the Central Intelligence Agency, he had visited *Moskva* twice and thought it was one of the most uniquely lovely cities in the world.

As he disembarked the Airbus, a flight attendant thanked Sokolov for flying home via Aeroflot-Russia Airlines. He proceeded down the gangway where he would, for the next while, be subject to the scrutiny of the Federal Customs Service. He had studied his documents meticulously to make sure he understood every piece of data and that all personal details were memorized. Sokolov even had a home address in Moscow. He had no idea where Parnell had come up with that. He just had to trust her that it would pass investigation.

Arriving at Passport Control he had to remind himself to get in the line for Russian nationals. He noticed that all the agents taking care of the returning travelers were women.

As he waited his turn, he occupied himself with a Russian language magazine that he had kept from his flight. He hoped that in doing so he could prevent anyone from engaging him in conversation. One elderly man started with some small talk. Morgan would just say, "*Da,*" without ever looking up from his reading. He felt rude but it succeeded. The offended man gave up and turned to someone else for dialog.

It wasn't long before Sokolov was at the counter. The agent processing his reentry didn't fit the stereotype of Russian workers of this sort. She was young and attractive. Unfortunately, her demeanor entirely fit the image typecast for Russian agencies' personnel. She was brusque and to-the-point. She gave her interviewee a smile, but it appeared so incongruous with her face that Morgan was afraid it would break it.

This was Morgan's first real test as Sokolov.

"Welcome home." She held Sokolov's Russian passport up for several very, very long seconds, comparing the photograph to the image of the man standing before her.

"Thank you. Glad to be back," replied Sokolov in perfect Russian. The Border Service agent, apparently satisfied that the two faces matched, turned her attention to the stamps in the red Russian passport.

"You've been away some time."

Morgan wondered if this was a test.

"Only a week. It just seems longer." He knew what the passport stamps and other documents said.

"Your address. Eastern part of city?"

"South. *Domashniy* is south of Moscow." But he knew she knew that.

"A house?"

"A flat." Then silently he wondered if she interrogated everyone like this.

The official of the Federal Customs Service began to type his address onto her Cyrillic keyboard.

Sokolov never blinked but Morgan's knees went weak. "Shit!" he thought.

After a moment of waiting on and then staring at the monitor, the inquisitor nodded.

"Flat number ten, Aleksandr Ivanovich Sokolov."

Morgan was in shock. "Thank you, God," he thought. Then he corrected himself. "Thank you, Betsy Parnell."

Morgan was afraid he was sweating. The woman completed the other documents required by her job and approved his return to *Rodina* by way of a forceful stamp onto the final page of his counterfeit document.

With a curt "*Spasibo*" she let him know to move on so she could pass judgement on the next Russian in line.

It was as tense a moment as Josh Morgan had ever had. He gathered up his paperwork and passport and moved along.

✦

It was seven o'clock and inside the walls surrounding the U.S. embassy in Moscow, staff members were saying their farewells to those of the diplomatic personnel who were remaining, however temporarily.

Among the procession of vehicles sat six Green Berets in their UAZ van. A U.S. Marine assigned to the embassy was behind the wheel. Master Sergeant Lechler was beside him. Sergeants Matheson and Jackson sat behind. In the rear cargo area, Jones, Aboud and Macduff sat among their ordnance with small weapons at the ready.

The three special operators in front had on white camouflage pants. The matching parkas were wrapped around their waists. Where their torsos were visible through the truck's windows, each SPIRIT wore causal civilian shirts and coats. Smith, Aboud, and Macduff were outfitted in their full snow camo suits.

Finally, at 7:30 AM, with the people leaving and staying having completed their goodbyes, the caravan began to roll through the embassy gates to make its way to Vnukovo Airport. The hardened operators in the back exchanged looks. Fluff let out a "whew" as Lechler smiled. The adrenaline began to pump through their bodies. They were finally deploying. Operation Nemesis, the "tip of the spear" for Operation Retribution, was finally mobilizing. And that's why they were here.

✦

Aleksandr Sokolov collected his single bag from the luggage carousel. His parka was slung over an arm. The airport was modern and only the Cyrillic letters on the signs made it look different from other major hubs. Well, that and the Russian soldiers in every part of the airport, most with the still pervasive *Avtomat Kalashnikova* weapons. In his previous two visits to Russia, Josh had landed at Sheremetyevo Airport. There was an occasional soldier around the terminal but nothing like the military presence here.

"Sign of the times," he told himself.

Sokolov approached his next point of inspection. The path through Customs Control split into two corridors. On the left was the Green Channel. The Red Channel was on the right. The signs identifying them as channels were written in both Russian and English, though the pronunciation of the Russian word translated as "channel" was really pronounced "corridor."

Sokolov walked under the "Green Channel" sign since he had nothing to declare. Josh hoped it would be less stressful than his last visit with the agent. He was sure his heart couldn't take another interrogation like that.

As with Passport Control, the Customs Control lines were quite long. The one for Russian nationals was longer than for non-Russians. Josh decided that, like Sokolov, many Russians worried about the looming conflict with the Americans had decided to get the hell out of Dodge, wherever their "Dodge" happened to be.

"No place like home," Morgan figured.

The former CIA officer figured that most of the people in the Green Channel were likewise citizens seeking the safety of the Motherland during the crisis. But Morgan thought that, if this thing blows up like it could – he almost smiled at his unintended pun – there would be no safe harbor anywhere in *Rossiya* or the U.S.

It took forever to get to the front of the line but – and he knew that it was because of the long lines – the inspection of his suitcase and the baggage of most of the people surrounding him was cursory. He was passed through in short order, too.

"Pays to be a Russian, I guess," as he noticed others undergoing a very rigorous check.

Finally, Morgan walked through some doors, guarded by a pair of soldiers and two other men in plainclothes, and into the main terminal. He remembered from previous trips that he needed to purchase a Troika card to get around on public transportation. As he was looking for a Mosgortrans ticket kiosk, he suddenly made eye contact with a man walking directly toward him.

235

"That's never a good thing when nobody's supposed to know you're here; let alone who you are," Morgan realized.

Just how long Josh had been out of the game came hurtling into his mind. Working for CIA he'd always prided himself in his ability to maintain his composure; to keep his cool no matter the circumstances. Right now, he really felt like running.

"But how silly would that be," he grasped, considering all the AK-47s around.

As the man grew closer, he smiled and extended his hand.

"Aleksandr Ivanovich!" he exclaimed and upon thrusting his hand into Sokolov's, he pulled him close for a manly bearhug, during which he whispered, "Orlov sent me."

Morgan's now broadening smile was real. It wasn't just because he apparently wasn't being thrown into the Lubyanka Prison at the like-named old KGB Headquarters. It was because suddenly he didn't feel like the Lone Ranger. Maybe he wasn't all alone in this, after all.

From its location west of Central Moscow, the drive from the embassy to the Vnukovo Airport would normally be about forty minutes. The combination of weather and traffic, along with the length of the caravan itself, made for slow going. The forty-kilometer trip took a couple of minutes over an hour.

About ten kilometers from the final turn to Vnukovo, the six Green Beret sergeants began their final preparations. It was snowing heavily, and the roads were somewhat icy. That was good.

"Mother Nature's on our side," observed MSG Lechler.

Sokolov and his new friend, Vladislav Larionovich Proskurkin chatted amiably about the weather and not much else. Morgan knew better than to discuss the particulars about himself, his mission, who Slava was, or why he was here until they were safely away from the ears that were undoubtedly listening electronically around Vnukovo.

Slava led Sokolov to the parking lot and his gray 2017 Lada Vesta sedan.

Once they were safely past the airport's exit, Proskurkin filled him in. He was SVR. He worked for *Direktor* Orlov. In fact, Pavel Semyonovich had become like a father to him.

"Your friend Ryan Crenshaw asked Pavel to send you some help. I am it."

"Sokolov" smiled because Josh Morgan was relieved.

"So where are we going first, Slava?"

"Have you slept?"

"Hardly at all."

"Then we will go to my flat first, Aleksandr Ivanovich, where my wife will prepare a meal and you will sleep."

Morgan wanted to press on but knew he was about to crash. He smiled again and said in Russian, "Pavel Semyonovich Proskurkin, it's wonderful to meet you."

The motorcade of embassy vehicles was approaching Vnukovo by way of Kiyevskoye Highway. A hard right onto Ulitsa Centralnaya, or Central Street and they were there.

The first third of the procession had made the turn when one of the sedans suddenly failed to negotiate the curve, slid on the icy surface onto the shoulder and partly off the road exactly where the elevated offramp from the Kiyevskoye Highway leveled out. The car behind it appeared to nearly rear-end it but managed to skid up slightly behind and to the left. The van behind it braked slowly straight toward the first sedan. The van's rear was slightly slanted to the shoulder. All the other cars managed to come to a complete stop such that none of them collided with another. But it was a mess. The first car would need some help getting back on the road so a congregation of U.S. Marines attending to the caravan ordered all the civilian personnel to remain in their cars.

While some of the Marines encircled the car to assess the means to right it, others crowded around the rear of the UAZ van. From its rear, shielded by their military brethren, sprang six men in snow camouflage pulling an array of likewise covered equipment – large cylindrical canisters, an elongated duffle and other packs. They fled into the wooded area inside Central Street's curve with SFC Fluff Jones covering their tracks in the snow.

On the other side of the street, two men in a Lada Vesta stared at the near-pileup.

Forgetting who was with him, Slava said aloud, *"Chertoviy amerikantsy."*

His passenger repeated in Russian, "Fucking Americans? What do you mean?"

Vladislav Larionovich Proskurkin was embarrassed. "I mean that Americans don't seem to be able to drive in weather when it's bad."

"I still don't get it."

"That is convoy from your embassy going to airport. They were ordered to leave country just as your president did to ours."

Morgan laughed. *"Chertoviy amerikantsiy."*

The embassy Marines quickly got the car straightened out and back on the road. As the cars resumed the last two-and-a-half kilometers to the airport to begin the process of assembling all the items and people for the trip back to the United States, six men hunkered in the snow to wait for their next move.

CHAPTER 28

Josh Morgan awoke from a satisfyingly deep sleep to the smell of a meal as appealing as that of any five-star chef he had encountered. Or maybe he was just hungry.

Normally he would consider three hours of sleep merely a long nap but today it felt like a snooze marathon. Refreshed somewhat from the time of slumber, he felt at least rested enough to begin his quest for answers.

Sokolov walked toward the aroma and upon entering the kitchen, his host's wife bowed, removed her apron, bowed again, and started rushing around to make the table ready for her guest.

Slava laughed as he apologized, "She is always nervous with guests in house. But that doesn't happen often."

Two children peeked around a doorway into the kitchen.

"Come, children," the father beckoned. Two identical twins about nine years old appeared from the next room and stood shyly at attention.

"This is Galina and Irina," he introduced. "They are loves of my life."

At those words, the childish reservation vanished, and the pair dashed to their father's lap.

"They are what I live for. It is for them I do this thing with you."

Sokolov envied the affection he saw in the family.

"I understand. I do."

✦

It was a power breakfast of some magnitude. Seven o'clock in the morning at The Four Seasons Hotel in Washington, D.C., and former U.S. President Trent Weston, former CIA Station Chief Ryan Crenshaw, and current MI-6 Station Chief Sir Albert McGinnis were already at breakfast at Seasons.

Crenshaw reported on an encrypted message he had received from SVR Director Orlov. Brief and to the point, it acknowledged the "tourist's" arrival. Period.

McGinnis reported that his country's Government Communications Headquarters had received no further intercepts that were unquestionably from parties associated with the previous communications.

"That makes sense, doesn't it?" remarked Weston. "Borzilov's in custody so there would be no need to try to contact him. For his part, his mission is pretty much toast. He's lying in a hospital bed and, despite the death of Vice President Logan and the others, the real target had to be Hendrickson."

"Indeed," agreed Sir Albert. "GCHQ is collating everything they've got from the Moscow area but with nothing to distinguish the contents; well, there are just too many blooming communications to sort through. I hope your NSA is having better luck."

"Except they're not looking – at least not with any objectivity," Crenshaw clarified.

"I'm absolutely gobsmacked at the inability of this government to see all sides of this."

Weston looked bewildered.

Sir Albert smiled. "Amazed."

✦

Maggie Loughlin had hardly slept. The little sleep she managed was right at the end of the night so that when she awoke, she was at first disappointed at waking and then devastated at the realization that none of what entered her mind was a bad dream. It was all too real.

She wasn't sure she could get through another day at the office. It was tempting to call in sick but, of course, given the current crisis and the shortage of personnel in the press department, she couldn't consider it. Besides, Maggie finally admitted, as bad as her day would be at work, it would be infinitely worse sitting at home with nothing to occupy her mind. The worst of it was that she couldn't talk to Morgan. She couldn't get any information about where he was or what he was doing. Or how he was – even if he was less than okay.

"Damn it, Morgan."

Without tears or further delay, Maggie got up from the couch and started to ready herself for work.

✦

Morgan finished his lunch. He was ready to get to work.

Galina and Irina stared at him but would look away and giggle as soon as he returned their gazes.

"Where to first?"

Morgan shared his idea. "To Borzilov's flat, I think."

"I agree."

Morgan thanked the lady of the house and knelt to say a special goodbye to the twins.

In a matter of minutes, the "two" Russians were on their way to the small apartment where Gennadiy Borzilov's family had lived upon returning from Washington, D.C.

✦

President Hendrickson was resigned to the fact that her course of action was the only option that made sense. General Richards supported the decision. The pair sat in the Oval Office alone. Prior meetings had always included the entire war planning team, but it wasn't necessary at this point. The plans were all in place. This meeting was solely about reporting progress and the general could handle that.

The previous updates were delivered by phone. Operation Nemesis and therefore the overarching Operation Retribution were indeed underway. Six SPIRITs were in position near the Vnukovo International Airport on schedule. In the middle of the night tonight, they would move to their final location.

"Madam President, if you wish to countermand your orders, this would be the time."

POTUS' demeanor gave no hint of uncertainty or trepidation.

"General, I think we're well beyond any theoretical point of no return."

"I agree, ma'am. The EMP is the primary weapon. The SNAP is our contingency. Personally, there's a part of me that would just as soon nuke 'em right off the bat."

The icy stare from the commander in chief told him he'd just been a little too exuberant about a nuclear holocaust.

"Can you update me about the other deployments. Summaries only, please. Just 'complete' or 'not complete' will be sufficient."

"I can say without qualification, ma'am, that all areas of deployment have been accomplished in record time. Ground personnel are in position on every border with the Russian Federation that we have access to. Aircraft are in place at every base we have in allied territory and are patrolling. Submarines are in place in the Baltic. Our entire Naval fleet is dispersed in strategic locations.

"In summary, Madam President, we have everything in place. Of course, much of our inventory was in place prior to the current crisis because of our NATO agreements and other treaties."

"Well done, general."

The Chairman of the Joint Chiefs and his superior covered a few additional details before she abruptly dismissed him.

As he walked down the hallway from the Oval Office, he griped, "Hell, I've got other things to do anyhow."

Well before reaching the West Wing's exit and his waiting car, the general already had retrieved a cigar from his pocket. Richards' aide held the door open for him as well as offering a lighter that he knew would be required.

As the Army General stepped into his car, he had only one word and it carried some measure of disgust: "Civilians!"

✦

Morgan/Sokolov kept a watchful eye down the hallway as Proskurkin prepared to pick the lock. As the real Russian wiggled the knob to prepare to insert the metal tools, the door opened without requiring them. The former and current intelligence agents leaned into the room for a quick look and, seeing it unoccupied, entered and closed the door behind them.

The living room was neat. It showed no signs of anything being amiss. They moved to the bedroom and then to a room where both children apparently slept. Inside it were a crib and a small bed. They inspected the combination kitchen and dining room. Nothing appeared disturbed.

Proskurkin gave Morgan a bewildered look. "We believe Borzilov's family was abducted to blackmail him into doing thing he did, but this shows no signs."

Sokolov headed to the small table that doubtless served as a nightstand. He picked up a cell phone and held it up to Slava. The man hesitated a moment before taking the phone and nodding.

"She wouldn't leave that," Slava said.

"Or that." Morgan pointed to an item on the dining table that he spotted through the door from the parents' bedroom.

Proskurkin followed him. Morgan picked up a cloth diaper bag.

"Everybody's gone, including the baby. This family doesn't have much. They wouldn't have two of anything, I suspect. Larisa wouldn't leave this behind."

"So, they *were* taken."

"I think so. My British contact gave me a general area where the family might have been moved but nothing specific. There's nothing here that helps."

Slava gathered up the diaper bag and the two investigators left the flat. As they entered the hallway, a pair of eyes looked through a cracked door that shut immediately when Slava took notice of them. He walked to the door and pounded on it.

"Intelligence Service. Open door!" he shouted loudly. "Open door or I will break it in!"

Finally, an older woman opened the door. Beside her was a woman of an age that she was probably the first woman's daughter. The younger woman held a baby in her arms and recoiled at the sight of the two agents.

Proskurkin softened his tone upon gaining entrance to the family's flat.

"We mean you no harm. We are worried about Larisa Borzilova and her children. When have you seen them last?"

The older woman shrugged. Her daughter moved behind her.

The Russian SVR agent asked again, "Have you seen them?"

Still no answer.

Morgan looked about the flat and observed a roomful of religious objects. Icons, crosses, and other Christian-themed items were everywhere.

"Mother, my name is Aleksandr Sokolov and I am assigned to work with the Church in the cases of members who may have come to harm."

As soon as Morgan said "Church," both the older and younger women crossed themselves.

"I'm sorry for the imposition but we are most concerned about your neighbors."

The older woman finally disclosed what she knew.

"It was late at night. I heard noises – voices – but couldn't understand them. They were trying to be quiet, I think. I peeked out my door as they were all leaving."

"You saw them? What did they look like?"

"I only saw from behind. But two men and woman."

That confirmed one theory that British Intelligence had, and that Sir Albert had passed along, Morgan knew. Thinking they had gotten all the information the women had, the two men excused themselves.

"*Spasibo*," Morgan offered and turned for the door.

"I got their car number."

Both men wheeled back around.

"License plate?" asked Slava.

"*Da*. Through our window."

The woman opened a small box adorned with the face of Jesus and retrieved a scrap of paper. She handed it to Morgan.

Scribbled on it was the number of the tags on the car. Morgan was grateful for the clue but wondered how they would use it.

Staying in character, Morgan crossed himself and said to the family, "Mother, Daughter, bless you and the child."

Exiting to the hallway, Proskurkin smiled at the work he had witnessed. "Very nice."

"If we can get anywhere near where the family was held, maybe this will help get some information from locals there."

The men were halfway down the stairs from the flat when Morgan suddenly exclaimed, "Crap! The phone!" He turned to return to the Borzilov flat. As he passed Slava on the way back up, the Russian held the phone up.

"Have it."

Morgan spun back around and fell in behind his SVR partner and followed him to his sedan. Once in the car, he tried to turn on the phone. It was dead.

"Sheesh! I need to go back up to get the phone's charger."

Proskurkin pulled it from his pocket.

"I have that, too. You talk sweet to grandmothers. I remember to collect evidence."

The SVR operative started the Lada, put it in gear, and pulled onto the street.

Sokolov located the Vesta's USB port and plugged in the mobile phone. It took a few minutes for the phone to charge sufficiently to power up. When it did, he saw that the device required a fingerprint or a four-digit passcode.

"Shit!"

"What?"

Morgan turned the phone's screen toward Slava. The American hoped that his counterpart had access to some of the resources of the Foreign Intelligence Service, but he suspected that, like himself, the man was on his own. So, it was almost certainly up to the two of them to access the data.

Morgan/Sokolov knew he had limited attempts so thought carefully about his choices of possible codes.

"Children's birthdays," remarked Proskurkin.

From a pocket Morgan pulled the cheat sheet that Crenshaw had prepared for him about Borzilov. Why he had thought to include the children's birthdays, Morgan had no clue, but there they were. He typed in Valeriy's on the Cyrillic virtual keypad. No success. He suddenly remembered that Russians would put day first, then month. He reentered the numbers. Still nothing.

Ulyana's date of birth brought the display to life. Morgan showed the instrument to Slava with a smile.

"Ah, mothers."

"They're the same everywhere, aren't they?" observed Morgan.

As they drove toward their next destination, Selyatino, Morgan worked through the various bits of data on the phone. His first digital stop was the call logs, both sent and received. He summarized what he saw.

"There are a number of missed calls from various numbers that were 'unknown.' There are no outgoing calls for…" Morgan performed some mental math. "…Nine days."

"They were taken then," concluded Slava.

"*Da*," Morgan agreed. "So, all those missed calls are over the same period.

Very few identified calls but…" He began counting. "…well, several calls during the same period.

"So, I'd guess those calls are from her husband, Gennadiy, but she was gone already. I have some of the numbers from the burners we have in our possession or from which we intercepted communications. We can compare them, but you've got to figure they're going to match. Right?"

The driver nodded his agreement.

"So, he's trying to connect with his wife and can't. That means he doesn't know where she is. Or at least not how to reach her."

"*Da.*"

"British intercepts will get us in the area in Selyatino. Maybe the license plates the neighbor gave us will help. Actually, the description of the car will probably get more results"

"I agree," Slava answered. "Perhaps, once we're there, things will begin coming together."

The drive from the Borzilov flat in Lyubertsy to Selyatino was just over an hour. The Vesta transporting the pair of investigators was nearing the turn off of the loop that took them around *Moskva* to the south, so they were about halfway to their destination, or about thirty-five kilometers out.

Morgan was uneasy at the speed of the vehicle along the snow-packed highway. It was a little too fast for his comfort, but he figured Slava knew what he was doing. It was snowing even more heavily now, and the roads were getting worse.

Morgan couldn't help thinking how beautiful the scenery was, though the area was all residential and commercial. They were well away from the iconic structures in Moscow. Still, the abundance of the white powder reminded him of home. Now "home" meant Washington, D.C. Of course, it used to mean Jackson Hole. His mind wandered to Maggie and what she was doing. Josh had lost track of what time it would be there, but his love was there, and he missed her.

✦

Maggie sat at her desk. She had much more work to do than yesterday. It helped distract her a bit, but she was working on a total of perhaps five hours sleep over the last two nights. It was taking its toll.

The day was significant. Congress would issue a Joint Resolution declaring that a state of war existed for the country. The president had tasked newly sworn-in Vice President Bauer to ensure that the votes were there. As president of the Senate in his new office and having just stepped up from his former office as Speaker of the House of Representatives, he was uniquely qualified to work with both houses of Congress.

It hardly mattered how qualified or unqualified Bauer was, the resolution was in no jeopardy of failing to pass. The mania that had gripped the war council was just as pervasive among the elected representatives in Congress.

War was inevitable. Retribution was required by the people of the United States and the governmental entity that represented them. The president should be relieved at the certainty of the authorization to proceed, given that Operation Retribution was already underway.

President Sandra Hendrickson would deliver a speech from the Oval Office immediately after the approval. Maggie was busily preparing a summary of the speech to distribute to the press corps at the conclusion of the address, based on the script that she already had.

The sun wouldn't set for another thirty minutes but it was almost dark already. The dense clouds that were dispensing the heavy snow shower blocked what little light might be left. The snowfall had been going on almost the entire day and was getting more pronounced by the hour.

The six operators were nestled in nearly two feet of the white stuff. The snowpack made concealment easier and the additional accumulation would help conceal evidence of their movement later in the night. With their high-tech layered clothing, staying warm in thirty-degree temperatures wasn't difficult. It would be somewhat more so during the night.

Morgan and Slava rolled into Selyatino around six. Morgan compared the numbers on Larisa's phones to the ones he had from her husband's and they matched. Knowing that was of no real help but the confirmation lent some credibility to their theory about Borzilov's not being able to reach her and that possibly spoke to the blackmail scenario.

The town had a population of close to thirteen thousand and was located in the Naro-Fominskiy District of Moscow Oblast, Russia. It was urban and that surprised Morgan. He wondered why the kidnappers, if indeed that's what they were, didn't select a more rural area.

But there were forested areas around and, among the residential developments, a few less densely housed neighborhoods.

This was going to be tougher than the American thought, and he had thought it would be nearly impossible. The British intercepts that Sir Albert McGinnis had provided only narrowed the search area to around a four-mile radius.

Morgan opened the Google Earth app on his smart phone and took the paper map from his coat pocket. He located the approximate center of the target area the Brit identified on the map and drew a freehand circle of the approximate region of accuracy. An area of about eight miles in diameter had seemed pretty precise to Morgan when his new MI-6 friend first detailed the area, but upon looking at the map while being in the area, it was still a sizeable region when you were looking for a specific house. Or apartment, or barn, or motel… The former CIA spook realized the men, woman, and their hostages could have been hanging out in any type of structure.

SVR Agent Proskurkin pulled to the shoulder of the road and took the paper rendering of the area from his passenger.

He noted, "About one-half of your circle is wooded. I would think they would want some place like that."

"Secluded. Right. But how can we cover such an area?"

Slava took Morgan's phone and zoomed in on the area he was talking about. He moved the area around the display.

"I don't know if the resolution is good enough to see everything, but I only see two things that are structures for sure. There could be more. But if we check this area, we can eliminate a lot of the target area very quickly, or…"

Morgan caught on, "…Or possibly get very lucky."

Proskurkin didn't look directly at his partner but smiled and nodded. He put the car in gear and pulled back onto the road. The snowfall had lessened somewhat. Still, it might be difficult to see a small road heading into the forested area. Driving southwest, the trees were on the right. Slava had started a navigation app on his phone and was watching the icon that represented the Lada as it moved on the digital representation of the road.

The Vesta hadn't reached a point that would be at the limit of their target area, but the street turned sharply away from the woods. He stopped in the middle of the thoroughfare. There were no other cars near them.

"Did you see a road of any kind leading into the trees?"

"No," answered a disappointed passenger. "Nothing that could possibly be one."

"We can't go any farther."

"Then neither could anyone else."

"Should we turn around and look again?"

A shake of the American's head and, "Let's make the left turn. Google Earth shows that we can follow through these neighborhoods and the street will eventually turn back toward our area. I think we should make sure we can eliminate this entire area."

"*Da*. I agree."

The pair drove through the residential area and the worry entered Morgan's mind that the people they were looking for could be in any of the houses. How would they know? There would be no way to realistically search every house in the town.

◆

The Joint Resolution passed with votes to spare. There were a number in opposition, but it wasn't close. The president composed herself as the producer for her televised speech counted the seconds down with her fingers until POTUS went on the air.

"My fellow Americans, it is with a solemn heart that I announce to you that Congress has approved a Joint Resolution that a State of War exists between the Russian Federation and the United States of America. I have genuinely mixed emotions in that, while I regret that the situation has come to this, I am grateful for the support of the members on both sides of the aisle.

"The challenge to our sovereignty by the cowardly, unprovoked, and outrageous attack on me, Vice President Logan, and the many others who were killed and injured cannot go unanswered. The Resolution of Congress doesn't permit an onset of war but rather affirms that it already existed and was initiated by the Russian Federation."

POTUS continued for only a few minutes longer.

"I have sent a letter to Russian President Tatarov by way of Ambassador Listunov stating the results of the Congressional vote and ordering the expulsion of all remaining diplomatic personnel from throughout our nation.

"I guarantee their safe passage from our borders. I do not promise to delay any actions I deem appropriate in response to…"

◆

After a few minutes driving through the homes in the outskirts of Selyatino, Josh and Slava found themselves returning to a southwesterly direction back along the edge of the wooded land that concerned them. They followed the road only a short distance until both knew they were well beyond the radius Morgan had drawn on the map.

They turned sharply north and then right and northeast toward town. They finally had covered the entire perimeter of the treed plot and had not seen an entrance into it on which a car could conceivably drive to a house or other building.

They repeated the process for two other large, wooded lots, and one smaller one. The results were the same.

The next one they surveyed led the men to a small road that almost went unnoticed, covered as it was by what had to be a day or two of snow. It was difficult, but the Vesta finally reached the end of the lane, only to find nothing there – no structure of any kind.

"Shit," said two voices in unison, one in Russian; the other in English.

With no room to turn around, Slava backed the car the entire distance back to the main road.

Morgan looked at the time. It was 9:30 PM. He was extremely disappointed with their results, though in truth, he'd expected nothing more.

A second road presented the same challenge. Navigating the narrow lane – not much more than a pair of ruts – left them nearly stuck twice. At one point, Morgan feared he would have to get out and push the vehicle. But then he had an even greater fear. What if they weren't able to free the vehicle at all? Fortunately, each time the car managed to spin out of the deep snow.

No sooner did they find enough traction to move forward from their situation than the Lada Vesta's lights lit up a small, but fairly well-built house.

They pulled close to the building. The two investigators gathered up flashlights from the back seat and approached the house. Morgan knocked on the door. Slava gave him a bewildered look, reached for the wooden entryway, and, with a powerful pull, ripped it open with a single yank.

Morgan and Slava shined their beams around the three rooms and found nothing of consequence. No one had been in this house for a long time. Morgan rested his hands on the back of a chair momentarily. He turned in a flash and kicked at nothing in particular.

"Why the hell am I even here?"

Proskurkin patted the American on the shoulder as he walked past him on his way to the door.

"More to do."

Ex-CIA Spook Josh Morgan fell in behind him.

Even with the urgency of their mission, the pair had to eat. They made the short drive to *Kafe Sakura V Selyatino*. Morgan tried the Pizza Primavera while his counterpart had the homemade borsch.

As they ate, the two men reviewed their map. They had eliminated about sixty percent of the area geographically but hadn't made a dent in the number of homes or other buildings their quarry could've been in because they hadn't covered any of the residential areas.

The two also had to sleep so they made the short trip to the *Hostel Moy Dvorik*. Unlike the last two nights, Morgan was fast asleep in no time.

CHAPTER 29

Day 14 – Friday

The six special ops SPIRITs had endured the day relatively comfortably and without hassle. That was no real surprise. Who would be walking through a wooded area along the major road leading to Vnukovo International Airport in the middle of a snowstorm?

They had held their position during the daytime. There was a constant flow of vehicles making their way to the airport and any movement might expose them to some sharp-eyed individual who would wonder what snow-camouflaged soldiers were doing walking through the small wooded area.

There was almost no traffic at 2:00 AM, though. Minutes would pass between cars and trucks. However, the move was perhaps the riskiest part of the operation. It certainly carried the greatest danger of being spotted. The trek covered nearly four hundred meters of open terrain to reach the southwest corner of the interchange for Ulitsa Centralnaya and the Kiyevskoye Highway. Complicating matters even more than the lack of cover was the fact that the entire roadway was lighted.

First, the operators went under the offramp from the highway to the *ulitsa* and then proceeded westward beneath the elevated Kiyevskoye. To the extent that they could, at each step of their hike the soldiers of Operation Nemesis used the road above them for concealment, along with its support columns. They moved slowly to avoid sweating. The perspiration would make the cold more difficult to bear.

Each SPIRIT moved in the tracks of the man ahead of him. The Green Berets carried all of the equipment they left the aircraft with – the SNAP, the EMP, all their survival gear, and their small arms.

Even for trained operators, carrying the array of gear they had was difficult. Each man's share was heavy. The snow was difficult to tread through.

With almost all of the road elevated where they hiked, the only ground-level road they crossed was where the cloverleaf from the eastbound side of the Kiyevskoye completed its arc to join the northwestern-bound Centralnaya leading to the airport terminals and other facilities.

Macduff was the last man crossing the terrain to the other side of the various sections of road that formed the interchange. This gave him the task of scattering the snow to cover the single line of tracks to prevent any attentive drivers on the road from becoming curious about them. This made his and his SPIRIT partner's progress much slower than their teammates.

There were three cars that came to their crossing point. They were a long way away and easily seen well in advance of their arrival where the SPIRITs made their way across the asphalt. Each time, between the first and second cars, and again between the second and the third, two men made their way successfully between them.

It was the fourth vehicle that presented the problem. About the time the two remaining sergeants were preparing to proceed across the road, a vehicle appeared from the direction of the airport. It was going much slower than the others had. Its pace was a crawl, even considering that the road was still covered with snow.

The problem was that, from the vehicle, a pair of spotlights illuminated the landscape on both sides of the road. The two SPIRITs froze, unsure if they could complete their crossing. They were caught in a barren triangular patch of land between the off-ramp from the Kiyevskoye Highway and Centralnaya. With no cover but a small stand of trees, loosely spaced and of relatively small size, the operators had a decision to make. Their choices were all poor ones.

If they retreated for the eastern side of the road from which they had come, it would mean slogging through the snow with their portions of the heavy gear. It would leave tracks where Macduff had just managed to repair the snow from their previous steps.

If they made a run for the cover of the overpass at the interchange of the two streets, they would likewise leave tracks that might get the attention of the occupants of the searching vehicle that had to belong to security personnel. Worse than leaving tracks, the two Green Berets feared they wouldn't make it before the truck arrived.

The final option, though risky, seemed to make the most sense. They dropped their packs and quickly covered them with snow. The two men dropped face-up in the snow and, as efficiently as they could, desperately raked snow over their bodies, including their faces.

Just across this only non-elevated section of road they had to deal with, Master Sergeant Lechler and the other three soldiers in the unit were likewise exposed. They spread the loose white powder over their gear and readied their weapons. The Operational Sergeant pointed at the tracks they left and SFC Jones rushed out to disturb the snow in an effort to disguise their true nature as human footprints. He had very little time. The security vehicle was less than a half-mile away. Deciding he had done as good a job as possible considering the minimal time, he darted back to his three fellow operators. The four knelt against a wall that supported the overhead portion of Centralnaya. The solid wall would provide a visual barrier that should shield them from the floodlights and the eyes of the vehicle's occupants. That is, if they weren't discovered before the vehicle got that far.

Having done all they could to hide themselves, all six commandos could only wait; two lying on one side of the road, the other four kneeling against a support wall on the other. Macduff and Aboud hoped the snow fully covered their prone figures. They were completely unable to see what was occurring around them. The first they would know that one or all of the SPIRITs had been seen would be when they heard the light tap-taps of suppressed weapons fire beyond them. The others that were hunkered against the wall each had weapons prepared to fire should MSG Lechler give the order.

A firefight would create a scenario that would most likely end their mission. Even if they prevailed, hid their victims' bodies, and moved on, the unattended vehicle and missing personnel at whatever office they occupied would lead to a search that they wouldn't be able to escape from.

✦

Inside the security vehicle, two men went about their responsibility to search the area around the airport, though less zealously than they should. The heightened tension with America resulted in increased watchfulness for the Russian soldiers and airport security staff. The two men in the light armored truck were, in fact, discussing the state of war that had been declared against Russia by the American president and speculating as to how far things would really go. So, as the two beams of light swept the areas on both sides of the truck, the Russian soldiers gave scant attention to what they might reveal.

The passenger-side beam moved slowly back and forth, lighting up the landscape. It passed across the retired airplane that rested silently on the ground in the interchange as a symbol that passersby were near an airport. It angled forward until it was blocked by the white wall that supported the road above them

The driver moved the beam of his spotlight about in similar fashion, paying as little regard to the terrain as his passenger was. He pulled slowly under Kiyevskoye Highway where it passed above them and stopped, leaving his brilliant light shining perpendicularly to the truck.

With his vehicle stationary, the soldier behind the wheel selected a cigarette from his pack and lit it. The two men carried on their chatter about the prospects of war beneath the overhead road for a couple of minutes. The driver scanned his side as they talked. The passenger's view was blocked by the highway support. He was completely unaware that, on the other side of the barrier, less than five meters away, four U.S. Green Berets were poised for a fight.

The passenger took a cigarette from his comrade and looked across the space to their left. The surface of the snow was lightly disturbed in a line extending to the far side of the road. The soldier pointed as he lit up.

In response, the driver moved his spotlight up and down the line of tracks. Finally, he made his judgement.

"Deer. From a few hours ago, I suspect. Not fresh."

The right-side soldier wasn't fully convinced and opened his door. He stepped to the front of the armored personnel truck for a better perspective.

The left-side occupant remained in his seat. He lowered his window and told his fellow soldier, "If you want to tromp around in snow for no good reason, go ahead. I'm staying in here where it's warm."

The man outside the military vehicle surveyed the area a short while longer, then returned to the warmth of the vehicle.

✦

Master Sergeant Lechler was the only one who had a clear view of the security vehicle as it had approached. His unit members were pressed as tightly as possible against the support wall, single file behind him.

Lechler had watched the vehicle approach. At one point, the ray of light from the near side of the truck shown a mere two feet from him before the vehicle passed beneath the overpass where its view was obstructed by the white wall against which he and his men were nestled.

As the truck reached the opposite side of the wall, the four men heard it stop. SFC Jones turned to face their rear in case someone approached from that direction.

The men heard a door open. Three or four minutes elapsed before they heard the door shut and the truck begin to move away.

The four SPIRITs remained in their positions until they were sure the truck was far enough away to move back to a location from which they could provide cover for their stragglers. Lechler gave everybody the all-clear and the two men lying in the snow opposite them arose, gathered their packs, and resumed the slow progress to catch up to their fellow operators, with Macduff covering the trail behind them.

✦

The current president had asked the former one to help in the first two or three days after the bombing at St. John's Episcopal Church. In the days since former Speaker of the House Aiden Bauer ascended to vice president and began taking on the responsibilities of that office, Weston hadn't received any requests for help. In fact, he hadn't heard from the Oval Office at all. Since President Hendrickson seemed to consider him a confidant, consulting with him on a number of matters, he found the lack of contact somewhat curious. He wasn't offended. POTUS had been pretty busy. Yet here he was in her office at nearly seven in the evening.

"Why now?" he wondered.

"Trent, I could use your help."

Though her visitor thought again, "Why now?" he merely said, "Of course, Madam President. What can I do for you?"

"After the approval of the Joint Resolution today, I've suddenly begun getting some pushback on the decision to launch an initiative against the Russian Federation."

"Is that what you're calling it now?" observed Weston silently. "An 'initiative?'" But aloud he said, "In what way?"

"Some of the networks and online outlets have spoken out in ways they haven't up to this point. The criticism has been sharp. I'm sure they're just playing devil's advocate. Maybe they're getting cold feet."

The mind of the man who had previously occupied this office was racing. "Or maybe you've been moving so fast that you haven't been listening."

After his private thought, he said, "I see. Are you having second thoughts?"

"Not at all. As you've agreed, this is the only acceptable course of action."

The former commander in chief verbalized his thought this time.

"I'm sorry, ma'am. In what way have I stated my agreement?"

The expression on the present commander in chief was of genuine puzzlement. The tilted head and the furrowed brow, along with the slightly agape mouth made her confusion clear.

"Mr. President, you sat in this very office and gave your support for the war effort."

"Madam President, I believe what I said was that I supported your preparations for war. My advice to you, if I may call it that, was that you knew too much to not prepare. But we are far past preparations now."

Weston could see that Hendrickson was grinding her teeth.

"So, you think a military reprisal is a mistake?"

"I'm not saying that, either. I'm suggesting that it might be premature. I fully supported your expulsion of the Russian diplomats, but I wouldn't have sought the war resolution just yet. We're just – what? – nine days since our conversation about preparedness. May I speak frankly?"

The president's words were abrupt and harsh. "It sounded like you were *already* being frank with me."

The terseness of the comment took Weston aback. He paused to keep his own irritation in check. Finally, he spoke with the practiced calm of a man who had served his country in many capacities and, during the years, had learned that cautious words always served him better.

"Just because the resolution has passed doesn't mean you have to act now. In fact, it could be a powerful tool for international pressure on Tatarov."

"So, you, too?"

The word "too" caught Weston's attention. He knew that the CIA director had voiced her own skepticism about the haste toward war and had been fired because of it. Well, technically it was for reaching out to Orlov, but that was a minor distinction, Weston believed.

"I'm sorry. Madam President. I don't understand."

"British Prime Minister Michaels called me to urge restraint. In particular, Michaels said that, while they will support us and would never publicly voice any disagreement, his government would prefer delaying action. Other of our allies' leaders have contacted me with similar issues. And heads of agencies in my own administration have voiced objections."

"Then perhaps caution is in order to…"

"Goddammit, Trent, they tried to kill me!" Hendrickson thundered. "They nearly killed my son. My husband and daughter…" She paused to collect herself.

"Regardless of your lack of enthusiasm, I need you to issue a declaration of your full support."

POTUS stood and walked around her desk to stand in front of the former president. She put her hands on her hips.

Most people would have dropped their head, fidgeted, and caved. Weston looked the president squarely in the eyes and declared, "I can't do that."

POTUS lifted her arms from where they rested and folded them, waiting for more from the seated man. No additional words came.

Sandra Hendrickson returned to her seat behind her desk. She had no idea what to say. For his part, Weston was a firm believer that, in situations like these, the first person to speak lost.

"I'm disappointed, Mr. President."

"Madam President, I can't in good conscience…"

"Damn your conscience," came the words, softly but with great malice.

"I urge you, Sandra. Delay this thing just a little bit."

"It's too late for that," she disclosed. "I already have operators in place outside Vnukovo International Airport in Moscow. They have a B-54B SNAP and a non-nuclear Electromagnetic Pulse device. If they aren't called off in sixty-eight hours, they have orders to execute their mission at discretion.”

Weston knew his face had gone ashen. It was the low-yield nuclear device that alarmed him. Morgan had already told him that soldiers were in Russia.

“God, Sandra! No! Call them off. Stop this nonsense before it’s too late!”

“I can’t do that.”

Weston thought she almost sounded as if she were boasting when she followed up with, “…in good conscience.”

The former President of the United States was vehemently opposed to acting this early in any form. But nuclear? He was shocked. And terrified.

One of Weston’s underlying principles as president, as CIA director, in every office he had held was that he would do whatever it took to avoid even limited nuclear engagements. He could never support any strategy that considered the so-called “tactical” nukes. But now he had confirmation that it was not only in the playbook; it was the primary option. And it was out of his hands.

In the back of his mind, he considered where this might lead. With two superpowers at war, the logical extreme was nuclear. He had mostly pushed that out of his thoughts.

Weston would’ve felt hypocritical in announcing support for Hendrickson simply because his supposed buy-in would be, in fact, a lie. It was a lie to the extent that he was actually a party to efforts underway to undermine the rationale for doing so. He wondered how Josh was doing. Was he meeting with any success?

He knew he would have to pass along the situation of troops on the ground outside the airport in Moscow.

“The airport… why is the ops team at the airport?” he puzzled. “They had to have infiltrated the country elsewhere. And a nuclear bomb, even a small-ish one, doesn’t have to be in a hyper-specific location. It only had to be ‘in the neighborhood,’ so to speak, of its target.”

He pondered the question as his Secret Service detail transported him back to The Four Seasons.

Secret Service Agent Jack Johnston knew his protectee well enough to know when something hadn’t gone well, but it was neither his place nor his nature to ask. He sat without comment in the passenger seat beside fellow agent Jeff Coulter, who had made the same assessment that Johnston had.

Suddenly, the two agents heard an exclamation from the seat behind them.

“Oh, shit! Damn it! No!”

✦

After their close call early in the relocation from their staging point, the six Green Berets had moved without incident and reached their final vantage point.

The highs each of the next several days were forecast to range from thirty degrees Fahrenheit to thirty-four. Overnight lows were also anticipated to remain fairly consistent at about nineteen degrees. Those were not outrageous temperatures. With seven layers of clothing, the SPIRITs could adjust as necessary. But they weren't adjusting much. Remaining hidden was the primary operational consideration until the moment they decided to execute. The immobility, with its lack of activity, made the cold seem more bitter than it would've otherwise been.

Each of the warriors made semi-snow caves and nestled their respective low-profile, single-man tents into them. They cut boughs from the evergreens surrounding them to camouflage the white shelters. Mostly the men lay on sleeping pads that were designed for sub-zero weather and the soldiers not responsible for lookout duty remained in their shelters in their sleeping bags.

They left their ordnance stowed for now. They would assemble the equipment at the opening of their window for discretionary engagement.

Until then, they remained hidden, eating cold rations and resting.

✦

Former Commander in Chief and ex-CIA Director Trenton Weston, ex-CIA Case Officer Ryan Crenshaw, and soon-to-be ex-CIA Director Elizabeth Parnell sat in Weston's suite at his hotel with the only one of them who would have his job after their mission was over. And that fact made MI-6 Washington Station Chief Sir Albert McGinnis the only one who had even the remotest possibility of providing direct support to the two men in Russia who were trying to avert a nuclear holocaust. Yet it was his very position that prevented him from exercising any of that power.

The group never communicated on the phone except to arrange meetings. The code was a simple one-word text. Weston had texted "hello" to them from his SUV and all except McGinnis were waiting for him at his hotel when he arrived. The Brit arrived at the same time as Weston and they rode the elevator to his room together.

A disbelieving collection of current and former government officials from two countries listened as their host explained what he had learned at the White House. Once they heard the plan and its current level of implementation, any reservations about their course of action evaporated.

"I suspected things were far along," admitted McGinnis. "My superiors must certainly know those details. I didn't need to."

"Why the airport?" Parnell got right to the issue that had troubled Weston.

"I gave that some thought after meeting with Hendrickson. My first thought was that the nuke was the primary weapon. I've decided it isn't. It's the EMP," he speculated.

Crenshaw spoke first. "They're going to take down a plane? That's not exactly the response I was expecting."

Parnell understood and cleared it up for the others.

"President Tatarov uses Vnukovo."

Each spoke their preferred expletive.

"Yes. They're going to take out the Russian president," Weston confirmed. "At least, that's what I think."

"That's all it could mean," agreed Sir Albert. "And, in a way, it makes sense. If the Russians were trying to take out your president... well..."

"We've got to get her to call them off!" exclaimed Crenshaw.

"Can't," countered Weston. "Or at least we don't have much time to. She's given them discretionary execution."

"What's that?" asked the former CIA spy.

Parnell spoke first. "They have a wave-off deadline. If they're not ordered specifically to stand down by that time, they go dark and take action autonomously and at their discretion. They will turn off their communications devices, except among themselves, and turn them back on every twelve hours for updates."

McGinnis sighed and placed his hand on his forehead. "When?"

Weston answered, "11:00 PM Sunday, Moscow time. 3:00 PM Washington time. At least that's when their discretion goes into effect. Actually executing depends on Tatarov taking off in his plane. Until then, the SPIRITs sit and wait."

"We have to let Orlov know. As SVR director, he can tell Tatarov, warn him not to fly," suggested Crenshaw.

"I'm not sure that's a good idea," warned Parnell.

Crenshaw looked confused.

Weston took up the explanation. "If we tell Orlov, he may do more than warn the president not to fly. They'll go after our guys, too, to make sure. That's what I'd do."

Everyone around Weston's hotel room agreed.

"I see your point," conceded Crenshaw. "We can't tell him about the nuke. But he still goes and finds it."

"And you run the risk of the Russians deciding on their own first strike. Orlov is trying to prevent the possibility of war, maybe nuclear. He finds out we're already about to start one..." finished McGinnis.

"So, it's pretty much up to Josh," summarized Crenshaw. "And he's got to get evidence while the president still has time to call this thing off. Something short of seventy hours."

"That's about the size of it. Assuming she can be persuaded to call it off," agonized Weston. "Hopefully Tatarov will do the smart thing under the circumstances and just hunker down."

"So how do we let Morgan know?" asked Sir Albert.

The same blank, worried expression was on everyone's face.

✦

Maggie was home. Soon she would go to bed and try to sleep, unless she decided to stay on the couch in front of the television again. She wished she could talk to Josh. She wished he was home. She wished they were both back in Wyoming, oblivious to the extent of the crisis.

Morgan hadn't even taken his personal cell. It was on the nightstand on his side of the bed.

The fiancée decided to reach out to Ryan Crenshaw to see if he had news of the fiancé.

✦

Ryan Crenshaw looked at his vibrating phone.

"any news," read the text from Maggie. Ryan hated not telling her of the current situation, but she didn't need the worry. Besides, what did he really know about Morgan? All that he knew was of the situation. Everybody involved had agreed that they wouldn't communicate except in the direst of scenarios. The current one fit but Maggie didn't need to know.

Josh's former college professor typed, "no news that's good news right?"

The issue with trying to reach Josh was that he got burner phones in Moscow. He hadn't called in and that was the only way they would know his number. It would be suspicious to SVR *Direktor* Orlov, who believed himself to be an equal participant in this venture, if they asked him to contact Morgan without telling him why.

In other words, they were dead in the water.

CHAPTER 30

Day 15 – Saturday

It was well before sunrise and, though it wasn't snowing, Selyatino's lights reflecting off the low clouds in the Russian sky indicated it was still overcast.

Both men were ready to resume their quest for evidence at 6:00 AM. His anxiety had kept Morgan from getting much rest; that and Slava's snoring, which indicated that he hadn't been kept from his slumber.

The men had studied the map intensely the previous night to try to determine a strategy that had a rational basis. They came up with nothing that would expedite their search. Proskurkin took Larisa Borzilova's phone from his pocket and began to comb through its data again. Morgan retrieved the Russian mother's diaper bag and rummaged through the contents. Suddenly, his eyes fixed on one item.

"Slava, how well do you think they've treated the mother and kids?"

"I don't know. Maybe pretty well until they no longer need them for leverage. Then who knows? Why do you ask?"

Josh Sokolov held up two bottles of medicine and smiled wryly.

"The baby might need these. And they don't have them."

SVR Agent Proskurkin smiled and nodded and began to search his smart phone for Selyatino business listings of pharmacies. None of the ones he found were open yet, so while they waited, without an effective plan in mind, the two went to breakfast.

As they ate, Proskurkin examined the medicine. "Do you know what these medicines are – mercaptopurine and methotrexate?"

"I have no idea," answered the American as he finished his coffee, "but I hope the little girl really needs them."

They identified the two closest pharmacies to their target area circled on the map, which contained the areas south and southwest of Selyatino and decided to drive to them when their opening times arrived.

The first was A-Mega and the two investigators were waiting in the parking lot when the store opened. They rushed in and spoke to the pharmacist as he began preparing for business.

Slava held up the two bottles and enquired whether the man had filled prescriptions for the two medicines recently. The man looked briefly at the bottles and answered with an immediate "no."

"Could you check with your other workers? It's important," Morgan asked.

"No other workers. Only me," the elderly pharmacist replied. He continued to set up for his work day.

Proskurkin asked, "Are there similar medicines that don't require a prescription?"

The store owner gave an annoyed glance over his reading glasses.

"*Nyet.*"

The two men started for the door. They halted their progress upon the pharmacist's question, "Have you tried the Gorzdrav?"

The pair of inquisitors suddenly felt very stupid.

The Russian turned to face the man. The American simply held up the bottles to look at the labels stuck to them. The name of the dispensing pharmacy was clearly printed on the containers – "Gorzdrav."

"Since medicine was filled at Gorzdrav Aptyeka in Moscow, perhaps it was refilled at same store here." The man seemed to take some pleasure in rebuking the men taking up his time preparing for customers.

Before Proskurkin could ask the question, the pharmacist said, "Three minutes," and gave the address.

"One last question, please. What are these medicines for?"

"A number of things. Taking both in combination, probably leukemia."

The two trained intelligence professionals immediately experienced a rush of sadness for a child they didn't know – for a child they suspected might already be dead. But not from a disease."

Slava looked especially bothered, Morgan saw, and knew it was because he had children.

The drive to the Gorzdrav Pharmacy was really closer to two minutes. It was west of A-Mega near the hospital. Its pharmacist was friendlier.

"Oh, my," came a sympathetic remark from the man upon looking at the bottles. "These are oral chemotherapy. Yes. We filled these few days ago. They're not something we ordinarily have in store. When woman called about them – I took call – I told her we would have to bring from Moscow. They were here that evening."

Both of the men trying to find evidence to stop a conflict between their countries felt a surge of adrenaline.

"It was odd that woman didn't seem too upset at delay. You should take these daily. And dosage is for small child. I would have thought she would have had greater urgency."

Morgan realized it wasn't the mother who had called. Likely the woman who was one of the abductors.

The man, in his early thirties, finally realized he was sharing a customer's information with these two men. He didn't know who they were, and he decided he should find out.

"I'm sorry. Who are you? Why are you asking these questions?"

Morgan saw his Russian counterpart begin to reach for his SVR credentials and interceded.

"I am the father of the baby Ulyana, who has the leukemia. The mother has taken our daughter and I'm afraid she won't take care of her. We've... uh, had some arguments."

The pharmacist's sympathy returned.

"I understand. I'm sorry. She's young?"

"Not even a year," replied the child's "father" with some anguish that wasn't entirely faked.

"At her age, I'm guessing acute lymphoblastic leukemia."

Of course, Morgan knew the man had no way of knowing for sure, but the word leukemia stunned him again.

"Yes. Her mother is travelling with our son, the baby, and three other people, I've learned. Do you have a name? Or description?"

The pharmacist nodded at the fake Russian who was asking the questions.

"Yes. Well, name. Not description."

The answer caused some disappointment to both of the men who were seeking the Borzilov family.

"They didn't come in. Since mother didn't seem as concerned as I thought she should be, when medicine arrived, I had courier take it to her. They gave address when they ordered. You know, it was surprise. Nobody answered door, but delivery driver heard people inside. He left package outside door. You can only do so much. Of course, they haven't come in to pay, but it's for child."

Morgan's and Proskurkin's excitement was equaled only by the increased tension they felt in finally making progress.

"May I have the address?"

The pharmacist had another bout of misgivings but upon seeing the excitement in the "father" at possibly seeing his child again, he began scribbling on a piece of paper.

Morgan snatched it out of the man's hand and thanked him for his kindness. Morgan thought to himself that the man had no idea what good he might've really done by helping.

Morgan and Proskurkin quickly moved to the door.

"Make sure your child takes her medicine. Dear girl."

In the car, Proskurkin gave Morgan a grievous look and expressed what Morgan had himself been thinking.

"You know this might not be the right place. No one answered the door. I would've given a fake address. And even if it's the right place, it may not give us the evidence we need to get your president to halt this nonsense."

Morgan grimaced. "Just drive."

While Vladislav Proskurkin started out of the *aptyeka's* parking lot, Morgan busily typed the address they'd just gotten into the nav app on his phone. The address was in the edge of a wooded area in a location they hadn't checked. It was, however, within the radius of the area the Brit said was the limit of their technology's accuracy.

It wasn't far to the southwest of the first forested expanse he and Slava had checked last night. And it was only minutes away.

When the American and the Russian arrived at the place indicated on the navigation app on Morgan's phone, it was indeed off the beaten path. If there was a house there – and the courier had said he left the prescriptions at one – it certainly wasn't visible from the street. The only hint that there might be something there that people visited was the slightly depressed section of snow that might be the road that Morgan's phone swore was there.

The space in the trees through which it went was about the width of a car. The only indication was that the surface of the snow was lower. So, if it was a drive into a house, it hadn't been used for a day or two. The snow shower had covered any tracks – or potential tracks, Morgan reminded himself – significantly, even though it had ended about twenty-four hours ago.

Proskurkin and his passenger looked at the spot that appeared to be the entrance to the address they were looking for. The pair exchanged an apprehensive glance. The driver shrugged and pulled cautiously onto the snow-buried path. Once he was off the main street, he came to a stop and reached under his seat.

"You never know," he said, and handed his counterpart an MP-443 Grach PYa identical to his own.

Morgan pulled the slide back and released it, chambering a round.

"*Da. Nikogda nye znayesh.*"

Slava eased forward, his only clue at the location of the road, or path, being the barely hinted at imprints of previous traffic. Only seventy meters off the paved road sat a rundown, but habitable, house. It was small and white. No vehicles were present, and no smoke was coming from the chimney. Neither pair of eyes saw tracks through the snow. Morgan noticed one other detail.

"No package near the door. Somebody retrieved the medicine," he deduced.

Proskurkin turned off the engine. He and Morgan opened their respective doors of the Vesta and stepped out. Slava took the lead. Morgan had no problem with that. He was an active intelligence officer. Morgan was a "former" one. Each man moved far enough around the two sides of the house to ensure that there wasn't an automobile behind the structure.

The SVR agent looked in a window on the southwest side of the house. After a moment, he lowered his handgun and returned to the front of the old *dacha*.

"Morgan!"

Ex-CIA came around from the northeast side of the house. Seeing his companion had put his gun down, he, too, lowered his from the ready position he had maintained during his survey of the property.

He saw the Russian walk up the steps onto the porch without reservation, so he did the same. The door was unlocked. Slava, though certain nobody was inside, still looked cautiously into the house as the wooden entry swung on its hinges. He walked in and inserted his gun in his waistband holster. Morgan put his in a coat pocket.

"This room."

Morgan followed as Slava led from the living area into an adjacent room on the left.

On a bed lay the body of a woman with a baby girl still wrapped tightly in her arms. Beside the bed was the body of a young boy on the floor with a pencil and a piece of paper, on which there was the unfinished drawing of a cat. There was no need to check pulses.

"I guess we're in the right place," said Proskurkin rather coldly. Morgan was disturbed at the sight, particularly of the children.

Larisa Borzilova had two bullet wounds in her forehead. Ulyana had one. Son and older brother Valeriy had one in the side of his.

Russian SVR operative Vladislav Larionovich Proskurkin assessed the scene.

"I would guess the mother went first. Then the boy and the baby last."

Morgan collected himself and joined the examination of the bedroom. On a table by the bed were diapers, powder, and a couple of bottles. Some baby formula and an empty milk container were there. There weren't any extra clothes for the mother and son.

"We suspected they would be dead," said Slava. "If they were going to kill them, why provide for them? In fact, why take them out of the apartment at all? Truthfully, I expected nothing when we started our search for a pharmacy that might have provided the medicines. Same reason. Why care for someone you are going to kill?"

"Maybe they didn't intend to kill them, if all went well with Borzilov's assassination attempt. If they were blackmailing him, as we think, and he succeeded in killing Hendrickson, maybe they were going to honor their part of the bargain. Perhaps they realized that Borzilov was 'bought and paid for,' as we say in the U.S., and that they could use him for other ops."

Proskurkin pushed the dead woman's legs away to make room for himself and sat on the edge of the bed.

"As you and I discussed, as I discussed with Orlov, and as you have said you discussed with your comrades back in your homeland, none of this would be necessary if this was an operation sanctioned by my country."

"I agree. Now we just have to prove it."

Morgan returned to the living area. His partner examined the bedroom a bit longer and, finding nothing in the way of clues, he joined his associate. When he entered the room, he saw the American holding up a bag.

"The medicine. Unopened. Must've been delivered about the time they decided to kill the family."

"*Da.*"

The men scrutinized the room. There wasn't much there. Nothing had been left behind by the kidnappers, it seemed. Even the logs and other items that were now only ashes in the fireplace had burned completely. There was no hint at what the other objects might've been.

Morgan and Slava opened every cabinet door, every drawer, and found nothing. They looked in every other room in the small structure with the same result. Morgan sat at the kitchen table, dismayed by the absence of anything useful in their quest to absolve Russia of culpability in the bombings.

The SVR agent looked on the dim side again. "This could've still been run by some rogue element in Russia. It would be hard for your woman leader to distinguish that from a sanctioned op."

Morgan thought of the Muscovite as a "glass half empty" sort of man. He hated to think so, but knew the man was right.

"So, what do we do? Give up?" asked the Russian spy. "I think we move on. There is too much at stake."

"I agree. Just don't know where this leaves us."

Morgan crumpled up the piece of paper on which the pharmacist had written the address of the house and tossed it toward the fireplace.

In an instant, a light clicked on. When he had walked toward the back of the house, before he knew that Slava had abandoned his search around the other side, he had seen a cardboard box partly covered with snow. He jumped and headed to a back door that he knew had to lead to the box's location. Proskurkin furrowed his brow, wondering what his friend was so excited about. Still, he rose to follow.

Just as he reached the back door, from just outside he heard, "*Spasibo tyebye, Gospodi!*"

"Why are you thanking God?"

His American associate was returning from his discovery. He dusted snow from the top of the box and grinned broadly.

"Trash!"

"You're thanking God for trash?" teased Slava Proskurkin, but he knew exactly why Josh Morgan was so excited. It might mean nothing, but their quarry had left something behind.

In a matter of minutes, the two investigators had every piece of refuse laid out on the kitchen table. There were scraps of food, paper towels, and newspapers. There were also plastic eating utensils and fast food wrappers from places in Selyatino.

But there was one feature on several of the pieces of trash that stood out noticeably. Both Joshua Matthew Morgan and Vladislav Larionovich Proskurkin had the epiphany, but it was the American who spoke first.

"These weren't Russians!"

CHAPTER 31

In the 19th Century, Emperor Alexander III asserted that "Russia only has two allies; its army and its navy." But, while the Russian Federation remained very self-reliant, with similar intentions and equal urgency to its enemy, it was circling the wagons. Shoring up alliances with friendly nations was paramount if they were going to assemble a coalition as formidable as the Americans had amassed.

Ambassadors from every ally had already conferenced with Tatarov in his office in Moscow. The leaders of members of the Collective Security Treaty Organization (CSTO) scheduled visits with him. The heads of state of Armenia, Belarus, Kazakhstan, Kyrgyzstan, and Tajikistan responded to the Russian president's request for a conclave in the Russian capital.

However, to display their boldness in the face of the actions of the American president and the meaningless vote by her Congress, Russian leaders weren't sitting back expecting all their friends to come to Moscow. Rather, they were reaching out to them.

So, the press announcement from the Kremlin reinforced its nation's fearlessness when it announced that President Tatarov would make a multi-nation trip, beginning with China and then moving on to North Korea and Syria.

Solidarity in purpose and defiance in the face of American aggression would be the theme of the trip abroad.

The CSTO meeting and the date of the president's friendship tour would be announced soon.

✦

A number of items in the box of trash held no meaning for their investigation, but Morgan and Proskurkin observed that some of the food wrappers and empty cigarette packages each had an identical characteristic.

Each was written in Arabic.

"Holy shit!" shouted Morgan in English. He covered his face with both hands as the pieces all began to assemble themselves in his mind. The only good thing about the truth was that it wasn't the Russians.

"No! No! No!"

Morgan got up and paced the room frantically. He looked at the Russian sitting at the table, bewildered at his friend's anxiety about this.

"Saudi Arabia. The Holy Islamic Republic of Saudi fucking Arabia!" The name of the country that had kidnapped former President Trenton Weston exploded in English.

"Why is that so bad?" asked the SVR agent.

His hatred of the Saudi government came rushing into Morgan's mind like a tsunami.

After his plan to try Weston as a war criminal fell apart, fearing that the wrath of the Great Satan might visit upon him personally, Saudi President Yasim al-Hashimi acceded to every demand the United States made of him. New president Hendrickson had managed her post-crisis position well. She conducted the negotiations without fanfare to avoid having the bluster of the Saudi president erupt into something of substance.

So, as al-Hashimi publicly continued his anti-American diatribe and threats at every opportunity, POTUS dismissed them as baseless posturing before his radical following.

But it was plain now that the belligerence hadn't been hollow, after all. Revenge was always a part of al-Hashimi's intentions, it seemed.

Morgan explained the unknown details of Saudi Arabia's involvement to Slava about what the U.S. had explained to the world at that time as the acts of a single terrorist.

"I say again, why is that so bad?"

Morgan wanted to rip the man's head off for his lack of understanding, as his confused look persisted. Morgan grappled for a way to clarify the basis for how horrible this development was.

"Oh, my!" Morgan suddenly whispered thoughtfully. After a pause, he continued, "Why *is* this so bad?"

He shook his head at his rant and the nonsense behind it.

"They weren't Russian!"

"They *weren't* Russian," echoed Slava.

"This is wonderful!" Morgan exclaimed finally.

"This *is* wonderful! Now you can tell your American leaders, and this will all go away."

The release Morgan had felt at the belief that the change of identity of the guilty parties was about to defuse the tensions with Russia fell apart.

"Not so fast," Morgan cautioned, returning to Russian. "It *is* wonderful news but I'm not sure it's enough yet. Remember, we're not doing this in any official capacity. My president won't take my word for it. I'm not even supposed to be here."

The Russian didn't seem to believe his American partner. "I liked the happier you better."

"Slava, you have the benefit of your *Direktor* knowing what you're doing. Hell, he *sent* you to do this. But what if you had set out on your on without his approval or knowledge? What would he do?"

Reality was starting to sink in for Proskurkin.

"Don't get me wrong, I'm going to pass this along, but I assure you; we're not done yet."

✦

CIA Director Elizabeth Parnell, like many in the government, had seen little sleep recently. Of course, the concern of others was mostly in moving the president's war plan along to a successful conclusion. Her agenda was just the opposite. She wanted the whole thing stopped.

It was seven in the morning. She had stayed in bed despite the fact that she had been wide awake since about three-thirty and had only managed fitful periods of sleep prior to that.

She had provided, along with the ones she had purchased for herself, three burner phones each for Crenshaw, Weston, and McGinnis. The one in her current use began to vibrate on her nightstand.

Knowing that Morgan had the number of the device, she excitedly reached to check the display. She didn't know the numbers of whatever phones he had procured in Russia, but she knew this one didn't belong to any of the three team members locally.

Parnell read the brief text and knew it was from their man in Russia.

"the ones who rented jezebel" was all the message said.

It took a minute to decipher the meaning, but when she did, she wasn't as surprised as she might have anticipated.

"Damned Saudis."

Saudi agent Fadi Al-Majeed had really been the one who used the boat named *Jezebel*, at least for a few minutes, and he was dead. His national support had rented it for him.

The DCI needed to let the team know, but that was secondary. She grabbed her Agency phone and dialed the number for POTUS. There was a momentary delay while she was announced to the president. The comment was succinct.

"The president can't speak to you right now."

"This is urgent."

The screener was unpersuaded, apparently having heard the "urgent" plea countless times before.

"I'm sorry."

Although she wasn't surprised at the snub, the director was pissed. She had already begun dressing even before she got word that POTUS was ignoring her.

Parnell rushed to her car and sped off toward 1600 Pennsylvania Avenue.

✦

"So where do we go now? Do we try to retrace their steps?"

Morgan shook his head and wagged his right index finger at his associate. He even smiled at the Russian.

"No, if they're still in the country…" He paused as soon as he spoke those words, realizing they might have indeed fled Russia.

He continued, "If they're still in Russia, they'll be at the Saudi embassy. Where else would they be?"

The two men were walking briskly toward the door to leave the house. The grisly sight of the bodies of the three Borzilovs caught the American's attention through the doorway to the bedroom. He hated to leave them without attention, but he never slowed down.

Inside the Lada Vesta, Slava was turning the key when Morgan's phone buzzed. He had expected a message from Betsy. He hadn't expected this message.

"same that happened to jezebel – ur 20 – 32h"

Slava saw the shock on his passenger's expression.

"What is it, Morgan?"

"Aleksandr Sokolov" knew time was growing short. The *Jezebel* had exploded into a million pieces in the waters of the Gulf Mariners Marina.

"So, an explosion will happen at my "20" – my location – here, in thirty-two hours," he thought. That could only mean one thing.

Morgan said to his driver, "Nothing. Everything's fine."

"Fucking politicians," he griped silently as Slava Proskurkin pressed the accelerator and headed for Moscow.

✦

Elizabeth Parnell, CIA director for only an indefinite period of time longer, had guessed correctly that the president hadn't thought to ban her from the West Wing.

She needed no identification to the guards at the gate to the White House complex, or into the West Wing. The guard announced her arrival to the president's personal secretary, Brianna Washington. The reply was delivered in a flash.

The guard had a look of complete puzzlement. "I'm sorry, Director Parnell. The... uh, the president can't see you... right now... she said."

Parnell had been delivering the president's intelligence briefings for several months now. Guard Oliver Blalock was dumbfounded that she appeared to suddenly be *persona non grata*.

"I'm sorry, ma'am."

"Not your fault, Oliver."

Parnell was considering what options she might have for bolting to the Oval Office.

"Good morning, Director Parnell."

Acting Press Secretary Maggie Loughlin hadn't slept much – again – and arrived at work a little early. She was startled when she saw one of her fiancé's "team members" in the lobby of the West Wing. Even though the CIA director was there most mornings to meet with the president, she was currently on the president's shit list. Somehow Maggie knew this had to do with Morgan.

"Good morning, Ms. Loughlin." An idea occurred to Parnell.

"Secretary Loughlin, do you have a moment?"

Maggie was flustered but managed a weak "of course."

She escorted Parnell toward her office, but when she reached the hallway where they would turn left to go there, the CIA chief turned right. The Secret Service agent posted by the Oval Office's door moved to intercept Parnell. He hadn't received notice that she would be coming.

"Good morning. Special briefing with POTUS," the director bluffed.

The agent didn't yield.

From the corridor leading from his office appeared Chief of Staff Noah Chandler.

"Betsy."

"Noah," she said with a smile.

"Can I help you?"

Betsy knew that Chandler wasn't a man easily conned. She decided to just be honest.

"Can I have a moment?"

The chief said nothing but turned to lead Parnell to his office. At the other end of the hall, Maggie knew nothing of what was going on, but she was distressed, nevertheless.

DCI Parnell only shared that she had information that might suggest the Russians weren't behind the bombings. She didn't divulge that Josh Morgan was the one who had uncovered the information; only that she had an asset on the ground in Russia.

Chandler pondered the disclosure briefly. Momentarily, without a word, he lifted his handset and called his boss.

"Ma'am, I believe it would be in the nation's interest to hear what Director Parnell has to say."

There was a pause.

"Yes, ma'am. We'll be right…"

Another pause.

"Yes, ma'am. Understood."

Relieved, Parnell stood to make the short trip to the president's office.

"Keep your seat, Betsy. She's coming here."

Betsy's rolled eyes were met with a shrug from Chandler.

"Am I so soiled that she doesn't even want me in her office?" the spy chief wondered.

◆

The roads were still a bit icy. In the best weather conditions, the drive to the Saudi Arabian embassy would take fifty minutes, but Slava made it in forty-five.

He parked the Vesta on the street not far from the diplomatic offices of the Holy Islamic Republic of Saudi Arabia.

"Aren't we a little obvious, Slava?"

"Doesn't matter. They know we spy on them all the time. We surveil everyone. They expect we'll be here, right here in this spot."

Morgan wasn't convinced. He shook his head and slumped down in his seat. His Russian driver made no effort to hide.

The pair watched a few cars come and go, but none was the one they were looking for.

"How do we know they'll keep the car?"

The SVR agent shrugged with a smirk. "Why would they change?"

◆

"I told you I didn't have time."

Director Parnell stood. "Yes, Madam President. Thank you for…"

"Please get to the point."

Chandler squinted at the tension that was apparent between the two women.

Though it wasn't her office, the DCI said, "Would you care to sit?"

"Won't be that long. The point?"

Parnell remained standing, as well. She explained what she had told Noah Chandler – asset on the ground, new information, casts doubt on Russian involvement, suggests the Saudis, and so on.

"Who's your asset?"

Betsy stalled. There was no way she would identify Morgan.

"I'm not at liberty to say, ma'am."

"Not at liberty?" POTUS' voice was very measured. The volume was low, but her words oozed contempt, an observation not lost on the woman's chief.

"I'm sorry, but, yes, ma'am."

"Is that all?"

"Well, I…"

The President of the United States spun around. "I have work to do."

And that was that.

Betsy Parnell hoped that Morgan hadn't burned his phone yet.

✦

Morgan would've trashed his phone by now but, quite frankly, it hadn't occurred to him until they parked near the embassy.

It vibrated.

He read "on your own"

The former CIA case officer massaged his temples with the first two fingers of each hand.

"On my own," he thought. "Isn't that always the case?"

✦

Maggie hovered around the West Wing lobby, hoping to get a word with Parnell on her way out. The director delivered a discreet shake of the head.

"Not now," Maggie understood. "She knows something but won't tell me."

She returned to the office she occupied that belonged to Marie Ginnetti. She knew she shouldn't, but she lifted her mobile phone, accessed Contacts, and tapped to dial a number. A familiar voice answered.

"Hello, Trent… I'm okay. Was wondering if there was any news." Maggie tried to keep her words veiled, but she really didn't know how to disguise her intended meaning.

"Can we talk later? I'll call when I'm free," came the reply. "Thanks, dear."

Maggie was annoyed at the abrupt ending to the call. But that it was abrupt made her sick to her stomach. She would try to work.

✦

Trent Weston had received a cryptic message from Parnell.

"screwed"

His phone chirped immediately after that message at the arrival of another.

"hello"

He knew that Crenshaw, McGinnis, and Parnell would arrive shortly.

✦

The deployment outside of Vnukovo International Airport was uneventful. SFC Jack Jackson and SFC Bull Macduff were on watch.

SFC Lucas Matheson was the Communications Sergeant for Operation Nemesis. He was the point man for communicating with the Special Forces Operational Detachment-B, or B-Team, deployed in Estonia. Cooley passed on the information he had learned that the Russian president had just announced that he would be flying to a handful of countries in the coming days.

Each of the six SPIRITs gave a thumbs-up to their teammates.

The weather had been partly cloudy with only an occasional flurry. There had been little wind for the last ten hours. Since wind determined the direction of an airplane's takeoff, it was important, though not essential, that the wind be coming from the team's backs. In that case the Russian president's plane would take off directly toward them.

The major factor in selecting their tactical position was that the prevailing wind direction in Moscow in winter was southeasterly. The primary runway at Vnukovo was northeast to southwest. It would require generally northerly winds to necessitate that departing planes take off away from the operators. And that almost never happened.

✦

The Embassy of Saudi Arabia in Moscow was designed such that many of the offices wrapped around the parking lot. It was difficult to get a vantage point to see inside the lot. A number of cars had come and gone but none had the license plate with the number that the Borzilova's neighbor had given them.

Having sat there for nearly ninety minutes, Morgan was growing impatient. It was getting dark.

"Screw this. We don't have the time."

The man in the driver's seat looked at him with concern. He knew their mission was important, but his fellow operator had a much greater sense of urgency than Slava himself had.

"What have you not told me?" he wondered.

Morgan's phone had a camera, though without the resolution of high-end smart phones. Nevertheless, Morgan needed to speed things up. He stepped out of the car and walked toward the entrance of the parking lot. He held his hand to his ear so that the phone's camera's lens faced away from him. He made two or three passes of the gate with the video running, speaking into the device to appear he was having a casual conversation.

When the American returned to the car and reviewed his video, he was extremely disappointed at its quality. He was unable to clearly make out any of the license plates he had recorded, and there were quite a few. He enlarged an area on each one. But despite the poor quality, his heart raced when he identified a number on two cars' plates that could, in fact, be the one he was looking for. Now that he knew which cars were possible matches, the former spy started to get out again.

Proskurkin reached behind him into a bag in the rear floorboard and retrieved a high quality, compact Nikon digital camera.

"Here." And he handed it to his American partner.

"You couldn't have given this to me earlier? While I was taking pictures with this damned phone?"

"Didn't know what you were about to do."

Morgan walked directly to the gate this time and, without any attempt at stealth, pointed the camera directly toward each of the cars of interest.

He returned briskly to the Vesta and enlarged the snapshots on the Nikon's display.

Proskurkin watched Morgan as he looked at the images. The American leaned forward and made some adjustments on one of them. He smiled and handed the Nikon to the Russian.

"Bingo."

✦

Betsy related her experience at the White House to Weston, McGinnis, and Crenshaw.

"We're going to practically have to get a video of the church bombing with a blow-by-blow confession." Betsy immediately regretted her unintentional, poor choice of words.

"I'm just saying we're going to have to have something unambiguous to get Hendrickson's attention. I'm not sure what type of evidence would make a difference."

✦

Morgan and Proskurkin waited hopefully to see if the black Mercedes-Benz with the matching plates would leave the embassy. Two hours passed. Then three. It was 9:30 PM when the vehicle left the compound

"We don't know what the people we're looking for look like. How will we know if they're the ones in the car now?"

"What does it matter if it's the same people?" insisted Proskurkin. "If the Saudis are behind this, whoever is in there might know."

"I suppose you're right, but we need information."

"*Da.* We do." Slava set his handgun on the seat beside him.

The SVR agent kept the Vesta close to the Mercedes, which seemed to be wandering aimlessly. The windows' tint was fairly dark, but under one street light, the driver was able to see inside well enough to say, "There is only one person in the car."

Morgan struggled to make the determination, but finally he did.

"You're right, Slava."

The Saudi made a stop at a convenience store. Josh and Slava drove past when the Mercedes pulled in, made a U-turn and came back to a spot near the store and parked. They waited in the Vesta sedan while the man they were tailing went inside. Morgan started fiddling with the camera.

"We're about to get our first good look at this guy. I want a photo."

The Saudi man returned from the store opening some sort of canned drink.

The ex-CIA officer began snapping away.

"What will you do with those, Morgan?"

"I don't know yet." He set the Nikon in his lap.

It was the Mercedes driver's second stop that interested the men tailing him. At 11:00 PM, he pulled up to the entrance of *Krysha Mira*. Instead of getting out at the "Top of the World," he remained seated until two passengers got in the car with him – a male in the front passenger seat and a female in the back. Morgan fired off a burst of photos of the pair.

"Two men and one woman," observed the Russian.

"I think the chances that we have the right people just went way up," concluded the American. Morgan snapped a few more photos and smiled.

The Lada Vesta pulled in behind the Mercedes as it left the nightclub.

It was only a fifteen-minute drive to another night spot. Night Flight, located on Tverskaya Street, was Moscow's oldest club. It wasn't a place frequented by many Russians. Only a select group of locals was rich enough and sophisticated enough to join the mostly international businessmen, tourists, and local expatriates who made up almost all of the clientele. Difficult to get into, it was pricey and hopping.

The three Saudis exited their sedan and the driver handed over control to the valet.

"Quick. Pull up there. We'll follow them."

Slava's snicker exploded with a laugh.

"We won't get in. We'll be laughed away the moment I drive up in this Vesta. And it's mostly for foreigners anyhow."

"I *am* a foreigner," the United States citizen reminded.

"That's not what your papers say."

Morgan reached into an inside pocket of his parka and pulled out a passport and opened it to his photo page.

"*Me llamo Alejandro Manuel Sanchez.*"

To Slava Proskurkin's astonishment, the identity of the man on the passport was indeed Alejandro Sanchez.

"A gift from my friend at CIA. Now pull around the corner and let me out."

The SVR started forward.

"Where do I meet you?"

"Sanchez" thought a moment. "Park where you can see the entrance and watch for me to come back out. If I'm alone, just pick me up. If I'm not…" Morgan wasn't sure how he wanted to finish the sentence.

"…Then just wing it."

Slava shrugged his lack of understanding.

"Just make it up as things develop."

The "Spaniard" exited the car and walked back around the corner toward the entrance of the nightclub. He looked around at the other businesses in the area.

"There you go," he said when he spotted what he needed.

Sanchez stepped past the line of partiers waiting to see if they would be lucky enough to gain admission to Night Flight. None were too happy at the sight of the pedestrian walking to the head of the line toward the gatekeeper. The bouncer had the type of physique you would expect anywhere in the world – stocky but fit and with a look that let everyone know that he wasn't one to be trifled with.

The man gave Sanchez an up-and-down, assessing the Spaniard for suitability for the club. Well before Morgan reached him, his hand was up, and he was shaking his head.

He stepped toward Morgan, who had decided that Alejandro Sanchez was going to have a bit of an attitude.

Before the man could speak, Morgan demanded in English with a Spanish accent, "I would like to go in."

"Go to the back of the line and wait your turn, if you wish, but I can tell you, you won't get in."

Sanchez huffed and assumed an aloof demeanor.

"Pavel said to speak with you personally, Dmitri." Morgan had heard a fellow nightclub employee call him by name. "You are Dmitri?"

"Pavel? I know more than one Pavel." His voice carried the highly suspicious intonation of one who had heard every trick in the book from people trying to con their way into the Night Flight. "Pavel who?"

"Shit! Pavel, Pavel. I don't know his name. Pavel at the Café Pushkin." The Café Pushkin was the nearby business Morgan had identified before approaching the entrance to the Night Flight. "I just ate there, and he said that this was the place to party… this…" Sanchez looked at the name of the club on the building. "…this… this Night Light." The Spaniard's smugness was irritating, even to the man who *was* Sanchez.

The hulking guard to the place was pissed.

"Flight. Night *Flight*, you fucking *zhopa*."

Normally Morgan wouldn't have liked to be called an ass. Sanchez certainly didn't and he didn't even know what it meant.

"Fuck you, *zhopa*, too." His taunt dripped with superiority. The man took a step toward him.

Morgan/Sanchez stepped back and threw up both hands.

"I'm sorry. This has just been a fucking awful day. The fucking airline just fucked every fucking thing up. Because of them, I'm wearing these clothes." Sanchez gestured with both hands up and down the length of his body.

"Does this look like Armani? Does it? I had to buy these clothes because I couldn't find a store with anything suitable. The airline assholes lost my luggage. So, I go to eat. Pavel tells me to come here. You won't let me in.

"At least I have my wallet. I'm not letting go of my cash." Morgan opened the wallet just enough to show a thick stack of U.S.-denominated currency

The bouncer's eyes fixed on the cash. The Spaniard began to put the money inside his very unfashionable parka and walk away.

"Sir…" The gatekeeper's tone changed immediately upon seeing the $2,400 that Morgan had gotten at the money exchange in Washington.

"Sir, you've had a terrible day. I think we can work something out."

Morgan/Sanchez squinted, and then smiled as if catching on.

"I see. Well, I've been terribly uncivilized. Let me make it up to you. How much to 'work something out,' as you put it?" he whispered.

The Russian bouncer didn't bother to whisper. He didn't care who witnessed the transaction. It was standard practice.

"One hun-… two hundred dollars… U.S."

"Two hundred? Two hundred is nothing. Here's three hundred. Do you have a suitable jacket and tie I can change into?"

The smiling bouncer never looked up as he counted his cash.

"I think we might."

And with that, he unhooked the gold snap of the thick red velvet rope from one end of the gold stands and allowed Alejandro Sanchez into Night Flight.

✦

In the Vesta, Proskurkin had just returned to the parking apace along the street after letting his associate out around the corner. He chuckled in amazement when he saw the bouncer cheerfully leading him into the nightclub.

✦

Inside Night Flight, the doorman provided Morgan a sport coat and tie that would pass the rigid dress code of the trendy club. That cost him another US$200 and the man made it clear that the cost was only for a "rental" for the night. The American tipped him an additional two hundred dollars if he would turn a blind eye if he happened to leave the place with the clothes. The man said nothing but took the cash and smiled. Morgan held up five additional twenty-dollar bills and whispered another request into the Russian bouncer's ear. He received another smile as they completed the transaction.

Morgan had considered how he wanted to approach the three people who had abducted and murdered Larisa Borzilova and her children. He thought of trying to pick them up. That certainly wouldn't have been an unusual occurrence at this nightclub. With many of the late-night partiers looking to hook up, men had a variety of choices, from professionals to merely other partiers looking for company. But what if the Saudis weren't interested? It would be hard to try a "Plan B" if that tactic failed.

While he considered other possible ways to persuade the two men and one woman to move outside, he surveyed the crowded room to see if he could even spot them.

Finally, Morgan/Sanchez spied them. He walked toward them and introduced himself. It took a near shout to be heard over the booming techno music.

"Alejandro Sanchez." He extended his hand but received none in return. All he got were icy, suspicious stares.

"Have it your way," Morgan said in English in response to the snub. He started to walk away, deciding that straightforwardness might be the simplest approach. "But this has to do with three bodies in Selyatino."

One of the men stepped forward immediately and grabbed Morgan's arm. Sanchez pulled it away, displaying as much offense at the Saudi's rudeness as he could muster.

"I have no idea what you mean," the Arab said.

"Very well, *amigo*." The Spaniard resumed his retreat from the trio. All three followed. This time it was the second man who stepped around and cut off his departure.

"Who are you?" The Saudi Arabian national stepped very close to Morgan and put his right hand against his chest.

Morgan looked down for a moment, then made eye contact and calmly removed the man's palm.

"I am simply someone who was trying to be a friend. Now, excuse me." Sanchez used the back of his right hand to push the man gently out of the way. "But if you don't know what I'm talking about, why are you interested?"

The first man pulled him back around to face him very forcefully. At once, a large, powerful hand pulled him away. The Saudi turned to see a serious-looking bouncer warning him with only his expression to lay off his friend.

Morgan thanked Dmitri and briskly headed for the exit. As instructed by Morgan earlier, the bouncer held the three Saudis back for just a moment before releasing them to go about their reveling. The three paused only momentarily before pursuing the man who had cryptically mentioned an act that no one should've known about.

Morgan's pace was rapid enough to keep his pursuers behind him but not so quickly to lose them in the crowd. He passed through the Night Flight door and sped up his escape.

As soon as it became clear he was heading for the gray Vesta, the first Saudi barked an order to a valet, who dashed away to collect the patron's Mercedes. The remaining man and the woman sprinted toward the Spaniard's car and stepped in front just as Morgan shut the door.

"Your turn!" Morgan told Proskurkin. "Get them to follow us."

Slava looked at him curiously and inched the car forward until the Arabs had to yield. As they did, one pulled a handgun and pointed at the two men in the car, though he didn't fire on the crowded avenue. The three murderers ran to their car. One man jumped into the driver's seat while the other man and the woman got in. The woman threw a few Saudi riyals as payment to the car attendant and they pulled away to try to catch up to their receding target.

"Where am I going?" a genuinely bewildered SVR agent asked.

"I dunno. Some dark alley, I guess. Let them catch us, but make it look good."

Proskurkin exhaled a huge gasp of air. "Are you sure this is a good idea?" He pressed the accelerator and moved away more quickly, but at a rate that would allow their followers to catch up. "I hope you know what you're doing."

"That makes two of us, pal."

The Russian spy weaved his way in and out of the traffic that was still heavy, even at this time of night. He made a few turns that took him to a more secluded part of Moscow. All the while, he adjusted his speed to appear convincingly like he was trying to get away while actually drawing in the black Mercedes Benz.

CHAPTER 32

Day 16 – Sunday

The following car closed the gap between it and the Lada Vesta, as its driver expertly allowed. The distance was reduced to less than ten car-lengths. Proskurkin had led the Saudi driver into the Yasenevo District of Moscow near the headquarters building of his own agency. He knew it well. His mind raced ahead in his intended route. The agent hoped he would time his and his American passenger's "capture" so that they were at the desired location.

It was just after midnight and the Russian finally had to ask, "What is your plan, Morgan? I mean, after we let them catch us?"

"We question them. Nicely," he said sarcastically as he retrieved his handgun. His Russian friend's was already accessible.

"What if they just shoot us as soon as they come to the car?"

"They won't."

Proskurkin looked at him questioningly.

"They'll want to know what I know," Morgan followed up.

Slava didn't know what had transpired in the nightclub. He'd been too busy driving to find out.

"If you say so." This time the driver managed a smile.

The Russian driver turned the Vesta into a closed alley. He sped near the barricaded end and braked quickly to a stop.

The black Mercedes swung around the corner and, seeing the Lada motionless with no escape, stopped forcefully. Nobody emerged for several seconds. Finally, the Saudi who had first challenged Sanchez when he introduced himself at the Night Flight, the apparent alpha, exited from behind the car's wheel and stood outside his door. The second male and the woman, guns drawn, walked deliberately toward the two men they had just overtaken. In a moment, their leader advanced more deliberately a few steps behind.

The gun-wielding pair approached cautiously, the woman on the driver's side, the man on the passenger's. The good guys had about a five-second strategy session while the bad guys completed their walk.

The alpha hung back on the driver's side only a few feet and ordered, "Out! Get out!"

Both men inside the car waited. The Saudi shouted louder, "Get out of the car!" Morgan and Proskurkin resisted longer, until the Saudi leader moved closer. He strode up on Slava's side and took charge, demanding that the men get out.

Upon the alpha's order, both men raised their hands. They each carefully lowered one hand to open the car door, stealthily gathering their handguns on its way past their laps. With their guns in hand, each opened his door and, stepping out, fired their weapons. Morgan pulled off two quick rounds to the beta male. Proskurkin fired a single shot with practiced accuracy into the right knee of the female Saudi agent. Morgan's target dropped immediately. Slava's victim's leg buckled under her and she twisted to the asphalt. She pointed her gun at the SVR agent, but his menacing look persuaded her not to try to fire. She dropped her weapon.

With one man dead and the woman wounded, Alpha frantically scrambled to retrieve his gun from inside his coat. Slava turned instantly toward him. The Saudi man, like his female agent, elected to stand down.

Proskurkin ordered the Saudi man and woman to lie face down on the alley's hard surface and place their hands on the backs of their heads. He watched them while Morgan put the body of the Beta male in the Vesta's trunk. Before he did, he ripped the lining out of his coat – he no longer needed it – and bandaged the knee of the woman. She trembled with pain but bravely refused to moan or cry. Proskurkin felt some detached admiration for her.

The men commanded their prisoners to get into the Vesta. Alpha sat in the front with the driver's gun pointed directly at him. They directed the woman to lie in the back floorboard. The SVR agent nodded toward the Mercedes and told Morgan, "Follow me."

Morgan started the black sedan and fell in behind Slava. The Russian drove a very short distance to the Insayd-Biznyes Hotel. Pulling into the parking lot, he lowered his automobile's window and motioned Morgan to a vacant spot. The ex-CIA Officer pulled in, turned off the engine and opened the back door of Slava's car. With handgun drawn, he ordered the woman up from the floorboard and sat beside her.

It wasn't time they felt they could spare, but after a short discussion, Morgan and Proskurkin decided they knew one place where they could carry on their conversation with their Saudi Arabian captives without interruption. It was 1:39 AM when the SVR agent and his American partner left Moscow's Yasenevo District and drove onto the highway that would return them to where they had been not many hours earlier.

✦

It was a remarkable recovery. President Sandra Hendrickson stood over her son, AJ, lying in his own bed in his room in the family quarters in the White House. She and Adam Sr. held each other tightly.

"Are you sure there's nothing I can get you?"

"Mom, for the umpteenth time, no. I'm fine. Just hand me my X-Box controls and go away."

The first gentleman leaned to tweak the nose of his son.

"I guess you are fine. Things seem to be getting back to normal very quickly."

AJ offered his parents a genuine smile. "Love you, Mom. Love you, Dad."

Mom and Dad left their son to his – well, to whatever electronic adventure he was about to enjoy. They felt blessed beyond words to see him home and on the way to a full recovery.

"I have something to tell you. I've been meaning to, but we just haven't had time to talk. I fired the DCI."

Adam Sr. literally leaned back and exhaled a deep breath. "Parnell? Wow!"

"Yeah."

"Why?"

Sandy told her husband the entire story of Parnell's decision to reach out to her counterpart in the Russian Foreign Intelligence Service.

Adam chose his words carefully. "And you're sure she didn't feel like she was just doing her job? I mean, gathering every perspective she could?"

Sandy bristled at what she perceived as her husband questioning her judgement.

"We're at war! I can't have people going behind my back."

"So aside from being – I don't know – disrespectful, what did it hurt?"

"What would people think?"

"What people? Did she tell anyone?"

"She said she didn't."

"Then what does it matter? Look at it as – I don't know – counsel. Sure, it might seem ill-advised…"

"*Seem?*"

"Okay. I suppose it was ill-advised, but maybe she's just trying to get more facts."

"So, now you're second-guessing me, too."

Though in truth, Adam Hendrickson thought perhaps things were moving a little fast on the war front, he had never remotely questioned her rationale for her executive decisions. He had never once considered that she had made them for any reason other than that she thought they were what was best for the country.

"No... no, not at all. Not ever, sweetheart."

The husband pulled his wife close and they sat on the couch of the executive residence. Sandy lay her head on Adam's shoulder.

"You know, they nearly killed our son."

The president's husband raised his eyebrows. "Gee," he thought. "That's the national interest?"

It was something over a half-hour when the four people in the Lada Vesta – well, five, counting the dead guy in the back – arrived at the turn into the wooded lot where the small white house sat. The lack of additional snow made their previous car tracks very apparent.

The Saudi woman was slumped over in pain in the back of the sedan. The Alpha Saudi Arabian man had realized quite some time earlier where they were headed.

Slava pulled up to the small *dacha*. Morgan had held his gun the entire trip. He stepped out first. Then Proskurkin exited the driver's side.

"Get out!" shouted the Russian.

Both Saudis hesitated. The SVR agent, grabbed the woman by the collar and yanked her hard out of the back seat. She fell to the ground roughly.

The male in the front seat rose slowly from the passenger side seat and stood.

Slava kicked the woman on her injured knee.

"Stand up!" He kicked her again. "*Pizda!*"

Despite her severe pain, the Saudi woman glared at her tormenter for calling her a "cunt."

Morgan wasn't sure if he was supposed to play "good cop" to his partner's "bad cop" or not, but the man's treatment of the woman genuinely bothered him.

"That's enough. We need her alive."

The Russian gave the American an irritated look before putting his foot onto the prone figure's face and pushed it roughly.

Morgan motioned with his gun for the male Saudi to walk around the car. Then he helped the woman to her feet.

"Get him inside," he said to Slava.

Slava winked at Morgan and took the man up the steps into the house.

The American put an arm around the woman's waist and she reflexively put hers around his shoulder. The pair walked slowly into the house.

"Thank you," the woman said.

Morgan set her on the couch. Proskurkin took both of the Saudis' coats. The coldness of the air was immediately uncomfortable to them.

Proskurkin ordered the man onto the couch., "What is your name?"

The man cut his eyes toward the Russian and remained silent.

Morgan looked at the woman. He asked more gently, "What is your name?"

She likewise held her tongue and received the butt of the Russian's pistol for her decision.

"You killed three people here," Morgan accused. "Why?"

She lowered her head but cut her eyes toward her questioner.

Morgan thought, "Kindness and compassion aren't getting me anywhere."

The two inquisitors left the man alone entirely.

Morgan decided to change tactics.

"You are trying to start a war between our countries. Why?" He noticed she really wanted to answer but did not.

The questions went on for four hours with no results. Both Saudis were well-trained.

Finally, Morgan spoke to Proskurkin. "I'm hungry. I'll go get something. Can I trust you to stay in control while I'm gone?"

Both men noticed trepidation in the eyes of the woman. The Saudi male showed no reaction at all.

"Just get some food," muttered the Russian.

Morgan left to go to a store. He wasn't sure he would find one open at six-thirty in the morning. And he wasn't entirely certain he could trust his SVR counterpart while he was gone.

✦

MSG Lechler and his team had less than eighteen hours before they went into "discretion" status.

SFC Cooley Matheson continued to monitor their link to their Command Center. The SPIRIT Team was concerned with two things. First, would they be called off by the B-Team, which was receiving orders from the Pentagon? Secondly, when would Russian President Tatarov depart for China and the other Russian allies?

Each question was a factor in the outcome of Operation Nemesis, and, on a larger scale, Operation Retribution.

MSG Lechler and SFC Bull Macduff spoke quietly. Each had a significant and unique role in the operation they were tasked with. Whether in the missile silos of the cold war or those of the present day, to the Green Light Teams of days past or the SPIRIT Teams that followed them, the higher-ups had always established a two-man rule. No single individual could initiate the execution of any type of nuclear option. Launching a missile required two keys and/or two codes. Therefore, detonating a B-54B SNAP also required the deliberate actions of two individuals. Lechler and Jones each had half of the code that could deploy their nuke.

And while the two-man rule dated back to the birth of the atomic age and carried on to the present, there was a major flaw in the thinking behind it. Should either of the two men die during the operation, the plan was wrecked. To ensure that they could complete their mission – at least with regard to Green Light and SPIRIT Teams – each owner of his respective half simply divulged it to the other.

Neither Lechler nor Jones had yet disclosed his half of the detonation code for the SNAP but, with the short time until they went dark and their discretionary period opened, they decided to do so. The nuclear device was "Plan B," but its use was still a possibility. In fact, should their primary plan fail, the bomb became the primary solution for almost immediate execution.

A half-hour before sunrise, SFC Lucas Matheson passed the latest information along to his team members who were positioned along an approximately twenty-five-yard-wide protective line. No stand-down order from their command team. No word of when the Russian president might be in his plane.

To a man, each SPIRIT felt that execution of their plan was more likely than not. In about seventeen hours, SFC Jack Jackson would assemble his Springer Drone. SFC Cooley Matheson would mount the EMP to it. SFC Bull Macduff would remove the canvas cover from the container housing the SADM SNAP and ready it for its lethal use. SFC Abe Aboud would inspect the drone's electronic control device and prepare to hand it over to Jackson. It would be a busy time immediately upon the commencement of the window during which they could act autonomously to launch the drone strike. That period would last no more than three days. If no opportunity arose to deploy the EMP, the orders to detonate the bomb became active. Sergeants Jones, Jackson, Matheson, and Aboud would retreat with all possible haste. Master Sergeant Lechler's and SFC Macduff's orders were to remain for an additional two hours to maintain "eyes-on" the SNAP to prevent it from falling into enemy hands. Then they would attempt their own withdrawal. However, both men being realists, they knew they had no chance of getting clear of the blast radius and had agreed to simply maintain their positions. They joked they would have the best view of the event.

The other four sergeants would at least have some chance to escape death by nuclear blast. Their plan was to commandeer a vehicle as soon as possible and drive like hell away from Vnukovo.

The comparatively small man-portable nuclear bomb, at three kilotons, would have a fireball radius of about 120 meters. Victims within it would virtually evaporate. The thermal radiation radius was just over three-quarters of a kilometer. The souls within this zone would suffer third-degree burns.

The real danger to Moscow itself would be from the radioactive fallout and the emotional damage of having witnessed the device successfully detonated on the soil of the Motherland.

Had the SNAP been the primary weapon in the United States' retaliatory strike, the designers of the war plan would have preferred to use it in a more strategic location, such as central Moscow or a military installation. As a secondary option that would be used only in the event that the EMP failed or that the soldiers were unable to deploy it, the planners felt they couldn't risk having the SPIRITs move from their position outside the airport. Besides, a mushroom cloud anywhere near the Russian capital would make its point.

So, the SPIRITs had their orders. All of them, but especially Lechler and Macduff, the Operational Sergeant and the SNAP Technical Sergeant, hoped for the successful execution of Plan A, the EMP deployment. Though capture might occur, it was infinitely better than having a front-row seat to a nuclear blast.

At seventeen hours and counting until communications blackout, their orders for now were to sit and wait.

◆

Ex-CIA spook and current kidnapper Josh Morgan arrived back at the safe house with water and food. The two Saudis were in generally the same physical condition as when he left. The woman had more bruises. The man, according to plan, was unscathed.

Morgan and Proskurkin questioned their prisoners throughout the day. Their frustration at the lack of results was growing but the situation required they keep their emotions hidden. They alternated interrogating the two terrorists. Occasionally they questioned them in tandem. They tried interspersing periods of silence with intense rounds of enquiry. Nothing worked. During the entire process, they continued to deprive the two agents of food or drink. They refused to allow them to go to the bathroom, hoping one or both would soil themselves. They weren't sure if the embarrassment would stimulate compliance or not, but it didn't matter. It had been seven hours and neither had suffered the indignity.

The American and the Russian were both unaware of the deadline they faced with U.S. Green Berets poised for attack. Yet they knew tensions were sufficiently high that hostilities could erupt at any point. Parnell's message to Morgan made him more keenly aware of the likelihood.

Desperate for a resolution to the crisis he faced at a personal level because of the crisis his country faced, Morgan concocted a plan.

The U.S. citizen scrutinized the faces of the Saudi Arabian agents, watching for their reaction to his question.

"Do you have children?"

The female agent's expression didn't change. Alpha's countenance, on the other hand, briefly changed at the enquiry.

"Small children?" came the follow-up.

The male's face tightened a little more. His brows furrowed. He pursed his lips.

Morgan had his answer.

In all the things Morgan had done during his time with CIA and since – burying bodies on his property, killing Everson Blake in cold blood – what he was about to do would be the most personally disturbing. He went into the bedroom where the bodies of Larisa Borzilova, Ulyana, and Valeriy lay.

Proskurkin wondered what the American was doing.

After a short delay, Morgan returned with the corpse of the infant. He had decided he wasn't capable of physical torture so attempting to inflict mental and emotional torment would have to do.

"Record this," he said to his Russian cohort without using his name.

Proskurkin propped his Nikon on a chair facing the Saudi Arabian pair and set it for video capture.

"Phone, too," said the American.

The Russian propped up his phone.

Josh Morgan felt physically sick for what he was doing, but the stakes were so high with regard to his country and even the Russian Federation, that he felt he would resort to anything.

The SVR agent started the video and watched as Morgan handed little Ulyana Borzilov's body to the woman. She recoiled at the touch of her cold, waxen skin to hers.

"Hold her."

Both Saudi agents' eyes widened. The man fidgeted in his seat. The woman pushed at the baby, doing everything she could to resist the demand.

"No! I will not do this!"

"What is your name?" Morgan shouted, forcing the stiff corpse into her arms. The woman held the infant at arm's length before setting her gently on the couch between her and her leader. Her tormenter thrust the lifeless baby immediately back into her arms.

Alpha shouted, "You're insane!"

"What is your fucking name!?" the American yelled to the woman.

"This is madness!" the Saudi male screamed.

"Your name!?" repeated Morgan, placing his gun against her left, uninjured knee.

The Saudi female began to cry. Her words were soft.

"Hishma el-Sawaya. My name is Hishma el-Sawaya."

She tried to set Ulyana down a second time, but, again, Morgan prevented it.

"What is his name?!" Morgan demanded, tilting his head toward her partner.

El-Sawaya looked fearfully at the man on the sofa beside her. Morgan pressed the barrel of his gun more forcefully against her left knee, while pushing his thumb against the bullet wound already in her right knee.

El-Sawaya jerked back and let out a muted scream. Her breathing turned into rapid gasps. She looked at Alpha again. Morgan pressed harder with his thumb and the handgun.

El-Sawaya blurted out, "It's al-Abdul. Jawhar al-Abdul." Her tears exploded in a mixture of pain and rage.

Al-Abdul surged for the woman. Morgan brought his handgun across the Arab's face. The Saudi man swung wildly and managed to connect violently with el-Sawaya's cheek and nose.

The former American spy knew the time had come to shift targets.

He snatched the infant corpse forcefully and shoved it into al-Abdul's arms.

"This is outrageous!" al-Abdul snarled.

Morgan leaned over the infant body to get right in the man's face.

"What's outrageous is killing three innocent people! What's outrageous is trying to kill our president! What's outrageous is trying to start a war between America and Russia. Why?" Morgan's voice was at full volume and the pitch increased with every syllable.

"Is your hatred for the United States that strong?!"

"Yes!" the Saudi leader finally bellowed, immediately dropping Ulyana's body to the floor. His effort to stand was aborted by Morgan's push to his chest.

"You are the Great Satan! You have tormented us relentlessly! The fool Russian would only cooperate if we had his family!"

Alpha's words became a diatribe, flowing past the man's ability to stop them. They poured out in a vicious stream of hatred.

"If he had succeeded, we would have been rid of your American president. But he couldn't. He was incompetent! But at least the fool started the war between your countries, as we wanted. Thanks be to Allah! Praise be to Allah!"

The suddenness and explosiveness of the admission startled both

Proskurkin and Morgan. A limp feeling overtook both men, each one stunned at the outburst and the realization that they had gotten the confession they were after.

"The Holy Islamic Republic of Saudi Arabia does not have the weapons to destroy America. We arranged for the Russians to do it for us."

Hishma el-Sawaya was aghast. She stared at her partner in disbelief. Jawhar al-Abdul slumped into the sofa as the weight of his acknowledgment that his country had constructed the plot between the two superpowers sank in. He inexplicably reached to retrieve Ulyana Borzilov's small body from the floor and set her gently on the sofa.

A few minutes of silence consumed the air. Finally, Morgan played the video on the phone to ensure that it had successfully recorded the confession. It was more important to have the confession on the phone than the camera so they could transmit it to others. Satisfied with the product and restarting it, he began to calmly ask al-Abdul questions.

The American lowered his tone, feeling that, having made his confession, the Saudi Arabian might respond if he appealed to his pride. So, over the course of the next forty minutes, Jawhar al-Abdul provided details about the plan to bring the Great Satan and Russia to war.

He detailed how they had approached Gennadiy Valeryevich Borzilov. He explained step-by-step how they had masterminded the plan at every phase. Al-Abdul even described their decision to kill their surrogate's family, explaining that he felt some remorse at the deaths of the children because he has children of his own.

The Saudi's face took on a look of puzzlement when Morgan had responded to the disclosure of his fatherhood with, "I know."

At the conclusion of the expanded confession, Morgan again checked the phone for a successful video. Confident that he and Proskurkin had reached their goal, he said to his associate, "Watch them."

The American tenderly lifted the body of young Ulyana Borzilov from where it lay on the couch between the two Saudi Arabians and carried her back to her mother and brother. His eyes misted at the thought of how he had exploited the youngest.

Morgan straightened the body of the mother and moved it to the center of the bed. He laid the boy on one side and returned Ulyana to her arms. With some difficulty, he closed the eyes of the family, and stood silently beside them. Finally, he placed the bedspread over them and left the room.

Morgan passed completely through the small living area without so much as a glance at the Saudis or his Russian partner.

He uttered, "Back in a minute." The words were so soft that Slava didn't really understand what the American had said but assumed the essence of the communication when the man walked outside.

Joshua Morgan sat in the driver's seat of the Lada Vesta. He rested his forehead on the wheel and thought about the Borzilov children and those that he might have one day. He thought about Maggie. He pounded his fist softly against the wheel. As his breaths turned into short gasps, he surrendered to his emotions and began to weep.

✦

At three-thirty in the afternoon, SFC Lucas Matheson received an update from the B-Team in Estonia. He relayed the piece of information along to the rest of the team. The Kremlin often timed its news releases so that they would make the early morning news in Washington, D.C. It was 7:30 AM in the American capital and the Russians had just announced that President Tatarov would depart Vnukovo International Airport tomorrow at 11:00 AM for his multi-nation coalition-building trip. The Special Forces soldiers' operational discretion commenced less than eight hours from now and the Russian president's flight would take off twelve hours after that.

"Almost time to saddle up, girls," Cooley's voice announced through the others' earpieces.

✦

Monitoring foreign countries' press releases didn't fall under the purview of the White House press department. Nevertheless, the staffers always took notice because of how such international news might affect the group's own work. Particularly now that a state of war officially existed between the United States and the Russian Federation, the significance of any reports from the enemy was greatly amplified.

Acting Press Secretary Margaret Loughlin sat at her desk and scanned the report that had just arrived by internal email. Maggie didn't "need to know" the operational details of Operation Nemesis, therefore she didn't. She was read in on the overarching Operation Retribution, though, even then, what she knew was largely summary in nature.

Because of that, the announcement about Tatarov didn't elevate her anxiety. It should have.

Just down the hall from her office, POTUS was on the phone with General Richards. The two were discussing whether there was any reason to stand down. Both were steadfast in their commitment to the war plan and agreed that there was not.

✦

Sleep had been hard to come by for DCI Elizabeth Parnell, so it startled her that she had actually been doing so very soundly when her phone played the tone indicating that she had a message. Only after seeing on the display of her official phone that nothing was there did the CIA director grasp that the text had been received on her current burner. Her pulse quickened and she became suddenly wide awake at the realization that the news would be from her unofficial operative in the Russian Federation.

"Shit!" she said aloud upon seeing the single word text. Despite the fact that it was only four letters long, she did a double-take.

"done" was the word that Morgan, Parnell, Crenshaw, Weston, and McGinnis had agreed would indicate that Morgan had uncovered irrefutable evidence that disassociated the Russians from responsibility for the bombings in the United States. They had also agreed that the corroborating documents or other proof would be communicated separately. It must be indisputable and in such a form that it would not be subject to interpretation or dismissible as hearsay.

So, under those guidelines, it was with no small sense of excitement that Parnell saw the word in digital form on her phone's screen.

"Done," she said aloud. She appreciated that Morgan wouldn't transmit that communication lightly, having full understanding of the rigid "ground rules" for defining success.

The director looked at the development with professional detachment. Solely as a practical matter, she only felt relief that it might divert her country and the Russian Federation from the road to war.

But Betsy couldn't help from feeling a sense of vindication, even in the midst of the gravity of the new information. She understood the logic for the president firing her, but on a purely personal level, she took comfort in the knowledge that she had been right about the thing that got her terminated.

Now, the important thing was to get the president to listen to her. She wasn't sure she could make that happen, and, having knowledge that operators were on the ground outside of Vnukovo and of their orders, she knew time was running short.

✦

Morgan knew that his Russian partner was obliged to report to Orlov and knew that he had done so several times during their quest for the truth. But he had a dilemma. The video was on Proskurkin's phone; not his. They had tried to figure out a way to get it onto Morgan's device, too, but each time they tried to text it, the transmission failed. And neither Morgan's nor the SVR agent's simplistic disposable phones had the equivalent of Apple's "AirDrop." The app was a feature on iPhones that would've allowed a direct transfer from phone to phone.

The pair of investigators had agreed to hand over any evidence they turned up to their respective homeland's intelligence agencies simultaneously. Morgan felt that allowing Parnell an immediate opportunity at disclosing the video to the White House was essential because of her cryptic message indicating that some military action was imminent. But he didn't know how to accomplish that. There appeared to be no way around letting the Russian give it to Orlov first.

However, there was a complication with that, as well. It was the same thing that prevented Slava from sharing the file with Morgan in the first place, or for sending it directly to Parnell from his phone, for that matter. The inexpensive burner phones that he had brought to share with Morgan weren't capable of texting as large a file as the videos. And the Nikon had no Bluetooth capability.

"I agree," Morgan finally conceded to Slava. "Our only option is to take it to Moscow and hand-deliver it to *Direktor* Orlov."

The former American spy looked at their captives. "What do we do about them? Take them with us?"

"I say we shoot them." Proskurkin meant it.

Morgan wouldn't have it. They took the dead Saudi's body from the trunk and put it inside the house. Morgan insisted that they allow al-Sawaya and el-Abdul the chance to relieve themselves and have some water.

Proskurkin rolled his eyes and shook his head. "Are your American spies all as soft as you?" He meant that, too. But rather than fight Morgan over it, he agreed to permit the bathroom break and a quick snack with water.

They found no rope but tore strips off towels from the kitchen. They bound the pair's hands and feet, blindfolded and gagged them, and ordered them into the Vesta's trunk. It would be over a half-hour drive. After that there would be additional time for Orlov to do something with the recording. Morgan didn't know what lay ahead operationally, but he was growing increasingly anxious about the amount of time that was elapsing. He accepted again that this was the only solution available.

The American and Russian got into the car and sped away with two prisoners in the rear of the sedan and leaving four bodies at the *dacha*.

✦

It was the answer Parnell expected but it pissed her off just the same.

Brianna Washington, the president's personal secretary, repeated, at her boss' orders, the exact sentence POTUS had said. Her voice quivered when she delivered it.

"Under no circumstances will the president speak with you today." After she communicated it, she felt bad.

Parnell hung up abruptly. She had to move to other options to get Hendrickson's attention. The DCI looked at her phone for the time.

"Eight-fifteen. Damn."

Parnell dialed the chief of staff. He was in a meeting with his boss and would be unavailable for at least an hour. The CIA director thought of asking his secretary to interrupt him, but since he was in the Oval Office, as soon as POTUS heard who it was, she wouldn't let him take the call.

The DCI dialed her burner phone. It was the first time during the operation that any of the players had used one for anything other than texts.

✦

"Yes," said former President Weston, with some confusion at receiving a voice call on this phone.

"We have a problem," came the frantic voice of Betsy Parnell over Weston's device. "I got the 'done' text from our guy. Just haven't had time to let you know. Trying to get someone to listen."

Over the next two minutes, Parnell explained to Weston everything she had tried.

"I'll call her." Trent Weston disconnected the call.

The ex-chief executive had the current one's direct number.

✦

Inside the Oval Office, Sandra Hendrickson glanced at the display on her ringing and vibrating phone. She huffed a brief expletive and ignored it.

"If you need to take that...," started Noah Chandler.

"If I needed to take it, I think I know I could have," replied his boss curtly.

POTUS started back with the discussion she was having with her chief. She stopped abruptly.

"I'm sorry, Noah."

"Not at all, ma'am. I understand that you have a lot going on."

Hendrickson took off her glasses and set them on her desk.

"First, I get a call from that damned Parnell. I don't have the time for her nonsense. Then I get the call just now from President Weston. I know the DCI got him to call somehow. With everything going on, I don't have time for him, either."

Chandler tilted his head and exhaled. "With all due respect, I don't think anyone could get him to call you if he didn't think it was extremely urgent. He's sat in this very office. He understands the burdens you carry as president. Don't you think you should...?"

"No. Now, where were we?"

Chief of Staff Chandler decided he would call Weston himself, but it would have to wait until this meeting was over."

✦

Never mind a suit and tie. Weston slipped on his greatcoat over slacks and sweater and collected his gloves.

"Jack, Jeff, could you guys please get me to the White House. It's important."

The two Secret Service agents assigned to him permanently went into action. Jeff Coulter rushed downstairs to ready their boss' SUV. Jack Johnston waited until his radio crackled with his partner's voice telling him that he had the vehicle and was at the front door of The Four Seasons.

The Senior Agent escorted Weston down the hall to the elevator and then both men proceeded to the lobby and out the door.

✦

As an SVR agent, Vladislav Larionovich Proskurkin's duties generally involved working in the field in other countries, since his organization's responsibility was foreign intelligence. Like Morgan, he was pressed into duty because of the extraordinary circumstances of recent days. Orlov trusted him.

When Josh Morgan and Slava Proskurkin arrived at St Basil's Cathedral on the southeastern end of Red Square, Foreign Intelligence Service Director Pavel Semyonovich Orlov was already there waiting for them.

"I understand you have been quite valuable to our countries in trying to prevent this foolish war," he said to Morgan.

"As have you, sir." The American extended his hand.

Proskurkin spent as little time as possible explaining what they had uncovered and the nature of the evidence they were turning over to him, on the phone and on the Nikon.

"I understand."

"You will provide a copy of the video to my friends in Washington before doing anything else with it?"

"You have my word, Morgan." The Russian chief spy extended his hand again. Morgan's stomach churned as he saw the proof of Saudi Arabia's sponsorship of the plot to assassinate his president and initiate a war between Russia and the U.S. leave his control.

Almost as an afterthought, Proskurkin handed the keys to Orlov and told him where the Vesta was and what the trunk held.

"They might be of value to us. However, they are diplomats so there might be some consequences in holding them."

Orlov smiled and waved over his shoulder as he left. His laugh gave Morgan the impression that the pair of Arab agents might never be heard from again.

CHAPTER 33

Twelve minutes after leaving The Four Seasons, Weston's SUV pulled alongside Lafayette Square and let DCI Elizabeth Parnell in. Another couple of turns and they were driving into the White House complex, past the guardhouse and up to the entrance of the West Wing.

Former President Weston sprang out of the black vehicle and practically sprinted to the door with Elizabeth Parnell trying to catch up. Weston led Parnell into the lobby and turned left. The few people who stood nearby just watched. Nobody had the nerve to try to stop a President of the United States, even a former one. He marched briskly down the hall toward the Cabinet Room, turned right into the corridor, bypassing Brianna Washington's station, pushed past a Secret Service guard and opened the door to the Oval Office.

An astonished Sandra Hendrickson saw her predecessor standing in the doorway. Her shock turned to outright anger when the man stepped aside to let the DCI walk in.

POTUS shot up from her seat.

"What the hell is the meaning of this?" She pressed the button on her intercom to call for Secret Service agents to come throw a former president out of his former office.

"You need to hear the director out."

President Hendrickson's face was crimson, and she stuttered, unable to get any words to come forth. Her trembling was visible. Her fearless chief of staff was dumbfounded at the sight of his boss so unnerved.

POTUS was beyond livid. Finally, she lifted her finger from the intercom and said. "Five minutes."

"We'll take as long as we need," Weston countered.

Without being asked, Weston sat on the loveseat at the center of the presidential office and motioned Parnell to sit beside him, completely taking over the unscheduled meeting. Chandler gathered his papers and rose to leave.

Weston spoke a one-word direction. "Stay."

The chief sat and wondered what the hell was about to happen.

Morgan and Proskurkin walked away from St. Basil's.

"Where do we go now?"

"To get a drink, Morgan. I could use one."

"Or two or three," his American counterpart added.

Slava was smiling broadly. His relief was much stronger than Morgan's. The American felt there was more to be done, given his awareness that there were likely American forces already on Russian soil. In addition, he had just seen the evidence he had intended for Parnell disappear with the Director of the Russian Foreign Intelligence Service.

As excited and hopeful as he had been ninety minutes ago, he had a gnawing sense that things weren't as settled as he'd hoped, and that they weren't going to be.

Maggie Loughlin was almost ill. She was standing by the door of her office at the end of the hallway that ran alongside the Cabinet Room when Weston and Parnell turned toward the president's office. And though he had seen her, Weston never acknowledged her.

With the DCI in tow, his demeanor made Maggie certain that something was dreadfully wrong. And her gut told her Morgan was in its epicenter.

The entire West Wing was abuzz at the reports of Weston storming through the halls to POTUS' office. Maggie thought she was going to throw up.

President Weston had turned the encounter over to Director Parnell. She explained in detail the results of her asset's work in Moscow. She didn't identify Morgan as the asset. Nor did she disclose the involvement of Weston, Crenshaw, and Sir Albert McGinnis. For his part, Weston was fully willing to admit his role in the affair but didn't think it was wise for the time being. The last thing the current president needed was to feel that her authority was further challenged and that she was being ganged up on. Weston decided he would confess to his part when the time was right.

POTUS was somewhat calmer, though she was still angry that the DCI was undermining her decisions.

"I'll ask you what I did previously. Who is your asset?"

"I'd rather not say right now, Madam President."

"Well, I'd rather you do."

Parnell gathered some resolve. "I *won't* say. Identifying the asset, even to you, might compromise further operations, should they be needed."

POTUS glared at the woman for her subordinance.

"What is this evidence?"

Parnell took a deep breath.

"It's forthcoming."

"'Forthcoming,'" snorted Hendrickson. "Is that some sort of code word for 'you don't know?'"

"The evidence is in the asset's possession. You can imagine the difficulty of getting it out of Russia. We no longer have the cover of our embassy now that all our diplomats are expelled."

Weston finally contributed to the attempt to persuade the president to tap the brakes with regard to the special operations underway outside of Moscow, at least until she saw the evidence that Josh had uncovered.

"Sandra…" The use of the president's first name brought a look of indignation. Weston reconsidered.

"Madam President, I would think the possibility of exculpatory evidence with regard to Russia being behind the attacks on your life would at least warrant additional caution until it can be substantiated. Perhaps a twenty-four-hour pause would be in order, to allow validation?"

"Mr. President, I've included you in most of the more substantive of my decisions since I've been in office, have I not?"

Weston nodded.

"At times, it has caused some consternation on the part of my party." This wasn't really true, but it would help make her point.

"But never did I intend to characterize this presidency as a sort of partnership…"

Weston stiffened at the implication and interrupted.

"I have never presumed it to be and have never offered advice when it wasn't requested. But frankly, Sandra, you're moving far too quickly here. The cost to delay action is nothing. The costs to the entire planet if you're wrong…? The consequences will be catastrophic."

President Sandra Hendrickson stood with her left hand on her hip and her right index finger pointing straight toward Weston. She shook it and opened her mouth. Words failed to come forth initially until she said, "Excuse me. I have work to so."

POTUS started to sit but instead shifted her finger to Parnell.

"And you…" She stammered a moment. "I expect your resignation immediately!"

Parnell stood and barked, "Well, I won't offer it. You're going to have to fire me and do so publicly. Ma'am, you're acting with undue haste. This sense of urgency… well, it's manufactured. This rush to action isn't warranted."

Weston stepped between the president and the DCI and gently turned Betsy's shoulder to direct her from the president's office.

Parnell stood her ground briefly before accepting that it was time to leave. As she reached the door, she turned and delivered her final comment with acquiescence and a touch of sadness.

"You're behaving dangerously, ma'am."

Weston simply said, "Madam President." And followed Parnell from the room.

President Sandra Hendrickson remained standing and had almost forgotten her chief of staff, who still sat in a chair along one of the Oval Office's walls, having never said a word.

"If you don't mind, Noah, I need a few minutes."

Chandler forced a smile and took his leave. He, too, wondered what the supposed evidence was. And who was this asset?

The chief started to his left down the hallway that led directly from the Oval Office to his own. Instead, he decided to try to catch Weston and Parnell before they left, so he backtracked to the hall that ran parallel to the Cabinet Room. He stopped where he would turn left toward the lobby.

He cautioned himself silently, "What would you say to them? Certainly don't need to get between them and POTUS."

As he remained in the middle of the corridor chastising himself, another thought occurred. He resumed his walk alongside the Cabinet Room until he reached the door of the acting press secretary. He watched Loughlin through the door momentarily. She sat with her left forearm on her desk and her right hand holding a pen to her mouth. She stared mindlessly at the TV on the wall, but Chandler knew she had no idea what was on it.

Finally, she turned to him with the same blank look.

"Maggie?"

Seeing her visitor, she literally shook the fog away and widened her eyes dramatically.

"Oh, hi, Noah. Sorry. Just deep in thought." The smile she gave him wasn't very convincing.

"Morgan still sick?"

Maggie seemed to be caught off-guard by the question.

"Huh? Oh, yes. Still under the weather. Better, though. Thanks for asking." Then she smiled the same insincere smile.

Noah Chandler smiled and nodded.

"Hmmm…"

In the southern suburbs of Moscow, in the Yasenevo District of Moscow, in the headquarters of the Foreign Intelligence Service of Russia, Pavel Orlov sat at his desk drinking his Russian Standard Vodka.

The video of the Saudi Arabian nationals was conclusive. Though the confession was extracted through coercion, there was no doubt it was genuine. The duress the pair were under in no way shaped el-Abdul's testimony. His speech was narrative. He was telling a story, rather than answering leading questions. Yes, it was authentic.

But Orlov had a decision to make. He had promised cooperation with the CIA director. He had promised his old acquaintance Ryan Crenshaw the same. The young American Morgan had asked him specifically and he had given his word that the video would first go to the CIA chief.

But this information is of the type that could totally refute the American president's assertion that Orlov's *Rodina* had planned and executed the bomb attacks against the American leader. President Tatarov could release the information to the world and completely humiliate the United States while defusing the crisis. Of course, providing the video to the Kremlin would disclose that Orlov had operated without authorization to collect this information domestically. Had he been wrong, he would have been made to pay. But since he was found to be right and had, in fact, proven the Motherland innocent of the deeds, he might be forgiven. Perhaps his countrymen would even view him as a hero.

The SVR *Direktor* considered his alternatives and came to a decision. It was the decision to have more vodka and watch the video again.

Director of Central Intelligence Betsy Parnell, former spook Ryan Crenshaw, and head of British intelligence in the UK's Washington embassy, Sir Albert McGinnis, sat around the table in the hotel suite of former President Trenton Weston. The host had ordered lunch for all.

Parnell looked at the time on her phone. Twelve-ten.

"Why hasn't Morgan contacted us? He should've reached out?"

"Exactly how was he going to get his collections to you, Betsy?" the MI-6 chief asked.

"I don't know," Parnell confessed, "but he had to know there was a way to get it to us. I mean, the nature of his evidence would have a bearing on the means to provide it to us. If it's documents, he just texts it to me. If it's going to stop a war, no need to be all spy tech and cryptic. Just get it to us. Covert be damned."

"I agree," said their host. "And I can attest, the young man is as resourceful as anyone I've ever seen, either when I was DCI or during my life outside the Agency. So, it makes me think something is preventing his getting it to us."

Ryan speculated, "Even if the Russians had it, they'd want to make it public, wouldn't they? I can't imagine they want war any more than we do. Right?"

"I go back a long way in this game, and I haven't figured the Russkis out. Have you?" McGinnis warned. "Betsy, do you fully trust Orlov? Do you have absolute confidence that he's really working with the same interests as we have? I don't. I'm sorry, but I have to say I don't."

"Absolute confidence? No. I don't have total confidence in many people, if anyone at all. But why would he agree to cooperate unless he's a true believer? There's nothing to be gained from it. And why would he send one of his agents to help Morgan? I think the odds are that he's on the level."

All acknowledged some agreement with the DCI.

"What if his agent's the bad guy?" Crenshaw worried. "I've been acquainted with Orlov for some time and I agree with Betsy. I think it's most likely he's really trying to help. Of course, I sorta got this whole ball rolling. Maybe that's just me not wanting to have screwed things up."

Weston thought for a minute and said, "Ryan, you might be onto something. One thing we haven't considered is that Russia really was behind the attacks. Then the Russian agent who is working alongside Morgan is trying to see what we know, guide the investigation to whatever end suits them."

Everyone groaned at the possibility.

Weston continued, "But, no, I think Josh would be onto him, if he's fake. I don't think he'd get played."

"What if something's happened to the lad?" McGinnis offered. "We don't know that Morgan sent the message."

"But he knew the code words," countered Director Parnell.

"Ah! Agreed," said the Brit.

◆

Josh Morgan and Slava Proskurkin sat in a bar, each finishing their second shots of vodka. The Russian's phone rang, and he stepped away from the table. The longer the disposition of the recorded confession took, the more the American's distrust of his Russian sidekick grew.

In time, Slava returned from his call.

"I ordered something to eat. Pickled vegetables."

Morgan decided he had to broach the subject.

"What do you think your *Direktor* has done with the video?"

"I'm sure he has done whatever your director and he worked out."

"But they didn't work out anything. At least, not that I know of. I was supposed to deliver the information."

"But you couldn't, could you?"

Morgan thought Slava was too content with the state of things.

The vegetables came along with another plate.

"Herring canapes," the Russian said.

✦

After forwarding the video, Pavel Orlov left his office at 9:00 PM. Before going home, he needed to decide what to do with the Saudis in the back of Slava's Vesta.

✦

As with most, if not all her predecessors, Sandra Hendrickson's closest confidant was her spouse. And like past presidents did, she believed, she truly valued his advice. After she shared the tale of her meeting – encounter was a better word, Sandy decided – she was troubled at the somewhat extended delay in her husband's reply. She sensed he was about to reveal some difference of opinion, and it made her mad before she even knew it to be true.

Sandy had described the rudeness of the ex-president, walking in uninvited and without announcement. She spoke of the insolence of the CIA director. How could Adam disagree?

"How can you think they acted appropriately?" she insisted, preempting any opportunity to voice disagreement.

She was relieved when he spoke.

"The way you characterized things," he affirmed, "then, yes, I believe they acted disrespectfully."

Sandy lay her head on Adam's shoulder.

"But can I ask one question?"

POTUS raised her head and delivered a caustic glance at the first gentleman.

"Honey…" he began, taking both of her hands in his. "What would it hurt to back off a little? At least take some time to see if this so-called 'evidence' materializes?"

The president stood to walk away. Her husband gently pulled her back to the sofa beside him.

"Sweetheart, please don't be mad at what I'm about to say." Adam looked Sandy directly into her eyes, leaning his head toward hers slightly. "Is it possible, even the slightest bit, that your urgency is being fueled by your emotions? Perhaps this is so personal that it's created a need for speed that isn't necessary."

POTUS pulled away from her advisor. He pulled her back and hugged her warmly.

"Sandy, I honestly believe you've approached this thing rationally, except in the area of timing. Your decisions have been well-thought-out. It's just your timetable is, perhaps, more compressed than it needed to be."

This time his wife didn't pull away. She lay against him. Finally, she ended the silence.

"You know I hate you, don't you?" Her smile underscored the sarcasm.

"Yes, sweetheart. I hate you, too," Adam said as tenderly as he could.

POTUS lifted her mobile phone and called her chief of staff.

"Brianna, would you get Director Parnell on the line?"

She gave her husband an insincere glare.

"I hate when you're right."

"Oh, you don't mind me being right," he responded. "You just hate being wrong."

The President of the United States gave her husband the finger, smiling the entire time.

✦

Ryan Crenshaw's phone sounded with the tone that informed him that an email had arrived. He read it and said hopefully to his guests, "Maybe this is what we've been waiting for."

The former Russian professor and former CIA station chief in Moscow lifted the lid to his laptop. He launched his decryption application. Then he opened his email and clicked to view the attachment. The photo was of the Statue of Liberty. He dragged the icon of the image file into the window of the software and clicked on "Extract."

The image began to dissolve into pixels that, in turn, began to resolve into three icons representing files with MOV extensions.

"Videos," Crenshaw informed the rest of the group.

While the four pairs of eyes watched the laptop's display, as if trying to speed up the decryption, the DCI's Agency phone rang. When she saw the caller ID, she shifted her gaze to Trent Weston, who saw in the director's face a nervous, confused look.

"Yes?" she answered. Parnell listened a moment before she leaned back in her chair and dropped her free hand to her side.

A few short phrases and remarks constituted her part of the call, punctuated with pauses of various lengths in between as she listened to her caller.

"Yes, ma'am... Yes. ma'am... That's quite all right... Yes. Thank you... Yes, ma'am. I understand."

Parnell's listening pause was longer this time, then she finally said, "As a matter of fact, we may be getting what you need right now."

Weston smiled at the thought that maybe the Sandra Hendrickson he believed he knew had finally reappeared.

✦

In Estonia, technicians attached to the Operational Detachment-B that was providing support for Operation Nemesis were counting down the final minutes until their A-Team's discretionary window opened. A flurry of communications was taking place as the B-Team reviewed orders and procedures with the six SPIRITs on the ground outside of Vnukovo. Among other items, the communications sergeant confirmed to their forward-deployed operators that no stand-down orders had been received from the Pentagon.

The two teams went through checklists for the EMP deployment and, as a contingency, the detonation of the SNAP.

✦

The four individuals watching the video files received from Orlov were flabbergasted at the content.

Weston's only experience in the spy business was as Director of the Central Intelligence Agency. He was never in the field. So, the sight of the interrogation and corresponding use of the infant's body disturbed him. He knew that such things happened but, sitting behind his desk at Langley, he was far-removed from the uglier aspects of fieldwork.

Seeing Josh in action in the recording, the former chief executive couldn't help being a little disappointed in him initially. Then the renewed recognition of what was at stake overwhelmed him and his feelings changed to one of profound distress that the young man he knew and admired was having to go to such lengths.

Still, the major takeaway from the images was that Saudi Arabia's al-Qaeda government had orchestrated the entire plot to kill Hendrickson and provoke a war between the U.S. and Russia by creating the appearance the Kremlin was to blame.

For their parts, Crenshaw, Parnell, and McGinnis were field operatives and, while none had participated directly in an operation as distasteful as what they were witnessing, they had each supervised those who had, or at the very least read the reports of black ops that had employed brutal tactics.

DCI Parnell made it only halfway through the first video before she was back on the phone with President Hendrickson, who personally took the director's call this time.

"It's the Saudis. No doubt. We have proof that you need to see."

The spy chief listened to POTUS' response and acknowledged it. "Understood."

Then to Weston, "We've got to go."

The ex-president said, "He should come," pointing to Crenshaw.

Betsy nodded.

"If you don't mind, I'd like to keep my knowledge of this operation hidden for now," requested Sir Albert.

"Agreed," said Parnell, as Crenshaw lowered the lid to his laptop.

There were no shaking of hands or other polite formalities. Parnell, Crenshaw, and Weston scrambled for their coats and headed for the door. They, along with their British friend, felt a great sense of accomplishment at uncovering the truth and were overjoyed that President Hendrickson was in the process of having the A-Team stand down.

✦

Hidden in the snow alongside the airport's boundary, six U.S. soldiers watched a security vehicle stop on the elevated portion of the Kiyevskoye Highway directly in front of them. The beam of the powerful spotlight mounted on the passenger side of the truck pierced through the trees as much as possible from its higher position on the highway.

All six operators recognized the markings on the vehicle. It was either the same guards that they had encountered when they were making the trek here, or some of their comrades.

But unlike in their previous near-confrontation, accompanying the motor vehicle was a pair of guards walking along the edge of the forest with flashlights almost as powerful as the floods on the truck.

Russian forces had no doubt stepped up security in preparation for the departure of the Russian president in a few hours. Communications Sergeant Matheson voiced a very brief sitrep to the B-Team in Estonia and switched his radio to his team's channel to concentrate solely on communications with them.

The men in the truck appeared to be more diligent than before, possibly because they had company on their watch. The light paused occasionally as it coursed across the ground below and adjacent the raised highway.

The ground patrol was even more conscientious about their work, moving slowly at the edge of the trees. They stopped frequently to examine anything that caught their eyes in the illumination of the handheld lanterns. Even in the dimness of the night, the frost of their breaths was evident.

✦

"Yes, sir. Copy that," acknowledged the B-Team Leader. He turned his attention to the Communications Sergeant and pointed to his radio.

"Abort!" he shouted. "Abort! Abort!"

The sergeant relayed the order.

"Abort! Abort! Abort! Eighteen Echo, abort! Abort! Abort!"

The communicator waited for an acknowledgement. None came.

"Eighteen Echo, abort! Abort! Abort! I repeat, abort! Abort! Abort!"

The sergeant tried desperately to contact the SPIRITs. He was aware of their situation and knew that they were probably maintaining radio silence during it, but he wanted to ensure they heard the order to stand down as soon as the situation had passed.

The sergeant looked at the captain who served as the Detachment Commander. He stood silently behind the radio operator as he continued his frantic transmissions.

◆

The SPIRITs watched intently as the patrol lingered in their area. Each wondered if the Russian security forces were somehow aware of their presence. The operators' index fingers rested against the trigger guards of their various shoulder arms, from the Master Sergeant's Colt M4A1 SOPMOD to Fluff's Heckler & Koch HK G28, and the others' preferred automatic weapons.

After a few tense minutes, both the truck and foot patrol moved a short distance along their routes, where they paused and replicated their survey of the area adjacent to their new location.

SFC Cooley Matheson started to reactivate his radio for external communications but looked at his watch before he did. Ten minutes after eleven. The Communications Sergeant removed his finger from the switch and the SPIRITs of Operation Nemesis began their communications blackout. Having gone quiet, the Special Forces soldiers' discretionary window had just opened.

The Green Berets would have to delay preparations for execution until the Russian security patrols were completely out of the area. But the wait hardly mattered. The team had almost twelve hours until the Russian president's planned departure from Vnukovo International Airport.

Deployment of the Springer Drone and the Electromagnetic Pulse device mounted on it was a near certainty now.

◆

The word had gone from the Operations Nemesis B-Team to the Pentagon. General Richards was relaying the information to the commander in chief.

The president saw the Oval Office door open and her secretary peek in. POTUS motioned toward her and the three guests entered. Hendrickson only recognized two of them, but introductions would have to wait.

Brianna Washington closed the door behind her. Hendrickson motioned her visitors to seats in the center of the room as she pushed her left hand upward from her forehead over her hair. As she listened to her Chiefs of Staff Chairman deliver the bad news, her stomach churned. POTUS paced behind her desk.

"I don't understand, general. I don't understand at all. We had until 11:00 PM Moscow time to wave them off. That's 3:00 PM our time. Is that not correct?" The woman's voice was growing in volume and pitch.

The three Oval Office guests exchanged confused, worried glances as they picked up on the substance of the phone call transpiring before them. Their exuberance transformed to gut-wrenching anguish in a moment.

The president ended the call with, "Keep me updated." She pressed the button on the desk phone and turned to the three people who had delivered the news that the Holy Islamic Republic of Saudi Arabia was the nation behind the attacks, the deaths, the injuries, the plot to point to Russia – behind all of it.

Hendrickson's tortured look told Weston, Parnell, and Crenshaw everything they needed to know. They understood without a word that the weight of the knowledge that she had committed the United States military to operations on the basis of erroneous assumptions was crashing down on Commander in Chief Hendrickson.

The "Most Powerful Woman in the World" appeared to be nothing of the sort as she slumped into her chair behind her desk.

"What have I done?"

CHAPTER 34

Day 17 – Monday

With the security forces well away from their location, the SPIRITs began inspecting the arsenal they had brought with them.

Sergeant First Class Jack Jackson had done a preliminary assessment of the Springer Drone on board the MC-130J. The device was battery-powered and was effective as a weapons platform or a surveillance device.

The backpack aircraft weighed about fifteen pounds but had a payload capacity equal to that. There were four wings of equal size. Large pins held them onto the body, allowing them to retract inward to lock in place. When the operator removed the bungee cords that secured them to the fuselage, a push inward unlocked them from their folded position, and they sprang open like a switchblade. In their flight positions, the wings spread to a span greater than the craft's length and provided enough lift that, with the propeller turning at full power, the drone could be hand-launched by a single man holding it over his head with a pilot controlling it remotely.

The aircraft was highly maneuverable and extremely fast. It was capable of carrying small missiles that were lethal on the battlefield when the targets were tanks, vehicles, or other land-based objects.

However, for airborne targets, the drone's missiles weren't as effective. Though incomparably fast for their size, they were incapable of intercepting jets. Even if they were, a target's speed, coupled with countermeasures such as chaff, made interception unlikely.

For such targets, The Defense Advanced Research Projects Agency, or DARPA, had developed small non-nuclear Electromagnetic Pulse devices. The EMPs had a limited range. They were effective to a radius of about one mile, but despite the limitation they were very powerful. The EMP the SPIRITs were going to deploy on the Springer Drone was of a type known as Explosively Pumped Flux Compression Generators. These E-bombs had banks of high-voltage capacitors that produced a very strong magnetic field. Then a fast explosion transferred an extremely high amount of energy into the magnetic field, compressing the field very rapidly. The pulse radiated away from the blast as electromagnetic energy that was capable of disrupting computers and other electronics, even causing permanent damage to the nearest such devices.

EMPs could knock out electronics in buildings, tanks, and, most importantly for this mission, jet airplanes. Anything controlled by a computer was extremely susceptible to disruption and damage from an EMP. Most modern aircraft were fly-by-wire, meaning computers actually controlled the various systems of the aircraft by interpreting the pilot's actions on sticks, levers, dials, and wheels and converting them into digital commands.

As with any advance in weaponry, countermeasures to EMPs were the focus of developers. Efforts to "harden" electronics, that is intentionally shielding electronics against the effects of electromagnetism, became critical next steps. Success varied. Tests of the SPIRITs' EMP demonstrated it to be highly effective against the most intensely hardened computers, if detonated in very close proximity to the target.

The simplest of the two primary weapons at the operators' disposal was the most advanced technologically, the B-54B SNAP. The Special Nuclear Armament Package required the technician to attach an interface to the control panel of the bomb that allowed operator inputs. The digital display prompted two users individually for his half of the code. The next prompt was for an entry to the countdown timer. The device would go into sleep mode until the SNAP Technical Sergeant entered a time from one minute to six hours. If he failed to enter a time within two minutes of the prompt, the device would time out. The two code owners would need to enter them again. The timer display would flash "EXECUTE?" until the "enter" icon was touched. When it was, the two halves of the code needed to be reentered and the minutes and seconds would begin counting down. So, while it required key entries, once they were accomplished the thing only had to sit there. No flying. No aiming. Just waiting for the display to read "00:00:00.".

All of the SPIRITs were confident things wouldn't come to setting off the bomb. At least all of them, especially Lechler and Macduff, *hoped* they wouldn't.

The drone, the EMP, and the SNAP all passed their respective checks upon setup. The final step was for Electronics Sergeant Abe Aboud to run diagnostics on each piece of equipment. All passed their final exams and the operators returned to their waiting game.

✦

Josh Morgan was exhausted, but sleep wouldn't come. He was concerned why he hadn't received the second of the two communications he had expected in reply to his "done" text.

He received the first – eventually. The American knew that it had to have taken some time for Director Orlov to transmit the videos to Crenshaw, so the fact that a while had passed before getting the one-letter text didn't surprise him. The message had been a simple "k."

The second message would confirm that the president had backed off from her intention to strike Russia, whatever form the attack was to take.

It was one-forty-five and Morgan had tossed and turned on Slava's couch.

He had watched the man with envy as he played with his twin daughters. Later, the soft moans and obvious activity he heard from husband's and wife's bedroom after they had gone to bed made him a little uncomfortable – and made him miss Maggie. He wanted to put tissue in his ears to muffle the sound of his hosts' passion, but he was afraid he would go to sleep and not hear the arrival of the expected communication.

Instead, he did his best to ignore the couple – both times.

✦

"So, it was Josh Morgan?" the president observed from the videos. "I suppose you sent him."

DCI Parnell admitted it with confidence. "I couldn't send one of my own people. I was way out on a limb and didn't want to involve anyone."

"Instead, you enlisted a civilian?"

The director hadn't thought of it like that. She viewed Morgan as a former case officer who had proved he could still operate in the field by his efforts to rescue the man sitting next to her. She didn't answer POTUS.

The president had fully explained the failure to get the order to the SPIRITs in time before they went dark. It was utterly agonizing to confess to having initiated the operation and then find out she had, as some had cautioned, acted with undue haste.

And now two nations were at risk of engaging in a war that could result in nuclear strikes. It suddenly occurred to Hendrickson that, if things proceeded according to plan, the only way to avoid a nuclear first strike by the U.S. soldiers deployed in Russia was for them to actually succeed in assassinating Tatarov.

"The simplest way to back off the edge of this cliff," Weston suggested, "is to get the Russian president on the phone and tell him not to get on his darned plane. The problem is this: He will certainly send his military to comb the area around the airport. They will find and engage our boys. And as tragic as that would be, it pales in comparison to Tatarov's forces finding an American-made nuclear weapon deployed within his nation's borders."

Nobody spoke, but the former occupant of the office he was sitting in thought again how foolish the current occupant had been to even consider the plan she signed off on.

"Nuclear bomb!" he thought. "Insane."

The president conceded that the Special Forces A-Team couldn't be allowed to bring the plane down.

"I'll make the call and deal with the consequences. But I'd like to continue considering other options before taking that step. Who knows what the Kremlin might do in" – she choked on the word – "retaliation for our attempt to assassinate their leader? All this time, I truly believed we were seeking retribution for that very act against me."

POTUS buried her face in her hands and slumped until her forearms rested on her knees.

"How long do you think you can wait?" asked Ryan Crenshaw.

POTUS shook her head. "I don't know. Tatarov's plane is due to take off at eleven o'clock Moscow time. We could call at ten-forty-five."

"What if he decides to leave earlier?" Crenshaw followed up.

"Ten. Ten o'clock," DCI Parnell insisted. "If you haven't gotten the SPIRITs to stand down before then, you have to make that call."

Parnell's recommendation sounded more like a command. But everybody in the room, including Hendrickson nodded their agreement.

"We still don't have a plan," reinforced Crenshaw.

"And I think we need to monitor news to see if Tatarov's plans change," stated the DCI.

POTUS said, "I'd get Chandler, but he's on Capitol Hill. I don't want to bring anyone in on this. There are so many leaks in Congress, even throughout this administration. Word of this gets leaked to the press, we may have a more serious problem than we already have."

Everyone agreed that the situation was fluid enough to require monitoring and that a leak would be catastrophic.

"Josh Morgan's fiancée is just down the hall," suggested Weston.

POTUS leaned back and stared at the ceiling. Finally, she leaned toward her desk and pressed a button on her phone.

"Yes, ma'am," answered the voice from the speakerphone.

"Maggie, would you come to my office, please?"

The president reflected on the situation while waiting for the acting press secretary to arrive.

"Might as well make this a family affair." Hendrickson looked at Parnell. "Do you think Morgan would be up for another job?"

"He might. I'll text him."

President Hendrickson shook her head. "No time for that. Call him."

A voice call was poor tradecraft, Parnell knew, but it didn't matter at this point. She dialed the last number Morgan messaged her from and hoped he hadn't already burned that phone.

✦

Josh Morgan slept on his co-investigator's couch in Moscow, Russia. It had taken some time, but he had finally dozed off. At 2:15 AM, the phone rang. The sleeper awoke with such a start that his feet fell off the end of the tiny sofa. Out of habit, he looked at the caller ID, not expecting to see a number. As predicted, it read, "Unknown Caller." He just hoped it wasn't some fluke wrong number. He stepped from Proskurkin's flat into the hallway.

"Yes."

✦

While Parnell dialed Morgan's latest burner phone number, Brianna Washington opened the door and announced Maggie's arrival. She stepped in and her heart sank. In the room were people she knew were involved in whatever dangerous thing Morgan was doing. Were they here because something went wrong? Did they call her in because something had happened to her fiancé?

Her breathing increased along with her pulse. Her head turned sharply toward the CIA director when she heard her speak on her phone.

"Morgan? Betsy Parnell."

Maggie had no clue what was going on, but Morgan was apparently well enough to take a phone call. Her knees nearly buckled in relief. Without an invitation, she sat down between Trenton Weston and Ryan Crenshaw. Both men reflexively took one of their friend's hands.

The president moved to where her DCI stood and reached for the phone. Parnell was relieved to see POTUS engaged and proactive, and gladly handed her the phone.

"Mr. Morgan, this is the president. I…"

For some reason, the president's attention was drawn to the quivering, auburn-haired young woman whose face shone with a mix of hopefulness and fear.

"Josh, hold on a moment." The president walked to her press secretary, smiled, and handed her the phone. "Can you keep it really short?" She smiled again.

Maggie clutched the phone with both hands.

"Josh?"

✦

Josh Morgan heard what might have been the most beautiful sound he'd ever heard.

"Maggie. Oh, I've missed you. I love you."

The pair, on different sides of the world, spoke for only a couple of minutes, but the conversation did both of them more good than they would've thought.

Morgan ended his part of the conversation by telling Maggie that he was fine and would be home soon. Confident that the president's call was the good news he'd been waiting for, he believed that he was, and that he would.

✦

Wife and mother Sandra Hendrickson reached for the phone in the kindest way she could and softly said, "Maggie."

Maggie whispered, "I love you, Josh," and handed the cell phone back to her boss.

The commander in chief placed the phone to her ear and took a deep breath.

"Josh, we have a situation. I'm afraid I have to ask for your help one more time."

Maggie was smiling at Trent Weston when she heard the president's words. Her head twirled around, and her hand went to her mouth.

The President of the United States described the entire operation and its current status to the man in Moscow, even though he was no longer in the employee of the Central Intelligence Agency. Maggie Loughlin was hearing the same explanation that her fiancé was, even though she wasn't cleared for it, either. The president didn't care.

"We don't have a plan for you. We'll try to come up with something, but felt you needed to be aware. And perhaps you can come up with something yourself. We don't have time for all this spy shit. No changing phones. No cryptic messages or codewords. You keep this phone. Parnell will give you my direct number. Don't hang up after she does."

POTUS handed the DCI her phone. While Parnell gave Hendrickson's private number to Morgan, the president called General Richards. The Chairman of the Joint Chiefs picked up immediately. Everybody did for the president.

"General, I need the precise location of your team at Vnukovo."

Richards balked, as he should have, and asked the nature of the request. However, when Hendrickson invoked her authority as the commander in chief, he had no choice but to obey her direct order. POTUS scribbled down the GPS coordinates as the general gave them to her and handed the paper to Parnell.

The CIA director relayed the location to Morgan.

"One last thing, Josh. You need to keep your Russian friend out of this."

"Proskurkin? Why?"

"If I'm him, I'm going straight to Orlov. Things are different now. This isn't about proving Russia wasn't behind the plot here. If they know we have boots on the ground, they'll go after them with prejudice. And they should. It's what I'd do. They won't take the chance that you'll be able to just waltz in there and talk these operators down."

"Betsy, I don't even have a car."

"Figure something out, Josh." She heard the sigh through the phone. "You have about eight hours."

"Okay. Got it."

"Oh, and Morgan…"

"Yes."

"Watch your back. They figure out what you're up to, you're not a friendly anymore."

"Gee, that's comforting. See you, Bets."

"Good luck, Josh."

Maggie was bewildered. Why was Josh doing this? Don't we have a whole government of people to do this? The president knelt before the young woman who had just hired on only two weeks ago.

"I know this makes no sense to you. I don't like the situation we're in, either. And I'm sorry to have to rely on Josh. And this whole thing… well, it's basically my fault. But this is where we are. And I need your help, too."

◆

In the Proskurkin flat, Morgan looked toward the doorway to the bedroom where Slava was stirring. His first task was to figure out what he was going to tell his host as his reason for heading out on his own. He decided not to.

◆

Maggie sat down behind Marie Ginnetti's desk. She had her orders. Keep her door closed. Don't answer it for anyone. She wasn't to answer the phone for anyone other than the president or DCI Parnell. Her job was to watch TV and surf the web. Her mission was to monitor any news coming out of Russia that might indicate awareness of the U.S. commandos on the ground there.

But, more importantly, she was to be especially alert for any news that Russian President Tatarov was altering his travel plans. Delaying them was great. Moving his departure up was potentially disastrous. If that happened, she was to call the president directly and immediately. If she didn't answer, Maggie was to try again while she ran down the hall to track her down, and so on.

Maggie got it. It might be as important as anything she would ever do, the president had said.

✦

Morgan launched Google Earth on his phone. The phone was horrible at processing data. It was slow and locked up frequently. Finally, it settled on the coordinates outside the Vnukovo International Airport. He would use a navigation app for directions – if he could secure a car, he reminded himself – but as a precaution, he wrote down the directions.

The former spy had learned a number of skills at The Farm, CIA's training facility at Camp Peary in York County, Virginia. There were quite a few that he never used, and never even practiced. Stealing a car might have been at the top of that list.

He wasn't really considering it, of course, even if he could really pull it off. For one thing, he might be apprehended by the police some time after the deed. Whatever he decided, Morgan knew he couldn't get caught.

He considered simply asking Slava if he could borrow his Vesta. That is, until her remembered that Proskurkin had left it with Orlov with two Saudi Arabian agents in the trunk. They'd had to take the Metro to the bar and then to the SVR agent's flat.

The Metro!

Morgan accessed maps on his phone. After a struggle with the phone's performance, he discovered that he could get from just outside Slava's apartment to the Kiyevskoye Metro station in central Moscow in about twenty minutes. From there, he could take the Aeroexpress directly to Vnukovo. It would be about a thirty-five-minute trip to the airport. All totaled, it would be about an hour from the moment he left Slava's apartment.

Problem was, the Aeroexpress' first departure wasn't for about three hours from now at 6:00 AM. Morgan saw that he could catch the line from where he was to Kiyevskoye at five o'clock but arriving at the airport at six-thirty-five was wasting a lot of the limited amount of time he had.

Another problem was that he would have to walk from the airport terminal or take a cab and be dropped off alongside the highway. Rail was out.

"I guess you could say this is a store for your convenience," he thought wryly.

Morgan's Google Maps search of convenience stores near Slava's flat had brought a touch of humor to his otherwise stressed-out mood. The "convenience store" located at Bolshaya Tulskaya Ulitsa, 2, was the *Секс-шоп «Он и Она»*. He calculated that it would be a walk of almost three-quarters of a mile to number two Grand Tula Street. At least the nature of the store's products should make it very likely that he would find someone there, even at – maybe especially at – this time of the night.

The American decided he had no better plan. In fact, he had no other plan of any kind. He hated that he had to go on without his Russian counterpart. Proskurkin had been instrumental in getting to the truth about the bombings. And Morgan felt he could trust him. Nevertheless, he understood the logic behind Betsy's instructions, and agreed with it.

Morgan put on his jacket, topcoat, and toboggan. As he closed the door quietly behind him, he donned his gloves and draped his muffler around his neck. Downstairs, he stepped out to a clear night. Even with the city lights, the brightest of the stars twinkled above. It was bitterly cold, even for Moscow in late January. Figuring the temperature to be around twenty degrees, he pulled his wool scarf more tightly to his neck and headed east.

The former spy knew he'd had it good using his job as a photojournalist as his cover. He rented cars and hotel rooms under his own name. The Central Intelligence Agency even got a break with regard to his expenses. When he wasn't freelancing, he was on assignment for some legitimate publication, even though it was always arranged by the Agency to get him where he needed to be. Since he was providing real stories and photographs, the magazine or news outlet paid his expenses just as they would anyone else.

So, Morgan griped, how was it that he was setting out through the snow at 3:45 AM to a disreputable "convenience store" trying to get a ride to go confront an Army Special Forces Team to convince them to abandon their mission?

✦

Maggie watched five televisions – or tried her best to. She wished she could get help, but her instructions were to fly solo. The host of stories on five different networks, mostly about war preparations, presented nothing new about President Tatarov's trip abroad. Comprehending what she saw was difficult enough, but she had to keep the volumes up, too. And filtering through five audio broadcasts was almost impossible.

In addition, while being bombarded with the sights and sounds of the television networks, she scoured the internet for information there.

She was grateful to the president for letting her speak with Josh, but in retrospect, she was even more fearful, now that she knew what he was up to.

✦

Morgan reached his destination. As he approached the "Sex Shop/He and She," he saw immediately that he was correct in thinking that he would find people there. He would have preferred another type of twenty-four-hour store, but an alternate choice would've meant a longer walk and more wasted time.

He entered and saw four people, all males, examining the wares lining the walls and on the shelves. Morgan tried to decide which one looked like the safest one to approach. A thought occurred to him that he shouldn't talk to any of them. Given the carnal nature of the store, he feared any potential source of transportation would get the wrong idea. Instead, he walked to the man behind the counter.

"I need a ride to the airport. One hundred dollars, U.S.," he said in Russian.

The man stared back at him silently and Morgan wondered if the man considered the offer a euphemism for a sexual proposal.

The American quickly clarified. "This isn't a come-on or proposition of any kind. I really only need someone to take me to Vnukovo. Your store was the closest one that is open."

The clerk continued his silence. Finally, he said, "Two hundred and I'll take you myself."

Irrespective of the dire emergency facing the United States and Russia, Morgan hated to spend money unnecessarily.

"One-fifty. And only if we can leave now."

The men stared at one another. Finally, the sex shop employee hollered, "Yuri. I'm leaving."

Holding a box of merchandise, a man Morgan assumed to be another employee peered from the doorway to a back room.

"I have to finish stocking."

The protest didn't slow down Morgan's driver.

"Watch the store."

Yuri slammed down the box and walked toward the front of Sex Shop/He and She, complaining loudly enough the entire way that the customers turned their attention from the DVD cover photos of naked women and men and the enticing packages of toys promising every conceivable manner of sexual satisfaction.

"Never mind him. He's always like that."

Morgan glanced over his shoulder at the screaming Yuri.

"He's just like his mother."

The American looked at Yuri's father and then at the bright lights above the door that identified its products.

"So, this is a family business?" Morgan meant it sarcastically.

"*Da.* This way."

Morgan's driver led him to the side of the store to a bright yellow, Lada Kalina Sport, probably six years old. It was larger than a Mini, though not by a lot. However, given that the passenger didn't have bags, it would be fine.

The pair got into the small Russian-made car. Before putting the key in the ignition, the driver said, "I need payment now."

"Half now. The other half when we get there."

"*Yebat tebya*! All now," The Russian insisted. He pulled his jacket back to show a knife tucked in his waistband.

Josh Morgan decided he'd had enough.

"Fuck you back, asshole! He pulled his topcoat back to show the handgun he had in his waistband. "Half now! The rest later! Or I can just take your car!" He shoved seventy-five American dollars into the man's fist.

The man waited before turning the key to start his car. He looked back at his passenger, tucked the bills in his shirt pocket, and smiled.

"I like you," he said, and patted Morgan on his leg several times rapidly.

The small Lada pulled onto the street. About one hundred meters behind them, another car did the same.

CHAPTER 35

Josh Morgan reviewed the map on his phone again, which confirmed that it should take about thirty-five minutes to get to his destination. His driver chatted amiably the entire way. The passenger had no desire for conversation, but he didn't need to speak. The driver filled the entire time himself, with stories about his family, particularly his wife, which consisted almost entirely of complaints. He speculated on the talk of war between Mother Russia and the United States. Ironically, he seemed to know nothing of the fact that the U.S. had already declared war.

Morgan occasionally grunted an agreement or said, "Really?" He was trying to come up with a plan. He thought it might be as simple as walking into the forested area where the GPS coordinates indicated they would be, and yelling for them. Wouldn't the simple fact that he knew they were there lend some credibility to anything he said?

Yes, he decided, simple was best. They either believed him, or they didn't. Just successfully contacting the SPIRITs was the hard part.

The yellow sedan neared the interchange. Before the Russian driver could make the right onto the offramp to Centralnaya and toward the terminal, Morgan said, "Straight."

The Russian was unconcerned about the seeming change in plans and steered his Lada from the exit lane. He figured his rider would tell him what to do next. Morgan said nothing for another two-and-a-half kilometers. Then, "There."

The Russian moved into the exit lane. His passenger pointed left, across the highway to a complex of businesses.

"Make the U-turn under the bridge and go there."

The Russian followed the directions and crossed under the Kiyevskoye Highway, entered the onramp back onto eastbound Kiyevskoye. Less than a kilometer later he turned right, then made an immediate right into the business center.

"Which?" The center had what appeared to be a sporting good retail/wholesale business, an auto service center, a few offices, and a grocery store.

"There."

The Russian pulled into a space near the grocery store.

"Should I wait?"

"No, this is where I get out." Morgan pulled out some cash.

"Are you sure we can't make it two hundred," the driver smiled.

The American smiled back but put only the remaining seventy-five of the agreed-upon one hundred fifty dollars in the man's hand.

The Russian – the American never got his name – gave another smile and a salute. He put his car in reverse and started his drive back to the Sex Shop.

Morgan never noticed the car that continued past the grocery store a short distance and parked on the side of the street.

The ex-CIA officer pulled his collar up. He went into the store and to its restroom. More than he needed to use it, he wanted some more time to think. There were no others in the restroom. He stepped into a stall, shut the door, and leaned back onto it. He rubbed his face with both hands and convinced himself that everything would be fine. Finally, he used the facilities, rinsed off his face, and went into the store to purchase a drink and some snacks.

✦

It was almost 9:30 PM, and most of the key personnel in the West Wing were still at their desks. That had been the usual practice since the bombing.

President Hendrickson had filled in her chief of staff about the new evidence and the looming mission execution by the SPIRITs. She sat in the Cabinet Room with Chandler and General Richards, along with other key members of her war team, trying to figure some way out of the mess they were in. Beyond that, if Josh Morgan wasn't able to call off the Army Special Forces, they had to develop contingencies for the certain reprisals by the Russians.

"We've discussed so much here. It's quite daunting. General Richards, please summarize the full range of scenarios."

The Chairman of the Joint Chiefs of Staff began to draw a crude flow chart on his iPad, which was projected onto the TV display. He drew a circle and labeled it "drone/emp."

"First, our team is already in their discretionary window. They can act autonomously at any time, and in any manner they deem appropriate. But here's the simple version.

"The preferred action is to launch the Springer Drone with the Electromagnetic Pulse device attached to approach Tatarov's plane as it is taking off. The operator will intercept the plane, leading it in much the way a hunter leads birds, so that, as the plane leaves the ground, the drone will swing parallel to it and slightly ahead. Because of the airspeed differential, the plane will gain on the drone. The drone operator will attempt to bring it directly under the aircraft, where the EMP Technician will activate the device's bank of capacitors. It only takes seconds to build the electromagnetic field. Then he'll initiate the explosion that will compress the field and send it out as a pulse, which should take down the Russian plane."

Richards drew a sideways "V" from the "drone/emp" circle he had drawn earlier.

"The SPIRITs either succeed..." – the general wrote "yes" on the top line of the "V" – "or they don't." He wrote "no" on the lower line.

"If they succeed, they grab the nuke and make their escape. They set timed charges for fifteen minutes to destroy any equipment they leave behind to keep it out of Russia's hands."

The presenter circled the "no" on his drawing and drew another sideways "V" from it. He wrote "unable" on the upper leg and "failed" on the lower.

"There are two ways that the drone option may not succeed. First, they might not get the opportunity to engage. Tatarov never takes off in the plane. Of course, it appears that will happen today. The second way is an outright failure. The target presents itself. Our A-Team deploys the EMP, but it doesn't bring down the plane."

Richards wrote "snap+72" beside the word "unable." He wrote "snap+0" beside "failed."

"The team's orders are to wait seventy-two hours after discretion onset. If the target never presents itself, they are to set the SNAP's timer to one hour and retreat to the exfiltration point. However, they will be checking in every twelve hours, should that be the case.

"But..." The general taps "snap+0" on his chart. "...If they deploy the EMP but are unsuccessful in downing the plane, or if prior to acquiring the target, they are engaged, they may detonate the device at their discretion."

The president's eyes grew wide. She interrupted her general.

"I'm sorry... what? They have orders to detonate a nuclear bomb without direct orders from me?"

The Joint Chiefs Chairman appeared confused.

"Why, yes, Madam President. The plans you agreed to are what I've just explained."

"I don't think that's what I approved."

"I'm sorry, ma'am." General Richards opens his printed copy of the approved, signed plan. "If they can't engage with the drone, there will be scheduled check-ins during the seventy-hour 'hold" period, but in the other circumstances…"

Heads all around the room nodded in confirmation of the Chairman's explanation. The president sat back in her chair and could only utter, "Oh, my."

The full ramifications of her orders were instantly clear.

✦

Suddenly there was a rapid knock. The visitor burst into the room without waiting for an invitation.

Acting Press Secretary Loughlin nearly shouted, "This is bad!" She fumbled for the controls to the huge television screen on the wall. The display changed to QNN's Tracy Adams, looking quite fatigued from the hours he had put in during the crisis with the Russian Federation, was recapping the "Breaking News."

"This just in: The Quantum News Network has just learned from an unnamed source that U.S. Special Ops teams are already on the ground in the Russian Federation. Details of the deployment weren't available. As you can imagine, QNN struggled with whether to report this development, but the news is already being aired on Russian television stations. To repeat…"

The Cabinet Room was deathly silent. Heads turned in all directions as the war planners wondered what traitor among them had leaked this news. Whoever it was might've just destroyed the last chance to avert a war.

The president finally spoke. She was calm and resigned to her unavoidable next step.

"Chief Chandler, would you get President Tatarov on the phone for me, please?"

✦

Russian President Boris Yaroslavovich Tatarov was already in the presidential aircraft when the call from the American leader came. As he often did, Tatarov spent the night on the plane preceding a trip. It was his way of acclimating to the routine of the journey, even if there wasn't a sufficient difference in time zone between Moscow and his destination to require a mental and physical accommodation to jet lag.

The Russian leader had heard the reports of the presence of U.S. troops in the Motherland and was infuriated. However, since the foolish American Congress had issued its declaration of war against the Federation, this was to be expected. Besides, he told himself, these reports were often wrong, simply the results of overzealous reporting by an unfettered American press.

"Too much freedom," he remarked in reply to his own observation.

His aide wondered at the comment but said nothing.

"So, what do I tell American president?"

Tatarov accepted the tea brought to him by another aide. He considered his options, all the while adding milk and sugar into his brew and blending the mixture with his spoon. He sipped his tea with his left hand, holding the saucer beneath the cup with his right.

The aide continued to wait for his answer. The president looked out the window of the Ilyushin Il-96 Quadjet, though there was nothing to see yet, except the interior of its private hangar. He set down his cup and saucer and tapped his right fingers rhythmically on the arm of his seat. He took another sip of tea, wiped his mouth with his napkin, and finally decided on his reply to the woman he had kept waiting on the phone.

He looked at the aide, and with a full measure of defiance, said, "Tell her nothing."

"Do I tell her you will speak to her shortly?"

"*Nyet*. Hang up."

"Sir?"

Tatarov gave a couple of backhanded waves, arched his eyebrows, and leaned his head toward his assistant in displeasure for being questioned.

The attendant decided he was going to enjoy this. And with that, he pressed the button to disconnect the phone with a certain amount of flair and a bow for his superior.

The aide and his boss smiled in satisfaction at one another.

"There!" said Tatarov.

He rubbed his hands together as if wiping sand from them.

"We will leave earlier," the president decided.

✦

Normally, anyone dismissing her as the Russian president had done would have angered Hendrickson, but the emotion that gripped her was fear. She already knew things were out of control. Now she was terrified at the sudden inevitability of the danger ahead and the conviction that she was powerless to prevent it.

Noah Chandler saw that she had hung up the phone without speaking to Tatarov.

His boss returned the handset to its base and rubbed the bridge of her nose with the tips of her left thumb and index finger. She looked at her staff manager and remarked matter-of-factly, "Hung up."

Chandler sat in the chair across from the president's desk.

"Perhaps you could make a statement... go on TV..."

POTUS stopped him with her quiet rebuttal, "And say what? Tell the world that the rumors are true? Announce publicly where our ops team is?"

Chandler understood. It was frustrating and frightful to not have a resolution to offer to his boss and friend.

Hendrickson and Chandler returned to the Cabinet Room.

"My friends, I believe we should spend our time preparing for the worst."

The certainty of retaliation by the Russian Federation had been a part of the thinking from the beginning, so plans were already in place. One-by-one, the chief of staff of each branch of the military summarized his part.

The Navy had submarines deployed in the Baltic. Nuclear warhead-tipped cruise missiles would reach Moscow in mere minutes. Of course, everyone realized that the Russians had subs parked along our shores, too. But the Navy Admiral serving as chief was confident that his sub-chasing subs had them all located and could take them out before they could launch.

POTUS thanked him for his report, though she was thinking that it would only take one missile from one Russian sub to get through, and…

The Air Force had two roles – offensive and defensive.

Of course, every attack jet and bomber in the U.S. arsenal was ready to throw everything they had at Moscow and Russian military bases around the world. And from Eastern Europe to Japan and South Korea, and domestically in Alaska, U.S. fighters were prepared to repel any Russian air attack.

Relatively new as a defensive contribution from the Air Force was the capability of F-35 Joint Strike Fighters to detect launches of intercontinental ballistic missiles and shoot them down in the early stage of their flights. This enhancement to the F-35s was expensive and many top military officials thought the adaptations were overkill. Another reason for the lack of enthusiasm among some defense department officials was that they believed the technology would be better used in other applications. Regardless, the innovative countermeasure to ICBMs was on a number of F-35s.

Most believed their use would likely be to interdict attacks from rogue nations like North Korea and Iran. Now it seemed like the first test might well be from Russian ICBMs.

Some F-35s were already deployed prior to the onset of hostilities with Russia, but others were rushed to bases in Japan, South Korea, Finland, and Estonia, close to Russia where they should be able to acquire ballistic missiles in their boost stages. Sensors on the aircrafts would detect the infrared signature of a missile's launch and determine its location.

The individual reports continued for some time. The president was attentive and comprehended each military branch's interdiction plan. But behind her focused exterior, Hendrickson's mind was awash with the hope that somehow Morgan could make contact with the SPIRITs before they executed their plan. She even considered that the Russian military taking out the operators might interrupt things long enough for a solution to present itself.

POTUS and Chandler worked through every scenario they could think of that might develop if Morgan wasn't successful in reaching the Operation Nemesis soldiers, or couldn't persuade them to stand down if he did.

If the nuke was detonated, there would certainly be a response. The president and her chief of staff decided that the United States could not appear weak, but more importantly, the U.S. had to try to prevent that retaliatory strike. They decided that Hendrickson would have to go on the offensive as soon as satellites determined that the Vnukovo bomb had exploded.

She would have to warn the Kremlin that the United States would respond in-kind, if Russia launched missiles. She would say that her action had been in response to Russia's attacks on America, even though she knew better now.

She would inform Tatarov that U.S. submarines were close enough that missiles would reach Moscow first. Hendrickson would say that American forces deployed throughout Europe with her allies would launch and hit Russian cities while their nukes were still in the air.

Of course, both the president and her chief of staff knew that many of Russia's missiles were already aimed at NATO allies and they were very, very close.

The president sighed deeply.

"Shit."

◆

The CIA director had gotten her own slap in the face. Parnell had received a call from the White House asking her to call SVR Director Orlov. As with the president, she had been hung up on, though not as immediately. Her Russian counterpart took the time to inform her that he felt betrayed. When they had developed the plan to defuse the tensions between their nations, he believed they were acting in partnership. Yet, the entire time, the United States was proceeding with military options.

Orlov's final comment was, "I thought we were working together to prevent war. Apparently, the war has already started."

Then he hung up.

◆

The SVR agent who had been trailing Morgan received a call from Orlov, bringing him up-to-date with regard to the suspected presence of American

Special Forces in Russia.

"*Da. Da, Direktor.*"

The agent listened to the scant, unsubstantiated information without comment. But when Orlov said that analysts and signals intelligence had yet to come to any conclusions about where the military teams might be, his agent said, "I have an idea of their location."

Then he explained to the Director of Foreign Intelligence where he was and why he was there.

◆

Josh Morgan decided he needed coffee, whether he had time or not. Strangely, his often-bizarre sense of humor had him silently humming "Back in the Saddle Again" at his apparent knack for doing field work in the stead of the Agency that had callously booted him out those years ago.

As soon as he finished his java, he would call Betsy to check in. He hoped she would have good news, but he knew she would've already called. Morgan would tell her of his simple plan to walk into the woods and say "hello" to a team of some of the most lethal warriors on the planet smack-dab in the middle of their operation.

"Maybe if I took coffee and doughnuts. That would smooth things over, I bet." The thought of sitting in the snow for breakfast with the A-Team made him smile.

He was inside the store, drinking his coffee with his left hand, while warming his right hand in his parka's pocket, where he kept his phone. When it vibrated, he felt it immediately and stepped through the door and outside for privacy.

Before he could tell the director his idea for approaching the soldiers and his joke about coffee and doughnuts, Betsy started giving him the scoop on just how things were.

"Well, shit."

"Yeah. So, you might have to hurry. I can't tell you that you won't have company soon. Or that things will work out. But that's the story."

"And you're sticking to it." He didn't feel much like smiling at his joke this time.

"Say, Morgan."

"Yes?"

"Thanks for this."

"Just remember, you owe me."

"Hey! No way. This is your country, too." There was a pause before the director added, "Okay. I owe you. Happy?"

"I'll be happy when I get home. See ya, Parnell."

"See ya, Morgan."

✦

Russian Federation President Boris Tatarov hung up the phone after his conversation with Director of Foreign Intelligence Pavel Orlov.

"*Kapitan* Patrushev. Come!"

The president's aide, Radoslav Victorovich Patrushev, was never more than a few steps away.

"*Da, Tovarishch Prezidyent?*"

"Please get the commander of the Main Intelligence Directorate on the phone."

The president had a mission for the GRU *Spetsnaz*.

✦

As he walked toward the wooded area where the Green Berets were supposed to be, Josh Morgan wondered if he would ever see Maggie again. Moments earlier, he had what seemed to be a straightforward, although likely dangerous plan to walk into an area where friendly forces were hidden and try his best to talk them out of starting a global war.

Now it was likely that bad guys were on the way. He realized he had been incredibly lucky when he had chased Fadi Al-Majeed across Mexico, New Mexico, and Texas to try to save the man who was now his friend, Trent Weston. But that understanding also gave him pause. He was out of his element. Even when he was with CIA, he wasn't normally involved with wet ops. He knew that he could only push the envelope so many times before he was chewed up and spit out, as his granddaddy Silas Morgan used to say.

The former CIA case officer was more correct than he knew.

"My friend, where are you going?"

Morgan knew the voice, even though he was oddly speaking in English. He turned to face his recent partner, Vladislav Larionovich Proskurkin and was only mildly surprised to see a gun pointing at him.

"Hello, Slava," Morgan replied in English.

"It seems that there are things you haven't told me."

"I'm real sorry about that, my friend. Would you put the gun away?"

"I think I'll hold onto it."

"I guess you got your car back."

"Director Orlov had someone deliver it to my flat during the night."

"Hmmm. If I'd known that, I might've borrowed it."

"Oh, but I couldn't have followed you here, Morgan. I say again, what have you not told me?"

"Not sure what you mean, Slava. I just needed a cup of coffee."

The SVR agent Morgan had worked alongside to dispel the misinformation of Russian responsibility for the bombings in the United States seemed more like an enemy now. He was approaching Morgan with his handgun at eyelevel.

"I believe you are here because you have U.S. Special Forces in the area."

Morgan took an exceedingly deep breath and remained silent.

"We are friends?"

"Well, I'm not feeling real friendly right now." Morgan pointed at the Russian's gun. "We'd be on friendlier terms if you'd put that away."

"Can't. Sorry. Nothing personal." Proskurkin moved closer to the American. "You were walking that way, right?" The Russian SVR agent motioned with his gun for Morgan to resume walking along the frontage of Kiyevskoye Highway.

Master Sergeant Tom Lechler was on watch. Alternating between the "natural light" spotting scope and the night-vision optics on his forehead, depending on which provided the best view of what was happening at Vnukovo International, the Operational Sergeant saw what he'd been waiting for.

The SPIRIT spoke quietly to his fellow operators on their radios.

"'Red Bear' appears to be moving," he said, as he watched the door to the Russian president's private hangar begin to rise.

His teammates all turned their attention to the Vnukovo runway. All except Fluff.

"Tom, we got something happening along the street. There are two guys heading this way. One has a gun on the other."

MSG Lechler replied without taking his eyes off the events at the airport.

"Damn! Keep an eye on it. But ignore it if it doesn't involve us."

Morgan stopped and turned to face Slava, causing the Russian to step back instinctively. The American put his hands down. "This doesn't make sense. What if I tell you everything? We can work this together."

"I think you will tell me everything and I will tell the *Spetsnaz* who are on their way."

A pulse like an electric charge shot through Morgan. It was all he could do to maintain some semblance of composure.

"I see. Why are they here?'

Slava's initial smile shifted to a look of genuine sadness.

"You have betrayed me. Already, your soldiers are in Russia. That you are here makes me suspect they are nearby. We will walk there and wait until the GRU arrives."

"If your army is coming, why are we going?"

"Simple, my friend. I want to see this through. And I want you to see what you have brought. When they arrive, we will watch from a distance."

Morgan hated where this had gone. He genuinely liked Slava but he couldn't let it end like this. He only hoped Proskurkin considered him a friend, too.

Based on his previous calculations, Morgan knew they were just over half a kilometer from where the operators were supposed to be. He didn't have much time. He turned around to face the Russian agent following him.

"Slava, I really wanted to tell you. If I found out anything, I was going to call."

"Keep walking."

Suddenly, a camouflaged armored personnel carrier sped past along the road. It braked to a stop at about the spot where the American ex-spy thought the SPIRITs would be hidden.

"Looks like time's up."

Morgan was conflicted about what was happening. If the operators completed their mission, the Russian leader would be dead, and war would proceed. On the other hand, if they were…

Morgan couldn't let himself think that way. Those were U.S. military down there, following orders and doing their jobs.

✦

Eight GRU *Spetsnaz* operators piled out of the truck and took defensive positions. Unlike the security guards on previous nights, these men weren't just shining spotlights. They were scanning the woods for heat signatures with thermal imaging devices. The two men with the devices saw the bright images against the dark background of the snow's coldness at the same time. They switched to night-vision goggles identical to those of their comrades.

✦

MSG Lechler listened to his teammates giving details about the just-arrived Russian Special Forces while he kept his attention fixed on the airplane just beginning to roll out of the hangar at the airport across the highway.

Lechler spoke quietly into his radio. "Fluff, you see this?"

"Roger that."

"Jack, can you get that thing airborne?"

"I'll need some cover."

"Copy that," said the Master Sergeant. "Fluff, how long can we hold them off?"

"Fifteen to twenty, tops."

SFC Jackson had already determined a path in the trees through which he could get the Springer Drone into open sky. The EMP might do its job from some distance away, but the assumption was that Russia would've hardened the president's plane as much as current technology allowed. It needed to be close to ensure success.

Lechler watched the Ilyushin Il-96 roll away from the hangar toward the far end of the runway. Jackson examined the display on the flight controller handset. All systems were between the lines for the drone.

"Now if we can just get the damned thing airborne," hoped SFC Jackson.

For his part, EMP Technician Cooley Matheson could accomplish his part of the mission from anywhere. Just a flip of a switch to activate the Electromagnetic Pulse E-bomb, followed by a press of a button to detonate the explosive charge to compress and discharge the pulse. Until then, he would help provide security for his team.

MSG Tom Lechler called out updates from his observation of the Russian president's plane. "Target has turned and is facing directly toward us. Prepare for engagement."

"Roger that," confirmed SFC Jack Jackson. "I need to get into position."

Lechler gave some thought to their situation. "Fluff, we can hold for fifteen to twenty?"

"Roger."

Lechler did some quick mental math. "Bull?"

Angus Macduff answered through his comm, "Go ahead."

"Set the SNAP. Thirty minutes."

"Say again."

"You heard me, Bull. Thirty."

SFC Macduff thought through his Operations Sergeant's logic. Bull knew that they could always disengage the countdown timer on the nuke. Assuming they lived long enough to do so. But if the drone deployment failed and they were all toast... "Copy that."

Since Macduff and Lechler had shared their codes, Bull needed no help setting up the bomb. He inserted the interface into the port on the backpack nuke. The display came to life.

"Code 1?" came the prompt. Macduff entered his half of the code.

"Code 2?" appeared on the digital display. Bull entered MSG Lechler's code.

"Time?" Bull quickly entered three-zero-zero-zero and depressed the button to enter.

Lastly, the red letters asked, "Execute?" SFC Angus "Bull" Macduff took a deep breath and said a quick prayer. Even with that, he hesitated before acknowledging execution with "enter."

The requests to reenter the two halves of the code were accepted with no delays. As soon as the final part of the code was entered, Macduff saw the red digital characters flash and turn to, "00:29:59," then "00:29:58."

"We can always turn the fucking thing off," he reminded himself.

✦

Inside the Russian Federation's equivalent to Air Force One, *Kapitan* Radoslav Victorovich Patrushev informed his boss of their imminent departure.

"Comrade President, we are about to take off."

"*Spasibo,*" acknowledged Tatarov. He swiveled his chair and locked it in place. The Russian president fastened the two pieces of his seatbelt together and stiffened in his seat. He hated flying.

The pilot's voice came over the speaker above the Russian leader's seat.

"Comrade President, we are performing our final preflight checks. Once final preparations are complete, we will proceed down the runway. We wish you an enjoyable flight."

✦

Operations Sergeant spoke through his comm.

"Drone?"

"Go."

"EMP?"

"Go."

It was EMP Technician Matheson's job to move to a suitable position for Drone Technician Jack Jackson to fly the plane toward Vnukovo Airport. Matheson began to crawl slowly through the snow toward the edge of the trees and open sky. As soon as he moved, he heard a whizz over his head and the crack of an impact on the tree just above him.

MSG Lechler ordered, "Fire! Fire! Fire!"

Four members of the SPIRIT Team returned fire. Two of the GRU soldiers fell immediately. The other *Spetsnaz* Special Forces dropped to cover behind their vehicle. Lechler kept his eyes on the Ilyushin at the far end of the Vnukovo International Airport runway.

Matheson continued to creep forward through the white pack of snow. Aboud, Jones, Jackson, and Macduff maintained fire. Hitting a target would be nice, but they were chiefly laying down cover for Matheson to advance to a place where he could launch the small aircraft with his EMP attached.

✦

"I'm cold. Can I at least put my hands in my pockets?"

Proskurkin smiled knowingly.

"What's in your pocket?"

Morgan sighed, "My gun. Well, your gun, actually." He carefully reached in his pocket and retrieved the handgun with his thumb and forefinger and moved to hand it to Slava.

"Drop the gun where you are."

Morgan complied with the order and the MP-443 fell through the white fluffy surface.

At the sight of suppressed muzzle flashes, the Russian SVR operative looked over Morgan's shoulder. The American launched himself toward his Russian friend.

Proskurkin got off a shot just before the American dove headlong into him.

✦

The crack of small weapon fire caused six SPIRITs to look to their left momentarily to assess the threat. Confident that they were not in immediate danger from the struggle that was going on a quarter of a kilometer distant, the six Americans returned their attention to the Russian soldiers before them.

✦

Morgan felt a piercing pain and a powerful jolt in the right side of his abdomen, below and to the side of his ribcage. Morgan kept driving his legs as he slammed into the Russian. Both fell to the ground. Proskurkin landed flush on his back with Morgan's weight knocking the wind out of him.

Morgan slammed his fist repeatedly into the side of the stunned Russian's face. Slava raised the gun. Morgan grasped the man's wrist and held it to the side as the Russian fired another round wildly into the sky.

Proskurkin propelled Morgan off of him with a heave of his chest. The former CIA officer tried to gain footing but stumbled backward.

The SVR agent looked around for where he had dropped his gun.

Morgan raced toward him, slamming his shoulder into his side. Both men slid along the snowy ground. Morgan turned to retreat to where he had tossed his handgun.

Both men groped beneath the snow, finding their MP-443 handguns at about the same time.

When Slava Proskurkin rolled over to point his gun, he saw a kneeling Josh Morgan with his already aimed. Two quick muzzle flashes dropped the SVR agent.

Morgan wasted no time collecting Slava's gun and heading across the street and toward the firefight raging there.

Assuming a position behind the GRU *Spetsnaz* Team, Morgan began to fire. He killed one of the Russians. Three of the *Spetsnaz* soldiers rose slightly to address the new threat behind them. Each fell in their tracks from the automatic fire of the SPIRIT Team.

Another fired and Morgan dropped to the ground.

✦

President Hendrickson sat in the Cabinet Room with a small group. Only Chief of Staff Noah Chandler, Chairman of the Joint Chiefs General Dwight Richards, and Vice President Aiden Bauer represented the war planning group. Former President Trenton Weston and Director of Central Intelligence Elizabeth Parnell were present, as were Acting Press Secretary Margaret Loughlin, former CIA Moscow Station Chief Ryan Crenshaw, and Richards' aide.

They had watched with dreadful anticipation the broadcast from Vnukovo International Airport. Russian TV was reporting on the early departure of President Tatarov on his trip to counsel with major allies of his war coalition. The reporter had informed the citizens of the Federation that the Kremlin had moved up the trip for security reasons due to the indication that American troops might already be on the ground in the Motherland.

✦

The Master Sergeant barked into his comm, "Cooley, that plane's starting to roll."

SFC Matheson said, "Almost there."

Four Sergeants First Class fired at their remaining adversaries while their team member crawled forward to launch the unmanned aircraft.

Matheson reached the designated area for putting the drone in the air. He stood and held the small plane above his head. A sharp pain stabbed his right shoulder, but he held his ground.

Drone Operator Jackson watched Matheson intently. When Cooley stood with the drone aloft, Jack revved the engine and the aircraft bolted forward. As soon as he felt the drone release from his grip, Matheson stooped low to retreat to his team members. As he dropped, a second bullet creased his left lower back. He fell to the ground.

"Target rolling! Target rolling!" shouted the Operations Sergeant.

"I'm airborne," reported Jackson. "Airborne! Airborne!"

The Drone Pilot turned his attention to the screen on his hand controller. The combination of thermal and night vision optics enabled him to see the view from the forward camera in the unmanned craft. In the distance he saw the presidential aircraft begin to roll forward. Jackson banked his small craft to the right and flew it to a place some distance from the runway before banking left to fly perpendicularly to where the Quadjet would roll.

Seeing the drone take flight, one of the Russians directed his fire to try to down it. SFC Matheson, though seriously wounded, fired and put two bullets through the GRU soldier. With only one of the enemy remaining, Lechler and Aboud moved to flank his position.

The Russian soldier knelt further behind his vehicle. Jones raced toward the truck and looked under it to see parts of the enemy soldier's body. He fired quick rounds into whatever he could see, while Lechler and Aboud darted around opposite ends of the armored truck to finish him off.

Jackson was concentrating solely on flying the drone. In the wide-angle image from the camera, he saw the Russian jet gaining speed up the runway. He kept the plane centered in the unmanned craft's sights. The Drone Pilot continually banked his aircraft slowly to the left to keep the Russian leader's jetliner centered in the crosshairs as it raced forward.

Master Sergeant Lechler ran across the road to check on the unknown friend who had come to their aid. The man he saw had a bullet wound through his abdomen and a crease across the left side of his upper torso. Lechler had a mission to complete and left the man to return to his team.

Fluff Jones kept watch for additional threats. Abe Aboud checked each of the fallen Russians and cleared their weapons. All the while, Jackson flew his aircraft, watching the Russian jet grow larger in the video display of his controller. He maintained a smooth bank, losing ground to the Russian president's plane but accomplishing its goal of intersecting the aircraft immediately after it ended its run and took flight.

The Springer Drone was in perfect position to pull in line with the runway at the precise moment to allow the plane to fly directly over it.

SFC Matheson, despite his wounds had limped back to his team member and would detonate the E-bomb as the Russian plane flew over it.

✦

As the television image showed the Ilyushin presidential quadjet began its roll down the runway, the U.S. officials held their collective breath, fearful of what they might see. It reached the halfway point of the strip, nearing takeoff speed. It continued its rollout for a short time longer. As it rose from the hard surface of the runway, the landing gears began to retract immediately.

POTUS asked her Four Star General, "When should it happen?"

"Ideally, it should occur just as it reaches the end of the strip or just beyond. Until then it won't have gained enough altitude for the Springer to slide beneath it."

Silence overtook the room again.

✦

Jackson was flying the Springer perfectly. Matheson prepared to deploy the EMP. With the drone closing in on the Russian jet and nearly in close enough proximity to execute, SFC Jones said, "Tom! Look!"

Crawling toward the team was the man who had fought alongside them. Knowing their position was secure, the Operations Sergeant moved to help him. He rolled Morgan over. The man was trying to speak. Lechler leaned closer and shook his head, failing to understand the words.

Matheson flipped up the cover over the red button that would detonate the E-Bomb, and positioned his right index finger over it, poised for Jackson's confirmation that the drone was in position with respect to its target.

The Master Sergeant leaned in again to try to make out the words of the wounded man in his arms. He placed his ear directly over the man's mouth. Suddenly, Lechler's eyes grew wide and he shouted to his team, as he heard one word.

Morgan whispered, "Charlemagne," and then passed out.

"Abort! Abort! Abort!"

SFC Matheson jerked his finger back from the EMP's detonation switch, returned the clear cover over it, and powered down his unit.

SFC Jack Jackson turned the Springer Drone to the west and away from Vnukovo. He armed its autodestruct sequence. The program would fly the craft for several miles, gaining altitude as it went. When it reached thirteen thousand feet above the ground, it would dive straight down, crashing itself. A small explosive device would detonate upon impact, destroying the highly classified electronics aboard the drone.

While Matheson and Jackson were securing their weapons, SFC Bull Macduff took care of one more important detail. He rushed to the SNAP nuclear bomb. The display read, "00:03:16" Then "00:03:15," before the SNAP Technical Sergeant pushed a combination of three keys. The prompt asked for code one. The Sergeant entered it. Then he entered the second half of the code, when prompted, and the device made a crackling sound like an LED TV does when powering down.

Six men watched as the blinking navigation lights of Tatarov's plane rose higher and disappeared into the distance. Their unknown partner lay in Lechler's arms.

◆

Just as in the United States anytime Air Force One left Andrews, the television station's camera panned with the progress of the jet toward flight. As the jet cleared the end of the pavement and began a steep climb and banked to the right, the general slapped his hands together and then pounded the Cabinet Room's conference table with a fist. The reaction so startled everyone that heads immediately turned to the man.

When each person saw the smile that accompanied his reaction, they, too, shared in his jubilant relief, exchanging high-fives and pats on the shoulder. A few shook hands.

POTUS exclaimed, "That's it?"

Joint Chiefs Chairman cautioned, "Not entirely. There's still the nuke, but something's happened or there would've at least been the attempt by the drone. I'd expect Operation Nemesis has decided not to execute. We'll know any moment now."

The people in the room wondered if they'd celebrated prematurely.

"How will we know?" asked the president.

"The television broadcast will end abruptly, ma'am."

Hendrickson shuddered and turned her attention back to the screen.

Three minutes passed; then four. A full ten minutes elapsed, and everyone's optimism was growing.

Finally, Richards proclaimed, "That has to be it. There's little realistic chance of the nuke being deployed now. We just have to wait now to get some status from the SPIRITs. That is, if they're able."

The comment dampened the relief of the group, but each person knew that the major danger had passed. Still, they waited.

CHAPTER 36

As soon as the drone, EMP, and SNAP nuke were secure, Matheson switched his radio to a different channel and made the first communication beyond the Operation Nemesis SPIRITs since just before eleven o'clock the previous night. He simultaneously enabled "team broadcast" mode, allowing the support team to hear every team member's comm.

"Wizard, Intermission. Repeat, intermission," he reported to the B-Team in Estonia.

"'Intermission' was the Operation Nemesis codeword that indicated they were awaiting further orders. It also conveyed that they were no longer on radio silence with twelve-hour check-in intervals. They were remaining live until further notice.

✦

The Communications Sergeant sat up straighter and gave a quick thumbs-up to his overwatch commander.

"Good copy. Good copy. Confirm intermission. Confirm intermission."

Though not as overtly celebratory as the group in the Cabinet Room in Washington, the B-Team was equally relieved.

A second transmission came through the radio. It was the voice of Master Sergeant Tom Lechler.

"Pass on 'Charlemagne.' Pass on 'Charlemagne.'" The entire support team looked around at one another to see if anyone had a clue what that meant. There were only shrugs, headshakes, and puzzled looks.

"Confirm. Good copy. 'Charlemagne.'"

✦

Inside the Cabinet Room, General Richards' aide answered the four-star general's personal phone that he always carried. Often, he spoke with the caller himself. Other times, based on the content or the caller, he handed the phone directly to the Joint Chiefs Chairman. This was one of those times.

"Nemesis Overwatch," he informed the general.

"Go ahead." Richards listened to the report and answered coolly, "Understood."

The caller added a comment that brought a smile to the warrior's face.

General Richards ended with, "Need regular updates, particularly casualties. Order 'Curtain call.' Repeat, 'Curtain call.'"

Chairman Richards handed the phone back to his aide. Hardened as he was by tours in Kuwait, Iraq, Afghanistan, and covert operations around the world, the news got to him. He looked straight at Maggie.

"Charlemagne," he relayed to her.

Everyone in the Cabinet Room knew the implication, but only Maggie choked up.

In their earlier meeting, when everyone else resigned themselves to the fact that they had exhausted their options and that it came down to Morgan reaching the SPIRITs, Maggie had gone off on them.

"That's it?! Well, that's just bullshit!!" she had yelled. "You're gonna just sit here and hope Josh can think of something? That's not acceptable! What's he gonna do if they don't believe him? They might think he's a Russian agent. There's got to be something you can tell him to say that will convince them! Damn it all! If you can't do more than that, none of you should be in your position."

Captain Dwight Richards had commanded then-Sergeant First Class Tommy Lechler in Afghanistan. During most of their ops together, they had used the same word to order an immediate stand-down – "Charlemagne."

The general had remembered that and hoped the Master Sergeant would, too, so he had suggested CIA Director Parnell pass it along to Morgan when she last spoke with the man on the phone.

Maggie tried to remain composed, but a few tears slipped through the façade. General Richards walked to her.

"I know I'm not supposed to do this, but…" And he put his arms around her shoulders. He simply said, "Well done, young lady."

"Josh sure owes you one, Maggie," a relieved Trent Weston said.

"Yeah? Well, you can be sure I'll collect," the fiancée said of her fiancé, her face finally breaking into a huge grin.

The group's break from worry and responsibility ended as they began to sort through their to-dos.

Richards had ordered the exfiltration process underway with the "curtain call" order. POTUS, the vice president, and chief of staff had to develop plans for dealing with the aftermath of the whole affair, not just from the fact that a commando unit was prepared to assassinate the Russian leader, but the fallout that was certain from falsely blaming the Russians for the attacks in the U.S.

"But, first things first," decided the president. "Maggie, are you up to a job?"

"Of course."

✦

In addition to being the drone pilot, SFC Jack Jackson was the Team Medic. Matheson's wounds were serious, but clean. He needed attention but Medic Jackson's bandages would hold. Josh Morgan, as they had learned his name was, was a different matter. Jackson had treated him to the extent he could, and though he was stable, he needed attention soon.

The man was in and out of consciousness. At one point, he awoke with a smile and said, "So that's it, huh?"

Lechler smiled and patted him on the shoulder, "Hate to tell you this, Morgan, but we still gotta get the hell outta here. With the sun coming up, that's gonna be hard."

SFC Jones came running through the trees. He and Aboud had loaded the bodies of the eight *Spetsnaz* soldiers into the rear of their own vehicle and covered them with one of the SPIRIT's sleeping bags. Jones drove the truck some distance and parked it.

Macduff had gone to the auto service business next to the store where the Sex Shop owner had dropped off Josh and stole a vehicle there.

Now that Jones was back, he went about the process of setting a charge to explode all the equipment they were going to leave behind. The only ordnance they were taking was the nuke.

Jackson continued to hover over their new team member. Josh stirred again.

"Could you do me a big favor?"

Jackson said, "I guess we sorta owe you one. Whacha need?"

"You know the guy down there?" He weakly pointed toward the direction of the store.

"The one you shot?"

"That's him. Well, would you take care of him? He's sort of a friend."

Jackson laughed. "I don't even know how to respond to that. Your friend?"

Morgan smiled and bobbed his head.

"Already looked at him. He needs attention, but he should be fine. We were just gonna leave him."

Morgan waived his hand vigorously. "No. We have to take him somewhere." His was slurring his words, and then he passed out again.

"We gotta roll, guys," said the Master Sergeant as he saw Macduff speeding up in an oversized SUV.

Jackson and Aboud dragged Morgan along and put him in the back of the truck. The SPIRITs all crowded in. Matheson carried the SNAP and set it in the rear cargo area with Morgan.

Jackson said something to Macduff, who, as soon as the last team members were in, put the SUV in reverse and backed up frantically.

He screeched to a stop and Jackson and Aboud ran into the field, and fetched Proskurkin. They weren't as fond of him as Morgan was, so they tossed him roughly in the truck and Macduff raced away.

The instructions were clear. Maggie would create a press release that would go out immediately. It would state that the United States was immediately standing down all military operations and lowering the readiness to DEFCON 3.

The release would inform the public that new intelligence had confirmed that the individual who had attempted to assassinate President Hendrickson on two occasions and had killed Vice President Logan and others was acting individually and that the government of Russia was not involved.

Maggie also had orders to spin the brief. The report would assert that the president had acted responsibly, given the intelligence and the confession of Borzilov, but that the U.S. intelligence agencies had continued to pursue every avenue and had uncovered new information that led to the truth.

The release would also relate the president's proposal that, if President Tatarov would likewise stand down Russian forces, they meet at the earliest opportunity to resolve any lingering misunderstandings.

Maggie's statement for the president would state that American operators were not presently, nor had they been on Russian soil. This was, of course, a lie, but if the Russians discovered the truth or, more worrisome, captured the SPIRITs, the fact the president lied about it would add little additional flame to an already roaring disastrous fire.

Maggie finished the draft and took it to the Oval Office.

President Hendrickson approved it as written. Furthermore, regardless that it was two-thirty in the morning, Maggie awakened the producers of the major television networks and other media outlets in the United States to tell them that the president would be holding a live announcement from the press room in the West Wing. She passed on that Hendrickson demanded that they all carry it live.

Nobody would be awake to see it in her country, POTUS knew, but the Russian president would be awake and right now, that was all that mattered.

✦

The SPIRITs received the order to initiate "Curtain Call." That was the codeword to stand down entirely from Operation Nemesis and initiate their exfiltration plan.

As they sped northward, the Communications Sergeant in their B-Team overwatch in Estonia made a call to a number in St. Petersburg.

About fifteen minutes after the ops team had left their position outside the Vnukovo Airport, a black armored personnel carrier identical to the GRU *Spetsnaz* soldiers' drove slowly along the frontage road beside Kiyevskoye Highway, looking for signs of their comrades.

Almost directly beside them, about sixty meters from the edge of the road, a tremendous explosion occurred. Initially, the driver backed hurriedly away from the spot, but, after some observation, he returned, and his team examined the site of the blast. Scattered throughout the area were pieces of items that appeared to be military. They found traces of blood, ammunition casings, and other signs of soldiers' presence.

The squad leader got on his radio and reported that they had found where the Americans had been, and that there were signs of a battle. But there was no trace of the other GRU forces.

✦

President Hendrickson wrapped up her press briefing.

"Finally, I want to personally thank the Director of Central Intelligence, Elizabeth Parnell, for her tireless efforts to discover the truth. It is unusual to call attention to anyone in our intelligence agencies, but Director Parnell was instrumental in resolving this crisis.

"I also wish to thank the members of the Russian intelligence community who assisted us behind the scenes to uncover the additional facts that have led to the peaceful conclusion to this unfortunate episode.

"We will have additional information tomorrow."

Probably nobody in the Kremlin would realize that anyone in their government had been helping the United States. To Hendrickson's knowledge it had only been SRV Director Orlov and the agent that accompanied and worked alongside Josh Morgan. Tatarov would likely think the comment was gratuitous window-dressing for the colossal disaster the

United States had created, but Orlov deserved to know that the U.S. was acknowledging his help. The "thank you" was sincere.

Virtually the full contingent of the White House press corps was present for the briefing. The news went across the globe at lightspeed.

Very soon after the briefing concluded, the President of the United States received a call from the president of the Russian Federation.

✦

Betsy Parnell watched the briefing from her office. Of course, the president had called her personally and offered a very gracious apology, along with a promise that her job was safe.

The director's phone rang again. She listened to General Richards' news and hung up.

Words failed her. The only thing that came was a sigh. She dialed her phone.

Trent Weston was awake, along with all the others who were involved in the unsanctioned operation in Russia, although at first it had just been an effort to uncover the truth about the events in Washington. In fact, he was in Maggie Loughlin's office next door to where she worked at Marie Ginnetti's desk.

✦

Ex-President Weston wiped away a tear.

"No, I'll let her know. Yes, I know you'd make the call, but I think I should tell her. Would you let Crenshaw and Sir Albert know? Thanks, Betsy."

Weston ended the call and decided this would only get harder the longer he waited. He walked to the office where Maggie was sitting. He peeked through the doorway to see her with her head on her desk. He knocked gently on the door and received a slight but heartfelt smile in return.

"Hi, Trent. Come in."

As soon as she saw the grim countenance on her friend's face, she was immediately on guard for bad news.

Weston pulled a chair around to Maggie's side of the desk. Now she knew it wasn't going to be good.

CHAPTER 37

Trent Weston took his young friend's hand.

"I'm afraid Josh has been hurt."

"Only hurt?"

Maggie's face was pallid, but without expression. Perhaps she had been through so much already, Weston thought, that she just couldn't express more emotion right now.

"Yes, for now. But it's serious. He's been shot – twice. Only one is serious. The medic on the SPIRIT team is tending to him. Those guys are as competent as actual doctors. And they're probably better than MDs when it comes to this type of scenario. But here's the problem…"

Maggie interrupted Weston with her correct guess at what he was going to say.

"They can't get him to a doctor without compromising themselves."

Weston took a long breath. "Yes. I'm sorry, Maggie, but that's right."

Maggie looked away and bit her lower lip.

"Maggie, you know I love Josh like a son, so I'm conflicted. But having sat in Hendrickson's place, and even Betsy's, I have to say that, with what's at stake, it's the right call. It breaks my heart, but I agree with it."

"I know. But it still sucks."

Weston waited to see if his friend would say more. When she finally turned to face him, the emotion he saw was anger.

"Josh has put himself out there twice…"

Weston hung his head because one of those times was to rescue him.

"… And this is the thanks he gets. Just hung out to dry."

"You're right."

"Excuse me. I have to go to the ladies' room." And Maggie left her office.

Trent Weston waited only briefly before he called his wife.

"Alicia…" He gave his wife the news about Josh and also about his conversation with Maggie.

"I'm coming over, honey."

"I thought you might. I hoped you might."

✦

In St. Petersburg, Russia, only shortly after arriving for work, *Stárshiy Leytenánt* Dmitri Larionovich Nezhdanov left his office to go home. The Senior Lieutenant wasn't feeling well, he had told Colonel-General Yarmolnik. His superior had huffed a complaint, but ultimately relented to permit his aide's departure.

It took less than ten minutes to arrive at his home. He had anticipated this trip – he just didn't know when he would take it – so his personal belongings were already packed. He carried them to his UAZ Combi. His personal vehicle was identical to the one he had provided for the American soldiers when they had first entered his country, except for the color.

The Russian soldier drove out of St. Petersburg on E95/P-23 for what would be his last trip in his country. He would drive for over eight hours.

✦

SFC Macduff pulled into the crowded parking lot of a hospital. They had been driving about an hour. In the parking lot, they spied a UAZ truck, similar to the Combi they had used after infiltrating the country. This one didn't have the cargo area. It was passenger-oriented. It was perfect. SFC Aboud pried opened the side door and reached forward to unlock the driver door. MSG Lechler slid in and hot-wired the vehicle. Jones was busy exchanging the truck's license plate with the vehicle's next to it, a very dissimilar sedan, while Jackson assisted the wounded Matheson into their new ride.

Once all the other passengers were in the van, Aboud set the SNAP in the floorboard in front of rearmost seat and then the medic, with Aboud's help, moved Morgan to that back seat. Jackson jumped in beside Morgan to continue providing medical treatment, although he had done about all that he could.

With new license plates that weren't associated with the truck they were borrowing, and with all personnel and gear inside, Lechler fell in behind Macduff as he drove the SUV to the front entrance of the hospital. The Operations Sergeant looked in his rearview mirror at Jackson.

"I don't like this."

The medic shrugged and replied, "Hey, what can I say? I promised the guy."

By the time he got to the front entrance, Macduff's only cargo in the SUV they had arrived in was Vladislav Proskurkin. The American soldier parked and entered the hospital. In Russian, he reported his "discovery" to an attendant at the front desk.

"I found this man by the side of the road. He's seriously hurt. Please get a doctor."

The attendant tried to convince the Good Samaritan that he should go to another entrance. Macduff sat on a bench and played the part of someone desperately shaken at the sight of the bloody man. So, hospital staff rushed to the aid of the patient who had been kept sedated with morphine.

As they scurried about, one rushing to find a doctor and one determining what he could do for the injured man, Macduff quietly stood and walked out the door to his waiting team members.

✦

Former President Weston had sent Secret Service Agent Johnston to pick up the former first lady. At 3:00 AM, Alicia Weston arrived at the West Wing of the White House. Her husband escorted her to where Maggie was working, trying to keep her mind off Josh and his condition.

"Maggie, may I come in?"

The acting press secretary rose and embraced her friend.

"You're coming with me, dear."

Alicia Weston led Maggie to the SUV that had brought her. Trent followed along, after letting POTUS know they were leaving. Agent Johnston drove them to The Four Seasons and escorted the party to the Westons' suite.

Maggie, despite her emotional state, fell asleep as soon as she lay down in the spare bedroom.

✦

Senior Lieutenant Nezhdanov was making good time, considering the condition of the roads. Snow had been falling, though lightly, for the entire trip. He was five hours along. His only stop had been to get fuel and relieve himself. Food and drink were among the things he had packed at his house, so he snacked and drank water as he needed to.

✦

In the same five-hour period, the Master Sergeant had driven his team west to the Russian town of Novosokolniki. The drive was completely uneventful.

Hospital parking lots were logical places to hide. There were quite a number of vehicles, and they came and went. The ones in the lots were often there for extended periods of time. SFC Aboud had the current watch in the UAZ that sat among the other vehicles at the Novosokolnicheskaya Interdistrict Hospital. Macduff, Jones, and Lechler slept. Matheson, though in pain, refused sedatives in case "something came up," but was sleeping, nonetheless. Jack Jackson, on the other hand, was awake. He worried that their extra "team member" wouldn't make it to their extraction point.

They had three hours until they made contact with their asset. It would take almost another two hours to get to their border crossing and ninety additional minutes to their extraction point.

✦

President Tatarov had called President Hendrickson immediately after her *mea culpa*, of sorts. He had only thanked her, sort of, for standing down from her nation's aggressive actions. It angered the American chief executive, but the man was right.

The two leaders spoke for only a short while but agreed to speak later in the day. The Russian president was stalling until he got more information about a firefight between unknown forces and a detachment of GRU *Spetsnaz* – a detachment that had been missing for a while. Searchers had discovered their bodies in their armored truck not far from the general area where they had last radioed in. They had all been shot. In addition, where the fight had presumably taken place, another unit had witnessed an explosion.

Hendrickson explained as much of the facts as she was comfortable doing. CIA Director Parnell, along with Department of Homeland Security Larson, National Security Advisor Templeton, and Director of National Intelligence Donleavy had all consulted with POTUS to develop talking points that were mostly true, but still shielded their SPIRITs, who were still in the process of leaving Russia. The outline had enough wiggle-room for further information based on the ultimate outcome.

Tatarov broached the subject of the intruders into his country near the airport through his interpreter.

"I can assure you, Mister President, that we do not currently have, nor did we have at any point, military forces in your country," POTUS' interpreter lied, as he passed on her words.

He continued to relay the commander in chief's explanation.

"I think it is logical to assume that those operators were Saudi Arabian, as well."

Hendrickson had already identified the Middle Eastern country to Tatarov as the nation behind the plot.

"We are continuing to gather intelligence, and, I can assure you, as we develop more information, we will let you know. We intend to take action, as soon as we understand the full range of facts."

Russian Federation President Tatarov didn't believe his American counterpart. Neither did the officials in the room with him who listened to the call on headsets.

"I see," replied Tatarov. His intelligence and political advisors had already reached the infuriating consensus that, if they were to step back from the brink of war, they might very well have to dismiss any notion of retaliating against the president for her soldiers' actions. It enraged everyone in the Kremlin who knew of the skirmish outside Vnukovo Airport that the American leader would suffer no consequences for her attack.

The telephone conversation ended with an agreement that both countries would stand down and that the two leaders would meet within a few weeks, followed by a joint press conference.

✦

The Russian Senior Lieutenant backed into the hospital parking lot as he had been instructed. It was well past dark, but the lot was nearly full. He found that his nerves were easing somewhat. Perhaps, he thought, his time alone was about to end. The company of the Americans would provide some sense of security because of their capabilities. On the other hand, he knew, if he were discovered to be in the company of foreign soldiers, the cost to him as a traitor would be more severe than for them. He would be of no value.

Following orders, Nezhdanov parked in the northwest-most corner of the lot. He turned his flashers on for fifteen seconds. Next, he got out of his vehicle and stretched for another fifteen before returning to the driver's seat, leaving the door open.

✦

The Green Berets watched the Russian junior officer proceed through his ritual, just as directed. They waited a full ten minutes. They had, of course, seen Nezhdanov when they first entered the country, so there was no mistaking his identity. What they needed to see was his attitude as he waited for them. The plan was that they would contact him within five minutes. By waiting longer to move, they might see if he had developed second thoughts. If he had made other arrangements, they might show up in the form of Russian security forces.

✦

Nezhdanov was indeed growing anxious. He sat in the van and considered if something was wrong. He decided to close the door and drive away. Just as he was reaching for the door's handle, Master Sergeant Lechler arrived from behind, using the truck's open door as cover.

"Keep the door open," ordered the Green Beret.

The asset turned with a start and started to point a gun at the man beside his car, who easily disarmed him.

"Get in the back seat."

Lechler took the wheel and started the engine. Before them, headlights lit up and another truck moved in their direction and pulled forward into the empty space beside Nezhdanov's.

"Open the side door and the front passenger door."

The Senior Lieutenant did as the SPIRIT told him.

The two side doors next to one another and the open passenger door obstructed the view of any unwanted spectators. Aboud moved his wounded friend Matheson to the center passenger area of the truck their Russian partner had brought. He sat in the seat beside him.

"Did you bring what we asked?" Lechler asked.

"Yes. In the boxes," acknowledged the Russian.

Aboud sifted through the cardboard containers, pulled out three sets of the items and handed them to SFC Jones, standing between the two nearly identical trucks. Fluff passed them to Macduff in the truck they had driven from the hospital where they had left Proskurkin.

The men in each truck closed their doors, and, within just a few minutes, inside each of the UAZ trucks, where U.S. Army Special Forces soldiers had formerly sat, were six members of the Russian GRU *Spetsnaz*.

Unfortunately, Nezhdanov had expected only six members of the U.S. Army for which he had to provide uniforms. Morgan would have to wear his own clothes.

The two trucks, with MSG Lechler taking the lead, drove out of the Novosokolnicheskaya Interdistrict Hospital's parking lot. SFC Jones followed.

The two-truck caravan headed due east for a short distance before turning south, then southwest. In just under two hours, one Russian and six American soldiers disguised as such, approached the Russian town of Lobok near the Russian Federation's border with Belarus.

The thinking had been that crossing into a country allied with Russia would be easier than crossing into Latvia, a NATO member. Russia had intensified its patrols along the borders with Estonia and Latvia since tensions had erupted with America, so even approaching those U.S. allies would have most certainly been very difficult. Plus, the drive to the Belarusian border was shorter for the U.S. commandos. That it was a longer drive for Senior Lieutenant Nezhdanov was irrelevant.

Intel was that there were no guards at Lobok. But about one-and-a-half kilometers ahead, vehicles were backed up in front of them. Cars were also backed up facing them. Perhaps word was out about them. Or maybe it was the overall condition of the hostilities that existed between Russia and America. Whatever the reason, there were guards where there weren't supposed to be any.

They had prepared for this. One variable worried them. How would the Russian handle the situation? Another kink in the original plan was the man in the back of the second truck who was near death. Morgan wasn't even supposed to be here. With the painkillers he had in him, he'd been floating in and out of consciousness, and when he was semi-awake, he mumbled – in English.

The Master Sergeant pulled into the lane of oncoming traffic, bypassing the line of cars in their lane waiting to be inspected before entering Belarus. SFC Jones followed. Cars swerved to get out of the way.

Nearing the head of the line, but beside it, and immediately ahead of them they saw two guards. One pointed his AK-47 directly at them. The second raised his hand, ordering them to stop.

The two trucks came to a stop. The first guard continued to hold his gun on them. The second walked to Lechler's side of the truck and ordered him to lower his window.

There was a delay of a couple of seconds in which the Green Beret Master Sergeant wondered if his Russian passenger would do his part. Just as Lechler decided he wasn't up to this, the man spoke.

"What is it you want? You are holding us up." Senior Lieutenant Nezhdanov jerked his thumb over his shoulder to the truck behind them to include them in the offended party.

The border guard looked at both trucks, civilian, without any military markings at all. Then he looked at the uniformed men inside. The trucks and their occupants were incongruous.

"Where are you going?"

Nezhdanov leaned across his driver to hand a folder to the guard.

"These men and I have been assigned to Hantsavichy Radar Station."

Russian Aerospace Defense Forces rented the radar station from Belarus. The Volga-style radar was designed to identify ballistic missile launches from Western Europe.

The Russian border soldier examined the documents in the folder. Inside it were authentic orders signed by the senior lieutenant's superior, Western Military District Commander Colonel-General Jaroslav Borisovich Yarmolnik. Like many military officers, Yarmolnik relied heavily on the people below him for the authenticity of the content of his daily tasks and trusted them that what was put before him was both necessary and genuine. So, when his aide had explained one set of papers as standard transfer documents for seven of his soldiers to Belarus, the head of one of Russia's five military districts mindlessly signed them.

The guard took his time. He closed the folder and handed it to Lechler, who passed them back to Nezhdanov. He pointed his flashlight into the interior of the UAZ truck. He walked to the back of the vehicle and directed his light through the rear window.

When he returned to the open window on the driver's side, he leaned closer.

"Why civilian trucks?"

"We are trying to be inconspicuous."

"Then why uniforms?"

"Because, if we need to exit the truck for any reason, we want to do so with authority." Nezhdanov outranked his inquisitor. "And so, if fools like you question our orders, we can demonstrate our position over them, as well."

The remark angered the man, but he dared not rebuke a superior. He could, however, make things inconvenient for him. He walked toward the second truck. Men in both trucks put their hands on their weapons. In the second truck were a man not covered by the orders, and a container holding a low-yield nuclear device. They might explain away Morgan, perhaps as a prisoner, but not the bomb.

As the overly zealous soldier approached the second vehicle, another guard, an officer, came to Lechler's truck and called the first soldier back.

Nezhdanov spoke to the new arrival as an equal and without contempt. He handed the papers to him with a smile but said nothing.

The officer glanced quickly through the papers. Without a word, he handed them to the driver and motioned the man in front of the van to step aside.

"I apologize for the delay."

"*Spasibo*," replied the Senior-Lieutenant, and Lechler began to move forward. The two trucks cut in front of the line of cars waiting for examination and crossed the border.

The soldier that had examined the two trucks so relentlessly followed the officer who sent them on their way. The pair spoke for some time. The question was posed why they were driving to a base when they could've easily reached it by helicopter. Finally, the officer got in his truck and radioed his superiors, who, in turn, contacted the office of the Western District Commander.

CHAPTER 38

Josh Morgan stirred in the second truck. Sergeant First Class Daquan Jackson felt the wounded man's forehead. His fever was still quite high. Jack was amazed that he had lasted this long. He hoped he'd make it. He'd kept them from executing a mission that had apparently lost its justification. The SPIRITs didn't know what had happened, but something had changed. And this man had stepped right into the middle of a firefight to give them the message.

"Almost there, buddy. You are one tough son of a bitch."

"Thanks," Morgan mumbled through the morphine.

"Got anyone back home?"

"Maggie. Auburn hair. Blue eyes. And really, really great..." He paused, "...personality."

SFC Jackson laughed aloud, drawing the attention of Fluff Jones in the rear-view mirror.

Morgan smiled, despite what he was about to say.

"Don't think I'm gonna make it."

"Don't say that. You're gonna get back to Maggie."

"Maggie," and he was out again.

✦

A junior officer at the Western District Commander's office announced the call. Colonel-General Yarmolnik listened to the queries coming from the caller and felt a gnawing uncertainty that grew into anger and then into panic.

He called to the aide who was filling in for Dmitri Nezhdanov and asked him to bring copies of the transfer papers he had signed a few days earlier. It took some time to locate the stack of documents. He thumbed through them once, and then a second time.

Colonel-General Yarmolnik grew impatient and walked to Nezhdanov's desk outside his office. The young officer filling in for the regular assistant to the commander glanced up with a genuine look of fright.

"Comrade Colonel-General, here are the papers, but there are no copies of transfer orders."

The commander seized the papers from his subordinate's hand and examined them one-by-one, dropping each document to the floor that didn't match what he was looking for. He reached the final sheet in the stack and stomped away to his office.

Yarmolnik fell into his chair and slammed his fist on his desk. He had no idea what was really going on, certainly not that his aide was, in fact, assisting American soldiers who had planned an attack on President Tatarov, but Nezhdanov had made a fool of him. That was as bad as anything else he could do.

The commander retrieved the phone and, with more composure than he truly possessed, informed the officer at the Belarusian border that the men he had located were deserters from the District Headquarters – that was what Yarmolnik believed was the case – and that he should detain them until receiving further orders.

His ire was unmanageable when he heard that the "deserters" had been allowed to cross into Belarus. He slammed his phone down and yelled an order to his temporary aide.

Soon the assistant had an officer on the phone and announced as such to Yarmolnik. The Colonel-General barked his order and ended the call without another word.

At Gorodok, less than fifty kilometers inside the Belarusian border, the mini-convoy turned southwest off of highway P115 onto P114. The Americans and their Russian asset were less than ninety minutes from their extraction point. However, the two UAZ trucks had picked up a clandestine third member of their convoy.

There weren't many side roads of any consequence along highway E95, where the vehicles had been traveling since leaving the roadblock at Lobok. So, even with the head start they had been allowed, it had proven relatively easy for the Russian Orlan-10 Unmanned Aerial Vehicle to acquire them, simply by following the road.

Colonel-General Yarmolnik had ordered the drone to move from its sweeps of the Russia-Belarus border. With real-time video downlink, the ground controller kept eyes on the trucks that the Western District Commander believed to be carrying deserters. Having acquired its targets near Gorodok, where highway E95 became P115, the craft simply trailed along at an altitude of twelve-thousand feet. Its only purpose was to track the traitors until they could be overtaken by the Russian Ka-226T Multi-Mission Helicopter already making its way to intercept the two vans.

Yarmolnik could have requested help from the Belarusian military, but he was determined that his own soldiers capture Nezhdanov and the men he had helped desert. The helicopter carried no armament but six of the seven seats available for passengers were filled with *Spetsnaz* troops. The seventh seat was reserved for Nezhdanov on the return trip so that Yarmolnik could deal with his former aide personally.

The other six deserters could be transported back in their own vehicles. Or they could be shot on sight. The Colonel-General didn't care which.

The Kamov-manufactured craft was flying at its usual cruising speed of around 210 kilometers per hour. Upon learning of the two vehicles' turn northwestward onto Belarusian Highway P20, the chopper assumed a due-west flight, cutting the corner to close more quickly on their quarry.

The drone flew almost directly above the Green Berets, and the ground controller was providing constant updates to the two-man crew of the Russian Ka-226T.

✦

Some thirty kilometers after making their northwesterly turn onto P20, Aboud informed his driver that they were approaching their exit. There was a small road turning left that led to the town of Bel'chenk. But the righthand turn they took was an even smaller road that led precisely to the middle of nowhere. In about six kilometers, the country road became an even smaller dirt path through a pasture, but that was of no concern to Lechler and Jones as they neared the end of their drive. The next thing on their to-do list was something often required of special operators. They would sit and wait. It was supposed to be for a very short while.

✦

The Russian Orlan-10 UAV followed the two UAZs until the controller watching the live feed was convinced that the trucks were going to stay where they were, at least long enough for the *Spetsnaz* troops to arrive in their helicopter.

Nearly at its maximum range and nearing the end of its allowable gas consumption, the drone received commands from its pilot miles away to head home to him, where it would deploy its parachute and float to the ground to be retrieved for refueling and its next mission.

✦

Lechler and Jones backed their vans into the densely wooded trees that lined the open area they had come there for.

All of the American soldiers left their trucks, except for the Medic Jackson, who remained with his patient. Senior Lieutenant Nezhdanov also remained in his van.

SFC Jackson was pleased, and surprised, to see that Morgan had improved some. He still had a fever, but it was lower. He remained conscious – mostly – though he wasn't entirely coherent when he was. The ex-CIA spy struggled to make himself understood and was mostly unsuccessful. As a courtesy, Jackson nodded and spoke the occasional "right" to the garbled utterances.

Sergeant First Class Matheson was also better and was manning his spot in the deployment.

Macduff set the canister containing the nuke in the front seat of his truck for a quick grab when their ride arrived. White phosphorous grenades were stationed around the interior of the two vehicles, including on the pile of clothing and other items that were no longer needed. Everything would be burned completely.

The six U.S. Army Special Forces soldiers never let their emotions show, but each was glad – even more than usual – to get this one behind them.

◆

The helicopter was cruising at one-hundred-forty knots, about one-hundred-twenty kilometers from its destination. At the current speed, it would reach its destination in less than thirty minutes. Passing the invisible line on the ground that maps called borders, the aircraft went dark. All navigation lights were turned off. Interior lights faded. Night vision gear was already worn by the four-man crew. The special purpose helicopter was becoming as invisible as it could, both visually and to radar.

The MH-60M Medium Assault Helicopter was a variant of the workhorse Sikorsky Black Hawk. It was of the type used in the raid that killed Osama bin Laden, outfitted to make it stealthier than the other variants. It had arrived from Estonia for refueling in Latvia, a NATO member and ally of the United States. The mission was to bring home six Green Berets and their other passengers.

They had been in contact with the Army SPIRITs. Though the conversation was professional and limited to details relevant to the extraction, the crew could tell the operators were ready to get the hell home.

The Black Hawk was exactly on schedule for their arrival at the extraction site.

Unfortunately for the men on the ground, the Russian Ka-226T was already there.

◆

Master Sergeant Tom Lechler heard the chopping of rotary blades that were significantly louder than he expected. He was also surprised that their transportation was already there. In Communications Sergeant Matheson's last contact with them, the Black Hawk crew reported they were still a few minutes out.

Lechler looked at Matheson. Both men trusted their guts immensely, and right now they were telling them something was amiss. SFC Matheson called the crew.

"Scarecrow. Scarecrow. This is Tin Man. Uh. Should we deploy smoke?"

"Negative, Tin Man. We are about ten mikes out."

Matheson looked around at his team members as the whirring grew louder and the limbs at the tops of the trees began to thrash about dramatically.

To his fellow SPIRITs, the Comm Sergeant radioed, "Heads down! Heads down!"

A light utility helicopter circled the edge of the field slowly. Inside, the pilot listened as the commander of the *Spetsnaz* troops in the passenger compartment looked at his GPS receiver.

"This is it," he confirmed.

The Ka-226T descended and hovered about fifteen meters above the snow-covered area.

The special operators opened the side doors and scanned the landscape through night-vision goggles. In only seconds, they saw the two trucks. The aircraft dropped to the ground slowly, and two of the six passengers spilled out in a rush, moving away from the helicopter. The four remaining soldiers assumed defensive positions in the cover of the aircraft.

"*Stárshiy Leytenánt* Dmitri Larionovich Nezhdanov. Traitor, we are here to take you back to the Colonel-General. Surrender and you won't be harmed. You and all of your comrades, step forward."

Believing they were only facing an office flunky and his friends, the GRU soldiers were less alert than they should've been. The squad leader and his companion began to move toward the two vans.

"This is your last chance, Nezhdanov," came the ultimatum. Along with the warning, the leader sprayed a burst from his weapon into the trees above the trucks.

Immediately, two shots into each of the advancing men dropped them in their tracks. Gunfire erupted from the men in the Ka-226T. Though it wasn't armed, the helicopter provided a strategic advantage for the remaining *Spetsnaz*, as it lifted them away from the ground and straight over the trees above the UAZs.

Now shielded from direct view by the trees, the soldiers communicated a tactical plan. In short order, the helicopter moved down the tree-line, dropped to about a meter above the ground, where the soldiers jumped out of the side facing away from their enemies.

The Kamov peeled away from the firefight, rose to an altitude of three hundred meters, where its pilot provided battlefield information to the four men on the ground.

The shooting stopped, as the Russians moved along the edge of the trees toward the men who were obviously much more than office staff and deserters.

The American unit was deployed to face outward from the trees. Now they found themselves facing an attack from a single side.

Lechler ordered his team into a different defensive formation. They scrambled to place themselves between their two vehicles, shielded from the Russians. They had few offensive options. The best they could do was maintain their positions and hope they could hold out until the Black Hawk arrived on the scene.

The four Russians coordinated their movements. It was clear that they weren't content to wait on reinforcements and were pressing forward. With guidance from the Kamov pilot, they inched ahead.

The woods were so dense that neither unit had clear shots. The Russian helicopter pilot began to side-slip toward his own *Spetsnaz* soldiers. Directly above them, the craft rotated under its blades until it faced directly toward the Americans' location and illuminated its floodlight.

The Green Berets jerked their heads away and flipped up their night-vision headgear. Simultaneously to the blast of light, three of the Russian soldiers advanced toward their adversaries. Firing as they moved, they closed the distance to sixty meters. The fourth man moved deeper into the forest.

The U.S. operators fired blindly until their eyesight recovered. Then they delivered their rounds with greater precision, but still couldn't get clear shots. The three minutes of gunfire seemed much longer. Finally, Aboud saw one of the GRU team members move through a clear lane. Abe dropped him with two rapid shots. Two of the attackers continued firing but remained in their positions. Sergeant First Class Jackson left his patient to assist in repelling the assault. He crawled toward the front of the vans.

All the while, a single *Spetsnaz* moved deeper into the trees and circled to a position behind the vehicles.

Nezhdanov managed to move from his front passenger seat across the console to the driver side door and lowered himself to the ground between the two trucks just behind Jackson. However, his position between the vans left him with no opening to fire.

Without warning, the clatter of an automatic weapon racking twice, and the cracks of two suppressed discharges came from immediately behind one of the UAZ vans. SFC Matheson fell with yet another wound, one that proved fatal. The double-tap repeated, and Fluff Jones fell to the side with a wound to his right shoulder blade.

The two other Russian soldiers down the tree-line began to advance with more haste while their comrade fired from behind the Americans' vehicle.

Another shot from the closest *Spetsnaz* soldier pierced Nezhdanov in the side of his neck and continued through his flesh to strike Jackson in his thigh.

Operations Sergeant Lechler fired at the soldier concealed behind the van but had no clear shot. Between the two vans, the U.S. soldiers were trapped like the proverbial fish in a barrel.

The single Russian could fire at will or bide his time as his comrades advanced.

Suddenly, glass exploded from the van beside the one where the Russian assailant was sniping from, as a round from the handgun of Josh Morgan burst through the side window and into the left ribcage of the soldier. The *Spetsnaz* attacker spun away from the impact and, now facing directly toward the American, received three more shots in rapid succession directly into his chest as his killer fired through the opening of the shattered window.

With the fourth round delivered, the former CIA officer dropped unconscious to the floor of the truck. The Russian soldier collapsed backward away from Morgan as he died.

Seeing the nearest attacker felled, Lechler and the remaining SPIRITs in the fight turned their full attention to the only still-existing threat.

Then a muffled, barely audible whirring noise sounded from the tree-line on the far side of the clearing. The forward-facing Black Hawk opened up with its M134 7.62mm miniguns, making quick work of the remaining two attackers. The stealth chopper elevated its attack angle toward the Ka-226T, which had turned to flee at the first sight of the Sikorsky helicopter. But it was pointless. The miniguns ripped through the skin of the smaller aircraft, striking both crew and crippling the chopper. The Russian helicopter crashed into the trees in a fiery ball.

The Black Hawk had revved up its two YT706-GE-700 engines as soon as the crew received word from SFC Matheson that the team was under attack. Now the modified craft hovered momentarily until Master Sergeant Lechler gave the pilot the all-clear.

The pilot dropped in as close as safely possible, and the two crew chiefs went to work. One was medically trained and began treating the wounded along with SFC Jackson, who, despite his own injury had already begun to check on his men.

Macduff and Lechler dragged Matheson's body to the chopper and returned to complete their final mission responsibilities, transporting the

SNAP to the Sikorsky, and disposing of signs of their presence.

Nezhdanov's wound, though bloody, wasn't as serious as it could've been, so he assisted in the work.

Aboud and Jackson carried the unconscious American civilian to his ride home. Regardless of the seriousness of the man's wounds, Jackson had decided there was no way the tough son of a bitch wouldn't make it.

With the remaining soldiers safely in the Black Hawk, Master Sergeant Tom Lechler set off the white phosphorous charges that would destroy all evidence that United States soldiers were ever in Russia.

The MH-60M Black Hawk cruised along not far above the tree tops, reaching Latvian airspace in about twenty minutes. All lights came on as the Sikorsky turned north toward Lielvārde, where it would land and refuel. The wounded would get treatment from the medical staff who were part of the forward-deployed forces rushed there in the lead-up to the almost-war.

There was little conversation among the warriors. They would mourn the loss of their friend in time, but for now they concentrated on the details of Operation Nemesis for their debriefing.

Master Sergeant Lechler reflected on the role they played in Operation Retribution, which really never came to be. He looked at Josh Morgan, sedated and quiet, and wondered how he came to be in the field near the Vnukovo International Airport, whispering a code word into the SPIRIT's ear as he fell into unconsciousness.

Lechler figured he would learn the backstory of Morgan's involvement in time, but his appearance likely saved the world from war, and possibly a nuclear engagement.

The Green Beret looked at the other men around the interior of the Sikorsky. He admired the courage of Senior Lieutenant Nezhdanov and his cool performance at the border crossing. It appeared the defector would survive to have a different life in the United States.

The Operations Sergeant closed his eyes to try to sleep and decided this was his last op.

CHAPTER 39

Day 18 – Tuesday

The trip to Landstuhl Regional Medical Center near Ramstein Air Base in Germany was a necessity for Green Beret Sergeants First Class Jones and Jackson. It was important for Russian defector Nezhdanov, too, and critical for Josh Morgan.

Landstuhl was the largest American hospital outside the United States. Located near the city of Rheinland-Pfalz, the facility had long been noted for the outstanding care given to U.S. military personnel stationed in Germany and the treatment it provided for thousands of other service members and civilians throughout Europe. It was also the go-to facility for military personnel involved in major engagements abroad, including Operations Desert Storm and Desert Shield.

Once the men returning from Russia had been treated at the forward operating encampment in Latvia and had received further treatment at the U.S. base in Estonia, the next step was to get them to Germany.

Morgan was stable, though still in serious condition. He was given a high dose of sedation, though not to the level that would induce a coma.

As soon as the transport landed at Ramstein and taxied off the runway, ambulances arrived to take the patients away.

Day 19 – Wednesday

Ex-CIA Officer Josh Morgan fidgeted, his first sign of activity for nearly twenty-four hours. His eyes opened just enough for him to see through tiny slits between his lids.

Maggie Loughlin was looking back at him. As she saw him coming to some semblance of life, her concerned look turned into an enormous smile.

It was a bit inconsistent with the tears that were forming.

"Hey, stranger."

"Hey, yourself," he mumbled. He squeezed his fiancée's hand weakly. "You're a long way from home."

"Just in the neighborhood," Maggie teased.

"Glad you could drop by," the groggy patient replied.

A soft knock on Josh's hospital room door got Maggie's attention. Just outside the doorway, five U.S. Army soldiers awaited an invitation to enter

"Ma'am, may we come in?" asked one.

Maggie looked to Morgan, who smiled and motioned them in.

"Of course," his fiancée agreed.

"I'm Master Sergeant Tom Lechler. This is Sergeant First Class Abe Aboud. And Sergeants Jones, Macduff, and Jackson. We wanted to check in on our team member. How you doing, pal?"

Morgan gave a thumbs-up with his free hand. His left one still had IVs attached.

"Never been better," he said sarcastically. "Actually, I'm pretty good – now." He looked at the lady beside his bed.

"This is Maggie."

"Guessed as much."

All of the Green Berets extended their hands.

"This is quite a guy you got here."

Maggie nodded and took Josh's hand. "I know."

"He sure saved our as... bacon. Twice."

Aboud asked Maggie, "When did you arrive?"

"About the same time he did."

"You work for the president, I hear."

"Yes. As soon as we got word that Josh was on his way here, she put me on an Air Force plane to get me here, too."

"So, Morgan, what's the prognosis?" SFC Jackson asked.

"Couple of days and then home. How're you guys?"

"I'll be limping a while, but not bad.," answered Jackson.

Jones gave his update. "Won't be throwing a football around with my son for a few weeks."

Jackson said, "Nezhdanov is good. His wound wasn't nearly as bad as it appeared. He's being debriefed as we speak."

The visitors engaged in a bit of small talk with Morgan and Maggie. Lechler finally remembered to ask Josh about something that had been puzzling him.

"About Charlemagne?" he began.

"General Richards," Morgan answered. "I needed an 'in' with you guys, if I found you. He passed it along to the CIA director, who passed it along to me. Good call, huh?"

"Very good call."

Maggie smiled, though she didn't divulge her part in arranging her guy's "in."

Morgan suddenly got very serious. "I'm sorry about Matheson."

All the SPIRITs nodded soberly.

"Good man," said Lechler. "Well, we'll leave you two alone. We're heading back to D.C. for some debriefing at the Pentagon."

"Then what?" asked Maggie.

"Wherever we're sent," replied SFC Fluff Jones.

"Except maybe for me, ma'am. I've been in this man's army since I was seventeen. Convinced them I was eighteen. I think I'm going to get acquainted with my wife and daughters."

The Master Sergeant's unit members looked at their Operations Leader. It was the first they'd heard about his intended retirement.

"Here. One of mine."

The Master Sergeant handed Morgan a piece of headgear, official inventory designation, "beret, man's, wool, rifle green, army shade 297." The flash of the 10th Special Forces emblazoned the green beret. The unofficial SPIRIT team member held the gift in his hand, speechless.

"It was a pleasure meeting you, Maggie," the Team Leader said.

Jackson looked at Morgan. "Keep your head down."

"Thank you, guys," a solemn Morgan said.

"Thank you, sir," responded Jones.

Each of the Operation Nemesis soldiers shook Morgan's hand.

"Ma'am," said SFC Jackson.

Maggie gave her guy a smirk.

"They wanted to check up on their 'team member?'"

"Yeah. Funny thing. They needed another guy for their pickup basketball team."

"And you got shot playing basketball?" Her eyes sparkled with her smile.

"Other guys were sore losers."

Morgan dozed off from time to time, while Maggie sat beside him.

A phone call came in to Maggie around noon. It was the president.

"Yes, ma'am. He's going to be fine. Of course, Madam President."

Maggie nudged Morgan gently from his sleep.

"The president would like to speak with you."

In spite of Morgan's disappointment in Hendrickson's rush to action and his disenchantment with her resistance to advice from the CIA director and former President Weston, he knew that POTUS had eventually come around. And he wasn't certain he wouldn't have acted exactly as she had, if it had been him making the calls. He was very gracious during their brief conversation.

When he finished speaking with the chief executive, he handed the phone back to Maggie.

"She wants us to join her and her family for a private dinner when I'm well enough. She couldn't speak highly enough of you, sweetheart."

Maggie finished the call with a few words and lay her head against Morgan's and the two silently enjoyed each other's company for a while.

Day 20 – Thursday

Josh Morgan was still in some pain, but he was thrilled to be riding down the hall in a wheel chair, pushed along by a Landstuhl Regional Medical Center nurse.

Maggie rode with him in the ambulance to Ramstein Air Base, where a private jet was waiting to take them home.

Soon after takeoff, the ex-CIA officer received a call from the current Director of Central Intelligence.

"Hi, Betsy. Yeah, I'm great. Nothing like going home to put a spring back in your step. Is your job safe?" he teased.

He listened for some time without speaking. Finally, he answered the director.

"If you'd asked me a few weeks ago, I think I would've said 'yes.' But you know, I'm about to be a husband…" He smiled at Maggie, "So I think I'm gonna just do the college professor thing."

He listened to Parnell make her case.

"Thank you, Betsy. Of course, I'll give it some thought, but I'm sure this is my answer."

The phone call ended, and Maggie looked at her fiancé with concern in her eyes. He knew what her question was going to be.

"Yes. She asked if I wanted back in. She said I seemed to be incapable of keeping my nose out of her business anyhow, so I might as well be working for her."

Maggie's eyes continued their enquiry to Morgan.

"I said 'no.'"

"Are you sure?"

"Yep."

Morgan put his arm around Maggie and pulled her close.

During the flight, Morgan had other calls – from Trent and Alicia Weston and Ryan Crenshaw, who was finally home in Texas with Amelia. Josh had spoken with all of them while in the hospital, but like the family they were, they wanted him to know they were thinking of him.

He and his former professor were about to hang up, when Morgan remembered to ask him a favor.

Ten minutes later, his phone dinged its announcement that he had a message.

"here's the number…"

"Maggie, would you mind if I make a call?"

Morgan dialed the number that Crenshaw had gotten from Pavel Orlov.

The phone rang on the other end and the answer came.

"*Da.*"

"Slava," Morgan replied.

The two men had a conversation in Russian that was much less strained than it probably should've been.

Morgan said, "Sorry about the whole shooting you thing."

Proskurkin replied that it was okay. He would've shot Morgan, too.

"You did shoot me!"

Both men laughed and moved past their encounter with the realization that each was just doing a job.

CHAPTER 40

Three Weeks Later

The summit between United States President Sandra Hendrickson and President Boris Yaroslavovich Tatarov of the Russian Federation cleared up little about the events that transpired outside Vnukovo International Airport and in the countryside of Belarus. The American leader stuck to her tale that both episodes were the responsibility of operatives from the Holy Islamic Republic of Saudi Arabia.

And the Russian leader was steadfast in his conviction that American Special Forces were behind everything that had transpired in his Motherland. Yet, in spite of the tragic deaths of sixteen of his military's finest, Tatarov viewed his acceptance of the American's explanation as a necessary concession in the interest of peace.

Ultimately, both presidents agreed to advance the narrative that the bombings were the work of a single lunatic, a rogue Russian agent. The decision to keep Saudi Arabia out of the story was a strategic one.

As the leaders of the two superpowers stood at their separate podiums in Rome, it was clear to each and every representative of the global media that, even in the context of the unparalleled events of the last few weeks, no real details would be forthcoming. Certainly nothing would be disclosed that wasn't already known or suspected. Still, the questions had to be asked, if not in the hopes that they would actually be answered, then at least the correspondents could bring their respective networks some attention.

"President Tatarov, the United States wrongly accused your nation of being responsible for the attempted assassination of President Hendrickson and the deaths and injuries of many more," summarized one reporter. "How do you get past that?"

For anyone schooled in interpreting people's reactions and deducing their true feelings, they would've known that the question touched a nerve. But the Russian leader stuck with his conciliatory tone.

"Since the attacks were carried out by a citizen of my nation, it would have been difficult not to overreact and assume, despite our protestations, that it was the work of the Russian Federation. So, in the interest of peace, you simply accept that individual states must prepare to act against an attack but have enough courage to continue to search for the truth and accept it when it is discovered."

A number of reporters wondered if Tatarov had really used the word "overreact" or if that was the interpreter's translation.

"President Hendrickson, you have stated that you now accept the fact that the attacks were planned and carried out by Gennadiy Borzilov without any support from a larger entity. Is that still your position?"

"It is, because it is the truth. Every agency and organization in my administration worked tirelessly to uncover the truth. We, of course, had to prepare to act, but, as you know, no military action was taken while we continued our investigation."

The rest of the press conference was just the same.

Of course, both SVR Director Pavel Semyonovich Orlov and SVR Agent Vladislav Larionovich Proskurkin could've laid waste to the narrative of the two presidents that Borzilov acted alone. However, each man chose to let peace take its course.

✦

Army Special Forces Master Sergeant Tom Lechler informed his superiors of his intention to retire. Their response was to ask him to complete one more operation. It required a four-man team. SFC Jack Jackson would be recovered sufficiently from his thigh injury. Abe Aboud's operational specialty wasn't needed, nor was Macduff's, but they were included to round out the squad.

✦

FBI Special Agents Russell and Jeffries entered Walter Reed to take another crack at SVR agent Gennadiy Borzilov, who was nearing full recovery from the injuries he sustained during his second assassination attempt on President Hendrickson. The two agents hadn't seen him for two weeks. Upon learning that his family was dead, he had become increasingly despondent and uncooperative.

When he had divulged what little information that he had knowledge of about the true nature of the plot to kill the American leader, he had done so out of love for Mother Russia. His only concern was stopping the wheels of war that were turning because of him. The war that would've occurred between the United States and the Russian Federation was one that both nations would lose.

Since then, he had refused to turn on Russia or the Foreign Intelligence Service for which he worked. He would never become an asset for the CIA or any other U.S. agency. He would never betray his countrymen.

As the agents turned the corner into the wing where they would find their prisoner, they saw a flurry of activity developing in the hallway. Medical staff were rushing into the Russian's room, followed by the Bureau guard who had been on-shift for the around-the-clock watch.

Miles Russell stopped at the doorway of the room. His fellow agent looked over his shoulder as both men struggled to let the scene before them sink in. Each was certain the man still handcuffed to the bed was beyond help when they saw the blood on Borzilov's wrist, as well as on his bed and the floor of his room.

The doctor and two nurses worked desperately to save the man, but in the end, he was beyond resuscitation.

While the doctor called the time of the Russian's death, one of the nurses told Russell and Jeffries that the Code Blue had alerted her station just as the government agents were arriving.

The Code Team left the room to the agents.

"It took lot of resolve to do that, didn't it?"

Jeffries could only agree with a nod of his head.

Gennadiy Valeryevich Borzilov had stripped small pieces of cloth from his sheet. Then he pulled a number of individual threads loose and twisted them together. Finally, he wrapped the string around the wrist of his handcuffed right hand, held one end in his teeth and the other in his left hand, slicing the improvised rope saw back and forth until it cut through his skin and his veins began to bleed.

Once enough blood had spilled from the wound, his heart stopped, and the code sounded.

"Wonder how long he had to keep at it until it opened him up?" Jeffries wondered. "Can't believe he could keep going after the cut started hurting."

EPILOGUE

Four weeks later

Josh and Maggie had been home for several weeks. She had returned to work only two days after they returned from Germany. Even though Josh had improved enough to manage for himself, she hated to leave him each day for the West Wing. There was work to be done in the White House press department and Marie Ginnetti was still on the mend. But Maggie just wanted to be home with Morgan.

During her absence to be with her fiancé at the U.S. hospital in Germany, Noah Chandler had juggled his schedule enough to supervise the press group staff, which had done a remarkable job carrying the load. To a person, each of the staff remarked to the acting Secretary how much they had missed her.

Obviously, none knew where she was or what she was doing because none knew of Morgan's role in an operation that they likewise weren't aware of. The official story was that she was handling a task for POTUS.

Trent and Alicia Weston checked in on Josh, as did Ryan Crenshaw by phone from Dripping Springs, Texas. Betsy Parnell also called on occasion, although she never again made mention of her job offer.

Today would help Maggie's situation immensely. The entire press group cheered as Press Secretary Marie Ginnetti walked through the door of the West Wing. She limped and had a few visible scars but was smiling.

All of the West Wing's officials were there to greet her, including President Hendrickson and Vice President Bauer. Chief of Staff Chandler was there. But even with all the political "royalty" present, Ginnetti first walked to Maggie Loughlin and gave her a big hug. She whispered her thanks into the ear of the woman who had so ably filled in during her absence.

"The president says you did a remarkable job. I can never thank you enough."

Maggie said, "I'm glad I was able to help." Then she followed up that truth with a lie. "It was my pleasure."

The West Wing workers shared cake for only a short while. This was, after all, the heart of the White House, and there was always work to do.

Maggie had respectfully cleared all of her belongings from Ginnetti's office in anticipation of her return. As she sat at her own desk, her boss knocked on her door. Maggie rose to assist her, but Ginnetti waved her away.

"I'm fine, dear. May I sit?"

"Of course, Secretary Ginnetti." She walked around the desk to sit in a chair beside the woman.

"It was 'Marie' when I left. It's still 'Marie.'"

"Yes, ma'am."

"Ah, that's better," said Ginnetti once she was seated. "Thank you again. Your work was nothing short of outstanding. I wanted to fill you in about a phone conversation I had with the president a few days ago.

"I've been serving in the government for thirty-something years and I'm about worn out. I've always been arrogant enough to think I couldn't be replaced. No... actually, I think it's more accurate to say that I worried each time I left a position about the person who would replace me. I've always taken great pride in my work and am not convinced many others do in Washington."

Maggie suspected where this was headed.

"I told the president I would be stepping down soon. I recommended you to replace me."

Maggie was just getting her life back, at least she was getting a better situation for her life. Her distress was difficult to hide.

Ginnetti grinned and placed her hand on her young protégé's.

"Don't panic, Maggie. We're talking about a few months; not a few days. Honestly, I want to spend some time with you. Not just training you but getting to know you. And knowing I have such a capable partner here now will make leaving easier when the time comes."

Maggie caught that her boss had said "partner" and not "assistant" or "subordinate," and was flattered at the choice of the word.

"I feel that I can accomplish so much knowing that you're here. And to tell the truth, I want to make a difference before I leave."

Maggie was grateful for the kind words. She was pleased that the press secretary wouldn't be hitting the road anytime soon, so she would have a lot of time to give thought to her decision. She had already seen the demands of the job. She wasn't sure she wanted it.

The two women spent another half-hour talking about purely personal things. Ginnetti asked about Josh. She knew about his role in the events in Russia. She asked when they might be getting married. Ginnetti showed

Maggie photos of her husband, children, and grandchildren. It was clear to the younger woman that the older woman's experience had changed her.

✦

Josh Morgan was reclined on the couch when Maggie got home from work. He looked at his watch.

"One-thirty? You get fired?"

Maggie flew into his arms and gave him a long, passionate kiss.

"Nope. I got offered the job permanently. Well, sort of."

She told Josh about the conversation with Ginnetti. The news was as unsettling to him as it had been for her.

"Wow. That's quite an honor. At least you've got some time before you have to decide."

"Exactly what I thought."

Ever the news junkie, Morgan had the TV on QNN.

"Wouldn't you rather be watching a comedy or something? I would think you've had enough of international affairs."

"You know, you're right. But I've got a better idea."

Morgan started to turn off the television but stopped at the sound of the synthesized music and words that were almost addictive to him.

"This is Tracy Adams with breaking news…"

Maggie had already started to head for the bedroom. She rolled her eyes and sat back down.

"Saudi Arabian President Yasim al-Hashimi is dead. Once again, Saudi President Yasim al-Hashimi is dead."

Inside the townhouse, eyes widened and mouths opened. Maggie put a hand to her mouth. Josh turned up the volume.

"The controversial leader of the al-Qaeda Party that toppled the Royal Family and seized control of the oil-rich nation was departing King Khalid Airport when his plane suddenly dove into the ground just off the end of the runway. According to witnesses, the aircraft appeared to lose control and drop from the air.

"At the same time, computers and other electronic equipment throughout the airport failed. Reports of other power interruptions were reported as far as a mile from the airport.

Maggie uttered, "Oh, my…"

A smile began to form on Morgan's face and grew as he said, "Son of a bitch!"

Maggie was puzzled at his words and more so by the mixture of happiness and satisfaction the smile seemed to convey. More than that, Morgan didn't appear to be terribly shocked at the news.

Josh smiled again. When he turned off the television, his fiancée was stunned.

"Don't you want to watch this?"

"No. I think I've got it."

The man stood and took Maggie in his arms and kissed her. She leaned back and looked into his eyes and arched her eyebrows flirtatiously.

"So…?"

Morgan said, "Right. Where were we?"

He took her by the hand to lead her to their bed. When the doorbell rang, the couple's first instinct was to ignore it, but in light of the events of the last couple of months, they decided to at least see who it was.

Josh whispered, "I'll get rid of them." He opened the door to find six men, who stepped into the room without invitation.

"Joshua Matthew Morgan?"

"What is this?" Morgan asked.

Maggie moved to him but was intercepted by one of the men.

"I'm sorry, ma'am…"

She tried to shake free but couldn't.

"Joshua Morgan, we have a warrant for your arrest. You have the right to remain silent. Anything you say…"

As the officer continued with the Miranda Warning, another turned Morgan around and began to apply the handcuffs. The man informing Morgan of his rights paused just long enough to say, "No cuffs." Then he continued.

"Maggie, call Betsy Parnell."

"Betsy Parnell? Shouldn't I call a lawyer?"

"Betsy first. Then a lawyer."

The men began to lead Morgan out of the apartment. He spoke over his shoulder.

"It'll be all right. I love you, Maggie."

Maggie's words faltered as she stared in disbelief.

"I love you, too, Morgan," finally came out, but the door had already closed behind the group.

The End

AFTERWORD

Novel - noun
>	a fictitious prose narrative of considerable length and complexity, portraying characters and usually presenting a sequential organization of action and scenes (from Dictionary.com)

I included the definition of "novel" to emphasize the fact that novels are, after all, fiction. I try to have as much fun as I can when writing a novel. I will be as accurate as possible when referring to real people, places, history, technology, etc. In most cases, I make up what I need to suit the story. Even then, I still try to represent the fiction in such a way that it is plausible.

For example, for this book, I wanted a drone, but didn't want it to be identical to what's really out there. So, I made one up. The "Springer" drone in this book is based on the Switchblade Drone made by AeroVironment (www.avinc.com).

And when I don't want to encumber readers with a preconception about a particular country, I make one up – like Terrador in *Half of Faith* – or I make material changes to the government – changing the Kingdom of Saudi Arabia to a terrorist-run Holy Islamic Kingdom of Saudi Arabia.

My goal with regard to my fictional creations is to craft them in such a way that, if they don't exist, they could, and, in the area of technology, to craft them in a fashion consistent with existing technology.

So, with that in mind, here are some examples of things from *SPIRITs of Retribution* that you might wonder about.

MADE-UP or REAL?

- A communications jamming device that can jam across multiple bands and over large areas – REAL
- A communications jamming device carried with the president in the same way that the Nuclear Football is – MADE-UP (as far as I know)
- Green Light Teams as I described them – REAL
- SPIRITs – MADE-UP

- SADM B-54 – REAL
- B-54B SNAP – MADE-UP
- 173rd Fighter Wing at Kingsley Field Air National Guard Base in Oregon training alongside the Finnish Air Force – REAL (2016)
- EMP Explosively Pumped Flux Compression Generators – REAL
- EMP as I described – MADE-UP (as far as I know)
- Springer drone – MADE-UP (Based on the Switchblade Drone by AeroVironment.)
- F-35 with anti-ICBM capabilities – REAL BUT NOT DEPLOYED (Being studied as of publication date.)
- Russian drone Orlan-10 UAV – REAL
- Russian helicopter Ka-226T – REAL
- MH-60M Black Hawk – REAL (Sort of. The available details about the modified helicopter in the Bin Laden raid are what I describe in the book.)
- U.S. and Russian small arms –– REAL
- Specific Russian vehicles – REAL
- Russian highways, streets, neighborhoods – REAL
- Area around Selyatino – REAL (In fact, if you search Google Earth for the area around Selyatino, you should be able to find the precise area I described when Slava and Josh are searching for the Borzilov family, right down to where they had to turn away from the first wooded area and then reacquire the tree line.)
- Pharmacies, stores, hospitals, hotels, etc. in Russia – REAL (Even "Sex Shop, He & She!")
- All businesses in the U.S. – REAL (Unless they're bad guys. Don't want to get sued!)

ABOUT THE AUTHOR

Rod Johnson has two passions in life – his family and writing. After years in the Financial Services industry, Rod retired to devote his time to both.

Among the author's influences are great novelists in the thriller genre such as Clancy, Ludlum, le Carré, and others. Nelson DeMille's *Charm School* is an all-time favorite novel and he admires Brad Meltzer for the breadth of his work across multiple genres and media.

Rod's dad was the first of his family to move away from the family farm to live and work in a city (population 5,000). However, with extended family remaining on farms and ranches, the writer "grew up country" and this upbringing is evident in some of his characters.

Spy thrillers are Rod's primary focus. His debut work, *Half of Faith*, is the first in the series of Josh Morgan Novels that carry the protagonist's name.

The writer's faith-based and inspirational articles have been published in national magazines.

Rod still spends much of his non-writing time in the outdoors. He loves flyfishing and photography and his family spends as much time as possible on their thirty-seven-foot sailboat, *No Regrets*.

If you enjoy plots with a myriad of moving parts, lived out in characters with compelling blends of virtues and flaws and complex personalities who struggle to balance their better selves with their hypocrisies, you'll love Rod's work.

The author still resides in a small north Texas town with his wife and daughter.